The Uncompleted Past

MARTIN DUBERMAN is professor of history at Princeton University. He was born in New York City and grew up there and in Mount Vernon, New York. He received his B.A. from Yale University and his M.A. and Ph.D. from Harvard.

Mr. Duberman is the author of *Charles Francis Adams, 1807–1886,* which was awarded the Bancroft Prize in 1962, and *James Russell Lowell,* which was a finalist for the National Book Award in 1966. He is also the editor of *The Antislavery Vanguard: New Essays on the Abolitionists,* published by Princeton University Press in 1965. Currently Mr. Duberman is completing a history of Black Mountain, the experimental college and community.

Mr. Duberman is also a playwright. His documentary play *In White America* had a run of 500 performances Off-Broadway (where the production won the 1963–64 Vernon Rice–Drama Desk Award), two national tours and a large number of foreign productions. One of Mr. Duberman's short plays, *Metaphors,* was part of *Collision Course,* which opened in 1968; another, *The Colonial Dudes,* was recently done at the Actors' Studio, and a longer play, *Groups,* had a workshop production at The Loft. An evening of two of his one-act plays, called *The Memory Bank,* opened Off-Broadway in 1970 and was published the same year. His new full-length play, *Payments,* will be performed at the New Dramatists in spring 1971.

THE UNCOMPLETED PAST

Martin Duberman

A Dutton Paperback

NEW YORK
E. P. DUTTON & CO., INC.
1971

For
Dick Poirier

SBN 0-525-47290-8

Contents

PART III
The Crisis of the Universities

PART IV

Preface

IN PREPARING these essays and reviews for publication, I was surprised to discover that I did not have to choose between a chronological or topical approach; when set out chronologically, the pieces, with only a minimum of rearranging, fell readily under three title headings. This surprised me because I hadn't realized that my "subject" had shifted so decisively (though not completely) from one period of time to the next. During the first period, 1962–65, the theme of my writing was almost entirely professional"; the articles from those years deal either with my special field of interest as an historian—the Civil War and Reconstruction—or with broader professional inquiries into the nature and boundaries of historical knowledge. From 1965 to 1968, a different theme prevailed: the Civil Rights movement and its offspring, the New Left. Then, beginning in 1968, a third topic came to be of paramount importance—the crisis in the universities.

The fact that the thematic focus of my essays and reviews has shifted through time would be of little interest if the shift merely signified some personal evolution. But many Americans (and especially those with backgrounds similar to mine—white, middle-class, Northern, liberal/radical, university-trained) not only share the concerns of these essays but also have shifted priorities between them in a way comparable to my own. Many, like me, started by being almost totally absorbed in specialized, professional problems, gradually became involved with public questions, tried to apply the insights of their profession to those questions (in my case, "historical perspective"), and recently, under a variety of pressures, have found the focus of their attention shifting from Civil Rights to the campus.

In the end, of course, I can only claim to speak in these essays for myself, and many of the views I express and the mode in which I express them are no doubt idiosyncratic (and to some extent, I hope, valuable because of that). But what finally convinced me that this collection might be worth publishing was the feeling that it articulated at least some of the issues and attitudes central to the sixties. This does not mean, of course, that the volume pretends to anything like an exhaustive commentary on the decade; a vast number of possible topics and events, from pop culture to lunar orbits, are absent. I have also omitted a subject that did absorb me during these years—the drama. Though I wrote a good deal for and about the theater in the sixties, I decided that those pieces, interior, reflective of personal matters, would be inappropriate in a volume chiefly concerned with public questions.

The title of this collection, *The Uncompleted Past,* is meant to convey my sense of the book's overriding theme: our uncertain conception not only of what the past was, but also of how it does—and whether it need—control the present. In regard to that theme, my view is that the past will always remain "uncompleted": we will never grasp its meaning whole, never understand its influence over our lives to the extent we might like, nor be able to free ourselves from that influence to the degree many might wish.

Rereading these pieces has made me aware of their de-

Preface

ficiencies, but I have tried to resist the impulse to tidy up the arguments and the prose. Instead, I have put my second thoughts into brief introductions to each piece. In a few cases the impulse to change a word or correct a punctuation proved so strong that I simply accepted the dictum that the only way to get rid of temptation is to yield to it. These few instances aside, the essays stand as originally written.

M. D.

PART I

The Profession
of History

THE ABOLITIONISTS
AND PSYCHOLOGY

The full-scale reevaluation of the abolitionist movement, which this essay called for, is now well advanced. In the past half-dozen years a number of studies by a new generation of historians have appeared, and almost all are sympathetic toward the movement (the most important, in my opinion, is Aileen Kraditor's Means and Ends in American Abolitionism). *Sympathy for the abolitionists has become so strong among younger historians that in 1965, when I was putting together* The Anti-slavery Vanguard, *a collection of new essays on the movement, I had difficulty finding any reputable scholar under forty who was willing to argue the traditional view of the abolitionist as a "meddlesome fanatic." Some of the older, more conservative historians feel that the balance has now tipped too far the other way, that the new generation of historians has over-compensated—the usual pitfall of "revisionism." This is not my view. I agree that a few scholars have let their zeal to defend the abolitionists take precedence over their obligation to understand them. But on the whole I believe the favorable view of abolitionism now current is no more than a long-delayed recognition of the movement's positive accomplishments.*

3

OUT of their heightened concern with the pressing question of Negro rights, a number of historians, especially the younger ones, have begun to take a new look at the abolitionists, men who in their own day were involved in a similar movement of social change. About both them and ourselves we are asking anew such questions as the proper role of agitation, the underlying motives of both reformers and resistants, and the useful limits of outside interference. From this questioning a general tendency has developed to view the abolitionists in a more favorable light than previously. As yet, however, it is a tendency only, and hostility to the abolitionists continues to be strong among historians.[1]

Perhaps one reason why no fuller re-evaluation has taken place is that historians have been made cautious by the fate of previous "revisionist" scholarship. We have seen how current preoccupations can prompt dubious historical re-evaluations. But this need not always be the case. Contemporary pressures, if recognized and contained, can prove fruitful in stimulating the historical imagination. They may lead us to uncover (not invent) aspects of the past to which we were previously blind.

"The Abolitionists and Psychology" was first published in *The Journal of Negro History*, July, 1962. It appears here as later revised for an anthology.

[1] I deliberately refrain from citing specific works and authors. In suggestions as tentative as mine, I have not thought it profitable to take issue with individuals. One point I do wish to make clear: I am not suggesting that *all* historians have viewed the abolitionists without sympathy or understanding. Louis Filler, Dwight Dumond, Irving Bartlett, Leon Litwack, Ralph Korngold, Louis Ruchames, Oscar Sherwin, and David Brion Davis have in varying degrees and with varying effectiveness demonstrated their sympathy. But they have not, in my view, as yet carried the majority of historians along with them.

The Abolitionists and Psychology

If historians need more courage in their re-consideration of the abolitionists, they also need more information. Particularly do they need to employ some of the insights and raise some of the questions which developments in related fields of knowledge have made possible. Recent trends in psychology seem especially pertinent, though historians have not paid them sufficient attention. It is my hope in this paper to make some beginning in that direction.

It might be well to start by referring to one of psychology's older principles, the uniqueness of personality. Each individual, with his own genetic composition and his own life experience, will develop into a distinctive organism. There are, of course, certain drives and reflexes which are more or less "instinctive." There are also a variety of common responses conditioned by our membership in a particular group, be it family, class, church or nation. These similarities among human beings make possible the disciplines of sociology, anthropology and social psychology, which concern themselves with patterns of behavior, and demonstrate that no man is *sui generis*. But it does not follow that the qualities which are uniquely individual are mere irrelevancies. As Gordon Allport has said, ". . . all of the animals in the world are psychologically less distinct from one another than one man is from other men."[2]

This is not to question, of course, the validity of attempts, whether they be by sociologists, psychologists or historians, to find meaningful similarities in the behavioral patterns of various human groups. The point is to make certain that such similarities genuinely exist, and further, to be aware that in describing them, we do not pretend to be saying *everything* about the individuals involved. Historians, it

[2] Gordon W. Allport, *Becoming, Basic Considerations for a Psychology of Personality*, Clinton, 1960, p. 23.

seems to me, are prone to ignore both cautions—their treatment of the abolitionists being the immediate case in point.

With barely a redeeming hint of uncertainty, many historians list a group of "similar traits" which are said to characterize all abolitionists: "impractical," "self-righteous," "fanatical," "humorless," "vituperative" and—if they are very modern in their terminology—"disturbed." The list varies, but usually only to include adjectives equally hostile and denunciatory. The stereotype of the "abolitionist personality," though fluid in details, is clear enough in its general outlines.

But did most abolitionists really share these personality traits? The fact is, we know much less about the individuals involved in the movement than has been implied. Some of the major figures, such as Joshua Leavitt, have never received biographical treatment; others—the Tappans, Edmund Quincy, and Benjamin Lundy, for example —badly need modern appraisal. And the careers and personalities of the vast majority of significant secondary figures—people like Lydia Maria Child, Sidney Gay, Maria Weston Chapman, Henry B. Stanton, and Abby Kelley Foster—have been almost totally unexplored. Whence comes the confidence, then, that allows historians to talk of "the abolitionist personality," as if this had been microscopically examined and painstakingly reconstructed?

Certainly the evidence which we do have, does not support such confident theorizing. In order to adhere to this conceptual strait-jacket, it is necessary to ignore or discount much that conflicts with it—the modesty of Theodore Weld, the wit of James Russell Lowell, the tender humanity of Whittier, the worldly charm of Edmund Quincy. This does not mean that we need leap to the opposite extreme and claim all abolitionists were saints and seraphs. But if some of them were disagreeable or disturbed, we want, in-

The Abolitionists and Psychology

stead of a blanket indictment, to know which ones and in what ways; we want some recognition of the variety of human beings who entered the movement.

It seems to me that what too many historians have done is to take William Lloyd Garrison as a personality symbol for the entire movement (at the same time, ironically, that they deny him the commanding leadership which he was once assumed to have had). Fixing on some of the undeniably "neurotic" aspects of his personality (and bolstered, it should be said, by the eccentric psychographs of other abolitionists—a Gerrit Smith, say, or a Stephen Foster), they equate these with the personality structures of all the abolitionists, and conclude that the movement was composed solely of "quacks." In doing so, they fail to do justice to the wide spectrum of personality involved; in fact, they do not even do justice to Garrison, for to speak exclusively of *his* oracular and abusive qualities is to ignore the considerable evidence of personal warmth and kindliness.

It may be that when we know more of other abolitionists, we may with equal certainty be able to single out qualities in them which seem palpable symptoms of "disturbance." But let the evidence at least precede the judgment. And let us also show a decent timidity in applying the label "neurotic." Psychiatrists, dealing with a multitude of evidence and bringing to it professional insights, demonstrate more caution in this regard than do untrained historians working with mere traces of personality. If the disposition to be hostile exists, "neurosis" can almost always be established. Under the Freudian microscope, it would be a rare man indeed whose life showed no evidence of pathological behavior. (Think, for one, of the admirable William James, who, as his devoted biographer, Ralph Barton Perry, has shown, was subject to hypochondria, hallucinations, and intense oscillations of mood.) I am not suggesting that all men's lives, if sufficiently investigated, would show equally severe evidence of disturbance. I mean only to warn that, given the double jeopardy of a hostile commentator and the weight of a hostile historical tradition, we must take special precaution not to be too easily convinced by the "evidence" of neurosis in the abolitionists.

And even were we to establish the neurotic component of behavior, the story would certainly not be complete. To know the pathological elements in an individual's behavior is not to know everything about his behavior. To say that Garrison, in his fantasy world, longed to be punished and thus deliberately courted martyrdom, or that Wendell Phillips, alienated from the "new order," sought to work out his private grievances against the industrial system by indirectly attacking it through slavery, is hardly to exhaust the possible range of their motives. We know far too little about why men do anything—let alone why they do something as specific as joining a reform movement—to assert as confidently as historians have, the motives of whole groups of men. We may never know enough about the human psyche to achieve a comprehensive analysis of motivation; how much greater the difficulty when the subject is dead and we are attempting the analysis on the basis of partial and fragmentary remains.

Our best hope for increased understanding in this area —aside from the artist's tool of intuition—is in the researches of psychology. But at present there is no agreed-upon theory of motivation among psychologists. Allport, however, summarizing current opinion, suggests that behavior does not result solely from the need to reduce tension, but may also aim (especially in a "healthy" person) at distant goals, the achievement of which can be gained only by maintaining tension.[3] Allport does not press his views,

[3] Allport, *op. cit.*, pp. 65–68.

realizing the complexity of the problems at issue. But his hypotheses are at least suggestive as regards the abolitionists, for their motives, rather than being solely the primitive ones of eliminating personal tension (under the guise of ethical commitment), may also have included a healthy willingness to bear tension (in the form of ostracism, personal danger and material sacrifice) in order to persevere in the pursuit of long-range ideals.

Acceptance of these suggestions runs into the massive resistance of neo-Freudian cynicism.[4] How old-fashioned, it will be said, to talk in terms of "ideals" or "conscience," since these are only unconscious rationalizations for "darker" drives which we are unable to face. How old-fashioned, too, to talk as if men could exercise choice in their conduct, since all our behavior is determined by our antecedents.

But the surprising fact is that such views are not old-fashioned. On the contrary, they have recently returned to favor in psychoanalytical circles.[5] Increasing dissatisfaction with the ability of behaviorist theory fully to explain human action, has led to a re-consideration of the role of reason and the possibilities of purposive, deliberate behavior. The result is the influential new school of "ego psychology," which views man as endowed with a considerable margin of freedom and responsibility, and which has restored to the vocabulary such "old-fashioned" terminology as character, will-power and conscience. Moral earnestness, moreover, is no longer equated with self-deception. As Allport has said, the very mark of maturity "seems to be the range and extent of one's feeling of self-

---

[4] Based largely on what people think Freud said, rather than what he actually said. See Philip Rieff, *Freud: The Mind of the Moralist*, N.Y., 1959.

[5] See, for example, O. Hobart Mowrer, "Psychiatry and Religion," *The Atlantic*, July, 1961.

involvement in abstract ideals."[6] Some of these new emphases had been prefigured in the work of such philosophers as Sartre, who have long stressed social action as a sign of "authenticity" in man.

But although all of this makes a re-evaluation of the abolitionists possible, it does not make one necessary. Men may now be thought capable of impersonal devotion to ideals, but this does not mean that the abolitionists were such men. Maturity may now be defined as the ability to commit ourselves objectively to ethical values, but it does not follow that every man who makes such a commitment does so out of mature motives.

Yet at least some doubts should be raised in our minds as to whether we have been fair in regarding the abolitionists as psychologically homogeneous, and at that, homogeneous in the sense of being self-deceived. My own feeling goes beyond doubt, into conviction. I do not claim, to repeat, that because the abolitionists fought in a noble cause, their motives were necessarily noble—i.e., "pure" and "unselfish," unrelated in any way to their own inner turmoil or conflicts. A connection between inner problems and outer convictions probably always exists to some degree. But an individual's public involvement is never completely explained by discussing his private pathology. Yet it is just this that historians have frequently done, and to that degree, they have distorted and devalued the abolitionist commitment.

To provide a concrete example, by way of summary, consider the case of James Russell Lowell, whose biography I am writing, and about whom I can talk with more assurance than I might some other figure.

His history seems to me convincing proof that at least *some* people became abolitionists not primarily out of an

6 Allport, *op. cit.*, p. 45.

The Abolitionists and Psychology

unconscious need to escape from personal problems, but out of deliberate, rational commitment to certain ethical values—recognizing, as I have said, that the two are never wholly unrelated. Lowell's active life as a reformer came during the period of his greatest contentment—secure in a supremely happy marriage, and confident of his talents and his future. His contemporaries agree in describing him as a gay, witty, warm man, without serious tensions or disabling anxieties. I have come across so little evidence of "pathology" in the Lowell of these years that when the standard picture of the abolitionist as a warped eccentric is applied to him, it becomes absurd.

And he *was* an abolitionist, though various arguments have been used to deny this. Lowell, it has been said, came to the movement late—and only at the instigation of his bride, Maria White, who was a confirmed reformer. He never fully committed himself to abolition, and finally left the ranks in the early 1850s. There may be some justice to these charges, but on the whole the argument is not persuasive. Given Lowell's youth (he was born in 1819) he could not have joined the movement much earlier than he did (which was around 1840), and there is evidence that he was involved in the cause before he met Maria White. The important point is that for roughly ten years he was unquestionably a serious abolitionist, both as an active member of the Massachusetts Anti-Slavery Society, and as a frequent contributor to abolitionist periodicals. The reasons for his drifting out of the movement are complex, but turn largely on the fact that his wife's death in 1853 destroyed the structure of his life and left him apathetic to public issues. (Might not this give added weight to the argument that it takes a reasonably contented man to interest himself in the problems of others?)

Even when it is admitted that Lowell was an abolitionist,

he is dismissed as not having been a "typical" one. But who was the typical abolitionist? Is the standard of measurement meant to be some outstanding individual—Garrison, say, or Theodore Weld—and is everyone else to be considered more or less of an abolitionist depending on how closely he approximated the personality structure of the model? But a man may be prominent in a movement without necessarily typifying it. And which of several leading—and very different—figures should be chosen as the model? The decision is likely to be arbitrary (and unconscious), varying with each historian.

Or is the standard of measurement meant to be some composite group of traits which accurately describe the large number of abolitionists, so that when any single individual fails to exhibit these traits, he may justifiably be dismissed as "the exception which proves the rule"?[7] This approach is more reasonable, but here again we run up against the old difficulty of drawing a genuinely valid group portrait. We know so little about the individual personalities and careers of the majority of abolitionists that it seems like putting the cart before the horse to even talk about a composite portrait. Certainly the one which is now commonly accepted ("impractical"; "self-righteous," etc.) fails adequately to describe many of the abolitionists about whom we do have information. I mean here not only Lowell, but a number of others. What I have seen in my researches into the papers of people like Edmund Quincy, Lydia Maria Child or Maria Weston Chapman (to name only a few of the more prominent), has created the strong suspicion in my mind that if their personalities were to be investigated in depth, they too would be found to deviate

[7] It is interesting that in its original form, the aphorism read: "is this the exception which probes the rule?"

from the accepted portrait in so many significant ways as further to undermine its reliability.

A conceptual scheme may yet be devised which adequately describes the motives and actions of most of the abolitionists. But if so, it will not be of the primitive kind thus far suggested. There is no reason why historians cannot legitimately investigate group patterns, but to do so meaningfully, they must become skilled in the techniques of sociology and other related disciplines. This takes time and inclination, and the historian, busy with his special interests and orientated towards the particular, rarely has either. Unfortunately this does not always prevent him from trying his hand, though the result has too often been the kind of elementary categorizing used to describe the abolitionists.

Opinions will continue to differ as to the best way of achieving desired social change. Our own generation's confrontation with segregation has made this clear. Many of us feel as strongly about the evil of that practice as the abolitionists did about the institution of slavery. Like them, too, we have scant faith in Southern voluntarism or the benevolent workings of time; patience and inactivity have not done their work. Naturally we would like to believe that our sense of urgency comes from concern for the Negro rather than from a need to escape from some private torment of our own. Because of this we are admittedly prone to credit our historical counterparts with the kind of good motives we would like to impute to ourselves. Our wish to think well of them may account for our doing so. But as Erich Fromm has said, "the fact that an idea satisfies a wish does not mean necessarily that the idea is false."[8] There is

8 Erich Fromm, *Psychoanalysis and Religion*, Clinton, 1959, p. 12.

13

much in the new psychology to encourage the belief that the idea is not false. At any rate, if we are to find out, we need less dogma, more research, and a chastening sense of wonder at the complexities of human nature.

LINCOLN AND THE
FIRST SHOT

The peripheral themes of this piece are ones which I refer to frequently (most fully in "The Limitations of History"): the importance of chance and of individual idiosyncrasy as elements in historical explanation; and the need for historians to become something like philosophers, willing to risk speculative appraisals.

CONDITIONS can be ripe for war without war occurring. Some catalyst is needed before a crisis erupts in war—an event which in itself may be trivial and, frequently, unpredictable. Those who believe in grand inevitabilities deny the real significance of the precipitating event. Intent as they are on establishing a rational world, these determinists prefer to discount the importance of all that is contingent and idiosyncratic. Yet it remains true that the world has sometimes turned on the most casual circumstances—a misunderstood word, a sudden rainstorm, a burst of temper.

The outbreak of the American Civil War is a case in point. It has alternately been seen as the inevitable result of "underlying forces," or as the unnecessary consequence of the hasty actions of a few men. The debate turns frequently on the actions taken by one man—Abraham Lincoln—during the crisis at Fort Sumter. Was Lincoln merely an instrument of fate—his actions preordained by inexorable historical forces—or did he have considerable margin of choice and room for maneuver? If the latter, did he use his freedom to maximize the chances for peace, or to encourage the tendency toward war?

The literature on Lincoln's role in the Sumter crisis is large and controversial. There is one school of interpretation—best represented in the views of Charles W. Ramsdell—which casts Lincoln as the villain who deliberately precipitated war. Ramsdell argues that Lincoln, in attempting to provision Fort Sumter, was consciously goading the

This review of Richard N. Current's *Lincoln and the First Shot* (J. B. Lippincott, Co., Philadelphia) appeared in *Book Week*, December 15, 1963. I have restored certain material, primarily a concluding section of three paragraphs.

16

South toward aggression in order to unite his own party and section.

A second influential view is that of the distinguished historians J. G. Randall and David Potter. It coincides largely with the official explanation Lincoln himself gave for the outbreak of war. According to this account, Lincoln reluctantly accepted the necessity of re-provisioning Fort Sumter only after his plans for maintaining an alternate symbol of Federal authority at Fort Pickens had gone astray. When finally convinced of the necessity of the Sumter expedition, Lincoln tried to make it as unprovocative as possible, believing there was a good chance the fort could be replenished peacefully.

A third version of Lincoln's role in the Sumter crisis has been given greatest currency by Professor Kenneth Stampp, who has adopted a position somewhere between the other two. Lincoln, Stampp argues, was well aware that war was likely to follow his attempt to relieve Sumter, but he accepted that probability (while still hoping for peace), in the name of preserving Federal authority and the Union. In any event, Lincoln was determined that if hostilities did come, the onus for their formal initiation should fall on the Confederates.

In an effort to evaluate these conflicting interpretations, Professor Richard N. Current, a distinguished Civil War scholar at the University of Wisconsin, has written *Lincoln and the First Shot*. After re-examining all the available evidence, he solidly aligns himself with the views of Kenneth Stampp.

Current maintains that Lincoln felt strongly from the beginning that Fort Sumter had to be held, lest capitulation there be taken by the Confederates as a tacit recognition of their independence. He preferred to hold Sumter without violence, but was aware that violence might well follow. He preferred that no shots be fired, but was determined that if any were, they should come first from Confederate guns. He preferred to preserve the Union by peace, but he would accept war rather than let the nation perish.

Professor Current presents his case with impressive authority and in sparse, lucid prose. With calm detachment and incisive skill, he politely dissects views that differ from his own (he is somewhat less polite, understandably, when dealing with the pro-Confederate polemics of Ramsdell and Company). In my opinion, he has made a commanding, persuasive argument.

There is only one major point on which further clarification would have been useful—that of "responsibility." Ramsdell, and Jefferson Davis before him, argued that the real aggressor in war is not he who fires the first shot, but rather he who makes the first shot necessary. This kind of "ultimate" responsibility is almost impossible to assign, since the argument can be carried backwards indefinitely. But if we focus on establishing responsibility for what happened at Sumter, the Ramsdell-Davis argument would seem to have some point.

It is true, as Current insists, that the Confederates were hardly passive recipients of Lincoln's policies. Davis' order to bombard Sumter was a deliberate decision to inaugurate hostilities. And yet Professor Current perhaps gives too short shrift to Davis' contention that his hand had been forced. It was impossible, Davis argued, to allow the peaceful provisioning of Sumter without seeming to give tacit consent to the continuation of a "foreign enclave" within the Confederacy's declared territorial borders. Passivity would have compromised the Confederate claim to independence and demoralized the Southern people.

Lincoln and the First Shot

Lincoln reasoned similarly in claiming he had no choice but to provision Sumter. It may well be that both leaders lost freedom of action because of the tragic logic of their positions. In which case, it would be more reasonable to argue that either Lincoln and Davis were both "aggressors," or that neither was, rather than to fasten major responsibility on one or the other. This is, more or less, the conclusion Current comes to in his closing paragraphs— but only after muddying the analysis somewhat by having singled out Davis for special censure earlier.

I wish, too—though this is perhaps asking for a work of speculative philosophy rather than sober history—that Professor Current had questioned Lincoln's basic premises more searchingly. These were, first, that the Union had to be preserved even at the risk of war and, second, that the best way of doing this was to maintain Federal authority at Sumter. The validity of these assumptions, especially the first, is not often questioned. They are, however, far from being unassailable. At the very least, they could do with more precise explication.

When Lincoln insisted that this "last best hope of earth" should not be allowed to perish, it was clear he had endowed the Union with mystical properties and hoped to dedicate the reconstituted nation to high and humane ends. The motives of those who since Lincoln's day have applauded the Union's preservation are somewhat less clear. It is a question whether today we glorify Lincoln's position in Lincoln's spirit: he wished to preserve the Union's spiritual potential; we applaud him for having preserved its power potential. So enamored have we become of our national power in the twentieth century that we automatically bless the forced reunification which made that power possible.

It is well to remember, too, that reunification *was* forced. In refusing to let the South establish her independence, Lincoln ignored what is supposedly a cardinal principle in the American creed—the right of self-determination. As David Potter has pointed out, there is considerable irony in the way we today applaud both the abstract principle of self-determination *and* Lincoln's refusal to let the South exercise it. Surely this is differential morality with a vengeance.

Even if we accept the *supreme* necessity of preserving the Union, there is still a real question whether Lincoln chose the right means for accomplishing that end. Professor Current describes, but does not really evaluate, the alternate policies of men like Secretary of State Seward, who shared Lincoln's goal but suggested different means for achieving it. Seward recognized that Sumter had become an explosive site and he thought it the wrong place to test federal authority—that is, unless one was willing to face almost certain war. He preferred to evacuate Sumter, maintain the symbol of federal authority at Fort Pickens instead, and then wait for a resurgent Southern Unionism to bring the seceded states back. Seward's vision was certainly defective. If nothing else, he put too much reliance on Unionist sentiment in the South. But his policies deserve to be evaluated rather than passed over, for it is possible that in the long run they might have produced happier results than Lincoln's. That is, unless one thinks that civil war and forced reunification were either the only or the best means of preserving the nation. But such means are not the usual signs of successful statesmanship.

It is not fair to expect Professor Current, given the kind of book he chose to write, to have raised these highly speculative and perhaps unresolvable questions. It might be more to the point to thank him for a splendid account, in terms of both narrative and analysis, of the Sumter crisis. Yet I have a nagging feeling that if we are to profit from historical experience it is just such "speculative" questions which must be raised.

HISTORY AS THEATER

This essay, the first of many pieces in which I mull over the perennial question of the "utility" of history, represents my views on the value of historical study at their most sanguine, a mood less frequent today than five years ago. The underlying premise of the piece—that a knowledge of past experience can provide valuable guidelines for acting in the present—is one I have come seriously to doubt; at the least, I would today insist on sharply limited definitions of "valuable," "guidelines" and "acting" (see "On Becoming an Historian"). In the same way, my charge to playwrights to concern themselves more than they have with the integrative aspects of human experience now seems to me to reflect a naïvely hortatory view of how artists choose and shape their materials.

I would say that today I retain considerably more faith in the integrative possibilities of human behavior than in the instructive potential of human history. Perhaps the affirmative mood clings more readily to an abstraction like "human potential" than to the specific activities—like reconstructing the past—to which human beings devote themselves.

Come, sit down, every mother's
son, and rehearse your parts.
—Shakespeare,
A Midsummer Night's Dream

I SUSPECT there are many besides myself who feel that historians are not communicating as well as they could, and that dramatists are not communicating as much as they might. It is the argument of this essay that the deficiencies of history and theater might be lessened if each would pay some attention to the virtues of the other.

First, however, I should make clear an underlying assumption: I believe the past has something to say to us. This may seem a truism, but an opposite view can be, and has been, cogently argued—the argument, if not the cogency, summed up in Henry Ford's statement, "History is all bunk." It is not my purpose to enter here in detail into the long-standing debate on whether history is or is not relevant to contemporary needs, can or cannot be objectively reconstructed, will or will not reflect the temporary bias of the historian and his culture. For the moment, I want only to make explicit my own premise that a knowledge of past experience can provide valuable guidelines, though not blueprints, for acting in the present. Those who do not share this assumption will hardly be concerned with the argument based upon it; there can be no wish to increase our awareness of the past if one holds that the past has no present meaning. And in the same way, those who believe that the theater is already rich

"History as Theater" was first published, under the title "Presenting the Past," in the Fall, 1964, issue of *The Columbia University Forum.* I revised it slightly when printed as an Appendix to the Signet paperback edition of my play *In White America.* It is that version which appears here.

enough in ideas and perspectives will have little patience with my further argument that its range needs amplification.

But to begin with history. Professional historians do, of course, worry about the shortcomings of their craft, but their dominant concern is with the difficulty of reconstructing past events "objectively." Handicapped both by the paucity of evidence and by the distortions in it which their own preconceptions introduce, historians have fits of self-doubt as to whether they are re-creating the past or merely projecting onto it their own, and their society's, transient needs. Yet few historians are concerned with shortcomings of another sort: whether their findings have much meaning for modern man. Too often today the academic historian seems to think his job is over once he has wrestled with the problems inherent in assembling data. He is, he would say, a scholar, not a policy adviser or a communications expert; it is up to others to draw and transmit the relevance of his findings.

Not only is the historian himself likely to be indifferent to the contemporary significance of his research, but suspicious of others who emphasize it; they are thought to be "propagandists." It is right, of course, to be on guard against any attempt to distort past evidence in the service of some present need. Yet such vigilance must be discriminating; a distinction should be made between reading contemporary meaning *into* the evidence, which is reprehensible, and reading it *from* the evidence, which is not. To do the latter is only to make explicit those conclusions already suggested by the data. The overt attempt to read "lessons" from history can, of course, be treacherous, but no worthwhile goal should be abandoned because it is difficult to attain. The effort to extract from the past something of use for our own experience is all that saves historical study from antiquarianism, the accumulation of detail for its own sake. If the past cannot be used—however conditionally—as a guide for the present, then its study is difficult to justify, at least to serious men. Historical writing becomes esthetics, the arrangement of past events in "pleasing" patterns, which, of course, can carry values of their own—except that historians have never been very good at esthetics. In asking them instead actively to search for "lessons," it should be stressed that no necessary threat is posed to historical objectivity. We would not ask historians to distort their findings, but to evaluate them, to be as eager to serve the living as the dead.

Assuming, then, that the past has some relevance for us, and that it is among a historian's proper functions—my own feeling is that it should be his preeminent function—to search for that relevance, it then becomes necessary to question the effectiveness with which such relevance (when found) is communicated. Since the invention of the printing press, the record of the past has been largely transmitted through the written word, and writing, a rational way of ordering and clarifying experience, makes an essentially intellectual appeal. Not always, of course, at the expense of the emotions: where the wish and skill are present, the writer can do much to evoke and engage our feelings. But the arousal of feelings is generally frowned on by the historian; emotion is thought to be an enemy rather than an adjunct of mind. Not surprisingly, therefore, historians have shown little regard for those literary skills best calculated to engage emotions. The majority of historians today eschew "lively" writing as a means of communication in much the same constricting way that they eschew relevance as its end. "Style" is thought to be an impediment to analysis, a frivolous sugar-coating repellent to those tough-minded heroes of the mind who prefer their ideas "straight."

Even were the historian more sensitive to the evocative potential of the written word, in immediacy he still could not rival the spoken word, which benefits from the direct confrontation of personality. In its beginnings, of course, the historical record *was* transmitted orally; in that sense, history began as theater. While no sensible person would advocate a return to this tradition, we may still wish to recapture something of its emotional impact. If we could bring the spoken word's immediacy and emotion to the presentation of history, a new richness of response, a new measure of involvement with the past, would be possible.

Almost all combinations of history and theater have been made by dramatists, with the result—as in Shakespeare's *Richard II* or John Osborne's *Luther*—that historical episodes have been used, shaped, and embellished for imaginative purposes. The past event becomes the occasion for a statement not in itself strictly historical. This is in accord with a writer's usual procedure; he transposes the raw material of experience, he makes it his own and, if he has sufficient insight and artistry, everyone's.

But the imaginative reworking of historical data is fundamentally inimical to what the professionals regard as "proper" history. The historian knows that his personality influences his interpretations, but this is not the same, he would say, as advocating such influence; a virtue should not be made of necessity. Control and restriction of interaction between the subjective historian and his "objective" materials is essential. This intellectual fastidiousness may severely limit the opportunity for speculation, but it also minimizes the risk of contaminating the data. The professionals, in short, prefer to emphasize information rather than informing.

Yet the contrast between the historian's "objective" presentation of the past and, say, the novelist's subjective reworking of it, is overdrawn. It describes the historian's intention more than his result, for in a real sense he too necessarily indulges in imaginative combinations of fact and opinion. Historical writing is never merely carbon paper, recording an exact facsimile of past events, but always consists to some degree of one man's idiosyncratic interaction with the data. It may be, too, that if the historian is ever to make widely relevant statements, he will have to become more consciously and extensively the philosopher *commenting* upon historical materials.

But if the contrast between the writing of history and fiction has been overdrawn, it is nevertheless a contrast the historian cherishes. He would protest being asked to play philosopher speculating on human ends, or psychologist investigating human needs, or novelist describing human conditions. He defines the role of a historian as simply one of collecting and recording what survives of past experience, *not* commenting upon it. Given this self-image, he objects especially to the "distortions" which a writer like John Osborne makes in the historical record when converting it for the stage. This, the historian would say, is adding immediacy and emotion to the past at the sacrifice of accuracy and intellectual subtlety.

An historian myself, I am sympathetic to these professional scruples even while not being fully convinced by them. Despite the risks, it seems to me worth searching for valid ways to combine history and theater, and not only to enrich historical presentation, but also to revitalize theatrical statement. For the benefits of a union between history and drama would not by any means be all on one side. If theater, with its ample skill in communication, could increase the immediacy of past experience, history, with its ample material on human behavior, could broaden the range of theatrical testimony. And there are grounds for believing that the theater's present range is badly in need of amplification.

The current mode of dramatic writing has been variously called the theater of the absurd, the theater of revolt, the theater of despair. The ugly, the empty, the irrational, the mechanical, the brutal, the apathetic—these are the dominant themes of contemporary theater. And they may well be the dominant themes of contemporary life. Perhaps today's playwrights, whose personal lives, we are told, have often been so melancholy, overdo the importance of these themes, confusing their own sorrows with the world's decline. But if the modern playwright has overdrawn the disintegrative aspects of modern life, it is not by much, judging from what we see around us. And the evidence of our senses is corroborated by the evidence of science. The portrayal of human behavior in the theater of the absurd closely resembles the description provided by sociologists, psychologists, and anthropologists. Man, these behavioral scientists tell us, *is* a creature who flees reality, who prefers comfortable deceptions to hard truths, whose yearning for approval drives him to think and act as his society dictates, whose libidinous instincts can propel him into brutal, selfish, destructive behavior. Thus the behavioral view of man seems to support the current theatrical view of man. If therefore, we take the function of drama to be the accurate reflecting of contemporary life, the state of our current theater must be judged satisfactory. Or, if unsatisfactory, only because our playwrights have not described the modern predicament with sufficient skill; the failure, according to this canon, would be one of execution, not intent.

It is possible to suggest, though, that the intent as well is too restricted. There is no inherent reason why drama need be limited to describing what *is;* it could also become concerned with what *might be.* One function of the theater should obviously be to reflect the actuality of life, but another might be to change it. Instead, by presenting man largely as brute, child or fool, the current theater fortifies and perpetuates those qualities. If men are told that they are at the mercy of impulse and irrationality, they become more likely to behave accordingly. Like it or not, the theater, partaking as it does of self-fulfilling prophecy, is a social force, though at present an inadvertent and negative one. Man's destructive qualities are real enough and must be faced. But other qualities—or at least potentials—are real as well, and they too should be brought to attention. At present they are not. Theater audiences see little to counteract the view that self-deception, hysteria, and savagery are synonyms for human nature.

Once again, the perspective of behavioral science is useful. Just as its findings validate the theater of the absurd, so they also support the need to supplement it. Psychologists and sociologists have made abundantly clear the immense plasticity and enormous adaptive power of human beings; if social demands and emphases are shifted, human action shifts accordingly. Thus, if we would not today celebrate man's innate goodness, we should be equally ready to recognize that nothing predetermines him to be cruel, vacuous, and selfish. As Berelson and Steiner point out in *Human Behavior,* man's "evil comes from frustration, not from inherent nature . . . he seeks acceptance . . . more than he seeks political power or economic riches, and he can even control his strongest instincts, the libidinous side of his nature, to this end." Man is not only a social creature, but also a social product. If challenged to do so, he is capable of using reason and will to develop integrative, and control destructive, impulses. Why should not the theater put such a challenge to him? Why could it not help to alter the destructive behavioral patterns it now merely describes? There is no inherent reason why drama cannot be an agency of amelioration as well as a voice of despair.

We need not be sentimental about all this and emblazon Victorian mottoes like SHINE IN USE on our playbills. I am certainly not suggesting that the theater of absurdity be supplemented by some crude theater of "positive thinking." I am suggesting only that since integrative experiences exist in our lives, they should also have some representation in our theater. Though despair and disintegration may well characterize the dominant mood today, they do not tell the whole story either of our present condition, or, more significantly still, of our potential one. The theater, by making room for a demonstration of other aspects of human nature, could help to see that the current mood of disintegration does not become the permanent one.

One way (though certainly not the only one) of demonstrating man's potential for a wide variety of experiences and behavior, is to put more history on the stage, either in fictional or documentary form. Both approaches have their drawbacks. Those characterizing fiction (à la Osborne) have already been discussed; my own experience with the documentary approach may serve to illustrate the special problems of that form.

In wanting to tell the story of being black "in white America" with the maximum impact, I thought it worth trying to combine the evocative power of the spoken word with the confirming power of historical fact. Yet I did not wish to sacrifice historical accuracy in the process. And so

History as Theater

I tried staging the raw material of history itself rather than a fictionalized version of it. The two modes of procedure, of course, are not entirely different—as I argued earlier. Using historical documents—letters, news reports, diaries, and the like—does not guarantee objectivity; it would be naïve to think that in selecting, abridging, cutting, and juxtaposing the materials of history, I was not also transmuting them. The past does not speak for itself, and the ordering intelligence that renders it, necessarily injects some degree of idiosyncrasy. The advantage of the documentary approach (if one is primarily interested in historical accuracy) is that it does at least minimize subjectivity and restrict invention. Its disadvantage (if one is primarily interested in making statements about experience) is that it circumscribes reflection and generalization. Instead of confining myself, for example, to the actual words John Brown spoke at his trial, I might have invented words to represent what I guessed to be his thoughts and feelings during his speech. In not doing so, I suspect that what I gained in accuracy I lost in insight. Truth of fact has less durable relevance than truth of feeling, for a fact is rooted in a particular context, whereas a feeling, being universal, can cross time.

There are, then, inherent difficulties in putting history on the stage: fictionalization can caricature the past, documentation can straitjacket it. Yet both techniques seem worth experimenting with, for history and theater, though the union be flawed, can contribute much to each other.

The great virtue of history, one the theater stands in need of, is that it counteracts present-mindedness—the belief that what *is* has always been and must always be. To have historical perspective is to become aware of the range of human adaptability and purpose. Thus the ancient world (and the eighteenth-century Enlightenment) saw man as a creature capable of using reason to perceive and follow "virtue"; the Christian view saw man capable of love as well as sin; the Renaissance believed that man's energy and will were sufficient to control both his personal destiny and his social environment.

Such views, of course, were philosophical models of what men could be, not necessarily what they were. But the dominant outlook of any period reflects actual as well as ideal behavior, for men build their self-images out of their experience as well as their aspirations. At any period, to be sure, ideal behavior is only approximated. Enlightenment France may have believed in the possibility—and necessity—of a rational life, but it was hardly free of sophistry and corruption; moderns have neither invented nor discovered man's capacity for the irrational and the vicious. But in other eras such qualities were not considered sufficient descriptions of human nature or insurmountable barriers to human aspiration; men could, they were told, resist their destructive impulses, could lead more than merely instinctive lives.

No doubt most of us today proceed on similar assumptions in daily life. But the assumptions get less formal recognition than they once did. We are not encouraged—in our culture generally, in our theater particularly—to recognize that human nature is malleable, capable of many forms and many goals. We are not encouraged to see that "absurdity" is only a partially true description of the way we live, and even more, that it tells us little of how we *might* live.

It is not the responsibility of the Albees or the Becketts to show us what we might be; their responsibility is to their own, not to all possible, visions. But for those concerned with the future as well as the present, something more in our theater wants saying. To recognize that human beings are curious, do strive, will reason, can love, is to wish for a theater that might express and encourage this kind of human potential—precisely because that potential is scarcely visible today. We need the theater of the absurd to dramatize our weaknesses and failings, but we also need a theater which might indicate our potential strengths and possible successes.

Putting history on the stage is hardly a cure-all. Not only does the technique, as I have argued, hold intrinsic difficulties, but it is true as well that historical theater would not necessarily be a theater of "affirmation"; undoubtedly much in man's past experience would underscore, rather than counteract, present pessimism. My only point is that the totality of past experience does include more than despair and defeat; there *is* material in history which chronicles achievement and possibility. Such evidence is around us today as well, of course, but we seem unable to use it; it may be a case of not being able to see the forest for the trees. This is exactly why an historical context may be needed if the "positive" aspects of human experience are to become accessible.

Merging the competencies of history and drama, therefore, could help to diminish the parochialism of both. Currently, historical study is fixated on past patterns and the theater on present ones; neither is sufficiently concerned with the future. If the variety of past experience could be communicated with an immediacy drawn from the theatrical idiom, both history and drama might become vehicles for change rather than only the recorders, respectively, of past and present attitudes. In being more fully exposed to the *diversity* of past human behavior, we might come to see that men (even if only *sometimes*) can give purpose and structure to their lives; can use the tensions of existence creatively, or at the worst, accept them with dignity; can, without sacrificing self-interest, treat others with respect and compassion. Such an awareness could be a useful corrective to the current penchant for underestimating ourselves, which, after all, is but one way of excusing and indulging our defeats.

THE ERA OF
RECONSTRUCTION

The opening paragraphs of this review continue the sanguinary mood of "History as Theater." Today I am less impressed with the similarities between the experience of the Civil War generation and our own than with the differences. I still think that we gain insight from studying the roughly analogous attitudes of an earlier generation, but given the differences in context and detail, I feel more hard-pressed than ever to spell out in any concrete way the nature of those insights.

The doubt I express here about the historian's ability to deal with questions of motivation, is one that has been of mounting concern to me—and one which I discuss at more length in such pieces as "The Limitations of History." Nothing has discouraged me more as a practicing historian, and particularly as a biographer, than the obstacles I find in the way of trying to understand the why in history. These, if anything, loom larger to me with the years, and I now doubt my statement that "we need not discuss individual psychology in order to derive instruction from history." Certainly the kinds of questions I have most wanted to ask of the past—matters of individual choice, consciousness and life style—cannot be satisfied without probing the sources of motivation.

WHAT does "popularization" mean? Two things: an effort to communicate specialized knowledge to the non-specialist, and a corruption of standards. The word has taken on a bad connotation—"popularizer" has become a calumny —because these two definitions have been equated; wide dissemination is thought to be the equivalent of debasement—an application to letters of that anti-democratic bias usually reserved for politics.

There has been reason enough for confusing the two forms of popularizing. Since the specialists themselves have eschewed—are often incapable of—communicating their findings, the job has been taken over by writers more interested in capitalizing on knowledge than spreading it, men skilled in producing instant sentences devoid of those nuances and uncertainties which are the authentic signs of knowledge in depth.

Fortunately there are some few specialists who feel the urgency and have the skill to share their knowledge, and who further realize that if they will not do their own popularizing, someone else will—badly. In the historical profession there is widespread disdain for scholars who do "popular treatments," a disdain which reflects, along with concern for preserving historical accuracy, a defensive lack of confidence. Historians are simply not sure that they *have* anything to communicate, which makes their contempt for the process understandable. Acres of antiquarian details they know they have, but whether these can be arranged into patterns that carry a usable message for the

This review of Kenneth M. Stampp's *The Era of Reconstruction, 1865–1877* (Alfred A. Knopf, Inc., New York) appeared in *Book Week,* April 11, 1965.

present, is a matter on which the profession, to put it mildly, has a certain want of confidence.

Historians of the Civil War and Reconstruction period (roughly 1820–1880) are more fortunate. They deal in themes of such obvious relevance to our own time that there is no difficulty extracting pertinent analogies. The issues faced by the Civil War generation are those we still face, though their focus has somewhat shifted—state versus national authority, the protection of minority rights in a system based on numerical majorities, the role played by political parties in adjusting interest conflicts, the utility of agitation in achieving social reform, and finally, of course, the place of the Negro in American life. In seeing how this earlier generation dealt with—or failed to deal with— roughly analogous problems, we gain insight into, if not answers for, our own.

Yet, sadly, it is not for these reasons that the Civil War period has found a large popular audience. The "buffs" who devour its literature by the ton care far less about the significant issues involved than about some fetishistic nonsense like whether or not Lee was wearing a hat at Appomattox. They see the history of the period almost solely as military narrative, and at that, military narrative in its narrowest sense. They seem unconcerned that the tactical lessons to be derived from dissecting Jackson's flank march at Chancellorsville have about as much meaning for techniques of modern warfare as a study of *Beowulf* for an understanding of Edward Albee. But perhaps irrelevance is the very source of their joy.

Kenneth Stampp, professor of American history at Berkeley, is one historian who refuses to pander to the fetishes either of antiquarian lay readers or of art-for-art's-sake scholars. He knows his specialty holds vital information for our own time, and he feels an obligation to give it general currency, especially the Reconstruction years 1865–1877 where dangerous myths still abound. The result of his concern is this lucid, literate survey in which he proves, in a little over 200 pages, that history can be made popular— i.e., digestible—without any dilution of subtlety or paradox.

What he has done is to distill those scholarly findings of the past two decades which have radically altered our view of Reconstruction, and which have desperately needed communicating to that larger public still feeding on destructive fictions. The view of Reconstruction which most Americans still hold (including sophisticates like James Reston) is that the period 1865–1877 was one of criminal mismanagement. Vindictive Northern radicals, according to this view, led an uncertain North away from the gentle policies of Lincoln, into the needless humiliation of a prostrate South. The radicals themselves were motivated by hatred, political advantage and economic self-interest— not by concern for the Negro. Against the protest of President Johnson, these radicals engineered first military and then "foreign" regimes in the Southern states; illiterate Negroes, corrupt Northern carpetbaggers and base Southern "scalawags" looted treasuries, tyrannized over the "better classes," and turned the state legislatures into obscene parodies of democratic government. Only in 1877, when Federal troops were finally withdrawn, did honesty and virtue return to the South.

Starting in the 1930s, an occasional challenge was made to this view of Reconstruction, a challenge which by the 1950s had grown to include almost every facet of the traditional picture. The process of scrutiny and revision still goes on, and at this juncture it is difficult to see through the debris left by the historical wreckers. An integrated synthesis of old and new is not yet possible, and Kenneth Stampp's book, therefore, is an interim report, an attempt to summarize for a general audience, without pretense to finality, the revisions which have thus far taken place.

Stampp makes clear that the older interpretation was not entire fabrication; vindictiveness, corruption and mis-government certainly existed. But we now know that there is so much more to Reconstruction that to talk exclusively of its sordid aspects is seriously to distort the story of those years. We now know that military government was in most places limited in strength and short in duration; that far from being brutalized, white Southerners were treated with astonishing leniency by their conquerors; that Andrew Johnson bears the major responsibility for the failure of his program, which, given its serious inadequacies, is not to be regretted; that both the extent and extravagance of Negro participation in the Southern state governments have been greatly magnified; that the carpetbagger and scalawag stereotypes are gross oversimplifications; that although the Reconstruction governments had their scandals, these were a national, not a sectional, phenomenon, the product of wartime demoralization, not of the special defects of Radical policy; that these Reconstruction governments, more-over, had many positive achievements to their credit, in-cluding the first system of free public education in the South.

As for the Radical Republicans who dominated the Re-construction experiment, their story is far more complex than was earlier believed. In dealing with the motives of these men, Stampp is at his most provocative. Rather than skirting or oversimplifying the difficult problem of motiva-tion, he deals with it head-on. Though his discussion is not fully satisfying, its limitations reflect far less on Stampp than on the built-in restraints of historical investigation.

Stampp believes that the Radicals were sincerely concerned about the Negro's welfare—a needed corrective to the earlier blanket denial that these men had any trace of idealism. But like the earlier view, the new one is essentially an act of faith. Just as it fit the purposes of a previous generation, hostile to the Negro, to devalue the commitment of Radicals pushing for reforms in his name, so it fits the purposes of our generation to see those same reformers in a more heroic light. It may even fit historical truth. But it might be well to recognize that present needs and past realities can get entangled. Ultimately, we lack the kind of intimate personality data that might allow for confident assessment of Radical motivation. Our psychologizing about them is based on imaginative (in both senses) use of fragmentary data, and our conclusions are likely to reflect our starting assumptions.

Stampp is most successful when exposing the inadequate premises which underlay earlier hostility to the Radicals —that men *never* mean what they say (if they are reformers), that they are really guided by the unarticulated, selfish motive, that they possess enough self-understanding always to be deliberative hypocrites and enough manipulative skill always to deceive others about their intentions. But when Stampp comes to argue his own position that "desire for justice" was a mainspring of Radical motivation, he is reduced to assertions rather than proofs. And the negative way in which he phrases them ("Their pleas for the Negro . . . cannot be discounted as pure hypocrisy") suggests an awareness that his case has not really been concluded.

Stampp's discussion of motivation, done as it is with maximum skill, perhaps holds an object lesson for historians. It may be that if they desire to judge the past in order to sensitize the present (a procedure I sympathize with) they will have to concentrate on actions rather than motives. It is safer, in terms both of evidence and metaphysics, to assert that the Radical program for granting civil rights to the Negro was a "good thing" than to argue that the men who advocated such a program did so for "good" reasons.

Stampp's book makes clear that we need not discuss individual psychology in order to derive instruction from history. Because he is not afraid to state opinions and to draw contemporary parallels, he has provided considerable matter for speculation, especially in regard to the ultimate cause of Radical failure to achieve equality for the Negro. Stampp hints, without insisting, that the root trouble lay in the underlying assumptions then prevalent in American society—the deep commitment to private property, limited government and the tenets of Social Darwinism. These values prevented giving land to Negroes, thus denying them economic security, discouraged continuing Federal intervention when Southern whites resorted to violence, and allowed a complacent belief that time would "gradually evolve" a solution for the race problem.

It is not clear that our value structure has changed sufficiently in a hundred years to justify greater optimism about the success of the Second Reconstruction. Yet values have shifted enough to give some ground for hope. Anyway, what choice is there but to hope?

THE LIMITATIONS
OF HISTORY

Parts of this essay are no longer congenial to me. Its mode of argument—abstract, generalized—I now find quite foreign. And though the essay does still represent many of my dissatisfactions with studying the past (especially the historian's inability to explain motivation), as regards some aspects of that study, the piece now seems to me rather too optimistic. For example, I'm inclined these days to doubt whether the study of past revolutions can yield even conditional guides for understanding present or future ones; currently, I am more impressed with the uniqueness than with the commonalty of events. I would now "justify" the study of history either on more general grounds (it makes us aware of the potential range of human behavior; it educates us in humility by showing how difficult it is to understand—and therefore to judge—men and events), or on negative grounds (it prevents others from claiming that history conveys clear-cut lessons). I am also more skeptical today about the historian's ability to make the past "relevant" even when, as this essay recommended, he does concentrate on analyzing essentials rather than cataloguing trivia: the historical evidence is too fragmentary and recalcitrant, the context of past (and present) experience too special, the historian himself too bounded by his culture.

In vain the sage, with retro-
spective eye,
Would from the apparent
what conclude the why,
Infer the motive from the
deed, and show
That what we chanced was
what we meant to do.
—Alexander Pope,
Moral Essays

IN the early decades of this century, the New History produced considerable ferment. Historians learned to challenge the platitudes and pretensions of their craft, and to
question both the reliability of their data and the quality
of perception which they brought to it. Time has dulled
these concerns; the New History has given way to the New
Complacency. Historians will still readily admit their im-
perfections, but with a detachment that suggests they no
longer feel very concerned about them. It is as if having
acknowledged their limitations, they now feel entitled to
ignore them—what we might call the confessional syn-
drome. Perhaps it is time to raise anew some questions regarding the value of historical study.

A useful distinction to begin with is that between human
behavior and human personality. By behavior I mean all
that can be observed and described by a third person—
externals, the world of action. By personality I mean that
tangle of individual strivings which underlies behavior—
the system of motivation at the source of the action.

"The Limitations of History" was first printed in *The Antioch Review*,
Summer, 1965. It appears here as later revised for an anthology.

Before Freud, behavior and personality were usually considered equivalents; personality, in fact, was defined as "the pattern of behavior characteristic for a given individual." Freud insisted that the individual personality underlay, but was not identical with, the individual's behavior. A man's personality, he insisted, is something more than the sum of his acts (just as it is also something more than the product of the cultural pressures around him). We cannot, simply by observing a man's behavior, deduce all there is to know about his inner strivings (just as these, in turn, cannot be fully accounted for merely by enumerating the domestic and community mores in which they were fashioned).

The distinction between behavior and personality can best be seen by singling out one behavioral trait—unselfishness, say—for closer examination, though my remarks could apply equally well to any number of other traits—apathy, friendliness, anxiety, optimism, etc. It is easier to observe and describe "unselfishness" in another than to account for it, for it can be produced by a wide range of personality drives. It can be motivated—to give only a few possibilities—by a fear of self-assertion, by genuine devotion to the object being served, or by a craving for admiration. To the outside observer, selfless behavior will always look roughly the same, even though it may be variously motivated. I say *roughly* the same, because there *are* subtle differences in the way individuals manifest their unselfishness and these subtleties do reflect the differences in motivation. But the distinctions are usually too fine to be readily identifiable, or to serve as tracers back to the motives themselves. It is true that when we observe the external world of action we always learn something of the private world of the actor; the contours of behavior will always reveal to some extent the individual's inner feelings and drives. Moreover, behavior and personality continually interact; they do not remain discrete units. Thus, an unselfish act may be initially motivated by a craving for admiration, but once performed, the act in turn modifies the craving, perhaps lessening, perhaps further stimulating it. But if behavior and personality are inter-related and interacting, the fact remains that they are not equivalents. We do not learn everything about an individual's personality simply by observing and describing the external pattern of his behavior.

All of which is prelude to a basic division between what historians can and cannot do. What historians can do, I believe, is describe past behavior, the external world of action. What they can do far less well is explain the personality strivings which underlie behavior; these are, indeed, largely closed to historical investigation.

Let me begin with that area in which historians are likely to be most successful—that is, the reconstruction of past behavior. Even here, the historian has difficulty. The accurate reconstruction of external events is jeopardized both by the partial nature of the evidence and by the personal preconceptions which the historian brings to it. Reconstruction is most difficult when the historian tries to *account* for past events rather than merely to describe them. It is easier, for example, to describe the milestones of our involvement in World War I—the various diplomatic exchanges, the international incidents, and so forth—than to explain their origins or to place them in some kind of "rank list" of relative importance in bringing on conflict. As soon as we try to analyze the cause of any event, or its effect on other events, we face severe epistemological difficulties.

The number of possibly relevant factors in explaining any event is very large. To be able to explain at all, we discard most such factors and single out a few for special emphasis. But it is difficult to know whether or not our choices are arbitrary. In "explaining" our entrance into World War I, should we concentrate on the international complications arising from submarine warfare or on Woodrow Wilson's Presbyterian background? If the latter, we are in danger of opening a Pandora's box of possibilities. But if we do not consider the personal backgrounds of the leading actors, we run the danger of omitting crucial elements in the explanation. What principle of selection, in other words, do we follow when accounting for an event or a sequence of events? Often historians deal with the problem impressionistically—that is, they use their "intuition" in deciding what is or is not relevant to a particular explanation. But "intuition," alas, has a disconcerting way of varying with individuals, so that we often end up with as many explanations for a given event as we have historians explaining it.

Even if we assume that the historian *can* reconstruct and explain past events, the question then arises as to what purpose this serves.

We are no longer so sanguine as to expect the study of events in the past to provide us with a detailed blueprint for action in the present or future. We recognize, for example, that no matter how much we learn of the contours of past revolutions, we will never be able to tell with certainty either how to avoid or how to produce one. There are too many variables through time; events are too embedded in their unique contexts to be readily interchangeable.

Yet no event is entirely unique. Similarities, even if only roughly approximate ones, can often be found between analogous events widely separated by time. Thus every revolution has had its "Thermidor," an onset of conservative reaction. It may not appear according to the same timetable in every revolution, nor manifest itself in exactly the same way, but it does seem to be a recurrent phenomenon. Such parallels suggest that a study of past revolutions can serve as at least a conditional guide towards understanding present or future ones. The analogy can only be rough, the similarities only approximate, but some information is always preferable to none. If we are aware of the consequences following upon certain decisions in the past, we will be better able, in approximately equivalent situations, to make more considered choices in the present.

But the emphases in historical writing are not usually placed in such a way as to encourage the past to yield even this limited applicability. Too often detail is accumulated and presented for its own sake, not as a foundation stone for some broader analysis. No bit of information is too small to be worth having when used creatively to form a larger mosaic, but all too frequently detail is elaborated *in vacuo,* the dead specifics of past action tirelessly rehearsed without any reference to a broader framework which might rescue the recitation from antiquarianism. A certain amount of such detail is necessary if we are to draw valid conclusions on larger questions, but too often the detail is allowed to stand alone, and the larger questions are ignored.

Such questions are always inherent in historical material, if we would trouble to see them. Thus, an historian of the American navy, instead of presenting endless details on outmoded ship construction, the dimensions and placement of gun batteries, or the minutiae of battle formations, could predigest these details and move on to an analysis of such broad problems as the relation between seapower and national strength, or the way in which a country's social structure can influence its command organization—to name but two of many possibilities. Or, more generally, military historians might transcend the archaic trivia of their material by converting military history proper into intellectual history; they could concentrate on what men have thought about war, rather than on the outmoded specifics of how they fought it. In this way they might do much both to interest and inform us: unlike Vauban, we do not fight wars today by building star-shaped fortifications, but like him, we do continue to wonder about the kind of military force necessary to maintain national security; unlike Frederick the Great, we have no concern with linear tactics, but like him, we continue to brood on the origins and use of power. Thus military history, if treated as the history of ideas, would have a better chance of speaking to us across the expanse of time. And this is but one way in which, by analyzing essentials rather than cataloging trivia, we might maximize the significance of past action for the present. None of this need be done self-consciously; if a book is structured properly, such speculative considerations could emerge naturally from the material without sacrificing narrative continuity or distorting the integrity of past events.

Using history as a tool for analyzing issues of continuing import has both rewards and risks. The reward comes from the satisfaction of making the past relevant, making it resonate for our times. The risk is that our histories will become obsolete as soon as the problems they are focused on cease to be of concern. But then we run that risk anyway. As different generations ask different questions of the past, our histories always become outmoded in part. It would be something, at least, if they were not entirely so at birth.

Even when historical writing emphasizes that which is of maximum relevance, it cannot be more than a tentative guide for present action. History, collective memory, is useful in much the same way that individual memory is useful (though perhaps not to the same degree, since history is the remembrance of the experience of others). In both cases the recollections, though likely to be partial, faulty, and distorted, are nonetheless indispensable, for through memory, be it individual or collective, we order experience, creating a basis for future action. Memory, then, is useful, even when not true—unless, of course, utility be a definition of truth.

The memory of past experience, however, is not the only possible guide to future action; in fact, it may not be the most important. In projecting a future course we should know more than what, individually and collectively, we have been; we should also know what we hope to become —and what we are capable of becoming.

History can tell us something of our capabilities—that is, if historians would aim at such discoveries—but psychology can tell us more; it can pierce behind action to motive, can examine those underlying needs which surface behavior often conceals rather than expresses.

History can tell us less of our hopes. If we wish to pass from discoveries about how men could behave, to decisions about how they should behave—from what is possible to what is desirable—we must move into the realm of ethics, the preserve of philosophers, poets, and prophets.

I suggest, then, a three-tiered (I am tempted to say ascending) structure: history—how man has behaved; psychology—how and why man does and could behave; "philosophy"—how man should behave. History as usually written freezes us at the first tier; we learn what men have done rather than what they could or should do. The historian might contribute something towards enlightening us on these other matters (as sage if not as scholar), but he chooses not to. He fears speculation and opinion; they are "subjective"; they are in contrast, he fondly believes, to the objective reality of his own reconstructions.

In one sense, despite himself, the historian does tell us something of our needs and goals, or at least of the limitations we must place upon them. For in describing past behavior, the historian educates in humility. He shows us that regardless of what might be the unlimited scope of our innate capacities and the boundless character of our utopian yearnings, the range for their expression is necessarily circumscribed by the way men have earlier channeled their capacities and defined their goals. What men may become will continue to depend on what they have been. The habit and authority of past patterns must ever limit and define future potentialities—a least until that visionary day when we can discover man's full nature and then agree upon how to utilize it. Should such a millennium occur, we would no longer either need or allow the past to define us. But until then, we shall continue to be creatures whose potentialities are historically conditioned.

Thus far, then, I have examined that area of past experience with which I think historians are best equipped to deal—namely, the external world of action. Even here, I have argued, the historian has no easy job. The reconstruction of past behavior is made hazardous by the limitations of the data, by the historian's preconceptions, and by inherent problems of causal explanation. Even when these obstacles can be surmounted, when past action can be both reconstructed and explained, its contemporary relevance is not always apparent. This is in part the fault of the historian himself, who tends to concentrate on details rather than essentials. But in part, too, it is a deficiency inherent in historical study, which, by definition, tells us more of what we have been than of what we might become. And in a revolutionary age such as ours, how we might free ourselves from the past and move beyond it seems more important to many than the past itself. But until our sciences have given us a complete model of human potential, and our humanities have then achieved a consensus on how that potential should be used, our very ability to free ourselves from the past will continue to depend on the extent to which we understand it.

And so—to emphasize the positive—one might say that the historian's power to reconstruct past action is sufficiently great, and the relevance of the reconstruction is sufficiently plausible, to make the effort worthwhile.

I have earlier stated, but not yet demonstrated, that historians cannot investigate past personality, that they cannot successfully recapture the private, inner world of feelings, drives, needs. One obstacle, though not in itself conclusive, is the historian's own distaste for such investigations. Historians, to oversimplify, tend not to be interested in personality—other than in its public manifestations. They have always been more concerned with how man functions and performs in society than how man lives alone, within himself. And this concentration has been steadily increasing in recent years, reflecting, no doubt, the trend everywhere towards impersonality. Most historians, to put it baldly, have become sociologists—indeed, amateur sociologists—though the label (even without "amateur" prefixed) might horrify them. Thus we have E. H. Carr, whom historians have rushed to praise, insisting that we reserve the word *history* "for the serious process of inquiry into the past of man in society."[1] We would all agree that the individual cannot be fully understood apart from his society, but what is too often made to follow, is that apart from his social role, the individual is not worth understanding. Such an attitude converts the historian's inability to examine individuality from a limitation into a virtue.

Further, it confirms those very traits of personality in many historians which first inclined them to join the profession. For historians, almost by definition, are men who shy away from the interior life, who are temperamentally drawn instead to the externals of behavior, to what is verifiable, concrete, susceptible of exact description—everything we sum up in the word "facts." In this regard, it is instructive that historians like to use the word "solid" in expressing their admiration for a particular work of history—as if the prime virtue was filling some literal void. For those who seek such "solidity," the elusive world of private feeling is unappealing, even threatening. Indeed "literal-mindedness" may have its very origin in a defensive flight from emotion (though many historians would no doubt insist that their avoidance is due to indifference, not fear).

There are historians, of course, who do not share the literal-minded temperament, who *are* interested in the interior world of personality. And some of them would no doubt claim that history allows them to pursue that interest, especially if they concentrate on writing either biography or the history of ideas. It is true that these two branches of historical study do entail some investigation into personality—but only some.

[1] E. H. Carr, *What is History?* (Knopf, 1962), p. 59.

The Limitations of History

It is a question whether the history of ideas is concerned with inner processes at all. As usually practiced, it focuses on distilled experience, an author's public formulation of his private confrontation with the universe. What is almost always slighted, perhaps necessarily, is the private confrontation itself, the nature of the inner experience which produced the formal work; and what is also slighted is the relationship between the two. It is true that if we pay attention to the patterns of imagery by which an author projects his ideas, these will sometimes take us into the emotional origins of those ideas,[2] but never, it seems to me, very far into them. Primarily, then, the historian of ideas deals with the result, not the process, of private experience. He can easily enough justify this concentration simply by defining his interest as in the ideas themselves, not in the private experience which produced them. He can thus with good conscience decline to concern himself with personality. But at the same time there should be no pretense that he *is* investigating it.

For the biographer, the situation is somewhat different. Some biographers also eschew any study of personality, in order, they say, to concentrate on the public career of their subject. But for many biographers, this solution is not satisfying. They feel that not even a public career can be well understood without reference to the inner strivings which underlay it. Moreover, they believe that the very logic of biography—the full portrait of an individual—demands some attention to the interior life. But although these biographers are, both by temperamental inclination and professional conscience, willing and eager to under-

[2] As, for example, the way Edmund Wilson's analysis, in *Patriotic Gore,* of the imagery of struggle and conflict in Holmes's writings establishes the crucial nature of the Civil War experience in Holmes's view of life.

take the job of personality analysis, they are usually un-able to perform the task, for the limitations of data can rarely be overcome.

Available historical evidence, even private journals and letters, contains only the traces of personality. It is a rare journal which is truly introspective, that is, which dis-cusses the author's motives and feelings as well as his activities. In some cases, omission of the personal com-ponent is unconscious, reflecting the author's limited self-awareness, while in others, it may be deliberate, part of the author's conscious effort to obscure or misrepresent his intentions. It is true that even when the record is rigidly impersonal, it usually manages, inadvertently, to reveal some personal data. But it is also true that even when the record is full of personal revelations, there are always tantalizing omissions, feelings which are unexplained, re-actions which are undefined. And often these omissions are in crucial areas. The skillful biographer, drawing on other sources and on his own intuition, can fill some of the gaps, but the limits both of evidence and empathy will leave the private record partially—and often notably—incomplete.

Take, for example, the case of George Washington. Few men have been the subject of such intense historical in-vestigation, yet we still know little of Washington's inner experiences. We can confidently describe the contours of his personality, such as his pronounced sense of public duty, but we can hardly begin to account for them, for the childhood experiences which are at their source, are almost entirely closed off to us. Even for Washington's adult life, crucial emotional episodes are unavailable. Not only do we not know what the quality of his love for Sally Fairfax was, we do not even know *if* he loved Sally Fairfax. In not knowing, we lose both the direct enrichment of personal empathy, and the indirect contribution such knowledge might make to our understanding of Washington's public career.

The limitations of data, then, usually force the biographer to confine himself to describing externals, the behavior of his subject. Thus the theoretical goal of biography, the depiction of the whole man, is in practice reduced to an unbalanced account which concentrates on action and slights personality—that is, if the biographer remains true to his material, rather than turning historical novelist and embroidering with imagined detail.

In fact, then, neither the biographer nor the historian of ideas, both of whom might be thought exempt from the usual limitations of historical investigation, can delve very deeply into the private experiences of figures in the past.

The appropriate question at this point is, "So what?" Are the private experiences of people long dead so important that historians need trouble themselves at their inability to recapture them? The answer, I believe, is a decided yes.

At the very least, the historian's inability to recapture the inner life runs counter to the vaunted pretension that he deals with "the totality of past experience." Either the historian must agree to trim this pretension to size or he must take refuge in the dubious argument that the private realm is so insignificant a part of past experience as hardly to count. I suspect that many historians actually believe the latter, though they would probably recognize that in the post-Freudian world this position is a bit awkward to defend.

But the inability to recapture the private realm raises more questions than merely history's pretensions. It also casts doubt on how well historians can reconstruct even the public realm. For how can we fully understand past actions without fully understanding what occasioned them? And to know what occasioned them requires a knowledge not only of the external circumstances which influence an event, but also of the internal strivings of those individuals who come to be involved in it. How, for example, can we fully account for Grant's refusal to retreat from Vicksburg after a series of failures, without a knowledge of his private needs, fantasies, fears? This, by itself, will not provide a full explanation, but without it, all other explanations must be partial. And if our understanding of past action remains partial, we cannot pretend to derive other than incomplete lessons from it. Is it possible to extract much of the meaning of a past event when we are unable to examine some of the crucial factors which produced it?

Beyond wanting to know about private experience for the light it throws on public action, it is important to recapture for itself. Unless we are put in touch—in life and literature—with the felt experiences of others, our own feelings atrophy. We need to be more than rationally *informed* about feeling; we need to *feel*—to respond directly with our own emotions to those of others. My conviction, perhaps idiosyncratic, is that the most profound experience available to us is the immediate sharing of the immediate feelings of our fellows. History, it seems to me, permits precious little of this direct sharing, for it cannot recapture those areas of private experience in the past to which our own feelings could most readily respond.

To respond with emotion is important not only as catharsis and communication, but also as a valuable adjunct to the learning process itself—at least to the kind of learning which leads to change and growth, rather than to the mere accumulation of data. Perhaps I can best explain what I consider the value of emotion to learning by using the analogy of psychotherapy. It is often the case that a patient in therapy can be brought to the point where he intellectually acknowledges the symptoms and even the sources of his neuroses. And yet he cannot abandon them, cannot really grow, until he can emotionally experience, can *feel*, that which he has already understood intellectually. In the same way, it seems to me, if we merely apprehend past events, without feeling their impact, they are not likely to inform us in the fullest sense.

Needless to say, we are not solely dependent on books for emotional vitality; there is also life itself. But if we value emotional response, there is reason to be unhappy at its absence from our studies, to which, after all, we give considerable time and energy. The absence is partly due to the built-in limitations of historical study. Historians, as I have argued, can but seldom put us in direct touch with the inner world. They can rarely appeal to our emotional sensibilities to the extent that a writer of fiction can. The novelist, for example, unlike the historian, *can* put us directly in touch with the emotions. He can freely describe that private world which the conscientious historian can at most only hint at, for he is limited not by data, but only by the extent of his own imagination.

Nor does it matter that the novelist is not describing the feelings of "real" people. This is quite irrelevant to the truth of his portrait, which will depend not on its correspondence to actual occurrences, but on its correspondence to what human beings are like. The validity of the novelist's insights ultimately depends only on the depth and clarity of his perceptions about people, and the skill with which he can communicate those perceptions. If he has these qualities, there is no limit to what he can tell us about the hidden world of personality, nor, as a result, any limit to the feeling response he can arouse within us. Fiction can sometimes deal in more profound truths than fact.

This is not to say that works of history are totally incapable of engaging our feelings. The historian may not be able to compete with the fiction writer in putting us directly in touch with the inner world, but there are other ways in which he can communicate and engage emotion: a recital of externals, even when we do not know their sources, can stir us deeply; so can language, if manipulated evocatively. If the two are combined—if "stirring" action is described in "stirring" prose—our feelings can be profoundly engaged. There is no doubt that a description of the Warsaw ghetto uprising, if done with a modicum of intensity and literary skill, is capable of moving us deeply.

Unfortunately most modern historians, even when they possess the requisite literary skills, usually eschew their use. The phrase "mere description" has become a standard term of opprobrium in the profession (rivalled only by the accusation of "popularization"). A neophyte historian who wished to study the Warsaw uprising would probably be advised to view it primarily as a problem in analysis. Avoid mere narrative detail, he would be told, and concentrate on such matters as the sociological background of the ghetto fighters; spare description and focus instead on an explanation of why the Jews in Warsaw rose and the Jews in Cracow did not. This kind of analysis, of course, is all to the good; I do not mean to disparage it. If intelligently done, it can do much to inform us. But need an appeal to our minds always be at the expense of an appeal to our feelings?

I am not making a plea for a return to descriptive history devoid of analysis. But I am concerned that our analytic history is so devoid of evocative description that where it nourishes at all, it nourishes only the intellect. We seem willing to put up with any amount of pedestrian detail so long as it contributes "information," but we are impatient with it when included "merely" to capture mood and evoke feeling. We distrust detail that speaks to our emotions, but not when it stultifies them. We seem suspicious of historians who excite us, but not of those who bore us.

It is, I suppose, unfashionable, if not worse, to see any merit in descriptive history. Yet the ability of literate, narrative history to engage our fantasies and arouse our feelings may explain why men like Herodotus, Gibbon, and Macaulay continue to find audiences—why, despite their suspect factual framework, they have managed to survive through time, while their "analytical" counterparts are ruthlessly and rapidly supplanted.

If the historian can be made aware of the inherent limitations of his profession, there is greater chance that he will be able to maximize whatever limited value the study of the past may have. This means putting aside some of the traditional pretensions of the profession, and these are not easy to surrender. Yet pretensions of any kind, as we know, can stand in the way of authentic accomplishment. They can prevent historians from performing well the roles for which they are suited. And there are such roles. For if history cannot be perfectly relevant, it can be partially so; if it cannot prescribe the future, it can conditionally guide the present; if it cannot recapture the feelings of men long dead, it can make at least a partial appeal to the feelings of men still living. History can do all these things—can, that is, if the historian decides that it must.

THREE HISTORIANS:
PERRY MILLER, BARBARA W.
TUCHMAN AND DAVID M.
POTTER

Though written at widely different times, the following three reviews have been brought together because in all of them I ask the same question: What makes for "good" historical writing? My attempt at an answer raises a number of controversial issues: the value of narrative history and of "popular" treatments; the comparative merit of approaching historical materials "subjectively" or "objectively"; the contrasting rewards (and pitfalls) that come from emphasizing the sociological or psychological component in past behavior.

PERRY MILLER's premature death in 1963 cut short one of the indisputably great scholarly careers—though "scholarly," connoting limited perspectives and dry acquirements, hardly does justice to his range and flair.

It was long known that Miller had been at work on a vast project, *The Life of the Mind in America*. Though few doubted the finished product would be of immense interest, equally few would have risked predicting that it would stand as his *magnum opus*; for this would have required Miller to surpass such brilliant earlier volumes as *The New England Mind: The Seventeenth Century*—so uncompromisingly Puritan in its integrity and profundity, in its insistent complexity. But one could at least be certain that because Miller himself looked on the "Life" as a major effort, it would be above the level of his *The Raven and the Whale*, a book he meant as a divertissement, but whose triviality and arrogance reflected all too well the minor nineteenth-century literary battles it chronicled. Every major writer is entitled to his aberrations, perhaps requires them; Miller's quotient, out of some dozen books, is unusually small. *The Life of the Mind in America*, as expected, does not add to the list, even though it comes to us in truncated form.

The grand design Miller outlined would have required nine "Books" (probably to fill two volumes). Together, as his wife, Elizabeth Miller, says in her foreword, they would have distinguished "the various strands of intellectual experience that went into the establishing of an American identity" from the Revolution to the Civil War. As outlined,

This review of Perry Miller's *The Life of the Mind in America* (Harcourt, Brace & World, Inc., New York) appeared in *Book Week*, August 29, 1965.

the Books bore such working titles as "Philosophy," "Theology," "Nature" and "The Self." At the time of his death, Miller had completed two of the Books—"The Evangelical Basis" and "The Legal Mentality"—and had begun a third, "Science—Theoretical and Applied." It is these, which Miller for the most part had thoroughly revised, that his wife has gathered for this volume. There can be no doubt of the rightness of her decision to publish this fragment of the whole, for though a poignant reminder of what might have been, it is also a brilliant confirmation of what had already been done.

There are lapses and lacunae, inevitable in an author who takes chances, who reads and judges independently, who insists on focusing not on all possible facets of an issue but on those that interest him—an author, in short, who stamps his personality, not merely his professional credentials, on every page. The only major disappointment, to my mind, is Miller's failure to clarify the *specific* influence of revivalism on the growth of reform activities in the early nineteenth century. That a causal relationship existed, we have long known; that it involved the evangelical emphasis on individual will power and the need for communal brotherhood, we have also known. It was to be hoped that Miller, who more than anyone combined the needed erudition and insight, might have extended and clarified the analysis. He has not. Though his narrative of the parallel progress of revivalism and "benevolence" is sprinkled with new insights (like the stunning analysis of Charles Grandison Finney's success), the interrelationship of the two movements is not explored in depth; Miller settled for the lame remark that although the connection "may be obscure," it certainly existed.

Nor is this the sole example of analytical failure. It is worth stressing that Miller was writing *his* book, not everyone's, but one has some right to complain when he *does* raise a problem and then promptly abandons it (as, for example, the relationship of revivals to capitalistic expansion). Just as the wit and grace of his prose carry us lightly over several less-than-light topics (canal-building, the civil law, etc.), so that same epigrammatic ease can mesmerize us into not noticing, or caring, that some issues are disappearing in literary sleight-of-hand (thus, extraordinary legal minds "almost miraculously emerged"—and no more said—during a period when the legal profession was at a low point in prestige).

Miller's most persistent refusal to prevent an analytical issue from turning into a mere literary device is his use of the Civil War. It may be that in some future section, he had intended to spell out the precise linkage between developing patterns in American thought and the holocaust of 1861. But he has certainly not done so in the text we have at hand. Instead, at given intervals, he apocalyptically reminds us that war will be the only "live option" which the emerging tendencies or evasions of the American mind will leave. Which may well be true, but we would prefer demonstration to assertion; Miller states but does not establish the organic connection between intellectual trends and the march toward Fort Sumter. The Civil War serves Miller as *deus ex machina*—but in the almost literal sense of a supernatural rather than logical culmination.

I would put in a quite different category another list of potential complaints against the book—the leisurely pace with which Miller approaches a point; his specificity; his insistence on detail; his intricacy of argument. These do not seem to me, as they may to others, defects at all. I believe they are, instead, part and parcel of Miller's special quality as an historian, the integral elements (at worst, the necessary elaborations) of his genius.

To be quite precise, Miller's handling of detail is what establishes in my mind his first-rate historical intelligence, or, to go even further, I would say that *only* when an historian treats detail as Miller does, is there a chance that first-rate history will be written. What he refuses to do, first of all, is dispense with detail; he *will* distill the essence, he *will* draw the broad conclusion, but *not just yet*. He insists that the reader first be given enough specifics to make him aware of the complexities involved in historical evaluation (which is to say, in understanding human beings). Yet Miller is able to luxuriate in the particular without losing himself (or the reader) in it. He is never the antiquarian amassing facts for their own sake (which really means for the antiquarian's sake); he, not the material, is the controlling force. Thus, the considerable detail he gives us on the life and writings of Finney is detail consciously chosen. He does not dump *all* he knows about Finney into our laps, as does the antiquarian; he selects what he has pre-determined is necessary for understanding the broader analysis he will shortly make of the significance of Finney's career.

And he does move on to broader analysis. In this, no less than in his insistence upon prior particularities, he is a model worth emulating. He knows that facts will not speak for themselves, will not form their own patterns; the historian must be the guiding intelligence, must himself extract the meaning from the data he has carefully assembled. Thus, after giving us considerable information about the pre-Civil War dispute over whether the law should or should not be codified, Miller explicitly draws its larger significance: the debate, consciously or not, was basically a contest between nationalism and cosmopolitanism, this in turn being "*the* American problem"—did patriotism consist, would identity emerge, within the context of isolated development or international culture? So persistently has Miller sketched the detailed background for this thematic statement that when it comes, we feel participants in drawing it; it is less a dictum handed down by authority than the shared discovery of reader and author. By having insisted that we first investigate *with* him the disjointed parts, he makes it possible for us subsequently to share the excitement (and even to some degree the sense of accomplishment) of the larger conclusions—which perhaps is only to say that among other things, Perry Miller is a true teacher.

A final aspect of the exemplary way in which Miller performs the historian's function is his willingness to extract guidelines for the present from his findings about the past. He concentrates his main energies on the job of historical reconstruction, but that done, goes on to relate it, in tentative and circumscribed fashion, to contemporary concerns. He is willing to attempt the role of sage as well as scholar, though without becoming ponderous or dogmatic. The effort alone some will call over-confident, inappropriate, misguided, but at least it does not reek of the academy's usual self-protectiveness. Miller will risk opinion and analogy; this makes him more vulnerable than those who refuse to suggest the meaning of their own findings, but also more relevant—and certainly more alive.

Perry Miller, in short, has left us more than his books—though these are great gifts. By his example, he has left, as well, a model of what it does (or should) mean truly to be an historian. It means insistence on enough detail to establish the complex particularity of men and events; it means, at the same time, pruning the irrelevant and building toward general statement; it means overt interpretation and an explicit avowal of findings; it means applying what we learn from the experience of yesterday to the needs of today. It means, in short, a determination to serve the present even while remaining faithful to the past.

BARBARA TUCHMAN's new book, *The Proud Tower*, attempts "a portrait of the world before the war, 1890–1914." Recognizing that some limits must be set to so vast a theme, she has confined herself to the United States and Western Europe, and within these bounds has selected eight topics for detailed treatment. These, so she tells us, are meant to concentrate on "society," but in fact range over politics, international diplomacy, culture and art.

The Proud Tower begins with a portrait of the English patrician class, focused on such choice specimens as the melancholy, caustic Lord Salisbury, the three beautiful Wyndham sisters, one of whom, Lady Elcho, carried on a discreet affair with Arthur Balfour for a dozen years, and the eighth Duke of Devonshire, described by a friend as "never angry though often bored." Following this pastiche of high life, and by way of contrast with it, Mrs. Tuchman surveys the Anarchist movement—men whose guiding vision of a better world led them to assassinate six heads of state within the twenty years preceding 1914. Chapters then follow on the United States (with special emphasis on Thomas B. Reed, "czar" of the House of Representatives), the Dreyfus Affair, the international conferences at the Hague in 1899 and 1907, Kaiser Wilhelm's Germany (with an extended portrait of Richard Strauss), the shifts of power in England after 1902, and finally, the European Socialist movement, especially as seen through the person of Jean Jaurès.

The Proud Tower requires its own evaluation, but first it might be useful to attempt a more general estimate of

This review of Barbara W. Tuchman's *The Proud Tower* (The Macmillan Company, New York) appeared in *The New York Times Book Review,* January 9, 1967.

Barbara Tuchman's accomplishments as a historian, for her work raises some fundamental questions about the nature and purpose of historical inquiry.

Her last volume, *The Guns of August,* earned wide acclaim and (not always a corollary) large sales. The enthusiasm was not, however, unanimous. Criticism centered on two aspects of a single assumption—that a prose style as vivid as hers must come at the expense both of analysis and accuracy. As a general proposition this is, of course, nonsense. The ability to write well (which must in any case be defined according to a particular purpose) is more likely to be a symptom of clear thinking than a substitute for it. Furthermore, the power to make the "mood" of the past immediate is as essential a contribution to "accuracy" as is any dogged accumulation of facts.

But Mrs. Tuchman's popularity is due to more than her skill with words. She has two other virtues often lacking in historians trained in the academy: she never loses sight of individuals, and she is not afraid to tell a story. These qualities, no less than her writing style, have led to criticism and misunderstanding.

Many historians today, in contrast to Mrs. Tuchman, are functioning as sociologists (without the sociologist's advantage of dealing with extensive data and live witnesses). They have become primarily interested in patterns of group, not individual, behavior, in what men share in common rather than what sets them apart. A similar impersonality has come to mark the historian's treatment of causality: the "large forces," the "underlying impulses of an age" are taken to be the significant elements in explaining past events.

Mrs. Tuchman believes that individuals are of interest for what makes them unique as well as typical. She believes, too, that "broader forces," though a necessary part of historical explanation, are not in themselves a sufficient explanation. She would never, in other words, want to study Lenin merely as a "typical revolutionary"; she would want to know about all those singular, unexampled traits which made him peculiarly Lenin. She would never assume that the "logic of events" dictated the course of the Russian Revolution; she would recognize that it might have turned out very differently had not a single man, Lenin, worked his influence, and had not elements of accident and unaccountability played their part.

Such a view of history is sometimes dismissed as "romantic." And in our age of collectivization and system-building, it is always suspect to pursue the individual and the particular. Yet, by her respect for the special nature of each person and each event, Mrs. Tuchman is able to suggest some of that complexity and chaos of historical procedure largely lacking in the work of the pseudo-scientists. What they exclude, she evokes: those irregularities of personality and incident which are in historical events an echo of our own untidy lives.

Mrs. Tuchman's descriptive narrative also serves a more sophisticated end than its detractors are willing to admit. An event's "significance" lies not only in some abstracted essence but in all the disordered detail which surrounds it. The willingness to "tell a story," moreover, and the skill at doing so, can do much to give us a "feel" for circumstances that is essential to our intellectual understanding of them.

The power of literate, narrative history to engage us on the level of feeling and fantasy may explain why historians like Herodotus, Prescott or Macaulay continue to find audiences even after their "facts," even their bases for selecting facts, have been found wanting. It may explain, too, why today so few people read the academic historians while so many read Barbara Tuchman. Without slighting the academic virtues of carefulness and depth research (though her research is almost wholly confined to printed sources), Mrs. Tuchman has filled her pages with individualized human beings subject to luck and whim, rather than with faceless automata carrying out "the spirit of the times." Indeed, she makes the very unmethodical quality of their "stories" an integral part of their significance. In other words, the past she re-creates is recognizably like the present; since we are thereby enabled to identify with the past, it becomes endowed with relevance. This is what most readers want, and they are not wrong in wanting it.

Admiring as I am of Mrs. Tuchman's aims and accomplishments, I was disappointed to find that her new book does not come up to the high level of *The Guns of August*. Many of her familiar virtues are in evidence. She can still strike off an epigram as apt in its insight as in its phrasing —like her reference to Mme. de Loynes, who presumably became mistress to Jules Lemaître "although some unkind gossip said their friendship was platonic." She shows, too, a continuing ability to bring clarity (not to be equated with oversimplification) to a welter of detail; her summary of the issues dividing Purists and Possibilists within the Socialist camp is stunning, and her skill in recounting the tedious maneuvers of the Hague Conferences of 1899 and 1907, without loss either of the reader's interest or of historical complexity, is a fine sample of her powers.

The Proud Tower also contains additional evidence of her narrative talents; the chapter on Dreyfus manages to separate the central issues of that affair without sacrificing the descriptive detail which does so much to recapture its dramatic intensity. Finally, as in all her books, this one is resplendent with people—not symbols or historical agents (though that, too, when pertinent) but marvels of idiosyncratic fullness. The book's superb photographs—huge portrait busts, direct, immediate, individual—are exactly right in underscoring her emphasis on personality.

Yet, for all its rewards, *The Proud Tower* is a good way from being an unqualified success—and its deficiencies are of a kind which could give ammunition to those who disparage Mrs. Tuchman's work in general. It would be a pity if her partial failure in one book should be allowed to obscure the richness of her talents and the rightness of her aims. In any case, the book's failings cannot be ignored.

There are, first of all, a surprising number of stylistic crudities and clichés for a writer of her power: the ideas of Nietzsche are said to have "rolled and billowed like storm clouds, beautifully and dangerously"; when Arthur Balfour succeeds as Prime Minister in 1902, we are told "the waves of change were already lapping at his feet." Sometimes, too, the writing is intrusive—not in service of the material but an end in itself. Mrs. Tuchman will sneak in an anecdote which bears slight or no relation to the discussion at hand, simply because it is amusing and she apparently cannot bear to leave it out. Or, she will allow phrasing to substitute for analysis, leading her into oversimplified statements of causality, which ordinarily she is too sophisticated to sanction. Thus, the cultivation and hedonism of Vienna at the turn of the century are explained this way: "The capital of Austria-Hungary had too many problems of political life too difficult to cope with—and so turned its attention to other matters." And Oscar Wilde's downfall is accounted for by some mystique of self-immolation: "Wilde, conforming to the duty of a decadent, was already engaged in destroying himself . . . satiety required that he must taste the ultimate sensation of ruin."

It is here, in treating personality, that the author's lapses are most disappointing, since she herself so often provides the standard of excellence. But what are we to do with a characterization of John Altgeld as "an almost demonic liberal," or with the statement that "nothing concerned [Henry] Adams himself more than money"? Though Mrs. Tuchman continues to be successful in not reducing her personae to abstract symbols, she is less careful about reducing them to their eccentricities. Her quick eye for the colorful quirk is sometimes too quick, as when it marks down Andrew White simply as a man with a passion for cathedral architecture and organ music. Nor can we be satisfied with short-hand judgments, even were they better phrased, which dismiss Strauss's *Don Quixote* as a composition in which "he let his affinity for realism run unreined," or which conclude that anarchists like Kropotkin, Malatesta, Jean Grave and Reclus "were not men of the ivory tower except insofar as their heads were in ivory towers."

These are matters of detailing. The most serious defect of *The Proud Tower* is structural. In attempting "a portrait of the world before the war, 1890–1914," Mrs. Tuchman has taken on an imposing assignment, one which can be accomplished, if at all, only when the historian has a clear conception of what he or she takes to be the central themes of the period. If Mrs. Tuchman has such a conception, she has not made it apparent. The book's eight chapters remain separate vignettes, unconnected by any thematic unity.

She offers an explanation for this, and on its face a plausible one: no tidy generalization, no neat package can or should be made, she writes in her foreword, of an age so heterogeneous. But this is an evasion. Some standard of evaluation did guide her decisions about what to put in the volume and what to leave out. This, in turn, presupposes some model in her head, conscious or not, of what the period was all about.

Admitting that her book is highly selective, she tells us she was guided in her choices by whether or not a given episode or personality was "truly representative of the period in question." But this is to suggest that a "representative" quality adheres to the material itself, and that the historian simply chooses which of several representative subjects to focus on. In fact, it is likely to be the historian who confers such values, not the material. It was Mrs. Tuchman who decided that the anti-imperialist movement in the United States and not the Populist movement was "representative" of the period. It was she who decided to end the narrative of American developments in 1902 rather than 1914, thereby omitting Progressivism entirely —a movement many historians would argue best represents the mood of this country in the pre-World War I period.

The subjective element is inescapably involved in the historian's choice of subject matter. But if this is not admitted, especially to himself, if the historian believes instead that the choice of what is representative or important is dictated by the material (and then, into the bargain, denies that the material *does* superimpose patterns), there is little hope that his study will show purposeful design.

This is not to say that a work of history which *does* have thematic coherence is necessarily more faithful to the evidence. It often happens that the "design" which a historian finds in the past corresponds less to what actually happened than to his own unconscious needs; he may be engaged not in extracting the past's "meaning," but in using the past for some metaphorical ordering of his own experience. But even this can be of more value than a book which never searches for meaning. The fullest measure of a historian's contribution may hinge not on its correspondence to actual occurrences but on the depth of his perceptions about the human condition and the skill with which he *uses* historical materials in order to make statements embodying those perceptions. For "even if history does not teach us," as Fritz Stern has remarked, "historians may."

If Mrs. Tuchman could have made explicit the subjective bases for her choices in *The Proud Tower*, if she could have given them shape and definition, she might thereby have raised them to the level of an organizing principle. As a result, her book could have taken on thematic coherence. But since she remains unaware of or embarrassed by her *modus operandi*, we have instead not a "portrait of the period," but random brush strokes, leaving a canvas unoccupied by any ruling vision.

I HAVE long contended (in those rarefied circles where such matters are debated—and usually with hyperbole) that David Potter may be the greatest living historian of the United States. With the additional evidence of his collected essays, I'm glad for the chance to say that in print, not least because Potter is little known outside the historical profession—in part because he has written only a few volumes (notably *Lincoln and His Party in the Secession Crisis* and *People of Plenty*), and in part because he has shied away from self-advertisement.

To call Potter the "greatest living historian of the United States" is, to be sure, a little silly; it's reminiscent of parlor games like "What five books would you take with you to a desert island?" There are so many kinds of excellence (and intelligence) that to select our "best" historian is inevitably to get involved in comparing apples and pears. The useful critical task is not to bedevil the nonproblem of whether Potter ranks 1, 2, 3 or 14, but to try to define what makes it so apparent to me (and to many others) that his work is indisputably of the highest quality.

The task is important not only in giving Potter his due but in trying to identify those features that mark historical writing of the first rank. There is no agreement among historians as to what those features are, and some who share my admiration for Potter may not share the reasons I assign for it. All I can hope to account for, in other words, is my own enthusiasm.

I believe, first of all, that Potter's eminence has less to do

This review of David M. Potter's *The South and the Sectional Conflict* (Louisiana State University Press, Baton Rouge) appeared in *The New York Times Book Review*, January 12, 1969.

with his special opinions than with the process by which he arrives at them, that his distinction is to be sought in his manner of address to a given problem rather than in the solution he offers for it. In this regard, his most characteristic stance is cautionary—he continually reminds us that history is made by historians. When evaluating a particular interpretation, Potter not only asks the traditional question, "How well does it fit the known evidence?" but also asks, "What was there in the background of the historian himself that led him to view the evidence in the way he did?"

Potter points out, for example, that the dispute among historians over the causes of the Civil War remains unresolved (and probably unresolvable) because it reflects philosophical as well as analytical conflicts. Disagreement over the comparative importance of such factors as the tariff or states' rights in bringing on the Civil War has been heightened by the underlying assumptions each historian has about the priorities to be assigned to three objectives: the abolition of slavery, the preservation of the Union and the avoidance of war.

Thus, J. G. Randall, preoccupied as he was with the evils of war, wanted to believe that armed conflict always can and should be prevented; this led him to stress "avoidable" mistakes when he discussed the onset of the Civil War and to minimize the fundamentally divisive nature of the slavery issue. More recently, historians have been preoccupied with the evils of slavery and the urgency of abolishing it. They have therefore tended to accept the outbreak of war in 1861 as inevitable, as the only possible instrument for destroying slavery.

Potter is troubled by historians defending one set of philosophical values as against another, because he believes the historian's proper function is not justification but explanation. He is troubled even when historians try to justify loyalties he himself shares. Though he has deep affection for the South (he was born in Georgia in 1910), he will not sanction any defense of the region that comes at the expense of historical understanding.

He will not, for example, accept the school of historical interpretation (best represented by the writings of William E. Dodd and Frank Owsley) that locates the South's distinctiveness in her "agrarianism"; that is, in her devotion to a democratic society based on production for use and typified by the independent yeoman farmer. In rejecting this view as too simplistic, Potter simultaneously rejects the antithetical interpretation (the one so popular with historians born in the North) that the South's identity is to be found in her devotion to a hierarchical society based on the production of staple crops for market and typified by the powerful white planter and his reactionary value structure.

Potter distrusts all such simple dualisms, all unqualified antitheses. The past, he believes, was no less intricate in its patterns and norms than is the present, and any historian who declares wholeheartedly for a single theme must sacrifice an awareness that paradox and contradiction are distinguishing elements in human history.

Those, for example, who insist that the yeoman farmer is the representative Southerner must ignore the abundant evidence that throughout history many Southern farmers have been not independent husbandmen but slaves or sharecroppers, men without options or opportunities. Those who insist on the contrary view that the normative South is one of large landowners, an authoritarian value structure and a repressive social system must view as extraneous all evidence (much of it well substantiated) that democratic impulse, social mobility and widely distributed ownership of land have also been defining elements in Southern history.

Potter's subtlety enables him to recognize the contradictions in historical data; his scrupulous honesty prevents him from resolving those contradictions by some neat formula. He frankly states that he finds evidence to support both the "democratic" and the "aristocratic" themes in Southern history. He admits, moreover, that he has no solution of his own to offer for the nagging question of whether the South has some distinctive identity—and, if so, of what it consists. He does suggest, characteristically, that the South's identity seems dualistic, that the region through time has been marked by both plebeian and patrician impulses, as well as by an almost obsessive need to be at once at odds with the rest of the nation and yet a part of it.

To some, Potter's confessed bafflement, his appreciation of divergent insights and his resort to paradox, may seem the equivalents of evasion, of the absence of organizing principles, even of a failure in morality. I myself felt two or three times while reading these essays that Potter's ability to see merit in almost all arguments and his distrust of any clear-cut position, signal some temperamental inability to choose. In the same way, his elegant balancing of opposites sometimes seems dictated more by stylistic than intellectual necessities; take, for example, his statement that "the cost of deep commitment is a certain measure, more or less, of intolerance" (how would he apply this to an A. J. Muste or a Benjamin Spock?) and "the cost of tolerance is a certain measure, more or less, of moral apathy."

But these occasions are rare. Far more often Potter's fine distinctions, his subtleties of perception, are what the complexities of historical evidence always require but almost never find. To read him is to become aware of a truth that only the greatest historians have been able to show us: that the chief lesson to be derived from a study of the past is that it holds no simple lesson—and the historian's main responsibility is to prevent anyone from claiming that it does.

THE POLITICAL ECONOMY
OF SLAVERY

Throughout this collection I frequently stress the view—which is commonplace—that the historian's personality colors his presentation and to that extent vitiates his pretensions to objectivity. But I also believe—though this review is one of the few places I so state—that the more the historian is aware of his subjective biases, the more likely it is that he will be able to confine them. Objectivity in a work of history becomes a possibility not, as is often thought, when there is an absence of opinion—an unattainable state—but when the historian makes an effort to discover his opinions and then explicitly labels them as such.

Having decided not to tamper with the original form in which these pieces appeared, I have let stand my references to Christopher Lasch. But I now regret them. I think the ambiguity of the Lasch article to which I refer in this review allowed for the interpretation I gave it, but as his subsequent writings and actions have made clear, Lasch does not hold some of the views I herein ascribe to him, particularly not the view that scholars should isolate themselves from the world. I was glad for the chance, four years later, to write more appreciatively of Lasch's qualities (see The Agony of the American Left*).*

EUGENE GENOVESE has been much in the news of late. He has spoken strong words about American intervention in Viet Nam, and he has declared himself a Marxist. The repercussions have been various: his professorship at Rutgers University became the central issue in the New Jersey gubernatorial campaign; both the Right and the Left pigeonholed and labeled him, and—ultimate accolade —*The New York Times* misrepresented him, suggesting he was opposed to coexistence and believed in the inevitability of world war.

This book is by *that* Genovese. But one would not know from the book itself. Whatever positions Genovese has taken in regard to public issues, they do not infect his scholarship. True, his focus of interest is economics, and he uses the concept of "class," but this hardly sets him apart from any number of colleagues who believe the war in Viet Nam and Capitalism divinely inspired. To the extent that "objective" is a useful descriptive term for any work of scholarship, it applies to *The Political Economy of Slavery*. This is not to say the book is faultless, only that its faults cannot be directly linked to its author's ideology.

The point is worth ramifying. It has become a truism that a scholar's personal assumptions (conscious or not) necessarily contaminate his data. And of course they do. But not perhaps to the extent we have assumed. We have grown too skeptical of reason—of a man's ability to use his mind in order to curtail his prejudices and transcend his provincialisms. If we would not today celebrate the supremacy of rationality, we need not deny its existence.

This review of Eugene D. Genovese's *The Political Economy of Slavery* (Pantheon Books, New York) appeared in *Book Week,* November 21, 1965.

A bizarre form of anti-intellectualism has been developing within the citadel of intellectualism—the universities. Its most recent spokesman is Christopher Lasch. In an essay in *The New York Review of Books* he has argued that intellectuals must function as intellectuals—that is, "neither as experts nor as rebels but as social critics." How one can be a social critic these days without being a rebel, or an intellectual without being an expert, is not made clear. Certain prescriptions are: intellectuals must avoid "empty moral protests"; they must spend their time instead in "better thinking, better scholarship." The underlying assumption, never made explicit, is that the powers of the mind (shall we say of self-objectification?) are so fragile that only by isolation from the corrupting influence of the arena can they be preserved. And so scholars are encouraged to turn themselves into little monasteries of the mind.

It is a disastrous suggestion. And typically twentieth century. A hundred years ago men were not bifurcated, compartmentalized. Even Emerson, so concerned with inner cultivation, so suspicious of restless action, warned the scholar against isolation: "You must, for wisdom, for sanity, have some access to the mind and heart of common humanity. The exclusive excludes himself." Talking only to fellow-intellectuals, participating only in academic rounds, narrows the scholar—and his scholarship. Conversely, involvement in the world can enlarge rather than distort his perspective. A variety of activities means a variety of human contacts; it means having one's frame of reference occasionally challenged instead of endlessly confirmed. The Prophets, after all, returned from the wilderness.

Eugene Genovese's book, therefore, signals more than an addition to specialized knowledge. It demonstrates by its objectivity that a scholar's active partisanship need not warp (perhaps it may even enrich) his professional contribution. It demonstrates further that specialization is neither a justification nor a sentence. All of which is a large tribute to Genovese and, if we would recognize it, to ourselves.

Astonishing as it may sound to the non-specialist (if he assumes Truth accumulates), historians still disagree about the basic patterns of life in the Old South. David Potter, probably our most subtle historian, sums up the pertinent literature this way: "After a vast amount of intensive study by many scholars, the essential structure of society in the ante-bellum South still remains in dispute." It is not clear whether the Old South was democratic or aristocratic, whether the planters or the yeoman farmers dominated the region, whether its institutions and attitudes were sufficiently unique to warrant calling it a separate civilization, whether slave labor brought the South prosperity or doomed her to backwardness.

On all these matters—and more—Genovese has much to contribute. At the risk of oversimplifying a complex book, it can be said that in general he returns to the traditional view of the Old South, the one which dominated historical thought before the work of such revisionists as Owsley, Craven and Randall. In Genovese's view, the ante-bellum South was controlled in every area—political, social, economic, psychological—by the values and needs of the planter class (with the corollary, of course, that the yeoman was insignificant in terms of power if not of numbers). The planters, moreover, produced a culture in sharp contrast to that of the North. At the root of this difference was the institution of slavery, an institution economically ruinous for the South. Slavery was inefficient as a labor force, retarded the capital accumulation that might have encouraged agricultural diversification and industry, and prevented the rise of any substantial home market.

These are the main but not the only themes Genovese treats. In passing, he deals with any number of controversial side issues. He denies that "capitalism" is an appropriate descriptive term for the Southern plantation system, rejects the common view that agricultural reform had made much headway in the region, affirms the expansionist tendencies of slavery, ascribes the low level of Southern market demand not to the self-sufficiency of the plantations but to the debilitating effects of the region's basic economic structure.

Few of Genovese's conclusions are actually new, and he makes no such claim; his book, he writes, "is an extension and refinement of arguments presented as long as a century ago." Since most historical "re-interpretations" represent nothing more than a return to earlier views recently out of fashion, Genovese is sensible to admit as much. But if anything, he is too modest. He brings enough new data and special insight to old arguments to warrant a claim beyond mere "restoration."

Rewarding as the book is, it has its difficulties. The main trouble is over-compression. Too many sentences (especially in the opening chapter) are theses in miniature, followed not by elaboration and illustration but by still further theses. We are often unable either to rebut or assent to a stated argument because we are given only its bare bones —and then hurried on to the next argument. There is such a thing as being too compact. It is fine to abstract the central issues from a body of detail, but enough detail must be given to make abstraction meaningful. It is obvious from Genovese's research that he had enough material to write a far larger, more leisurely, book; it is a pity he did not.

We could have profited, for example, from more detailed

definitions. In denying the "capitalistic" nature of the Southern economy, Genovese fails to make clear what does or does not consitute a capitalistic structure. In the same way, he provides no precise standards for deciding when a region may properly be described as "economically stagnant"—when present income yield is low or when future prospects seem dim? Since Genovese's conclusions are often categorical, he had a responsibility for laying out with equal rigor the premises on which he based those conclusions.

As his argument stands, I am not convinced that the Old South was in serious economic trouble in the 1850s—though the chance of *continuing* prosperity may have been slight. Even if we accept the view that by the 1850s the planters were already in difficult straits, we are left in doubt as to the root cause. In accounting for the failure of economic reform, Genovese seems uncertain whether to emphasize the built-in deficiencies of slave labor or the hide-bound value structure of the master class—whether, in other words, to stress institutional or psychological factors. Both were of course contributory, but their priority of importance as well as their inter-relationship needs further clarification.

Such disagreements and doubts necessarily arise when dealing with a book that has risked a synthetic reading— to some degree they testify to its provocativeness. Even the disagreements must be tentative: it will take time to digest and debate a work whose findings range so widely. In any case there is no doubt that *The Political Economy of Slavery* is an important book, and my own view is that both its major and minor themes are impressively and persuasively stated. Apparently Genovese already has in progress several other studies on the Old South. If they are as rich as this one, they cannot come too soon.

THE NORTHERN RESPONSE
TO SLAVERY

The following essay elaborates two themes which I had earlier begun to explore in "The Abolitionists and Psychology." Again using the abolitionists as a case in point, I try to discover more in this piece about whether the insights of psychology can be used to illuminate the study of history, and whether past experience can be used to illuminate our own. I continue to argue both questions throughout this volume, without resolving either to my satisfaction; the closest I have come to date is in the last essay of the collection.

THE abolitionist movement never became the major channel of Northern antislavery sentiment. It remained in 1860 what it had been in 1830: the small but not still voice of radical reform. An important analytical problem thus arises: why did most Northerners who disapproved of slavery become "nonextensionists" rather than abolitionists? Why did they prefer to attack slavery indirectly, by limiting its spread, rather than directly, by seeking to destroy it wherever it existed?

On a broad level, the answer involves certain traits in the national character. In our society of abundance, prosperity has been the actual condition—or the plausible aspiration—of the majority. Most Americans have been too absorbed in the enjoyment or pursuit of possessions to take much notice of the exactions of the system. Even when inequalities have become too pronounced or too inclusive any longer to be comfortably ignored, efforts at relief have usually been of a partial and half-hearted kind. Any radical attack on social problems would compromise the national optimism; it would suggest fundamental defects, rather than occasional malfunctions. And so the majority has generally found it necessary to label "extreme" any measures which call for large-scale readjustment. No one reasonably contented welcomes extensive dislocation; what seems peculiarly American is the disbelief, under *all* circumstances, in the necessity of such dislocation.

Our traditional recoil from "extremism" can be defended. Complex problems, it might be said, require complex solu-

"The Northern Response to Slavery" was first published in *The Antislavery Vanguard: New Essays on the Abolitionists,* Martin Duberman, ed. (Princeton University Press, 1965).

tions; or, to be more precise, complex problems have no solutions—at best, they can be but partially adjusted. If even this much is to be possible, the approach must be flexible, piecemeal, pragmatic. The clear-cut blueprint for reform, with its utopian demand for total solution, intensifies rather than ameliorates disorder.

There is much to be said for this defense of the American way—in the abstract. The trouble is that the theory of gradualism and the practice of it have not been the same. Too often Americans have used the gradualist argument as a technique of evasion rather than as a tool for change, not as a way of dealing with difficult problems slowly and carefully, but as an excuse for not dealing with them at all. We do not want time for working out our problems—we do not want problems, and we will use the argument of time as a way of not facing them. As a chosen people, we are meant only to have problems which are self-liquidating. All of which is symptomatic of our conviction that history is the story of inevitable progress, that every day in every way we *will* get better and better even though we make no positive efforts towards that end.

Before 1845, the Northern attitude toward slavery rested on this comfortable belief in the benevolence of history. Earlier, during the 1830's, the abolitionists had managed to excite a certain amount of uneasiness about the institution by invoking the authority of the Bible and the Declaration of Independence against it. Alarm spread still further when mobs began to prevent abolitionists from speaking their minds or publishing their opinions, and when the national government interfered with the mails and the right of petition. Was it possible, men began to ask, that the abolitionists were right in contending that slavery, if left alone, would not die out but expand, would become more not less vital to the country's interests? Was it possible that slavery might even end by infecting free institutions themselves?

The apathetic majority was shaken, but not yet profoundly aroused; the groundwork for widespread antislavery protest was laid, but its flowering awaited further developments. The real watershed came in 1845, when Texas was annexed to the Union, and war with Mexico followed. The prospect now loomed of a whole series of new slave states. It finally seemed clear that the mere passage of time would not bring a solution; if slavery was ever to be destroyed, more active resistance would be necessary. For the first time large numbers of Northerners prepared to challenge the dogma that slavery was a local matter in which the free states had no concern. A new era of widespread, positive resistance to slavery had opened.

Yet such new resolve as had been found was not channeled into a heightened demand for the abolition of the institution, but only into a demand that its further extension be prevented. By 1845 Northerners may have lost partial, but not total confidence in "Natural Benevolence"; they were now wiser Americans perhaps, but Americans nonetheless. More positive action against slavery, they seemed to be saying, was indeed required, but nothing too positive. Containing the institution would, in the long run, be tantamount to destroying it; a more direct assault was unnecessary. In this sense, the doctrine of nonextension was but a more sophisticated version of the standard faith in "time."[1]

One need not question the sincerity of those who believed that nonextension would ultimately destroy slavery,

[1] Arresting slavery's further spread, Lincoln said, would "place it where the public mind shall rest in the belief that it is in course of ultimate extinction. . ." ("House Divided" speech, June 16, 1858, Roy P. Basler, ed. *The Collected Works of Abraham Lincoln,* New Brunswick, 1953, II, 461.)

in order to recognize that such a belief partook of wishful thinking. Even if slavery was contained, there remained large areas in the Southern states into which the institution could still expand; even without further expansion, there was no guarantee that slavery would cease to be profitable; and finally, even should slavery cease to be profitable, there was no certainty that the South, psychologically, would feel able to abandon it. Nonextension, in short, was hardly a fool-proof formula. Yet many Northerners chose to so regard it. And thus the question remains: why did not an aroused antislavery conscience turn to more certain measures and demand more unequivocal action?

To have adopted the path of direct abolition, first of all, might have meant risking individual respectability. The unsavory reputation of those already associated with abolitionism was not likely to encourage converts to it. Still, if that doctrine had been really appealing, the disrepute of its earlier adherents could not alone have kept men from embracing it. Association with the "fanatics" could have been smoothed simply by rehabilitating their reputations; their notoriety, it could have been said, had earlier been exaggerated—it had been the convenient invention of an apathetic majority to justify its own indifference to slavery. When, after 1861, public opinion did finally demand a new image of the abolitionists, it was readily enough produced. The mere reputation of abolitionism, therefore, would not have been sufficient to repel men from joining its ranks. Hostility to the movement had to be grounded in a deeper source—fear of the doctrine of "immediatism" itself.

Immediatism challenged the Northern hierarchy of values. To many, a direct assault on slavery meant a direct assault on private property and the Union as well. Fear for these values clearly inhibited antislavery fervor (though possibly a reverse trend operated as well—concern for property and Union may have been stressed in order to justify the convenience of "going slow" on slavery).

As devout Lockians, Americans did believe that the sanctity of private property constituted the essential cornerstone for all other liberties. If property could not be protected in a nation, neither could life nor liberty. And the Constitution, so many felt, had upheld the legitimacy of holding property in men. True, the Constitution had not mentioned slavery by name, and had not overtly declared in its favor, but in giving the institution certain indirect guarantees (the three-fifths clause; noninterference for twenty-one years with the slave trade; the fugitive slave proviso), the Constitution had seemed to sanction it. At any rate no one could be sure. The intentions of the Founding Fathers remained uncertain, and one of the standing debates of the ante-bellum generation was whether the Constitution had been meant by them to be a pro- or an antislavery document.[2] Since the issue was unresolved, Northerners remained uneasy, uncertain how far they could go in attacking slavery without at the same time attacking property.

Fear for property rights was underscored by fear for the Union. The South had many times warned that if her rights and interests were not heeded, she would leave the Union and form a separate confederation. The tocsin had been sounded with enough regularity so that to some it had come to seem like hollow bluster. But there was always the chance that if the South felt sufficiently provoked she might yet carry out the threat.

It is difficult today fully to appreciate the horror with

---

[2] For a sample pamphlet exchange, see Lysander Spooner, *Unconstitutionality of Slavery* (Boston, 1845), and Wendell Phillips, *Review of Lysander Spooner's Essays on the Unconstitutionality of Slavery* (Boston, 1845).

which most Northerners regarded the potential breakup of the Union. The mystical qualities which surrounded "Union" were no less real for being in part irrational. Lincoln struck a deep chord for his generation when he spoke of the Union as the "last best hope of earth"; that the American experiment was thought the "best" hope may have been arrogant, a hope at all, naïve, but such it was to the average American, convinced of his own superiority and the possibility of the world learning by example. To-day, more concerned with survival than improvement, we are bemused (when we are not cynical) about "standing examples for mankind," and having seen the ghastly deeds done in the name of patriotism, we are impatient at signs of national fervor. But 100 years ago, the world saw less danger in nationalism, and Americans, enamored with their own extraordinary success story, were especially prone to look on love of country as one of the noblest of human sentiments. Even those Southerners who had ceased to love the Union had not ceased to love the idea of nationhood; they merely wished to transfer allegiance to a more worthy object.

Those who wanted to preserve the old Union acted from a variety of motives: the Lincolns, who seem primarily to have valued its spiritual potential, were joined by those more concerned with maintaining its power potential; the Union was symbol of man's quest for a benevolent society —and for dominion. But if Northerners valued their government for differing reasons, they generally agreed on the necessity for preserving it. Even so, their devotion to the Union had its oscillations. In 1861 Lincoln and his party, in rejecting the Crittenden Compromise, seemed willing to jeopardize Union rather than risk the further expansion of slavery (perhaps because they never believed secession would really follow, though this complacency, in turn, might only have been a way of convincing themselves that a strong antislavery stand would not necessarily destroy the Union). After war broke out the value stress once more shifted: Lincoln's party now loudly insisted that the war was indeed being fought to preserve the Union, not to free the slaves. Thus did the coexisting values of Union and antislavery tear the Northern mind and confuse its allegiance.

The tension was compounded by the North's ambivalent attitude toward the Negro. The Northern majority, unlike most of the abolitionists, did not believe in the equality of races. The Bible (and the new science of anthropology) seemed to suggest that the Negro had been a separate, inferior creation meant for a position of servitude.[3] Where there was doubt on the doctrine of racial equality, its advocacy by the distrusted abolitionists helped to settle the matter in the negative.

It was possible, of course, to disbelieve in Negro equality, and yet disapprove of Negro slavery. Negroes were obviously men, even if an inferior sort, and as men they could not in conscience (the Christian-Democratic version) be denied the right to control their own souls and bodies. But if anti-Negro and antislavery sentiments were not actually incompatible, they were not mutually supportive either. Doubt of the Negro's capacity for citizenship continually blunted the edge of antislavery fervor. If God had intended the Negro for some subordinate role in society, perhaps a kind of benevolent slavery was, after all, the most suitable arrangement; so long as there was uncertainty, it might be better to await the slow unfolding of His intentions in His good time.

And so the average Northerner, even after he came ac-

---

[3] On this point see W. S. Jenkins, *Pro-Slavery Thought in the Old South* (Chapel Hill, 1935), and William Stanton, *The Leopard's Spots* (Chicago, 1960).

tively to disapprove of slavery, continued to be hamstrung in his opposition to it by the competitive pull of other values. Should prime consideration be given to freeing the slaves, even though in the process the rights of property and the preservation of the Union were threatened? Should the future of the superior race be endangered in order to improve the lot of a people seemingly marked by Nature for a degraded station? Ideally, the North would have liked to satisfy its conscience about slavery and at the same time preserve the rest of its value system intact—to free the Negro and yet do so without threatening property rights or dislocating the Union. This struggle to achieve the best of all possible worlds runs like a forlorn hope throughout the ante-bellum period—the sad, almost plaintive quest by the American Adam for the perfect world he considered his birthright.

The formula of nonextension did seem, for a time, the perfect device for balancing these multiple needs. Non-extension would put slavery in the course of ultimate extinction without producing excessive dislocation; since slavery would not be attacked directly, nor its existence immediately threatened, the South would not be unduly fearful for her property rights, the Union would not be needlessly jeopardized, and a mass of free Negroes would not be precipitously thrust upon an unprepared public. Nonextension, in short, seemed a panacea, a formula which promised in time to do everything while for the present risking nothing. But like all panaceas, it ignored certain hard realities: Would containment really lead to the extinction of slavery? Would the South accept even a gradual dissolution of her peculiar institution? Would it be right to sacrifice two or three more generations of Negroes in the name of uncertain future possibilities? Alas for the American Adam, so soon to be expelled from Eden.

The Northern Response to Slavery

The abolitionists, unlike most Northerners, were not willing to rely on future intangibles. Though often called impractical romantics, they were in some ways the most tough-minded of Americans. They had no easy faith in the benevolent workings of time or in the inevitable triumphs of gradualism. If change was to come, they argued, it would be the result of man's effort to produce it; patience and inactivity had never yet helped the world's ills. Persistently, sometimes harshly, the abolitionists denounced delay and those who advocated it; they were tired, they said, of men using the councils of moderation to perpetuate injustice.

In their own day, and ever since, the abolitionists have faced a hostile majority; their policies have been ridiculed, their personalities reviled. Yet ridicule, like its opposite, adoration, is usually not the result of analysis but a substitute for it. Historians have for so long been absorbed in denouncing the abolitionists, that they have had scant energy left over for understanding them. The result is that we still know surprisingly little about the movement, and certainly not enough to warrant the general assumptions so long current in the historical profession.

Historians have assumed that the abolitionists were unified in their advocacy of certain broad policies—immediate emancipation, without compensation—and also unified in refusing to spell out details for implementing these policies. To some extent this traditional view is warranted. The abolitionists did agree almost unanimously (Gerrit Smith was one of the few exceptions) that slaveholders must not be compensated. One does not pay a man, they argued, for ceasing to commit a sin. Besides, the slaveholder had already been paid many times over in labor for which he had never given wages. Defensible though this position may have been in logic or morals, the abolitionists should perhaps have realized that public opinion would never support the confiscation of property, and should have modified their stand accordingly. But they saw themselves as prophets, not politicians; they were concerned with what was "right," not with what was possible, though they hoped that if men were once made aware of the right, they would find some practical way of implementing it.[4]

The abolitionists were far less united on the doctrine of immediate emancipation—at least in the 1830's, before Southern intransigence and British experience in the West Indies convinced almost all of them that gradualism was hopeless. But during the 1830's, there was a considerable spectrum of opinion as to when and how to emancipate the slave. Contrary to common myth, some of the abolitionists did advocate a period of prior education and training before the granting of full freedom. Men like Weld, Birney, and the Tappans, stressing the debasing experience of slavery, insisted only that gradual emancipation be immediately begun, not that emancipation itself be at once achieved.[5] This range of opinion has never been fully ap-

---

[4] See, for example, L. Maria Child, *The Right Way the Safe Way* (New York, 1860). After the Civil War began, the abolitionists modified their stand on compensation—thus showing that "pragmatic flexibility" of which they were supposedly devoid. In the winter of 1861, Garrison got up a petition to compensate loyal slaveholders, and in 1862, most abolitionists gave enthusiastic approval to plans for compensated emancipation in the District of Columbia.

[5] For sample abolitionist writings advocating gradual freedom, after apprenticeship, see L. Maria Child, *Anti-Slavery Catechism* (Newburyport, 1836), pp. 18–19; J. A. Thome and J. W. Alvord to T. Weld, February 9, 1836, *Letters of Theodore Dwight Weld, Angelina Grimké Weld, and Sarah Grimké, 1822–1844,* eds. G. H. Barnes and D. L. Dumond (New York, 1934), I, 257; C. K. Whipple, "The Abolitionists' Plan," *The Liberty Bell* (1845). Even Garrison was at first willing to hold newly freed slaves in "the benevolent restraint of guardianship" (*Thoughts on African Colonization* [Boston, 1832], pp. 79–80). Donald Mathews has pointed out to me that Benjamin Lundy in *The Genius of Universal Eman-*

preciated. It has been convenient, then and now, to believe that all abolitionists always advocated instantaneous freedom, for it thus became possible to denounce any call for emancipation as "patently impractical."

By 1840, however, most abolitionists had become immediatists, and that position, "practical" or not, did have a compelling moral urgency. Men learned how to be free, the immediatists argued, only by being free; slavery, no matter how attenuated, was by its very nature incapable of preparing men for those independent decisions necessary to adult responsibility. Besides, they insisted, the Negro, though perhaps debased by slavery, was no more incapacitated for citizenship than were many poor whites, whose rights no one seriously suggested curtailing.

The immediatist position was not free of contradiction. If slavery had been as horrendous as the abolitionists claimed, it was logical to expect that its victims would bear deep personality scars—greater than any disabilities borne by a poor white, no matter how degraded his position. Either slavery had not been this deadly, or, if it had, those recently freed from its toils could not be expected to move at once into the responsibilities of freedom. This contradiction was apparent to some immediatists, but there was reason for refusing to resolve it. Ordinarily, they said, a system of apprenticeship might be desirable, but if conditions to emancipation were once established, they could be used as a standing rationale for postponement; the Negro could be kept in a condition of semislavery by the self-

<hr />

cipation printed many plans for gradual freedom (e.g., in the issues of September 5, 12, 15, 1825), but, discouraged by the lack of response, Lundy finally discontinued doing so. Thus it might be well to ask whether the abolitionists, in moving steadily toward "immediatism" (a shift largely completed by 1840), had not been driven to that position by the intransigence of their society in the preceding decade, rather than by any inherent "extremism" in their own temperaments.

perpetuating argument that he was not yet ready for his freedom.[6]

Moreover, any intermediary stage before full freedom would require the spelling out of precise "plans," and these would give the enemies of emancipation an opportunity to pick away at the impracticality of this or that detail. They would have an excuse for disavowing the broader policy under the guise of disagreeing with the specific means for achieving it. Better to concentrate on the larger issue and force men to take sides on that alone, the abolitionists argued, than to give them a chance to hide their opposition behind some supposed disapproval of detail.[7] Wendell Phillips, for one, saw the abolitionists' role as exclusively that of agitating the broader question. Their primary job, Phillips insisted, was to arouse the country's conscience rather than to spell out to it precise plans and formulas. *After* that conscience had been aroused, it would be time to talk of specific proposals; let the moral urgency of the problem be recognized, let the country be brought to a determination to rid itself of slavery, and ways and means to accomplish that purpose would be readily enough found.[8]

No tactical position could really have saved the abolitionists from the denunciation of those hostile to their basic goal. If the abolitionists spelled out a program for emancipation, their enemies would have a chance to pick at de-

[6] See, for example, James A. Thome and J. Horace Kimball, *Emancipation in the West Indies* (New York, 1838), pp. 83, 85, 108.

[7] For sample awareness of the dilemma inherent in "plans," see William Jay, *An Inquiry into . . . the American Colonization, and Anti-Slavery Societies* (New York, 1835), p. 197; "Instructions of the American Anti-Slavery Society to Theodore Weld," February 20, 1834, in Barnes and Dumond, *Weld-Grimké Letters*, I, p. 126.

[8] See, for example, his speech "Daniel O'Connell" in Wendell Phillips, *Speeches, Lectures, and Letters* (Boston, 1891), Second Series, pp. 384–420.

tails; if they did not spell out a program, they could then be accused of vagueness and impracticality. Hostility can always find its own justification.[9]

A second mode of attack on the abolitionists has centered on their personalities rather than their policies. The stereotype which has long had currency sees the abolitionist as a disturbed fanatic, a man self-righteous and self-deceived, motivated not by concern for the Negro, as he may have believed, but by an unconscious drive to gratify certain needs of his own. Seeking to discharge either individual anxieties or those frustrations which came from membership in a "displaced élite," his antislavery protest was, in any case, a mere disguise for personal anguish.[10]

[9] I am not suggesting that all those who opposed immediatism were necessarily opposed to emancipation; no doubt some of those in opposition objected only to the means, not the end. I know of no way, though, to measure accurately the proportionate strength of the two groups, nor, more complicated still, the degree to which each actually understood its position.

[10] In pointing out what seem to me certain inadequacies in this stereotype, I do not mean to imply that no psychological or sociological explanation of the abolitionists is possible. Wide personality variations among individual abolitionists is not incompatible with their sharing a few traits in common—these traits being the crucial ones in explaining their "reform motivation." But if so, these common traits have not, in my view, yet been delineated. Which is not to say that they did not exist, nor that they may not be successfully isolated in the future. There could, for example, be some point in examining the "sociological truism" that "when family integration weakens, the individual becomes available for participation in some kinds of collective behavior" (Leonard Broom and Philip Selznick, *Sociology*, New York, 1957, p. 406), or the suggestion by Seward Hiltner that "the person who is vociferous and diligent on behalf of minority groups may be impelled by unsolved authority problems" ("Psychology and Morality," *Princeton Alumni Weekly*, September 22, 1964). Then there is the possibility, first suggested to me in conversation with Silvan Tomkins, of a connection between "being good to others" and an unfulfilled (because frightening) need to get close to people; by expressing concern for the unfortunate it becomes possible to discharge safely (because impersonally) some of the pent-up need for warmth and affection. Needless to say, all the cautions I try to outline in this essay against current psycho-social interpretations of the abolitionists, would apply to any future interpretations as well.

A broad assumption underlies this analysis which has never been made explicit—namely, that strong protest by an individual against social injustice is ipso facto proof of his disturbance. Injustice itself, in this view, is apparently never sufficient to arouse unusual ire in "normal" men, for normal men, so goes the canon, are always cautious, discreet, circumspect. Those who hold to this model of human behavior seem rarely to suspect that it may tell us more about their hierarchy of values than about the reform impulse it pretends to describe. Argued in another context, the inadequacies of the stereotype become more apparent: if normal people do not protest "excessively" against injustice, then we should be forced to condemn as neurotic all those who protested with passion against the Nazi persecution of the Jews.

Some of the abolitionists, it is true, *were* palpable neurotics, men who were not comfortable within themselves and therefore not comfortable with others, men whose "reality-testing" was poor, whose life styles were pronouncedly compulsive, whose relationships were unusual compounds of demand and phantasy. Such neurotics *were* in the abolitionist movement—the Parker Pillsburys, Stephen Fosters, Abby Folsoms. Yet even here we must be cautious, for our diagnostic accuracy can be blurred if the life style under evaluation is sharply different from our own. Many of the traits of the abolitionists which today "put us off" were not peculiar to them, but rather to their age—the declamatory style, the abstraction and idealization of issues, the tone of righteous certainty, the religious context of argumentation. Thus the evangelical rhetoric of the movement, with its thunderous emphasis on sin and retribution, can sound downright "queer" (and thus "neurotic") to the twentieth-century skeptic, though in its day common enough to abolitionists and nonabolitionists alike.

Then, too, even when dealing with the "obvious" neurotics, we must be careful in the link we establish between their pathology and their protest activity. It is one thing to demonstrate an individual's "disturbance" and quite another then to explain all of his behavior in terms of it. Let us suppose, for example, that Mr. Jones is a reformer; he is also demonstrably "insecure." It does not necessarily follow that he is a reformer *because* he is insecure. The two may seem logically related (that is, if one's mind automatically links "protest" with "neurosis"), but we all know that many things can be logical without being true.

Even if we establish the neurotic behavior of certain members of a group, we have not, thereby, established the neurotic behavior of *all* members of that group. The tendency to leap from the particular to the general is always tempting, but because we have caught one benighted monsignor with a boy scout does not mean we have conclusively proved that all priests are pederasts. Some members of every group are disturbed; put the local police force, the Medal of Honor winners, or the faculty of a university under the Freudian microscope, and the number of cases of "palpable disturbance" would probably be disconcertingly high. But what *precisely* does their disturbance tell us about the common activities of the group to which they belong—let alone about the activities of the disturbed individuals themselves?

Actually, behavioral patterns for many abolitionists do *not* seem notably eccentric. Men like Birney, Weld, Lowell, Quincy—abolitionists all—formed good relationships, saw themselves in perspective, played and worked with zest and spontaneity, developed their talents, were aware of worlds beyond their own private horizons. They all had their tics and their traumas—as who does not—but the evidence of health is abundant and predominant. Yet most

THE PROFESSION OF HISTORY

historians have preferred to ignore such men when discussing the abolitionist movement. And the reason, I believe, is that such men conform less well than do the Garrisons to the assumption that those who become deeply involved in social protest are necessarily those who are deeply disturbed.

To evaluate this assumption further, some effort must be made to understand current findings in the theory of human motivation. This is difficult terrain for the historian, not made more inviting by the sharp disagreements which exist among psychologists themselves (though these disagreements do help to make us aware of the complexities involved). Recent motivational research, though not conclusive, throws some useful new perspectives on "reformers."[11]

A reaction has currently set in among psychologists against the older behaviorist model of human conduct. The behaviorists told us that men's actions were determined by the nature of the stimulus exerted upon them, and that their actions always pointed towards the goal of "tension reduction." There was little room in behaviorist theory for freedom of choice, for rationality, or for complex motives involving abstract ideas as well as instinctive drives.

Without denying the tension-reducing motives of certain kinds of human behavior, a number of psychologists are now insisting on making room for another order of motivation, involving more than the mere "restoration of equilibrium." Mature people, they believe—that is, those who have a realistic sense of self—*can* act with deliberation and

---

[11] For recent discussions, see R. S. Peters, *The Concept of Motivation* (London, 1958); Gardner Lindzey, ed., *Assessment of Human Motives* (New York, 1958); Robert C. Birney and Richard C. Teevan, eds., *Measuring Human Motivation* (New York, 1962); Erich Fromm, "The Revolutionary Character" in *The Dogma of Christ* (New York, 1963).

The Northern Response to Slavery

can exercise control over their actions. This new view presumes an active intellect, an intellect capable of interpreting sensory data in a purposive way. The power of reflection, of self-objectification, makes possible a dynamic as opposed to a merely instinctive life. Men, in short, need not be wholly driven by habit and reflex; they need not be mere automatons who respond in predictable ways to given stimuli. Rather, they can be reasoning organisms capable of decision and choice. Among the rational choices mature men may make is to commit themselves to a certain set of ethical values. They are not necessarily forced to such a commitment by personal or social tensions (of which they are usually unaware), but may come to that commitment deliberately, after reflective consideration.

The new psychology goes even one step further. It suggests that the very definition of maturity may be the ability to commit oneself to abstract ideals, to get beyond the selfish, egocentric world of children. This does not mean that every man who reaches outward does so from mature motives; external involvement may also be a way of acting out sick phantasies. The point is only that "commitment" need not be a symptom of personality disturbance. It is just as likely to be a symptom of maturity and health.

It does not follow, of course, that all abolitionists protested against slavery out of mature motives; some may have been, indeed were, "childish neurotics." But if we agree that slavery was a fearful injustice, and if motivational theory now suggests that injustice will bring forth protest from mature men, it seems reasonable to conclude that at least some of those who protested strongly against slavery must have done so from "healthy" motives.

The hostile critic will say that the abolitionists protested *too* strongly to have been maturely motivated. But when is a protest *too* strong? For a defender of the status quo, the answer (though never stated in these terms) would be: when it succeeds. For those not dedicated to the current status quo, the answer is likely to be: a protest is too strong when it is out of all proportion to the injustice it indicts. Could any verbal protest have been too strong against holding fellow human beings as property? From a moral point of view, certainly not, though from a practical point of view, perhaps. That is, the abolitionist protest might have been *too* strong if it somehow jeopardized the very goal it sought to achieve—the destruction of human slavery. But no one has yet shown this to have been the case.[12]

At any rate, current findings in motivational theory suggest that at the very least we must cease dealing in blanket indictments, in simple-minded categorizing and elementary stereotyping. Such exercises may satisfy our present-day hostility to "reformers," but they do not satisfy the complex demands of historical truth. We need an awareness of the

---

[12] In this regard, there has been a persistent confusion of two separate indictments against the abolitionists: first, that they disrupted the peace, and second (in the classic formulation given by Daniel Webster), that they "bound more firmly than before" the bonds of the slave. It is undeniably true that the abolitionists contributed to the polarization of public opinion, and to that extent, to the "disturbance of the peace" (which is not the same as war). But it does not follow that because they stirred up passions, they made freeing the slaves more difficult. This would be true only if it could be shown that the slaves could have been freed *without* first arousing and polarizing opinion. The evidence does not seem to support such a position. In all the long years before the abolitionists began their campaign, the North had managed to remain indifferent to the institution, and the South had done almost nothing, even in the most gradual way, toward ameliorating it. Had the abolitionists not aroused public debate on slavery, there is no guarantee that anyone else would have; and without such a debate it seems unlikely that measures against the institution would have been taken. The fact that the debate became heated, moreover, cannot wholly be explained by the terms in which the abolitionists raised it; what must also be taken into account is the fact that the South, with some possible exceptions in the border area, reacted intransigently to *any* criticism of the institution, however mild the tone or gradual the suggestions.

wide variety of human beings who became involved in the abolitionist movement, and an awareness of the complexity of human motivation sufficient to save us from summing up men and movements in two or three unexamined adjectives.

Surely there is now evidence enough to suggest that commitment and concern need not be aberrations; they may represent the profoundest elements of our humanity. Surely there are grounds for believing that those who protested strongly against slavery were not all misguided fanatics or frustrated neurotics—though by so believing it becomes easier to ignore the injustice against which they protested. Perhaps it is time to ask whether the abolitionists, in insisting that slavery be ended, were indeed those men of their generation furthest removed from reality, or whether that description should be reserved for those Northerners who remained indifferent to the institution, and those Southerners who defended it as a "positive good." From the point of view of these men, the abolitionists were indeed mad, but it is time we questioned the sanity of the point of view.

Those Northerners who were not indifferent to slavery— a large number after 1845—were nonetheless prone to view the abolitionist protest as "excessive," for it threatened the cherished values of private property and Union. The average Northerner may have found slavery disturbing, but convinced as he was that the Negro was an inferior, he did not find slavery monstrous. Certainly he did not think it an evil sufficiently profound to risk, by "precipitous action," the nation's present wealth or its future power. The abolitionists were willing to risk both. They thought it tragic that men should weigh human lives in the *same* scale as material possessions and abstractions of government. It is no less tragic that we continue to do so.

PART II

The Movement

THE NEW EQUALITY

Nat Hentoff's The New Equality *marked an early recognition of the growing split between radicals and liberals. While writing this review of the book, I came to understand better than I had before that my own inclinations and sympathies lay with the radicals. But like Hentoff (at least as he then presented himself), I still have some lingering attachment to the liberal views that the federal government is a useful agency for social reform and that a "coalition of the concerned" can be a significant lever for pressuring the government to act.*

The recent emphasis by radicals on localism and decentralization seems to me all to the good as a way of reinvigorating democratic procedure. But I think there is a danger that decentralization might be viewed as a panacea, as a means sufficient in and of itself to solve our social problems. Many of our ills, in fact, are national phenomena and require the resources and power of the federal government for their solution.

It seems to me that liberalism, in the sense of state interference and regulation, has never been given a real chance to prove its effectiveness as a tool for substantive change; it has "failed" because the executive branch of the federal government has bungled some of the opportunities provided by Congress— as, for example, with Civil Rights legislation or the poverty program—and because the Congress itself reflects the divided purposes of the electorate.

In saying that I still have some faith in the state as an agency of reform, and yet at the same time claiming in several later pieces that I am "most at home in the anarchist tradition" (which deplores statism and "governing"), I am obviously involved in a contradiction. I would rather call it a paradox, the one Marx himself embraced when he sanctioned the state as a temporary expedient but also clung to the hope that once its mission was accomplished, "government" would wither away.

On all these matters, though, my views are unsettled, and throughout this section I continue to re-argue (with myself and others) the value and possibilities of decentralization, coalition politics and the like (see especially "The Relevance of Anarchy" and "Black Power and the American Radical Tradition").

IN the current deluge of "civil rights" literature, this excellent book is unlikely to get the wide reading it deserves. Which is too bad, for it is one of the few to put "the movement" in a broader context, to deal in recommendations as well as jeremiads, and to adopt a radical as opposed to a liberal stance (that is, dealing in essentials rather than palliatives).

The book has faults, largely organizational. Since they are not significant when weighed against the suggestive contents, it is better to list them now and be done. First, the argument does not "build"; it is episodic rather than cumulative. The chapters are more a series of self-contained essays than well-related units of a whole. Second, too much space is given to summarizing and rebutting the views of others. Some of this is necessary and some of it is brilliant (the devastating but not vindictive critique of Mailer), but there is too much rehashing of the obvious (the defective arguments of John Fischer).

Against these minor faults, *The New Equality* has major virtues. The radical approach is what gives the book its special flavor and importance. This is not one more panegyric to the "American genius for compromise," nor yet another bit of self-congratulation on the "slow but sure" progress in this best of all possible countries. Our large failures are writ large and their gruesome human toll bluntly counted.

None of this is shrieked. The defects of tone we sometimes associate with a radical stance are absent. There is no claim here on a monopoly of truth, no attempt to blue-

This review of Nat Hentoff's *The New Equality* (The Viking Press, Inc., New York) appeared in *Book Week*, August 9, 1964.

print the One Way to Salvation, no trumpet calls to the righteous for a cleansing and a violent rebirth. Hentoff is dispassionate and detached. He thus makes his hard-nosed analysis the more persuasive, and his message the more urgent.

Actually he has three interrelated messages. The first concerns the widening chasm between the white "moderate" and the Negro "activist." The moderate position, he says, is that epitomized by the *New York Times:* concerned and well-intentioned, but willing to tolerate only polite forms of protest. The activist position is that epitomized by the Harlem minister who told Hentoff, "Freedom is never voluntarily given up by the oppressor. We're going to have to be out on the streets a long time." The argument between moderate and activist represents contrasting attachments to order and justice. The moderate, who already shares in some of the "good things" of life, prefers to believe that social justice can be achieved without "unduly" disturbing social order. The activist, who sees little in that order worth preserving, believes that considerable tension and conflict are concomitants of meaningful change.

There is a growing impatience—which Hentoff shares —with the built-in evasions of the moderate position. In practice, "gradually" has often meant "glacially," and even were the phrase now to carry overtones of real advance, it might no longer be sufficiently rapid to satisfy the Negro's impatience or to sustain his hope. Certainly "gradualism," even if genuine, would not be enough to win back those Negroes who have become convinced of the Muslim contention (all too reasonable) that the whites will never fully "make good." To this extent, white racism has already created its own virulent, irreconcilable counterpart.

Aside from being "too little, too late," the moderate position suffers from the optimistic defect of placing too much faith in man's "conscience." Here is Hentoff's second theme. An appeal to morality, he argues, a reliance on the white man's guilt, is in itself an insufficient guarantee of reform. Conscience has brought some improvement in the Negro's status, but only some. If fundamental change is to come— and nothing less will do—"the movement" must organize and demonstrate its power. The hostile or apathetic white majority will not surrender its privileges unless frightened or forced into doing so: the dictum that "power only respects power" is as true of our domestic as of our foreign Cold War.

In this sense the activists are tough-minded realists. Their refusal to place entire faith in an appeal to conscience, or in the benevolent workings of time, separates them from the genteel main stream of the American reform tradition. That tradition has always been grounded in a double optimism—that the world can be made better, and that this can be done through an appeal to "right reason" rather than force and fear. The activists share the belief that the world can be made a better place, but they put their faith for change in power, not good will. To this degree, they are more in the tradition of European radicalism than American reform.

The civil rights struggle is growing more radical in ends as well as means. Hentoff's third and most far-reaching theme is that the struggle must increasingly orient itself toward larger goals—not merely an ending to segregation, but the restructuring of our society. Hentoff reflects the growing view among civil rights leaders that merely trying to win full partnership in American life is not enough. The view has two sources, one "intellectual" and one tactical. The first, represented by James Baldwin and Lorraine

Hansberry, is that partnership may not be desirable because the firm is corrupt. The root fear of the Baldwins, in
part based on a romanticization of Negro-hipster-slum life,
is that the Negro might exchange whatever uniqueness his
sufferings have given him for a mess of middle-class white
complacencies; he might surrender spontaneity and sen-
suality for the desiccated rituals of bourgeois life.

A second source of protest against aiming the civil rights
movement solely at assimilation comes from tactical rather
than ideological considerations. The view here is that although full participation in American life may be desirable,
it will not materialize unless the basic assumptions of our
society are first challenged. The Negro will never be fully
accepted until the value structure which has so long denied
him is itself overhauled. Until then, he will be given partial
concessions only, just enough semblance of good faith to
pacify the gullible—or the tired.

Both these sources—the intellectual and the tactical—
are moving the Negro protest into a deeper form of social
criticism, one which sees racism as a symptom rather than
the entire embodiment of our social rot, and which calls
for fundamental political and economic changes beyond
civil rights. Specifically, the Federal government must be
brought to exercise its powers in a full-scale assault on
poverty, unemployment and education. The problem of
poverty underlies the problem of civil rights; the inequalities of American life are phenomena of class as well as
color. And it is essential, Hentoff argues, for the underprivileged and poor of all colors and backgrounds to recognize their kinship. In his view, a neo-Populist alliance is
called for—one which would unite the American underclasses in a concerted drive to acquire power in the name
of·making fundamental changes in our society.

The possibility of such an alliance, as Hentoff himself shows, is highly uncertain. Low-status whites are often those most hostile to Negroes. Their prejudice is part of their essential protective equipment; it could be surrendered only if a new scapegoat could be found for their frustrations—possibly the wealthy and privileged. The Negro poor, on their side, "are far too preoccupied with survival and the particular afflictions of being black to think in terms of a potential alliance between them and the white poor." But some leaders of the protest movement, men like Bayard Rustin, are thinking increasingly in terms of the broader alliance, and the successful experiment in co-operation in Crystal City, Texas, may encourage further efforts at concerted action. Yet the obstacles to a coalition of the poor are formidable. Not only the specific obstacle of color prejudice, but the inhibiting effect of our middle-class value structure (not confined to the middle-class) with its emphasis on what is safe and secure, and our reform tradition of piecemeal adjustment.

Hentoff's argument, then, can be summarized as follows: There are fundamental inequities in American life which call for fundamental reforms; these reforms require the full weight and support of the Federal government behind them; the government cannot be brought to exercise its weight unless "encouraged" to do so through political pressure from below; the best way to exert such pressure is through an alliance of the poor, a coalition transcending the civil rights issue.

It is this last leg of the argument which is the most wobbly. Hentoff does not pretend that the alliance can come about easily, but he does see it as the only real hope for revitalizing the country. Many will agree, which makes the unlikeliness of the alliance all the more depressing.

SAMMY DAVIS JR.'S
AUTOBIOGRAPHY

In rereading this piece, I was struck that even when dealing with matters quite different from those in Part I, I again focus my complaints and disappointments on not knowing "what accounts for the man . . . what goes on inside of him." This focus, together with my insistence that Sammy Davis Jr.'s story not be read as a prototypical one, makes me see clearly that I am centrally concerned, perhaps even obsessed, with the particularity of a given person or event.

WE have recently learned much of the Negro's mistreatment, but the trials of a single man, when recounted as vividly as Sammy Davis Jr.'s are in his lengthy autobiography, renew and redouble the shock. As a teen-ager in the Army, he is relentlessly taunted by his fellow soldiers: in what appears to be a gesture of friendship, they offer him a bottle of beer; he accepts it, hopefully—it is a bottle of urine. In enlightened New York City he is refused entry (*after* World War II) into the Copacabana, El Morocco and Lindy's. And his marriage to May Britt brings down on them both a torrent of execration and obscenity which can only be called insane. It is here, in describing his relationship with May Britt, that Davis conveys the full dimension of American racial hatred. Threatened with violence, heaped with abuse (sample letter before their wedding: "Dear Nigger Bastard, I see Frank Sinatra is going to be best man at your abortion . . ."), they react with a courage so free of self-pity that in the same breath you want to cheer them and curse the maniacs who pursue them. "Dear God," Sammy Davis Jr. asks, "will it ever end? Will I ever be able to be like everybody else?" It is *the* rhetorical question.

Yet, in certain crucial ways, Sammy Davis Jr.'s experiences as a Negro have not been typical, less because of his unique gifts and uncommon success than because of his special background. He was, to be sure, born in Harlem. But he had two unusual advantages: he never spent a day in its schools, and in a real sense he had a father.

This review of Sammy Davis Jr. and Jane and Burt Boyar's *Yes I Can* (Farrar, Straus & Giroux, Inc., New York) appeared in *The New York Times Book Review,* September 19, 1965.

From age three he was on the road, performing in a trio with his father and Will Mastin. His energy and curiosity were spared the usual schoolroom burial. He was with people who cared about him, and his drive was channeled into a field where a Negro could find at least some opportunity. Few boys born in Harlem have been that lucky. In one sense his background worked against him: his father (and the show business milieu) shielded him so completely from the usual anti-Negro venom that when he later encountered it in the Army the impact was devastating. He had not been educated in servility, had not learned to play Tom—that broken nose is one result.

If there are problems in treating Sammy Davis Jr.'s story as emblematic of the plight of Negro America, there are obstacles of another sort in reading it as personal narrative. The primary one is that *Yes I Can* is an autobiography written by three people. I assume that Davis taped his reminiscences and that Jane and Burt Boyar turned the tapes into a continuous narrative. Except for the first 100 pages, where the broken sequences quite literally suggest splicings, the Boyars have done a skillful job. But their skill is part of the problem.

One need not question the integrity of anyone connected with this book in order to recognize that mediation by third parties necessarily contaminates an auto-biography. Language and form are central, not incidental, to autobiography; they carry values and emphases which are (or should be) crucial indices of personality. When one man's experiences are filtered (to any degree) through someone else's prose, the experiences themselves are altered. To evaluate this book at all, we must proceed on what we know is a false assumption: that every sentence represents Mr. Davis and no one else. If the portrait is not a fair likeness, he must nonetheless abide by it, for he has allowed the book to bear his name.

The image which emerges from *Yes I Can* is vivid. We see a man of immense drive and vitality, spontaneous, clever, generous, sophisticated about people (and loyal to those he likes), aggressive, egotistical, tough-tender. Still, we do not know him. We come away with little idea of what accounts for the man, almost no sense of what goes on inside of him. It is a book about actions, not motives, what the man does, not what drives him to do it. We are given considerable detail about "intimate" matters, but they tend to mask rather than expose the individual. Perhaps it is a case of confusing Confessions with Autobiography. There is a common assumption nowadays that if we divulge our behavior in certain "taboo" areas such as sex, we have thereby revealed the whole of ourselves—as if our identity consisted of the sum of our socially disapproved acts.

In embracing this thesis, Mr. Davis does not spare himself. He lets us know about his failures in friendship and love, his greed, even how he could use color "as a cop-out for any impulse I'd felt like indulging." And his confessions are in good taste—he neither conceals nor belabors the lurid details. Nor does he use them for secondary gains: the book is honorably free of mere scandal-mongering, of calculated humble-pie, of weaknesses unveiled only to off-set dramatically his later virtue. His revelations seem to represent an honest effort to show us how he is (or was before the stability of his marriage to May Britt). But confession cannot alone confer understanding. There must also be introspection. It would be unfair to expect intense self-scrutiny from a man whose specialty is entertainment, not psychological analysis—except that he claims such insight.

"Baby," he once remarks, "I know everything wrong

that I ever do—and I don't need a psychiatrist to tell me why I keep doing it." If so, why not share the knowledge with the reader? Why be reticent in the area of why and so frank in the area of how? Can it be that it is now permissible to reveal everything except thought?

Such introspection as we get tends to be colored with the supernatural. At one point, desperate at the emptiness of his life, Davis tries to head his car over a cliff; at the last moment the transmission snaps in half and the car slams to a halt "as though a huge hand had reached out and was holding it, preventing it from going over. . . . God had had His arms around me again." We are here in the realm of folk religion, of signs, omens, direct interventions. And it is the optimistic American brand: God intervenes to save, not punish, to lift up rather than smite down. Such "theology" goes in natural tandem with boosterism: "Man . . . can move into any shaped house he wishes to build. . . . If he works steadily toward his goal, eventually he accomplishes it." We are dealing with fantasies of omniscience, not realities of human limitations. I, for one, prefer the language of psychiatry which Mr. Davis scorns.

Nor is this the only place in the book where the Rotarian note is sounded. Davis goes to England to perform, and is treated everywhere with dignity. Naturally enough, he gives serious thought to settling there. But no: "America is still the best country in the world." Why?—despite all the hardships, it was possible for Davis to become a star in America. "It could never have happened for me in England. . . . Social equality is all they have for the Negro there." One hopes this is a deliberate sacrifice of logic to patriotism.

Sammy Davis Jr. the booster manages to exist side by side with Sammy Davis Jr. the swinger. Most of us harbor a variety of personae with little discomfort. But what gives

Sammy Davis Jr.'s Autobiography

this autobiography special fascination is that it presents a man who seems to sum up in his person so much that is contemporary in the American style—and the pieces are taken from all levels of our culture. We have echoes of James Bond: heading home from the downtown bars "with the freshest, best-looking tomatoes in the whole grocery store skipping along behind me"; drinking Cokes out of a silver goblet; doing forty around the curves; playing Monopoly at six A.M. with solid gold pieces.

We have themes reminiscent of Norman Mailer and *the* American Dream—power as salvation, trying to buy immunity from hate and pain by getting "big" (sexual inference intended), when that doesn't work, getting *bigger*. We have scenes, too, from the *Ladies Home Journal:* addressing Queen Elizabeth after a command performance as Your Majesty—"a phrase the grandeur of which one can never fully understand until one is saying it to a person who is actually entitled to it."

There are any number of subthemes equally revealing of the national pace and mood: staging marriage to a Negro girl, in order to stop unfavorable publicity—the public man replacing the private one, the image becoming the actuality. An endless round of parties with interchangeable people—perpetual motion to fill a spreading void. Wild spending sprees for bizarre luxuries—blatant materialism which has little to do with love of money or possessions, a lot to do with trying to purchase definition. Ignoring or minimizing mounting debt and declining health—that insouciant American optimism which takes no problems seriously because it assumes all are self-liquidating. And so forth. . . . It should be remembered that—on Davis's part —these attitudes are self-confessed excesses. Since his marriage they are apparently behind him—if not us.

Possibly Sammy Davis Jr. is (or was) able to represent

so many varied segments of Americana, from Babbitt to Warhol, because as a performer he has a built-in view of life as a series of roles and "bits." He *knows* that he is "on" most of the time, he mocks himself for playing roles even as he does so: Charles Good Son; Charley Modest; Charley Star. (Not the least of his American-ness is the insistent self-derision.) As for the "bits," they are as essential an expression of today's jet-set heterosexuals as "camping" is of homosexuals.

The "bit" technique goes like this: At all cost one must avoid the stigma of being too serious; to do so, you stick a self-mocking label on any scene in which you might be caught displaying deep emotion. Thus: "I don't want to do the 'engaged-couple bit,' but . . ."; or "I don't want to do the 'expectant-father bit,' but . . ." If one further masks the scene with a heavy dose of banter, it finally becomes permissible to express feeling. Doing "bits" with people is the "in" way of establishing fellowship. They allow one to show affection while ridiculing it, to be sentimental while appearing tough. It is a technique much superior to camping; the camp *must* treat the serious unseriously, the bit-player *may* be serious so long as his approach is ironic.

Autobiographies usually aim at one of two goals: presenting the individual experience, or using it to illustrate some larger historical theme. Sammy Davis Jr.'s autobiography focuses on neither. He has been unwilling or unable to make his story a depth analysis of self, and his history has been too special to serve as a prototypic tale of the Negro in America. And so we have a presentation which fluctuates between personal narrative and sociological suggestion, a fluctuation often absorbing, often unsatisfying.

HOWARD ZINN'S
THE SOUTHERN MYSTIQUE
AND
SNCC: THE NEW ABOLITIONISTS

The references in this review of Howard Zinn's two books to the "quiet confidence" of young radicals and to the possibility of moving "with high speed towards social justice" may have accurately reflected the mood of four years ago, but today they read like caricature. Yet if optimism has passed (as well as some of the organizations that embodied it—like the early SNCC), it does not stand as proven that we lack the ability to make a new world—only that the American majority currently lacks the will. Faced with this fact, the activist minority has fragmented, some rejoining the apathetic many, others taking refuge with the revolutionary few. My own feeling is that some progress in some areas (like school integration) continues to be made, but at a pace so glacial and in a spirit so confused, that one would have to be preternaturally optimistic (even for an American) to bet that it can keep abreast of the accelerating forces of social disintegration.

RADICALISM is returning to American life. It owes its initial rebirth to the civil rights movement, but men like Bayard Rustin and others less well-known are now moving beyond the race problem to broad social criticism. These new radicals increasingly see racism as but one symptom of our social malaise, a symptom which itself can never disappear until a broader attack is launched against the value structure which maintains it—against the preference for order, compromise and cliché over justice, principle and reality, against all that has turned us from a revolutionary outpost into a conservative bulwark.

The new radicals do not pretend to have any long-range strategy or detailed ideology; they are undogmatic, unsentimental and unhysterical. Despite their anger and disgust at the banalities and evasions of American life, their tone is one of quiet confidence. They are optimistic not only about the country's potential, but—and this is perhaps basic to any reform impulse—they are optimistic also about the ability of individuals to ascertain and manipulate reality. In this sense, the new movement marks a restoration of human confidence, the flowering of post-Freudian homiletics: neither our individual nor our collective past need determine our present goals; neither biology nor history is enough to prevent our planning rationally and acting

This review of Howard Zinn's *The Southern Mystique* (Alfred A. Knopf, Inc., New York) and *SNCC: The New Abolitionists* (Beacon Press, Boston) appeared in *Partisan Review*, Winter, 1965.

Howard Zinn's *The Southern Mystique* and *SNCC*

boldly. We are far more free—and thus far more responsible—than the determinists have told us. The new radicals insist, in short, that we may choose what to make of ourselves and our world.

Though the radicals in our midst are few and exert little power, at least they do once more exist, and their influence might yet lead us out of the post-New Deal morass. If so, we will owe much to those activists in the civil rights movement who first pointed the way, and to those intellectuals (often activists themselves) who first saw and schematized the broader possibilities of the movement. In this last group the preeminent publicists have been Michael Harrington and Nat Hentoff. Now there is Howard Zinn.

Zinn represents an emerging breed of scholar-activists. In his early forties, he has behind him a Beveridge Prize for his first book, *LaGuardia in Congress,* seven years of teaching history at a Negro college—Spelman, in Atlanta —and extensive involvement as adviser and participant in civil rights activities, especially those of SNCC. His two new books combine a scholar's knowledge and an activist's experience, which are used to inform his theme, not to exhibit himself. Thus both books are personal without being egotistical, are authoritative but free of pedantry, and are passionate without being suspiciously agitated. The common theme of the two books—a theme which is rationale and emblem for the whole new movement of social criticism—is that it is within our power to move with high speed towards social justice. *The Southern Mystique* outlines the reasons for this optimistic belief; *SNCC: The New Abolitionists* gives us the concrete experiences of those who have carried the belief into action.

Zinn's optimism, it must be emphasized, is not about what has been done, or even what necessarily will be done, but only about what *could* be done were we to become aware of the rich possibilities for change and determined to utilize them. This qualified optimism rests on both theoretical and specific considerations. Zinn draws the theoretical testimony from a variety of post-Freudian commentators—Kurt Lewin, Dorwin Cartwright, Harry Stack Sullivan, Gardner Murphy—all of whom believe in the transcending power of the immediate. Habitual behavior, according to these social psychologists, can be radically and drastically changed, even when deeply rooted. No determinant, be it instinctual or traditional, need preclude the alteration of behavior. And behavioral transformations, moreover, need not be preceded by intellectual ones. The opposite is often true: forcing changes (through legal or extra-legal pressures) in the way people act, can, by transforming the personal and social environment, produce changes in the way people think.

When Zinn applies this body of theory specifically to the race problem in the South, his optimism is supported by many specific examples of changes already wrought in that region. Though the white Southerner, Zinn tells us, does care about segregation, he cares about other things more —about his job, staying out of jail, the approval of his neighbors, community peace, keeping educational and entertainment facilities open. Furthermore, the mystique which sees the South as utterly different from the rest of the nation, is mistaken. The South may be racist, provincial, conservative, fundamentalist, nativist, violent, conformist and militarist, but these are national not merely regional qualities, American not Southern genes. Sectional differences, in other words, are differences of degree not kind.

Zinn argues this position brilliantly and with solid evidence. Only one reluctant reservation is necessary. That is, whether his optimistic diagnosis is applicable everywhere in the South. When he says the white Southerner has "no special encumbrances that cannot be thrust aside," I doubt if this is equally true for all Southerners. Perhaps Atlantans have "no special encumbrances," but can the same be said about the whites in Plaquemines or Sunflower counties? In such places the devotion to segregation may be so intransigent, that it does take precedence over all other values—including money, education and peace—just as the commitment to fundamentalism, nativism, etc., may be so fanatical that it is not susceptible to any but the most gradual inroads (which is not to say that the assault should be gradual). If the attitudes in such areas are variations on common national themes, they are so pronounced as to be almost new tunes.

None of this is exactly news to Howard Zinn. Knowing the South as he does from first-hand experience, he is well aware of the bitter inflexibility of certain areas within it. If he underplays this side of the picture, therefore, he does so knowingly, for a deliberate purpose. And that purpose is to encourage us to act. Too much has been said about the difficulty of producing change in the South (and in the nation) and not enough about its feasibility. Zinn deliberately stresses positive opportunities in order to counteract that mystique of intractability which for too long has served as rationale for pessimism and apathy. Zinn is here the true activist: he emphasizes those aspects of social reality best calculated to encourage involvement. He knows that the hope for significant change in this country is tenuous; he also knows that significant change will be *impossible* if we continue to dwell on the obstacles and to downgrade the possibilities. We are never in short supply of gainsayers, those eager to justify their complacency by magnifying the obstacles on the path to change. Zinn wants to prevent the number of these gloom-and-doomers from becoming so large that they will turn into self-fulfilling prophets.

Zinn does more than tell us that a new day is possible; he also shows us something of what it might consist of. His second book, *SNCC*, along with being a history of the organization, is also a history of those enrolled in its ranks. The everyday joy and terror of these SNCC workers in the South are taking on dimensions larger than the life most of us live. Certainly the joy is enviable—a warm, purposeful camaraderie—and even the terror suggests a self-confrontation most of us would welcome were the price not so high.

It is difficult, as Zinn says, not to romanticize these young adults. Yet there is no need to embroider. In their depth of feeling for each other and for their cause, in their simplicity and courage, they stand out against a purposeless, sterile backdrop in something truly like heroic outline, showing us what might be hoped for when the barriers that artificially separate people are broken down. They have lived under field conditions, of course, which by everyday standards are themselves artificial. Intimacy among them has been allowed to ripen through constant contact and mutual reliance, and has been further intensified by common dangers and goals. Then, too, they have had the rare fulfillment of knowing that their energies are employed in meaningful work.

As our society is now constituted, such conditions cannot be widely reproduced. The "new day" is for most of us still beyond reach. But thanks to Howard Zinn we have caught a glimpse of its splendors. Mama Dollie spoke to the right man.

JAMES MEREDITH
AND LEROI JONES

JAMES MEREDITH'S MARCH
IN MISSISSIPPI

LeRoi Jones's public statements since the time I wrote this review have further emphasized violence, racism and separatism. Though I still deplore those sentiments, the continuing indifference or hostility of the white majority to the Negro's plight makes me more understanding today of the psychological and perhaps even tactical necessity of Jones's position. Because of this, I now feel less ready than I once was to lecture Jones, especially since what I labeled "wild distortions" three years ago ("these are the last days of The American Empire") no longer seem quite so far-fetched.

Though slightly out of chronological order, I have inserted here a second, more favorably disposed article on James Meredith. Doing so helps to relieve some uneasiness I still feel at expressing distaste for Meredith in the first piece. I keep telling myself that it's silly to feel no white has a right to disparage any black, but I keep feeling it anyway. Maybe one reason is that I myself have never done much of anything in regard to the Civil Rights movement other than to write about it and to contribute a little money; certainly I haven't personally suffered or sacrificed for it the way many others have.

JAMES MEREDITH is the man who integrated "Ole Miss." LeRoi Jones is the man who called Andrew Goodman an "artifact." Needless to say, I was prepared to find Meredith's book admirable and Jones' distasteful. It has not been that easy.

Like almost everyone of my age, education, and section, I of course regarded Meredith's assault on the State of Mississippi as heroic. And still do. But one can admire an act without being attracted to the man who performs it, and certainly without thinking well of the account he subsequently writes of it.

One part of my trouble is that I do not believe in Divine Missions, let alone Divinity. The other part is my distaste for the military personality. James Meredith is convinced of the former and personifies the latter. I take him here at his own evaluation; the emphases are his, not mine, and he places them relentlessly lest we be tempted to inquire into other aspects of his personality and experience. Again and again he speaks of his "Divine Responsibility," of pursuing his Destiny, of carrying out his Mandate: "At a very early age I had established the . . . goals to be achieved on the way to my final destiny"; ". . . it appeared to me that the particular steps that I had chosen to take in an effort to carry out the mandate of my Divine Responsibility had been proper and timely"; ". . . my belief in my supernatural or superhuman powers was another important factor. Whether it was true or not, I had always felt that I could stop a mob with the uplift of a hand. . . . Because

This review of James Meredith's *Three Years in Mississippi* (Indiana University Press, Bloomington) and LeRoi Jones's *Home: Social Essays* (William Morrow & Co., New York) appeared in *Book Week*, April 24, 1966.

of my 'Divine Responsibility' to advance human civilization, I could not die."

In the very first paragraph, Meredith announces that he is "a soldier at heart" and goes on to say that if there was anything he ever wanted to be "it would have been a general." Throughout the book he employs military terminology: he is the aggressor in a war, he plots his strategy, he knows his enemy, and when in the end he finally wins his degree, it is his "battle citation." Meredith of course *was* in a war, and no doubt only a man of his intensity and certitude could have seen it through successfully. But the pervading element of grandiosity, à la MacArthur–de Gaulle, is nonetheless disturbing. That Meredith's Napoleonism is self-admitted makes it less, not more attractive, for it is proclaimed with an innocence, a guilelessness, that suggests self-delusion. He seems unaware that there could be grounds for embarrassment in viewing himself as The Chosen Vessel of the Lord.

"I have never made a mistake in my life," he asserts, "because I never make arbitrary or predetermined decisions. Every decision made and every action taken is always an impersonal result of the processing of every available bit of data." (Once, though, he does admit to "an arbitrary decision"—the result of "failing to apply my decision-making formula.") The computerized mentality so candidly—so proudly—displayed carries some eerie echoes of Dr. Strangelove. That movie, it is said, exaggerated, but no sentence in Terry Southern's screenplay is more improbable—or shocking—than this one from *Three Years in Mississippi:* "I not only want the right to participate in an established government, but I have the desire to fashion a better government . . . not only the right to be an employee in a nuclear plant, but the desire to build a better and more effective bomb."

The deterministic tone of Meredith's narrative, the stolid, resolute quality of his prose, reflect his impersonality. He believes Society must be placed above Self, and that events are shaped by forces larger than the individual. The result is that all the people in his book, including himself, emerge as cardboard figures. Thus Constance Baker Motley, key to the Ole Miss fight, is not in any sense brought to life as a person. She, like everyone else in the book, plays out her assigned role in the inexorable historical process—one more cog in the machine. There is a curious irony in the fact that Meredith, an individual who did so much to change long-standing patterns, has little belief in the importance of individuals.

If we could excise the postures and banalities from *Three Years in Mississippi,* we would have a book of value, especially as a primary source. Meredith has given us a case history of one of the key episodes of recent decades; he not only narrates the events but also prints many of the central documents—court decisions, correspondence with university officials, depositions and testimony, excerpts from his own speeches, articles, TV appearances and private mail. Much of this information only Meredith could have provided, and at many points he fills out our understanding of events with new details. Thus he makes it clear that his temptation to leave Ole Miss was not due primarily to bad grades; he shows that the pistol Cleve McDowell (the second Negro student to gain admittance to the university) carried and that ultimately led to his dismissal, was necessary for self-protection; he rehearses the controversy surrounding his 1963 speech to the annual convention of the NAACP (though in this instance his justifying comments are not persuasive, for reading his declaration in the speech that the pending March on Washington would "not be in the best interest of our cause" and

his Horatio Alger preachments to Negro youth on the supreme importance of establishing good credit ratings, I was
not surprised that many in his audience were offended).

Throughout the book I kept being brought up short by
the astonishing parallels in rhetoric and attitude between
Meredith and any earnest, high-minded American of the
mid-nineteenth century. Meredith's optimism, his religiosity, his boot-strap theory of self-help, his belief in our
country's "manifest destiny," in ethical absolutes and in
man's power to control and change his world, are all of a
piece with a frame of reference no longer widely held (at
least in intellectual circles). There is an antique—and appealing—ring to Meredith's statement that "the very existence of the human being makes everything possible"
—yes, even rapidly changing the Southern status quo.
There is an almost antediluvian—and less appealing—ring
to Meredith's perfervid patriotism: "America is a great
nation. It has led the world in freedom for a long time . . .
I have read widely and have traveled a good deal, and I
am firmly convinced that the American nation is truly the
greatest among nations."

To read LeRoi Jones' collection of essays immediately
after finishing the Meredith book is to jump, with a shock,
into a radically different milieu. If Meredith has all the
nineteenth-century pieties (and strengths), Jones has most
twentieth-century doubts (and subtleties). Where Meredith believes in God, Progress, Nationalism, Society, Morality, Self-Help, Jones believes in Skepticism, Violence,
Alienation, Personalism, Hate. There is little the two men
share and that little—a belief in the waning energy of the
white man, an insistence on the need for Negro unity—is
used to make very different statements: Jones wants the
Negro to get out of this Gomorrah, preferably leaving behind a trail of blood; Meredith wants to join it, infuse it

with new life, and he believes this can, should and will happen.

Jones at his best—in the early essays of 1960–61—is obviously the more probing, wide-ranging, subtle mind. He is very knowledgeable and very bright. He has a wild sense of humor, with enough irony left over for occasional self-mockery. He questions, pokes, rants. He is capable of an oblique, original perspective. He loves tilting at the Majority's Truth, puncturing the mindless slogans by which we live (often replacing them with slogans of his own, and often as mindless: the March on Washington was a "night-club act"; Nkrumah, Sukarno, Nasser and Castro are models of responsiveness to the needs of their people).

So much for Jones at his best. Much more often in these essays, and especially in the later ones, he is at his worst— far more hysterical, self-indulgent, murderous, than in any of his previous work (except perhaps his recent "novel," *The System of Dante's Hell,* a series of elliptical scrawls which reads like a parody of Burroughs parodying Hemingway). Most of these essays are full of private hangups and wild distortions: ". . . these are the Last Days of The American Empire"; Cassius Clay demonstrates "that a new and more complicated generation has moved onto the scene," etc., etc.

Jones likes to call his irresponsibilities "the craziness of all honest men." The craziness, at least, can be easily admitted. Moving beyond Malcolm X (who is beginning, by contrast, to sound like a good, gray prophet), Jones insists that the Black Man is "a different *species,*" a species, moreover, "that is evolving to world power and philosophical domination of the world." Black men must concentrate on becoming ever more Black—whatever that means. They must take steps to ensure their separation from the white devils. They must have their own nation, for, like the Germans, they need *Lebensraum* in which to grow. But before

James Meredith and LeRoi Jones

they move out, blood must flow, must "erupt like Mt. Vesuvius to crush in hot lava these willful maniacs who call themselves white Americans." And—in another disastrous echo of Nazism—Jewish blood especially must flow: "In Harlem it is almost common knowledge that the Jews, etc. will go the next time there's a large 'disturbance,' like they say . . ."

My main reaction to these ravings is not anger or fright, but boredom. They are so obviously the effluvium of a disturbed man that they cannot even be taken with the seriousness we accord polemics. Jones is pursuing private catharsis, not communication; there is no room at all for exchange—and apparently Jones couldn't care less. No doubt my boredom is what he hoped for; it confirms his expectations of how a decadent, "dead-loined," smug materialist (i.e., a White) would react to the hip, soulful, virile truth-seeking of a POWERFUL BLACK WRITER. To which I can only repeat—I'm bored. Bored by categories. Bored by pretense. Bored by lectures. Bored by bearded oracles.

Bored and a little (very little) sad. The last essays in this collection obviously mark the disintegration of a talented man—the man who wrote "A Poem for Willie Best," *Dutchman, Blues People.* The first piece in this volume, an essay written in 1960 called "Cuba Libre," shows that same talented man, a man, above all, with a fine sense of the concrete, the precise detail which encapsulates, embodies truth. In the 1965 essays, all is awash in rhetoric, platitude, diatribe. Jones can no longer be bothered with detail. Now he is possessed by visions: BLACK REVOLUTION, BLACK NATIONS, BLACK ARTS. No vision can afford the dilution imposed by particulars. No intelligence can do without them.

JAMES MEREDITH set off on his march to demonstrate that Negroes had "nothing to fear." Could he have believed this? It seems inconceivable that a man brought up in Mississippi could really think that we have now reached the point where Negroes no longer need worry about physical violence. Only a few years ago, when trying to integrate Ole Miss, Meredith personally experienced the Anglo-Saxon wrath which awaits those who boldly challenge established patterns. Surely Meredith does not actually believe that in the three years since then, white attitudes have been so revolutionized that Negroes in Mississippi could troop off to the polls without any fear of retaliation. What then was in his mind? Why did he originally state his purpose in words which could not possibly comport with his, or anyone's, realistic assessment of conditions in Mississippi?

No one can speak for Meredith other than Meredith. Moreover, it is possible he did not fully articulate even to himself his motives for undertaking a new assault on Mississippi, that he acted, in other words, out of the same combination of personal and public, unconscious and conscious drives which go to make up most human behavior. Yet at the risk of both presumption and over-simplification, it is possible to see in Meredith's act a rationale and significance apart from his stated purpose. Such an "explanation" may be no more than my own projection onto another man's action. But since the purpose of a symbolic gesture like Meredith's is to bring as many people as possible, through

This piece on James Meredith's march in Mississippi appeared (under the title "James Meredith, Optimist, Gives Fuel to Pessimism") in *The Village Voice*, June 16, 1966.

whatever variety of personal identifications, into sharing a common goal (such as integration), there is no need to apologize for making his march "our own."

What Meredith was saying to me, when he set out for Mississippi, was not that reasons for fear no longer exist, but that because they *are* still present, they must be continually faced. Danger, death, must be risked. Not to risk them, to bow to the implied threat, is to guarantee a continuation, perhaps even a worsening, of inequity. And the risk, Meredith seemed to be saying when he set off alone down the road from Memphis, must be assumed on an individual basis. The government can pass laws, the official forms of compliance can be registered, but significant change comes when individuals facing their own fear inspire similar confrontations in others—in those on both sides of the issue.

What would have happened had Meredith not been shot, had he completed his march without being harmed? Would he have thereby demonstrated—in accord with his stated purpose—that Negroes no longer have grounds for fear? Hardly. The common reaction, I suspect, would have been that he was lucky, protected by fame and publicity. The average Negro tenant-farmer would never have been foolish enough to imagine that his own anonymity and helplessness would prove safeguards of equal weight. Indeed the shock with which news of Meredith's shooting was received was based on the widespread feeling that in his case "they wouldn't dare!"

But they did dare—or someone dared. It does not help to say (even if we could be sure the statement was true) that surely the white majority in Mississippi did not approve. Death in the civil rights struggle has almost always come at the hands of one, or a few individuals. If most white Mississippians would never "go *that* far," the important point is that the Mississippi ethos turns up the Byron de la Beckwiths with enough regularity to cast doubt on whether they can accurately be called "mavericks."

If Meredith had not been harmed, in other words, his march would have demonstrated little more than his own courage, a quality we have long been familiar with. Now that he has been shot, the effects of the march are likely to be more extensive, though not in the direction Meredith hoped for. That is, few Mississippi Negroes will now be encouraged (if they ever could have been) to believe either Meredith's stated or implied purpose, either that they have little to fear, or that a confrontation with their fear, however "soul-enriching," will be unaccompanied by physical injury.

Few men have the resources (whatever their complex origin) to face up to such consequences. And one would be as sanctimonious in telling men that they should, as one would be naïve in expecting that they will. The more likely and probably more human (there is something supra-human about Meredith) response in the Negro community will be a redoubling of fear. And anger. And disillusion with the benefits of continued reliance on the tactics of non-violence.

The civil rights movement, under the weight of accumulated frustrations, had begun to shift ground before James Meredith's march, a shift dramatically symbolized by the recent change of leadership in SNCC. Given the usual distortions of the press, it is not easy to know what the assumptions and goals of Stokely Carmichael's "Black Panthers" really are, but their rejection of "politics" and their emphasis on "blackness" are unmistakable signs of heightened alienation. And who can say that their discouragement, their refusal to participate further in official assaults on segregation, is other than an appropriate response to the seemingly endless evasions of white America? Unfortunately their own approach seems even less promising, based as it is on a black variation of the separate but equal theme, on a suicidal rejection of allies.

Promising or not, the ranks of the disaffected are bound to be swelled by the abrupt end which came to James Meredith's march. His intended purpose was to encourage further participation by Negroes in "the American way," to enkindle their hope in the possibilities of participation. The effect is likely to be the reverse. It is hard to feel encouraged at the prospect of a bullet. It is difficult to feel hopeful when even a James Meredith can be shot down. Meredith, the congenital optimist, has unwittingly given fuel to the growing pessimism within civil rights ranks.

FOUR STUDIES ON
THE NEW LEFT

*The themes of this review are reiterated in several of the later
pieces in this section: my admiration for the New Left; my belief that anarchism is at the root of its family tree; and my fear
that its chances for growth and for the assumption of power are
slight—but not, as many are saying, so much because of its lack
of ideological underpinnings as because our society has never
provided fertile ground for the nourishing of radical protest,
ideological or not.*

ABOUT three years ago a flood of books began to appear on civil rights. Now the child of the civil rights struggle— the so-called New Left—is beginning to receive the same attention. Much information on the New Left (also known as "The Movement") has been available in *Dissent, Liberation,* and *Studies on the Left,* and occasionally in more general periodicals such as *Partisan Review, Commentary, The Village Voice,* and *The New Republic.* In following this varied literature, however, it has not always been easy to grasp the origins, character, and relationships of the different groups which make up the Movement. These matters are more readily developed in full length studies. A few valuable titles have already been published—notably *The Radical Papers,* a collection of essays edited by Irving Howe—and still others (most promisingly a volume by Jack Newfield) are announced. Of the four books under review, three are decided contributions to understanding and evaluating developments on the Left. The fourth, by Phillip Abbott Luce, is a decided hindrance.

In *Radicalism in America,* Sidney Lens, one of the editors of *Liberation,* has attempted—and to my knowledge it is the first such attempt—to write a one-volume history of American radicalism. It is often and truly said that today's young radicals lack interest in—indeed are scornful of— earlier radical movements. In this sense they are true revolutionaries: almost nothing in the past seems to them worth

This review of Sidney Lens's *Radicalism in America* (Thomas Y. Crowell Company, New York); Paul Jacobs and Saul Landau's *The New Radicals* (Random House, Inc., New York); *The New Student Left,* edited by Mitchell Cohen and Dennis Hale (Beacon Press, Boston); and Phillip Abbott Luce's *The New Left* (David McKay Co., Inc., New York) appeared in *Book Week,* May 29, 1966.

emulating or preserving. Lens, at least by implication, wishes to bring the New Left into the mainstream of American dissent—a tradition which would include Tom Paine, Samuel Adams, the utopian communitarians, the abolitionists, the Molly Maguires, the Wobblies, and the various followers of Marx—in order to enrich the perspective of its members and to make the movement seem more "American."

Lens has carried out his assignment with mixed success. My main quarrel with *Radicalism in America* is with its undefined point of view. The discussion of the period since the Civil War emphasizes the labor movement and the fluctuating fortunes of American Marxist organizations, and says almost nothing about the Radical Republicans of the 1860s who fought to extend civil rights to the Negro or about the Populists of the 1890s who worked to improve the farmer's lot. (This latter seems an especially unfortunate omission because so many of the young radicals—to the extent that they view themselves historically—identify with the Populist effort to form an alliance of the underclasses.) It is possible to justify these omissions by defining "radicalism" so rigorously—for example as "anti-capitalism" —that the Populists and Radical Republicans become mere "reformists." But if Lens has used such a strict standard, he does not say so. In his brief introductory remarks, he tells us only that radicalism can be identified in history as the effort "to make men equal in fact as in theory." However banal that may seem, it is perhaps the only definition of radicalism that would include enough of the various forms of social protest in America to add up to a "tradition."

Yet under this definition why do the Populists and Radical Republicans fail to qualify, or indeed the New Freedom, the New Deal and the Great Society as well? To include such movements in the radical tradition may be to dilute it hopelessly, to make it indistinguishable from liberalism. But to confine radicalism to those enlisted against capitalism, is to reduce the ranks so drastically that it becomes all but impossible to talk of a viable tradition.

If Lens fails to deal with this basic dilemma, he has nonetheless produced a concise, reliable survey based on the best available secondary accounts. And it is good to have at hand a survey of American history in which the hero is for once the committed outsider; instead of the usual paean to Samuel Gompers for cutting skilled workers in on a share of the capitalist pie, we have a sympathetic account of "Wild Bill" Haywood trying to organize the unskilled as a preliminary step to overthrowing capitalism; instead of reading how Woodrow Wilson made the world safe for democracy by going to war, we learn how Eugene Debs and other Socialists fought to keep the Wilson Administration from destroying democratic liberties at home; instead of dwelling on Roosevelt's success in patching up the capitalist system, we hear of the efforts of men like Norman Thomas in behalf of those like the sharecroppers who had been forgotten or ignored by the New Deal. If America is not applauded on every other page for the unparalleled achievements of its civilization—the usual survey procedure—we are still left with the realization that somehow it has always managed to produce men and women to fight against the established inequities.

The recent revival of this tradition of protest is expertly traced by Paul Jacobs and Saul Landau in *The New Radicals*. Their book consists of two parts: a long introduction which describes the membership, programs, and prospects of New Left organizations such as SNCC, Students for a Democratic Society (SDS), the DuBois Clubs, and the Progressive Labor Party, followed by the major documents that illustrate the varying perspectives of these groups.

Given the rapid shifts of personnel and tactics within the Movement, and of national and international developments that affect it from without, only an interim report on its activities is possible. But as an interim report, the Jacobs and Landau book could hardly be better. They write with a rare blend of sympathy and objectivity; though closely identified with the Left, they are capable of pointing out its weaknesses. Their major concern is the lack of a coordinated program or "ideology." This is a criticism increasingly heard, and within the New Left itself. But there is reason to believe that lack of ideology is less a serious deficiency than a source of strength.

Those who call for "ideology" are rarely clear about what they mean. If they mean the need to develop a program of tactics for achieving power (for example, "coalition" politics), then "ideology" seems all to the good—so long as the tactics do not harden into an inflexible formula, always self-defeating in our fluid society. But if those calling for "ideology" mean the formulation of a set of assumptions which explain how society has functioned and should function, then I believe the call is better resisted. The trouble with any all-inclusive theory—as we supposedly learned from the fate of Marxist analysis—is that it obscures as much as it explains, that it achieves clarity by ignoring diversity.

Those who call most loudly for theoretical rigor on the Left seem usually to have in mind some variation on Marxist dogma. Yet the more I read about the younger radicals, the more convinced I am that if any theory is congenial to their mood and style it is not Marxist Socialism but philosophical Anarchism, which properly viewed is an *anti-*theory. By "anarchism" I do not mean, of course, the popular stereotype which mistakenly equates it with nihilism and terror. I mean the speculative writings of men such as

Four Studies on the New Left

Proudhon and Prince Kropotkin. Their critique of modern industrialism and statism, their distrust of all forms of authority and coercion, their stress on individual sovereignty, their belief in the values of spontaneity and simplicity, their quest for a community based on voluntarism, mutual aid, and decentralized decision-making—all seem to me remarkably in harmony with the views of the young radicals of today (including, paradoxically, some radicals on the Right). Yet I have seen almost no awareness in New Left writings of this natural affinity, almost no recognition that anarchist literature could enrich the Movement's thought and place it within a relevant historical context.

To discover how campus radicals, a major group in the movement, do view themselves, the best guide is *The New Student Left*, edited by two seniors at Oberlin. An anthology of articles written between 1961 and 1965 by radical undergraduates who are mostly affiliated with SDS, it is an impressive collection. Many of the essays are eloquent, searching, and constructive. And all are honest. There is no slighting the complex nature of our social ills and remedies, the discouragements of community organizing in the ghettos, the frustrations of dealing with a national Administration which manages to emasculate radical demands by pretending to meet them. Just as these undergraduates reject easy optimism, so they reject easy theorizing. They distrust generalizations and abstractions, leaning instead to programs which are tailored to local needs and promise immediate results. But some of them do express discontent with the limited achievements of piecemeal activity, and therefore an increased susceptibility to the call for ideology.

It is fortunate that this anthology allows young radicals to speak for themselves, for otherwise we would never recognize them in the portrait offered by Phillip Abbott Luce's *The New Left*. Luce is a defector from the Marxist wing of the Movement which he defines to include the DuBois Clubs, the Progressive Labor Party (whose magazine Luce edited), and various splinter Socialist and Trotskyite youth groups. Taken together they have minimal strength and represent only a fraction of the New Left. But one would never know this from reading Luce's clumsy and myopic book—and that is its chief danger.

To be sure, the antics and foibles of certain elements in the Marxist wing (especially those of the Progressive Labor Party—known by other members of the Left as "Mau-Mau Maoists") deserve to be displayed. But unfortunately Luce persistently suggests that in describing the Marxist wing of the Movement, he is in fact describing the whole of the New Left. Occasionally he does seem to recognize that there are important distinctions, but only to revert over and over to terminology which by innuendo (the "leftward drift" of SDS) or outright assertion ("the original New Left . . . has succumbed to the rigidity of the Communist mentality") equate the two. Luce is no less misleading about some of the organizations which he defines as part of the Marxist camp. To say, for example, that the Communist Party "not only was, but is, the dominating influence" in the DuBois Clubs, is to make a simple-minded confusion between Communism and Marxism, and also to ignore the wide range of ideological commitments which actually characterizes DuBois Club members; indeed, Jacobs and Landau in their book refer to the "ideological laxness" of this group. If Luce's distortions are not the product of deliberate malice, then he must be convicted of stupidity. In any case, his book will delight J. Edgar Hoover.

The fate of past movements for radical reform in this country and the current hostility to the New Left remind me of Justice Holmes' remark that men talk in superlatives and then make changes in detail. Even small changes, of course, are worth working for, and there is always the hope of achieving larger ones. Certainly the failure to do so will not be for want of a new crop of energetic, idealistic young radicals. They represent only a minority of even their own generation, but it is an immensely attractive minority— skeptical, tough-minded, loyal to people rather than to ideas, determined to unite principles and policy, willing to give of themselves with a remarkable lack of posturing or self-aggrandizement. If they can somehow manage to come into possession of power, we might once more have a country that acts on the principles rather than the rhetoric of democracy.

JACK NEWFIELD'S
A PROPHETIC MINORITY

One obstacle to the growth of the New Left pointed out in this review (and in Jack Newfield's book)—the escalation of the war in Vietnam—has proved instead to be a stimulant. Until now the growing disillusionment with the war among the general populace prevented the New Left from being wholly isolated and thereby worked against its repression. Yet repression remains a distinct possibility. As the Vietnam war moves toward settlement, and as the New Left (especially SDS) broadens its target to include the entire "system," it may well find itself once more a small and despised minority—and to that extent once more vulnerable to McCarthyite persecution. Even without such a development, there are certain "natural" limits, it seems to me (that is, natural as of 1969), to the potential growth of SDS. I try to spell these out in a later piece, "The Prospects for SDS."

JACK NEWFIELD's lucid, compassionate articles on politics in *The Village Voice* have made many look forward with anticipation to his first book. The anticipation was not misplaced. *A Prophetic Minority* is the best single volume available on the New Radicalism of the Left. And a fine book on that subject means a fine book about America.

A host of organizations are usually included under the blanket label New Left, but Newfield, in a much-needed clarification, reserves that term for the "humanist and existential" members of Students for a Democratic Society (S.D.S.), Student Non-Violent Coordinating Committee (S.N.C.C.), and more localized groupings like the Free Speech Movement at Berkeley and the Mississippi Freedom Democratic Party. He places the Progressive Labor Party and the W. E. B. DuBois Clubs in a separate category, which he calls the Hereditary Left, arguing that these groups are in fact not new but only an ideological extension —often staffed by the actual children—of the old Marxist-Leninist Left of the 1930's. This distinction is entirely valid and should give pause to those who argue from what we might call "the F.B.I. syllogism": all radicals are Communists; S.D.S. is confessedly radical; therefore, S.D.S. is Communist.

In fact, the Maoist Progressive Labor Party—and to a lesser extent the Marxist DuBois Clubs—are fundamentally antithetical to the mainstream of the New Left as represented by S.N.C.C. and S.D.S. The best word to describe the Progressive Labor Party is "rigid": it stresses orthodox

This review of Jack Newfield's *A Prophetic Minority* (The New American Library, Inc., New York) appeared in *The New York Times Book Review,* October 23, 1966.

thought, tight organization, strict discipline, conventional culture. S.N.C.C. and S.D.S., on the other hand, are opposed to all forms of authoritarianism; they believe in decentralization, informality, free expression, experimentation and—love. (True, the last is rapidly disappearing in S.N.C.C., and for the best of reasons: the white love object respondeth not.)

Newfield's own allegiance is strongly with S.D.S. It is, he thinks—and I agree—the most promising expression of this generation's search for a politics rooted in ethics, for a "moral equivalent of war," for a society actually rather than rhetorically dedicated to the greatest good for the greatest number. Newfield hopes that S.D.S. might eventually set its impress on an entire generation rather than merely expressing its better tendencies, that in deeds as well as vision S.D.S. might be remembered as a "prophetic minority."

But his sympathy does not interfere with his judgment. Newfield neither minimizes the faults of the New Left nor ignores the obstacles to its further growth. In his preface he states his intention "to write a document at once fraternally supportive of this New Radicalism and candidly critical of its excesses and shortcomings." Himself one of the early members of S.D.S., Newfield has the insider's sympathy to carry out the first part of his intention; a reporter of impressive objectivity, he has the conscience to complete the second part.

His chief criticisms of the young radicals are two: they have been short on positive alternatives to the national shortcomings they so acutely pinpoint; and they tend to a romantic, transcendental view of life which sometimes precludes rational analysis. They have not, for example, examined all the ramifications of their call for "participatory democracy" (*can* the poor make technical decisions about the poverty program?). This in turn is part of a larger tendency to see the underclasses as inherently noble and virtuous. (In this last regard, a recent Louis Harris poll is illuminating: only 24 per cent of "underprivileged" whites support Negro protest demonstrations as compared with 57 per cent of upper-income whites.

Aside from these internal failings, Newfield sees two external obstacles to the movement's growth. One is a reinvigorated McCarthyism directly tied to the escalating war in Vietnam. The connection between military and domestic policies was stated long ago by Woodrow Wilson. On the eve of delivering his war message to Congress in 1917, and in anguish of spirit, he confided to Frank Cobb, editor of the *New York World*, "To fight you must be brutal and ruthless, and the spirit of ruthless brutality will enter into the very fibre of our national life . . . the Constitution would not survive it . . . free speech and the right of assembly would go . . . a nation couldn't put its strength into a war and keep its head level; it had never been done."

Wilson's words were accurate prophecy—as true now as fifty years ago. We are already seeing their truth: Julian Bond has been refused his seat in the Georgia legislature because of his opposition to the Vietnam war (also, of course, because he is a Negro, but the Vietnam reason was considered persuasive enough to serve as a public pretext); the Michigan legislature has banned Communists from speaking on campuses; the Justice Department has hounded the DuBois Clubs; Congress is considering a bill providing prison terms for anyone aiding "the enemy"; and the House Un-American Activities Committee is investigating the dangerous heresy of being against war. Should the Vietnam conflict escalate still further, "all bets," as

Newfield puts it, "are off on the future of the New Left. Its élite will be drafted, its organizations pilloried and red-baited, its idealism shattered, its mentality turned underground." In other words, it will meet the same fate that overcame the promising radical movement of the pre-World War I period.

The second obstacle to growth is less obvious, no less insidious: "the culture's spongelike genius for either absorbing or merchandising all dissent." Jules Feiffer once summed it up in a cartoon where for seven frames a Negro man looking much like LeRoi Jones berated a white one with a stream of abusive epithets; and in the eighth the white, looking sheepishly pleased, paid his money and asked if he could come back at the same time next week. The flogging itself, not the reasons for it, provides the allure. By treating protest as catharsis or entertainment, the country has managed to dilute, almost negate, its impact. LeRoi Jones becomes a TV personality and *Playboy* prints an account of the New Left side by side with its fold-out nudes. All of which brings to mind Ruskin's bitter remark: "I show men their plain duty and they reply that my style is charming."

Newfield's ability to register criticism and doubt along with sympathy and hope should not be taken as a sign that his book is one of those evenly balanced, academic accounts that uses objectivity as a substitute for feeling. The book's chief triumph is its tone, an uncanny blend of equity and engagement. One part of Newfield is a man of fairness: he will not embellish or exaggerate, he will not engage in polemics. The other part is a man involved with his world. Though conscientious, he is not disembowelled; though he strives to be fair to those with whom he disagrees, he can be eloquent about those with whom he sympathizes. And even where he disagrees, as with S.N.C.C.'s new philosophy

Jack Newfield's *A Prophetic Minority*

of Black Power, he is not the Olympian judge full of assumed superiority, but the loving friend heavy with concern.

I do not mean that *A Prophetic Minority* is faultless. The second half of the book (and especially the brilliant discussion of the "generational gap" between New Left and Old) seems to me a good deal more interesting than the first. The opening chapters on the background and founding of the New Left are less exciting because they work over ground already covered by earlier books, notably Howard Zinn's *SNCC: The New Abolitionists*. More troublesome is Newfield's tendency to journalistic shorthand; he fails to put flesh on some of the terms he uses—"humanist," "anarchist," "middle-class," "existential," etc. Since these abstractions carry a variety of meanings and a wealth of emotional cargo, it would have helped to know precisely how he defines them.

But if *A Prophetic Minority* is not faultless, it is very good. The story it tells should alone win for the New Left the additional converts it so much needs and deserves. If not, perhaps some will be brought over by the realization that the adherence of a man like Jack Newfield, with his large talents and sympathies, is itself strong testimony to the New Left's merit.

THE RELEVANCE OF ANARCHY

In this essay I try to develop further my contention that the New Left has close affinities with philosophical anarchism and that an awareness of those affinities could provide a useful perspective for the Movement (an awareness which has in fact developed since this piece first appeared).

Much additional evidence has accumulated in the past three years regarding one sub-theme of this essay—the anarchist view that the innately "good" infant is ruined by "bad" institutions; it was publicized by the debate surrounding the appearance of books by Konrad Lorenz and Robert Ardrey on human aggression. As might have been predicted, I have been persuaded in that debate by those arguing against the view that aggression is instinctive rather than cultural. My own efforts at educational reform (see "An Experiment in Education") have further convinced me that our institutions, rather than "human nature," bear chief responsibility for the deformities we see around us.

THERE has recently been a modest upsurge of interest in Anarchism. Several excellent volumes have appeared on the movement in the last few years,[1] and a fledgling group known as the New York Federation of Anarchists has formed (true to Anarchist principles, it has a "spokesman" rather than a leader, and refers to itself as a "discussion group," not an organization). But as yet interest in Anarchism is minimal, which to my mind is unfortunate, for Anarchism has, I believe, remarkable relevance for certain contemporary problems and particularly for those pointed to by the emerging "New Left."[2]

The blanket term "Anarchism" does not do justice to the varied movements and personalities usually subsumed under its label. The more one reads of Pierre-Joseph Proudhon

"The Relevance of Anarchy" appeared (under the title "Anarchism Left and Right") in *Partisan Review*, Fall, 1966.

[1] Since 1962 we have had two histories of the Anarchists and two anthologies of their writings. George Woodcock's *Anarchism* (Meridian, 1962) is a brilliant volume, written with the special insight and eloquence of an adherent, while James Joll's *The Anarchists* (Eyre & Spottiswoode, 1964) is a sophisticated, though less compelling and comprehensive analysis. The anthology edited by Irving L. Horowitz, *The Anarchists* (Dell, 1964) concentrates on the "classics" of Anarchist literature, while Leonard Krimerman and Lewis Perry in *Patterns of Anarchy* (Anchor Books, 1966) have collected less familiar writings and have excerpted and introduced them with so much skill as to give us a fully realized portrait of the movement, one true to its complexities. There had already existed a considerable library on Anarchism—for example, the works of Max Nettlau, G. D. H. Cole and Rudolph Rocker—but the four new volumes, authoritative and fluent, make the ideas and events of the movement more accessible than they have been.

[2] In using the term "New Left" I exclude certain groups frequently admitted under that title—the Progressive Labor Party and the DuBois Clubs—which are more correctly seen as continuations of the old Marxist Left, disciplined, bureaucratic, ideological, anti-Bohemian. By "New Left" I mean especially SNCC and SDS, but also more localized groupings like the Free Speech Movement at Berkeley (FSM) and the Mississippi Freedom Democratic Party (MFDP).

or Peter Kropotkin and the more one learns of the way the
movement differed from country to country and from period to period, the less confidently one speaks of *the* Anarchist tradition. Its internal variations were pronounced. The
peasant Anarchists, especially in Spain, were fiercely anti-
industrial and anti-urban and wished to withdraw entirely
from the State to live in separate communities based on
mutual aid. The anarcho-syndicalists of France put special
emphasis on the value of a general strike and looked to the
trade unions as the future units of a new society. Bakunin
advocated violence, Tolstoy abhorred it; Proudhon believed in retaining individual ownership of certain forms
of property, Enrico Malatesta called for its abolition in
every form; Max Stirner's ideal was the egotist engaged in
"the war of each against all," Kropotkin's was human solidarity, a society based on the union of voluntary com-
munes.

These are only some of the divisions of strategy, personality and geography which characterized the Anarchist
movement. What bound these disparate elements together
—what makes plausible the term "Anarchism" in reference
to all of them—is their hostility to authority, especially
that embodied in the State, but including any form of rule
by man over man, whether it be by parent, teacher, lawyer
or priest. The Anarchists were against authority, they said,
because they were for life—not life as most men had ever
lived it, but life as it might be lived. Anarchists argued, in
a manner reminiscent of Rousseau, that human aggression
and cruelty were the products of imposed restraints; the
"good" infant was ruined by "bad" institutions. They insisted that the authoritarian upbringing most children were
subjected to stifled spontaneity, curiosity, initiative, individuality—in other words, prevented possession of themselves. If they could be raised "free"—economically freed

from the struggle for existence, intellectually freed from the tyranny of custom, emotionally freed from the need to revenge their own mutilation by harming others—they could express those "natural" feelings of fraternity and mutual assistance which are innate to the human species.

Since Freud's return to Calvin, we are far less certain than the Anarchists about the infinite goodness of the "unspoiled" child. Aggression, conflict and frustration may be maximized by our culture, but those qualities do not seem wholly cultural in origin. Yet if advances in psychological understanding have made the Anarchist view of human nature appear too uncomplicated in its optimism, they have, in a more circumscribed way, given that view certain new supports. Norman O. Brown's reading of the Freudian legacy has reinforced Anarchist emphasis on the destructive influence of imposed restraints. Erik Erikson (along with Hartmann, Kris and others) has defined "natural" stages of development each of which marks an advance of mixed loss and gain, but an advance clearly preferable to the impairment which results when development is interfered with by adverse environmental influences. And psychologists like Saul and Pulver, if less eminent and sophisticated than Brown and Erikson, are employing rhetoric and drawing conclusions still more directly reminiscent of the Anarchists' optimistic terminology:

[If] . . . loving, understanding respect for [the child's] needs and feelings [is] provided . . . then the child gradually becomes socialized of its own accord with a minimum of tyranny and discipline . . . hostility, violence, and cruelty of all sorts, including wars and self-destructiveness, have their ultimate source in the minds of improperly matured men; and they are prevented by proper childrearing.

The Anarchist belief in the harmonious possibilities of human development—and the threat to that development posed by a hostile environment—is neither utopian nor outmoded; with some psychologists it finds partial, with others almost total, confirmation.

Additional support can be found in certain practical experiments undertaken in recent years. In the Scandinavian "adventure playgrounds," where children are given materials with which to build but are spared adult supervision, individual initiative and friendly cooperation turn out to be mutually supportive rather than mutually exclusive. And in A. S. Neill's Summerhill self-regulation does lead both to personal independence and to a recognition of the inviolability of others; indeed Summerhill is, in miniature, an Anarchist new world come to pass.

The Anarchists' distrust of the State as an instrument of oppression, the tool by which the privileged and powerful maintained themselves, is generally associated with nineteenth-century "classical" liberalism, with John Stuart Mill and, in this country, with the Jeffersonians. But by the end of the nineteenth century and increasingly in the twentieth, liberals began to regard the State as an ally rather than an enemy; only the national government, it was felt, had the power and resources to accomplish regulation and reform, to prevent small groups of self-interested men from exploiting their fellows.

Today the pendulum has begun to swing back again. In the liberal—but more especially in the radical—camp, the federal government has lost some of its appeal; veneration is giving way to distrust; from an instrument of liberation, the central government is once more being viewed as a bulwark of conservatism. This shift is the result of accumulated disappointments. The regulatory agencies set up to supervise the monopolists have been discovered to be operating in the interests of the monopolists; farm-subsidy

programs have been exposed as benefiting the richer oper-
ators while dispossessing tenant farmers and sharecroppers;
the urban renewal program seems to be aggravating rather
than alleviating the housing problems of low-income
groups; civil rights legislation has added to the sheaf of
paper promises without making any notable dent in existing
inequities; the poverty program begins to look like one
more example of the fallacy of treating symptoms as if they
were causes; and the traditional hostility between big government and big business has given way to a cozy partnership whereby the two enterprises have become almost indistinguishable in interest.

The result of these—and other—experiences is disillusionment with government, with the honesty of its intentions and, far more disheartening, with its ability—even
had it the best will in the world—to accomplish needed
reforms. Thus Paul Booth, national secretary of SDS, has
recently said, "Real change doesn't come from bureaucratic
liberal institutions, or from legislatures. Laws always get
passed, but the poor are still poor." SNCC as well as SDS
has shifted to "localism," to community organizing, "participatory" democracy, decentralized decision-making and,
on a personal level, to a freedom in dress, speech, sexual
mores, etc., which suggests a belief that ultimately salvation must come on an individual basis.

Like the Anarchists before them, these young radicals
care much less about participating in the American Dream
(a hope which in 1960 had been chief impetus for the
Greensboro sit-ins) than about restructuring it. They desire not further "progress," as this society currently defines
it in terms of greater efficiency and wealth, but rather, as
George Woodcock has said of the Anarchists, "retreat along
the lines of simplification." They represent, again like the
Anarchists, an ascetic, moralistic urge to cultivate the vir-

tues rather than to gratify the appetites, and they associate the virtues with poverty, with a rural "peasantry" and with those déclassé urban elements whose "anti-social" (even criminal) behavior echoes in exaggerated form their own alienation. In all of this, the young radicals of SNCC and SDS are far removed from the Marxists' stress on economics, fear of the *lumpenproletariat*, distrust of cultural experimentation—though many persist in claiming that the New Left already is Marxist (the FBI-HUAC view) or should become Marxist (the Old Left view).

As the New Left represented by SNCC and SDS shifts away from faith in the federal government, it has begun to employ rhetoric traditionally associated with the Right: the supreme value of the individual, the need to dismantle centralized authority, to resist bureaucratic invasion and to develop self-help, self-reliance, self-respect. The Left has begun to draw the equation long favored by the Right: that "centralism" and dehumanization go hand in hand, or alternately, that individual autonomy is a prerequisite for character. And this, ironically, at a time when the Right itself has begun to vacate that position in response to the growing partnership between big government and big business. Thus the two ends of the political spectrum in this country have started to converge—at least in terms of vocabulary, if not in terms of interests or goals.

But the Anarchist tradition is not of equal relevance to the New Left and to the traditional Right, except that it feeds their shared distrust—in one case burgeoning, in the other diminishing—of centralized power. The Right has never been so much anti-authority, as simply anti- one kind of authority—that associated with the federal government. To the Right, authority has been bad when it emanates from Washington, but good when associated with the Church, the Law, the schoolroom, the home, the Anglo-

The Relevance of Anarchy

Saxon way. Far from being hostile to established opinion, the Right galvanizes its legions in its defense. On the other hand, New Left organizations such as SDS and SNCC distrust authority in a more inclusive way. They do not believe in *any* established pieties—in thought, dress, speech patterns, art forms, social and sexual behavior, politics, or even in stimulants (pot not booze). They are conscious rebels against all imposed patterns, established institutions, received verities. SNCC and SDS are thus genuinely revolutionary: they see almost nothing in the past—and certainly not in the present—admirable enough to preserve. (The Right is prone to admire anything associated with the past—or rather with the myths it has invented about the past.) The New Left stands in direct descent from the Anarchists, who always stressed, and not only rhetorically, the values of spontaneity, experimentation, "primitivism," individual style and free expression.

Though Anarchism and the New Left are separated by wide differences, as, for example, the Left's reliance on politics, with its implied acceptance of "organization" and "government," the Anarchists did formulate some of the problems and did define many of the attitudes which are once more prominent. Hence, in seeing how an earlier generation of radicals of roughly comparable temperament sought its answers, today's New Left might better articulate its own. Yet to judge from their formal writings, SNCC and SDS seem little aware of their Anarchist forebears. Such an awareness will hardly provide today's radicals with a definitive style or with ready-made solutions, but it could lead them to clarifications and to further lines of inquiry.

CONTAINMENT AND CHANGE

*There is one observation I would like to add to this review,
though it is peripheral to the subject at hand. The essays by
Carl Oglesby and Richard Schaull, the one a direct participant
in, the other a sympathizer with, radical politics, demonstrate
how misleading it can be to settle for grab-bag labels like the
"New Left." Oglesby's economic determinism (as well as his
call for an alliance with the Right) and Schaull's Christian
radicalism are probably not representative positions within
the New Left. Yet to leave these men out of a discussion of
New Left tendencies is not only to ignore the diversity to be
found within the Movement, but to deprive ourselves of the
insights their divergent perspectives suggest. The point, I believe, relates to matters larger than the New Left; it is at base
a protest against the common habit of devaluing the particular
in the name of some presumed (and occasionally real) advantage to be gained from emphasizing commonalties. As I
make clear in a number of pieces, an awareness of singularity
is central to my definition of what it means to be a good historian (and even, I suppose, a good person). This bias has its
dangers, too—not seeing the forest for the trees. But I think it's
better to run that risk than not to know a forest has trees.*

THIS impressive, somewhat flawed book consists of two separate essays, one by Carl Oglesby, past president of Students for a Democratic Society, and the other by Richard Schaull, Professor of Ecumenics at Princeton Theological Seminary. The two essays are very different in assumption, tone and content. What binds them together is their common devotion to revolutionary change.

Oglesby's essay is concerned with American foreign policy. Some will call it a polemic, which it is not, others a tour de force, which, and in the best sense, it decidedly is. It is not a polemic because it does not rely for its force on the distortion or omission of evidence—no more distortion, that is, than is unavoidably present in any "thesis" book. Oglesby's range of inquiry, knowledge, and reference is unusually full; literary allusion and historical analogy are alike incorporated with ease and pertinence. Even where Oglesby's facts and arguments are familiar (as in his discussion of the origins of the Cold War), he states them with so much pungency, so much controlled, ironic passion, as in impact to be new. The power of his intelligence and the amplitude of his writing talent combine to produce a string of fresh, even memorable statements. An example: "If it were not for the tanks, the planes, the submarines, the missiles—where would the economy be? Which is very much like asking: If it were not for the heroin, where would the junkies be? Obviously: in hospitals undergoing very painful therapy. Perhaps even of a revolutionary nature."

Oglesby's indictment of our foreign policy is severe, and

This review of Carl Oglesby and Richard Schaull's *Containment and Change* (The Macmillan Company, New York) appeared in *The Village Voice*, May 11, 1967.

on the whole, persuasive; in regard to Vietnam, entirely so. Each of the standard arguments used by the Cold Warriors to justify our presence there, he in turn examines, and in turn strips to its essential vacuity: (1) "We are legally obliged to fight." Answer: the SEATO pact is full of escape clauses, and in any case no state has ever, will ever, or need ever, abide by a treaty harmful to its interests. (2) "We are responding to an emergency plea from the Vietnamese People." Answer: we have never heard from the Vietnamese people, only from the elitist groups which rule them. (3) "Our global reputation is at stake." Answer: it is indeed, our once-proud reputation as symbol and champion of the aspirations of the common man. (4) "We are resisting an invasion." Answer: even if one concedes that Hanoi created and continues to control the NFL, the basic question remains: why have so many South Vietnamese responded? Northerners account for no more than 20 per cent of the total NFL force, and anyway, if the presence of foreign troops is sufficient to deflate an army's claim to nationalist revolutionary status, then what will we do with the fact that General Washington's troops were outnumbered at Yorktown by their French allies? (5) "If we fail to contain Them here, we shall have to contain Them someplace else." Answer: this "domino" theory rests on a premise we have not acknowledged: that nationalism, especially the Asian variety, threatens American economic imperialism. It rests, too, on the arrogant assumption that all the Vietnams are our possessions, to be disposed of according to our interests, even if these run counter to the aspirations of their own people.

Oglesby's analysis of our Vietnam position is the more devastating because he places it in a broad context, treating it as only the latest, if most horrendous symptom, of long-standing American attitudes. He dissects with special skill the theory (perhaps best articulated by W. W. Rostow) that America, selfless and altruistic, is only interested in collaborating with the revolution of rising expectations throughout the world, in helping under-developed nations to import our technological revolution in order to advance democratic values and to improve the material well-being of the local populace.

Lovely in theory. And convenient as official rationale. But how about actual practice? The record, as Oglesby lays it out, is not lovely, nor convenient.

Consider Paraguay: United States aid is a major prop for the regime of dictator Alfredo Stroessner; regrettable, one of our Embassy officials in Asunción admits, but after all, Stroessner is anti-Communist, and "a sure anti-Communist, no matter how despicable, is better than a reformer, no matter how honest, who might turn against us."

Consider Haiti: Duvalier's government has received more than $57 million in AID support and almost as much in loans from the World Bank and the Ex-Im Bank; his own person is protected by a 20,000-man palace guard trained by U. S. Marines. The Haitian people, in turn, have the lowest school attendance in the hemisphere, the fewest hospital beds, the lowest per capita income ($70).

Consider Jamaica: it is rich in sugar, tourism, and bauxite, yet the country is in debt and 93 per cent of its people earn less than $500 a year. Where is the wealth going to? To American corporations, to Alcan, Alcoa, Kaiser, and Reynolds.

There are numerous such examples. The list is depressingly long: our support in Brazil of the plutocrat opposition to Janios Quadros; our sale of F-86 Sabre-jet interceptors, C-47 and C-130B transports, and Sikorsky helicopters to South Africa, whose racist policies we officially deplore; our successful attempt to overthrow President Arbenz in

Guatemala because his agrarian reform program included taking over certain unused lands held by the United Fruit Company; our recent intervention in the Dominican Republic which, based on hysteria and hearsay, ended in destroying the democratic regime of Juan Bosch; etc.; etc.

In short, the pretense that our foreign policy brings democracy and prosperity to the masses is simply that—pretense. It is designed consciously to deceive others and unconsciously to soothe ourselves. In fact, Oglesby argues, our statesmanship has always held uppermost in view not the welfare of the country being "assisted" but the profits of our own business community. "The main nut and kernel of American foreign policy from its earliest days onward," he writes, replacing the official explanation he so successfully demolishes with a "key" of his own, is "to ensure the availability of fertile frontiers to American business."

In drawing this indictment, Oglesby tries not to oversimplify. He acknowledges sources and attributes of our diplomacy other than business profit. He explicitly states, for example, that the AID (and even the CIA) is sometimes involved in genuine efforts to produce social reform; that the Peace Corps does embody a wish to be of help to other people; that the Asian Rice Institute in the Philippines holds out hope of being of real value to the Asian masses. But Oglesby admits these exceptions only to deny their significance. "All imperialisms," he writes, "have produced their mercy angels." Basically, overwhelmingly, America is not the friend but the enemy of the revolutionary movement in the under-developed world to establish governments responsive to the needs of their people and to use their resources to create a better life for the many.

As a description of our foreign policy of, say, the last twenty years, Oglesby, it seems to me, is unquestionably right (though even within this restricted time span, it is worth pointing to Ronald Steel's recent observation in *The New Republic* that "the United States has not only accepted land reform and nationalization in such countries as Bolivia, Indonesia, and Algeria, but even aided the expropriating regimes with food and money"). When Oglesby's generalization is applied to less recent history, it is less persuasive; and when he calls business profit the kernel of our foreign policy "from its earliest days onward," he is forced into some considerable sleights of hand with historical evidence.

When he writes, for example, that in our war with Spain "we had no time for pietistic hogwash; we were openly in the business of protecting business," it can only be that he is ignorant of the widely accepted conclusions of Harvard historian Ernest May that we embarked on that war primarily because of popular indignation in this country over Spain's mistreatment of the Cuban people. Or when, still more sweepingly, Oglesby writes that "we were never isolated and never isolationist. From the beginning, we had a Department of State and we were always directly interested in the power struggles of the commercial European states," he vastly underestimates the determination (one could almost say the obsession) of our early statesmen to avoid European entanglements, fearing as they did that these would compromise our identity and our independence.

These distortions are chiefly disturbing not because they misrepresent this or that episode in our past (such misrepresentations can be accepted, after all, as inevitable by-products of any attempt at thematic statement), but because they are part and parcel of a larger distortion, namely, Oglesby's view that human events can be accounted for almost wholly in terms of economics. "Reality" lies in questions of dollars and cents; if one wishes to know the actual, as opposed to the professed motives of human behavior, look to the pocketbook (thus Oglesby can announce that it was "the more practical arguments about money and land that won the Revolution the decisive support of early American conservatives"; he doesn't specify whom he refers to here, but certainly John Adams, everybody's "early American conservative," will not fit the bill).

All of this may sound very tough-minded of Oglesby, but only if one still wears the spectacles of the 1930s, seeing a munitions maker behind every statesman, a scheming capitalist behind every humanitarian reformer. At times Oglesby sounds like the very re-incarnation of Charles Beard (welcome proof that New and Old Left can meet, if only on the basis of surrender), as when, in a direct paraphrase of Beard, he refers to the American Civil War as our "national trauma to settle the dispute between the planters and industrialists"—a view which has not held currency for about twenty-five years.

Economic determinism seems to me a curious position for a man of Oglesby's idealism to wed himself to. For an idealist, supposedly, is one who believes in the possibilities of our better nature (such as the ability of a benevolent ideal of, say, fraternity to over-balance the drive toward, say, material self-interest). But if human affairs have been exclusively characterized through time by rapacity, aggrandizement, deception, and greed, the record will not, to put it mildly, inspire much confidence in the possibility of a more benevolent future. Which is not to say the record should be falsified in order to give balm to our fantasies of perfectibility, but only that I would think it difficult for Oglesby to remain an idealist if he reads human history the way he apparently does. He might answer, of course, that the American record (or, to further limit it, the American record in foreign policy) is not to be equated with the human record. But if this answer provides an escape from the horns of the dilemma, it does so at the expense of reason.

There is yet another, and perhaps still more serious objection to Oglesby's economic determinism. Because it maximizes the role of profits and minimizes the role of ideas in history, it encourages us to believe that in the specific case of the Cold War, our leaders care nothing, or next to nothing, for the anti-Communist ideology they mouth. Yet it may well be that the deepest cause for concern is that they do believe what they are saying. Their talk of making the world safe for democracy and material well-being, is not simply a smokescreen to conceal their wish to make it safe for American business (at least not consciously, which is the level at which Oglesby debates the matter). Johnson and Rusk are apparently convinced (at least at times) of the truth of their rhetoric, indeed at such moments it is not rhetoric to them at all, but the expression of a sincere belief in their missionary role. They are dangerous not only because they have become the willing tools of American business, but because as well, they are the unwilling prisoners of their own altruistic fantasies. It is hard to know which is worse: a statesman who cynically uses the rhetoric of benevolence to conceal his self-interested policies, or one who genuinely believes that rhetoric but then consistently chooses policies which run counter to it. It is, if you like, the choice between Scylla and Charybdis. The point is that both the monster and the whirlwind are elements in our foreign policy, and if we are ever to survive the double hazard, to steer that narrow course between, we must be aware of both, and not merely one.

Compared with Oglesby, Richard Schaull is a sobersides. He is less daring in his analysis, less apocalyptic in his vision, less dramatic in his presentation. It may be a matter of style—or simply of age. Schaull is of an older generation and he frankly admits that he finds himself "in the unenviable position of being caught somewhere between two worlds." He has spent most of his life "working for reform within the established order," twenty years of it in Latin America as pastor, teacher, and general secretary of the Brazilian Student Christian Movement. But now, Schaull tells us, he is "obliged to give priority to revolution," and this is tantamount to admitting that the whole orientation of his earlier life no longer seems relevant. It takes stature to make such a statement, and this confers on his opinions deserved weight.

All the more, because Schaull does not pretend to be a twenty-year-old, ever ready, ever new. He knows that he carries with him a certain amount of irreducible refuse from the past. Though he sympathizes with "the new mood of the new generation," he does not ignore the fact that he belongs to another. His hope is "to turn this handicap into an advantage by undertaking the task of interpretation and mediation." The hope is modest and honorable, though not, to my mind, more than partially realized.

Perhaps I am not qualified to judge his contribution, which is not merely a polite way of saying that I do not admire it. The fact is that our frames of reference are far apart. Schaull's theological orientation, his attempt to find, behind "the layers of metaphysics and religiosity," a Christian perspective "on history and on the possibilities for the fulfillment of human life that is radically oriented toward the future," is to my secular soul, misguided, irrelevant, or both. This is not to say that the religious analogies Schaull deduces are tortured or imagined, but only that their usefulness seems marginal. I don't find it necessary, for example, to recall that the Messiah was abandoned by His disciples, in order to realize that "we should have no illusions about political movements." Nor do I first become aware of the truism that suffering and defeat are necessary milestones on the road to fulfillment after learning that through the crucifixion of Jesus, a new man, the second Adam, was born.

These analogies may be real, but are they, for that, useful? Unless I mistake the mood of the New Left, a theological metaphor, however pointed, is more likely to blunt than to sharpen understanding; most of today's young radicals will be angered not inspired by religious injunctions. Their orientation is not to God, the supernatural, the claims of other worlds, but to man, the here and now, the necessities of this world. It is not merely religion from which they cannot or will not learn, but any form of past experience. They trust only what they have themselves witnessed; they do not care for the benefit of other people's accumulated insights (if that is what they are). In this they are very wise and a little foolish; wise because they wish to test everything for themselves, accepting no premise or authority which cannot be corroborated by their own experience; foolish, because in acting like victims of amnesia, they bring on themselves a certain amount of avoidable pain.

If the young radicals whom Schaull addresses are able to surmount the theological focus of his remarks, they might well profit (as I did) from his incidental comments. These I found far more interesting than the framework in which he sets them, though I'm afraid Schaull had hoped we would care about the framework, too.

The most valuable part of his essay is the answer he gives to the question "what is to be done?", the procedures he outlines as holding out most promise for radical success. Basically, he advocates the tactic of guerrilla warfare—not, of course, in the literal, military sense of taking to the woods, but rather its political equivalent. That is, Schaull advises the formation of small groups which will concentrate on "liberating" large institutions. These groups may establish a base either inside or outside of a given institution, as specific circumstances dictate, but in any case, they will be disciplined, they will work toward the goal of renewing a single institution, and they will be content, at least for a time, with limited advances. Once the successful renewal of one institution is achieved—like a defense factory—other central institutions related to it will necessarily be affected—like the military.

Schaull is surely right in pointing out that those who have earlier tried to work for radical social transformation have always found themselves "confronted by a total system—a complex of attitudes, institutions, relations, and power alignments—which blocks fundamental changes in society." I think he is also right—at least at this point in our national life, when there is no possibility of forming a radical political coalition strong enough to capture power and to change institutions by fiat—in saying that the guerrilla tactic is the only one which allows any point of radical entry into the interlocking directorate of American institutional life.

But if his argument seems valid, it is, for that very reason, a sad index to radical expectations. For if "guerrilla warfare" is the radical's chief hope, it is not a very promising hope. The only specific examples Schaull can point to in proof of its effectiveness are not encouraging: the Freedom Democratic Party in Mississippi and the community organizing projects in various urban ghettos. Being an honest man, Schaull can say no more than that the FDP may prove able to change the political order in Mississippi, and that the participation of the poor in urban affairs may have "unforeseen consequences in city life and politics." Perhaps they may, but thus far the results inspire marginal optimism only.

And speaking more generally, I think Schaull underestimates the capacity of our society to co-opt dissent, to
give just enough head to its guerrillas (be they in the
church, the universities, the federal government, the press,
or wherever), and to bend just enough to their projected
reforms, to dissipate the call for change without in essence
changing anything. Perhaps this is too pessimistic a view.
Perhaps if radicals did work in more tightly organized
groups, with more sustained effort and toward more clearly
defined goals, they could better circumvent institutional
resistance or better withstand institutional embrace.

This is probably true in regard to the institution I know
best—the university. At Princeton, where I teach, there are
a number (I sometimes think a large number) of younger
faculty members who believe in the necessity of radical
changes in the educational structure. But each tends to
pursue his individual protests and experiments in isolation. There has not been a combined effort (which would
include as well, radicals from the student body—and they
do exist, even at Princeton) of the kind Schaull suggests,
that is, one which would establish a sense of group identity,
a clear definition of goals, a flexible, but determined plan
of action, a willingness to engage in limited but sustained
attacks on various fronts.

The promise such an approach holds out is that "profound and necessary changes in the social order can take
place without the threat of total social disintegration"; if
the guerrilla strategy succeeds, in other words, the more
apocalyptic, bloodier forms of revolution would become
unnecessary. Those who prefer the visions of Marat will
see in Schaull's modest suggestions all the earmarks of a
"liberal betrayal." But to the extent that any path to social
change is available which promises at once to be radical
and peaceful, Schaull has probably delineated it.

Certainly his suggestions seem more promising than

Oglesby's, who, in a rather cryptic close to his own essay, suggests aligning the New Left with the Old Right. Both groups, Oglesby feels, are "in the grain of American humanist individualism and voluntaristic associational action." Here he confuses, I believe, a similarity of rhetoric with a similarity of goals. Both New Left and Old Right are increasingly using the same language—"self-reliance and self-help," "the sacredness of the individual," the need for de-centralization, the dangers of federal power and bureaucracy—but this does not mean that they hold the same ultimate values. The Right continues to believe that men fail willfully, that life's prizes do go to the hardest-working, the most enterprising, the "fittest," that the poor are by definition undeserving. The New Left believes, to the contrary, that society makes the major contribution to individual failure, that those who receive the largest share of society's rewards are usually its most unscrupulous members (while the poor, in human terms, are usually its "best"), and that anyway, most such rewards, especially material ones, are not worth having.

To link these two disparate groups, as Oglesby seems to advocate, is comparable to yoking a horse and a husky to the same wagon. As they head off in separate directions, they're just likely to smash that wagon to pieces.

THE PROSPECTS FOR SDS

This article was written in response to a list of seven questions submitted to a number of people by the editors of Partisan Review. *I confined myself to commenting on their last question only: "Do you think any promise is to be found in the activities of young people today?"*

In the two years since this was written, SDS has shown a substantial increase in membership. Nonetheless—for the reasons outlined in the piece—I think the organization's strength may have peaked, which would mean it will never enroll more than a small minority of the campus population. Since I admire SDS, I hope my estimate is wrong. And there are grounds for thinking it might be. The "emotional identification" with the underclasses which I discuss as a prerequisite for sustained commitment to radical protest might not be as crucial as I thought, or if it is, it might be achieved in ways I had not envisioned—for example, by subjecting students (as during the Chicago Democratic Convention) to the kind of brutality the underclasses have long known. As more students take part in some form of moderate protest—a peace march, say, or a campus protest against defense contracts—and are clubbed to the ground for it, they do learn something of what it means to be an outcast. If radicals are not born but made, the process by which they are made has been greatly advanced in this country during the past two years.

I'LL address myself to your last question. Specifically, I'll deal with the college population, because as a university teacher that's what I know best and because such promise as commentators find these days tends to center on the renewed social consciousness represented by campus groups like SDS.

The promise, I think, is limited—not because only a fraction of students is involved with groups like SDS but because only a fraction is likely to be. The large majority of undergraduates is career-oriented, concerned with making a place inside the system rather than with correcting its abuses. Most students see their four years in college as an opportunity—a joyless duty—to begin the trek toward expertise, toward achieving the status and security of a specialist.

This does not mean that they are unaware of our society's ills. On the contrary, they are often knowledgeable about our problems: about urban decay, the civil rights stalemate, the maldistribution of income, the defects in our educational policy, the military-industrial complex, the banality of our culture. Nor is it accurate to say that they are indifferent to these problems. Some undergraduates are notably troubled; others worry from time to time about this or that issue; almost none are merely cynical or content to repeat comfortable clichés about the poor being always with us.

But awareness of social ills is not enough to move the majority of students (or adults) into action against them. Thus while many admit sympathy for the aims of SDS, few

"The Prospects for SDS" was part of a *Partisan Review* symposium, "What's Happening to America," printed in the Winter, 1967, issue.

The Prospects for SDS

join it. Why? In part because most undergraduates share the national value structure—its faith in the benevolence of time and the Deity, its assumption that all problems carry their own solutions, its tendency to equate normality with "moderation." And these values prevent undergraduates no less than the rest of the nation from crediting the need for immediate, large-scale readjustments.

Then, too, their very knowledge can, paradoxically, inhibit any impulse to engage in protest. For not only do they know the details of social malfunction, they also know the futility of all past movements in this country for correcting it. Believing that the past does—must—repeat itself, they discount in advance any current or future hope for the success of radical protest. One can recognize that this assumption is convenient—it allows the undergraduate to pursue his private goals on the grounds that public ones are unattainable—yet also recognize that the assumption has considerable validity. The fact does remain, however much one regrets it, that the history of radical protest in this country is the history of impotence. True, the slaves were freed—but Southern intransigence seems to have played a far greater role in producing that result than did thirty years of abolitionist agitation. True, the New Deal eventually took over some of the reforms long advocated by Socialists—but with the double result of bolstering capitalism and destroying the Socialist movement itself.

Why then do *any* undergraduates become involved in organizations like SDS? Surely those who do participate are no less knowledgeable about American history or contemporary politics than those who do not. Yet somehow in their case tasting the apple produces neither skepticism nor paralysis. Why it does not is difficult to say. For one thing, those who join SDS do not accept the national hierarchy of values, do not, that is, place order above justice, compromise above principle, property rights above human rights. But another factor, less tangible, may be more significant in explaining their activism. Let me approach it indirectly, by way of an anecdote.

A few weeks ago I asked Jack Newfield, political columnist for *The Village Voice* and author of *A Prophetic Minority*, to talk to my undergraduate seminar at Princeton about the New Left. The meeting was prolonged and intense. Afterward, I asked Newfield what his reactions were to the undergraduates. I found his answer illuminating. He had been, he said, greatly impressed with their knowledge, intelligence and seriousness. They had listened to his indictment of American life with close attention, most had acknowledged its force, had seemed to agree that "something must be done"—and even that SDS seemed a promising vehicle for doing it. Yet, judging from student comments since, not a single convert to SDS was made.

The reason was pinpointed by Newfield himself: he was struck, he said, by the absence of "personal pain." Such sympathy as had been generated for his views had been grounded in logic. Newfield and his Princeton audience had reasoned together; problems had been analyzed, arguments tested, conclusions reached. Something like a rational consensus had been achieved. But what Newfield could not communicate (and not because he lacked the eloquence) was what it means to *feel* defeated and despised, to belong emotionally to the ranks of the dispossessed.

This, I think, gets to the heart of the matter. The average undergraduate can objectively understand the plight of our underclasses, but because he can establish no linkage between it and his own experience, he does not feel that plight. He cannot make the emotional identification with the disinherited which is essential to a *sustained* commitment in their behalf.

And this is true even of those undergraduates who are themselves from lower-class homes—as they are in increasing numbers. They may have belonged materially to the underprivileged class, but not psychologically; they may have shared the hardships of poverty, but they did not share the culture of poverty. Their very presence in a college testifies to their own (at the least, their parents') high level of motivation, to their desire to participate in the benefits of the "system" and to their belief that they will be allowed to participate.

It is thus no surprise to find that most undergraduate members of SDS come not from lower- but from middle-class backgrounds. Reversing the situation of their lower-class campus contemporaries, these middle-class SDS members have managed an emotional identification with the deprived without in their own lives having actually experienced any material deprivation. How this emotional identification became established is the question of central importance. Could we answer it, we would be a long way toward a psychology of social protest. But we cannot answer it—not now, and probably not ever. There are (and will always be, I believe) two chief obstacles to achieving an answer: the reasons for "identification" are probably as varied as the number of individuals involved; and further, any investigator attempting to analyze those reasons will be hampered by his own assumptions, often unconscious, about protest activity. Given this double subjectivity we must expect a range of "explanation" running from "unresolved authority problems" to "natural compassion for suffering humanity."

The central point, in any case, is that even fewer undergraduates have experienced the psychological sufferings of the underprivileged than have experienced the material ones. The large majority on any campus, including those from "deprived" backgrounds, has known little despair. Most undergraduates are self-confident, energetic, untried, undefeated. The world does lie before them like a land of dreams. They have not known enough private pain to identify on a gut level with the underclasses. And by the time they have—by the time, as adults, they do meet with their natural portion of affliction—they will spend their energies trying to deny and conceal it, for in America calamity is not considered part of the human condition but rather the result of personal inadequacy. Thus our adult population, even after encountering its private tragedies, is no more likely a candidate for protest activity than the campus population which has not.

One cannot wish pain upon the undergraduate; it will come soon enough. But until that experience, one cannot expect deep compassion for suffering or deep commitment to its eradication—other, that is, than in its intellectual, which is to say, its attenuated form.

MARTIN LUTHER KING JR.'S

WHERE DO WE GO FROM HERE: CHAOS OR COMMUNITY?

This review brings up several themes mentioned elsewhere. First, my belief that lagging progress in Civil Rights is due less to lack of legislation than to a failure to enforce the considerable legislation already on the books—a failure which reflects a weakness of will not only on the part of the executive, but more basically, on the part of the white majority. Second, my belief that federal power as an instrument of social change has been rejected too completely by radicals and that it remains a useful adjunct to the current radical stress on "neighborhood action." Of course federal power in behalf of the underclasses can be activated only if a majority (or substantial minority) of the electorate exerts the needed pressure. But the hope of organizing such a pressure group has in the past few years become, as we all know, a dim one. Thus, like King, I find myself pinning my hopes on a coalition politics whose prospects, at least for the foreseeable future, are not bright. All of which places me, I suppose, somewhere in that unpopulated zone between liberalism and radicalism.

IN terms of character alone Martin Luther King is a phenomenon. He learned long ago that white hatred of Negroes reflects white, not Negro, deformities, and this has allowed him to feel compassion for the oppressors as well as the oppressed, to grow in strength even while surrounded by vilification. But recently the personal attacks on King have come from less traditional sources and must therefore have proved a greater challenge to his equanimity. Some of the advocates of Black Power and of black nationalism have begun to treat King's insistence on nonviolence as a prehistoric relic, and to mock King himself, with his appeals to religion, to patience and to conscience, as an irrelevancy. Their scorn has been modified in recent months by King's outspoken stand against our policy in Vietnam, but ironically that same stand has brought denunciation from a different quarter in the Negro community—from the established civil rights forces led by Roy Wilkins, Ralph Bunche and Whitney Young.

Faced with abuse on all sides, King has not only remained temperate but has continued to seek reconciliation —both within the Negro community and also in terms of a larger alliance with disaffected whites. At the same time, he has continued to speak his mind, refusing to let pleas for tactical caution obscure the imperative responsibility he feels (which every citizen should feel) to apply ethical standards to international as well as domestic questions. To have managed all this in the face of heavy pressures and wounding accusations bespeaks a character of rare

This review of Martin Luther King Jr.'s *Where Do We Go From Here: Chaos or Community?* (Harper & Row, New York) appeared in *Book Week,* July 9, 1967.

stability, breadth and integrity. What a pity he will never be our President.

King's new book, *Where Do We Go from Here?*, is his attempt to summarize the recent conflicts within the civil rights movement, to consider the larger context, both national and international, which helps to account for these conflicts, and finally, to suggest possible lines for action. King is far more successful, it seems to me, in dealing with the first two of these considerations than with the third, in part because of his tendency when speaking of the future to substitute rhetoric for specificity, in part because of the difficulties of analyzing this complex, appalling moment in our nation's history. That King succeeds as well as he does is additional tribute to the unruffled intelligence of this unendingly impressive American.

The book begins with the question "Where are we?" King, in answering it, makes some subtle and needed distinctions. He rightly insists, first of all, that the disruption of the civil rights movement cannot be explained, as it so often is, by resort to pat answers. The simple equation which has the white backlash growing solely out of Watts and Black Power is inadequate. The hard truth is that the decrease in white sympathy preceded those developments. With Selma and the Voting Rights Act, one phase of the civil rights movement ended—the easy phase—where white sympathy could be readily engaged against the outright brutalities of Southern life. But as King puts it, "To stay murder is not the same thing as to ordain brotherhood." Public indignation against the Bull Connors was achieved far more easily than was the follow-up commitment to eradicate discrimination in housing, jobs and schools—in other words, to establish equal rather than improved opportunities for Negroes.

White America showed its reluctance about equality before Watts and before the emergence of Black Power, though these developments have since served as convenient excuses for still further delays. The reluctance showed in polls which indicated that 50 per cent of white Americans would object to having a Negro as a neighbor and 88 per cent to having their teenage child date a Negro. It showed in the refusal to implement vigorously civil rights legislation—a refusal which has left segregation the overwhelming pattern of our schools (84.1 per cent in the 11 Southern states), which has left Negro voter registration in Virginia, Mississippi, Louisiana and Georgia still under 50 per cent (and barely above it in four other Southern states), and which has made a mockery of open-occupancy and equal job opportunity legislation. In short, only a small minority of whites are yet authentically committed to equality, and it is this, not Negro "irresponsibility," which has prevented greater progress. The urban riots and the slogan of Black Power, as King says, "are not the causes of white resistance, they are consequences of it."

Though King's indictment of white America is as severe as it is justified, he follows it, curiously, with some optimistic predictions. The line of progress, he points out, is never straight: setbacks, disappointments, even retreats mark every movement for substantive social change. The current doldrums in which the civil rights movement finds itself were both predictable and natural, and Negroes should not, therefore, fall into pessimism or defeatism. The Negro has already won a great deal, King argues, especially in the intangible realm of heightened self-respect, and "no matter how many obstacles persist the Negro's forward march can no longer be stopped."

King bases this prediction on prescriptions which may not be filled. First, he advises black people to increase their efforts at amassing additional political and economic power. Here he agrees with the advocates of Black Power even while objecting to the way the Stokely Carmichaels have substituted for programs, slogans which imply separatism and violence.

Yet when King himself comes to spelling out a program for pooling black resources, economic and political, its stock generalities prove vulnerably close to Carmichael's sloganeering. He calls on the Negro to use his buying power to force policy changes among business concerns, but he gives no specifics as to which forms of selective buying might prove fruitful or which businesses might be the most useful targets. Likewise, when he calls on Negroes to develop "habits of thrift and techniques of wise investment," he says nothing about how these qualities may be inculcated, about where the average Negro is to find the money with which to make wise investments, or, finally, whether such middle-class "virtues" are indeed those to be highly prized and cultivated.

King does not believe that the Negro community, even if it can be brought to unified effort, will by itself have sufficient strength to achieve its goals. He understands well the bitterness and frustration out of which many Negroes, especially younger ones, have turned to black nationalism and separatism in a search for structure and purpose in their lives. But the nationalist path, King insists, can lead only to disaster; it represents what Bayard Rustin has called the "no-win" policy, the mistaken notion that there can be a separate black road to fulfillment outside the main stream of American life. What is needed instead, King argues, is a continuing (perhaps one might better say, reinvigorated) coalition between Negroes and whites, a coalition which will be strong enough to exert real pressure on the major parties to become more responsive to the needs of the poor. Only such a coalition can requisition the billions of dollars needed to correct the hard-core inequalities from which the American poor, white and black, suffer.

King's position seems to me impeccable in theory, but it suffers, as he himself must realize, from the lack of available allies for the coalition he advocates. He speaks, for example, of a large group of poor whites who in reality share common grievances with poor Negroes. But reality, as we all know, is only one, and probably one of the weaker, wellsprings of human behavior. The real question is: Can the poor whites in America be brought to recognize their common interest with poor Negroes, or will the transcending power of racism continue to prevent such a merger? Historically, the evidence is not encouraging; with the brief and limited exception of the Populist era, poor whites have put race before all other considerations—including self-interest.

And yet what other than coalition politics can King recommend? Feeling as he does that the American Negro's future rests in his own country—not in Africa, not in a union of the dark people of the world based on some mystical abstraction like *négritude*—King must then find a way to encourage American Negroes to believe that they in fact have a future (that is, an equitable one) in this country. The most hopeful path continues to be the old one of coalition politics, and it is that path to which King adheres. But at this moment in our national life the brutal fact is that coalition politics is a slim hope only.

This is a fact that King, for both tactical and temperamental reasons, cannot afford to acknowledge. Its admission is impossible tactically because it might precipitate the Negro community into the arms of black nationalism, and this, in King's view, would mean a dead end. Its admission is impossible temperamentally because King's personal optimism is deeply ingrained. He believes obstacles are always surmountable, given sufficient will and faith. He believes American racism can and will be overcome, that the goal of "genuine intergroup and interpersonal living" can be reached, though the way be difficult.

Since the grounds for such hope have in reality become tenuous and since King chooses, for reasons of tactics and temperament, not to acknowledge that fact fully, he is forced to fall back on rhetoric as a substitute for argument, to rely on eloquence to camouflage the lack of supporting data. Thus his discussion of future prospects contains more exhortation than sustained analysis: "there is nothing to keep us from remolding a recalcitrant status quo with bruised hands until we have fashioned it into a brotherhood"; "dark and demonic responses will be removed only as men are possessed by the invisible inner law which etches on their hearts the conviction that all men are brothers and that love is mankind's most potent weapon for personal and social transformation."

Exhortation, alas, even were it less pious, will not be enough to overcome the complacency and racism of the American majority or to restore the faith of the disheartened, alienated minority. It is far from clear what, if anything, can. The national prognosis remains poor until something—probably only an event of catastrophic proportions such as a major war or depression—plunges us to a level of despair, and thus of self-confrontation, which could, ultimately, lead to renewed health.

TWO STUDIES OF THE
BLACK COMMUNITY

The trend toward "separatism" in the sixteen-to-twenty-five age group of the black population which I pointed to in this review has clearly accelerated in the past eighteen months. How much it has accelerated, and what the comparative strengths are of the numerous organizations and ideologies competing for the black young, seem unclear—at least to a white outsider. My feeling, expressed at greater length in "Black Power and the American Radical Tradition," is that the "identity" aspects of this "separatist" development are promising, the "racist" ones alarming. But again, I feel uneasy, as a white, pontificating on the subject—more uneasy, perhaps, than in time will seem appropriate.

IN his foreword to Gary T. Marx's study of Negro attitudes, Bayard Rustin comments that Marx "tells it like it is." One thing is certain: he tells it in a way that sharply challenges certain popular stereotypes of Negro thought.

By using a carefully constructed questionnaire, by sampling a variety of geographical regions, social and economic strata, and by analyzing the resulting data with an admirable blend of precision and sophistication, Marx has come up with some surprising conclusions. Among the more eye-opening are these: there is *less* anti-Semitism in the Negro community than in the country as a whole; civil-rights militancy is greatest among those Negroes who hold stable, high-status jobs, who are socially mobile and who are well educated—the protest movement, in other words, is the product of relative affluence, not despair; civil-rights "victories" do not turn good radicals into pacified liberals, but rather make those radicals still more radical; only a tiny minority of the black population sanctions violence, and even fewer sympathize with the Muslim program of separation.

There is no doubt that Marx's study is an eminent example of opinion research, one carried through with estimable honesty and sensitivity. What is of doubt is whether his findings, completed over a year ago, remain applicable. The interviews on which Marx based his study were conducted in late 1964, and he finished his analysis of them in the fall of 1966. During that two-year period, a number of significant events occurred: Watts, the shooting of Meredith in Mississippi, the death of Malcolm X, the birth of

This review of Gary T. Marx's *Protest and Prejudice* (Harper & Row, New York) and Paul Jacobs' *Prelude to Riot* (Random House, Inc., New York) appeared in *The New York Times Book Review*, January 21, 1968.

Black Power. Despite these upheavals, Marx believes, and I think he is right, that, as late as the fall of 1966, no major shift had taken place in the attitude of the Negro community. Anger did increase and so did the appeal of separatism and violence, but the increase was sensationalized by the press out of all proportion to its magnitude. The dominant Negro mood continued overwhelmingly to favor integration, to be loyal to the United States and optimistic about the prospect of achieving social change within it, to disapprove of riots and of virulent anti-white and anti-Semitic sentiments.

The question which then arises is whether a significant shift in Negro attitudes has taken place in the past year— that is, since Marx's book went to press. At present the Negro mood seems to me too mercurial, and our techniques for measuring it too uncertain, for anyone to pronounce on the matter with confidence. One problem (and this may have been only a little less true of the 1964–66 period) is that any given individual in the black population probably contains within himself a variety of conflicting emotions. He may feel friendly toward a Jewish civil-rights worker and fury toward a Jewish grocery-store owner; pleased that his salary has gone up and outraged that he continues to be paid less than his white counterpart; proud to be an American but also proud of the new African states where blacks fully control their own destinies.

Poll that individual on Monday, and he will answer your questions according to whichever sentiments happen to be currently, and transiently, dominant (and also, of course, according to how he perceives the man asking him the questions). Poll him again on Wednesday, and his responses might be the exact reverse of those given two days before. This ambivalence is clearly revealed in a survey just released by *Fortune*. Three out of four Negroes inter-

Two Studies of the Black Community

viewed felt their condition was better than it had been in recent years; at the same time almost half were angrier than they had been a few years ago, with only about one in ten less angry. It seems apparent, therefore, that in the year since Marx's book went to press, the Negro community has become both more hopeful and more wrought-up. This comes as no paradox or surprise, for we have long known that "rising expectations" increase rather than lessen militancy.

Another trend, less familiar, and only hinted at by Marx for the 1964–66 period, has, I believe, recently quickened in an alarming way. I refer to the increasing alienation of the sixteen to twenty-five age group in the black population. The recent *Fortune* study, for example, shows that nearly twice as many Negroes from that age group reject integration as a primary objective as do their elders. To the *Fortune* survey I would add a few additional bits of evidence.

The first is from a black teacher in Harlem. Returning there recently after completing his undergraduate work at Notre Dame, he was surprised to find, he said, that "nine out of every ten youngsters in Harlem are now black nationalists." The same opinion is held by a twenty-five-year-old white man I know who has been living and working in central Harlem for the past three years. He, too, insists that "nationalism" has captured the young and that for them the goal of integration is "dead, stone-dead." He adds that "nationalism" comes in a variety of brands, ranging from a positive identification with Afro-American history and culture, to the more racist varieties that call for separation from the "white devils" and the establishment of an independent black state.

The loyalties of the youthful nationalists in the ghetto are divided, in uncertain proportions, between a bewildering host of competing organizations and ideologies, the best known of which are those of Elijah Muhammad (apparently the largest), of Malcolm X and his heirs, of the Yoruba Temple, and of the movement known as the "five-percenters." In the ghetto, as elsewhere, a profound generation gap exists, and those who under-sample youthful opinion fail to gauge the extent of current disillusionment. It is not clear if it is the racist brand of nationalism that has captured a majority of the ghetto young, but apparently it has captured a considerable minority, and a determined minority can set the tone and establish the options which their fellows, however reluctantly or apathetically, will accept.

One large explanation for the increasing cynicism and hostility of the ghetto young is provided by Paul Jacobs's report of what life is like for the minority poor in Los Angeles. The book's full title, *Prelude to Riot: A View of Urban America From the Bottom*, may sound grandiose, given the limited scope of the study. But I think Jacobs is right in believing that the patterns he has uncovered in Los Angeles hold, despite minor variations, for all American cities.

Jacobs is especially interested in the way minorities are treated by the governmental institutions that constantly impinge on their lives: the police department, the welfare bureau, the public employment services, the housing administration, the schools and the health services. Ironically, these institutions (the police department and the schools excepted) were created by the larger society to serve the needs of the poor. In practice, as Jacobs's investigations make abundantly clear, they provide minimum service and maximum manipulation, bias and humiliation. We have known this, of course, for some time. Indeed one of the sources of our national paralysis in dealing with the problems of the cities may be the numbness which has followed the constant reiteration of what is wrong and why.

Jacobs manages to pierce that numbness, to make the suffering concrete, the indignities fresh. He does so because of his skill as an investigator and reporter. By exposing himself to some of the actual experiences that the minority poor undergo, and by reading widely in documentary sources, he has combined the immediacy of a personal account with the verisimilitude of an objective survey. Moreover, though concentrating on a single city, he has been shrewd enough not to bury us in detail. He shifts briskly from topic to topic—and this rapid change of subject, along with the lucidity of his prose, fixes the attention. Only in his brief conclusion does he falter; in those final few pages, as he moves from describing what is wrong to suggesting possible solutions, his generalizations turn vapid and his prose soggy.

Yet we should not expect Jacobs to provide "answers" when our society as a whole has failed to grapple with the ills of the ghetto. That failure is not grounded on the sudden eclipse of human ingenuity or on the inadequacy of material resources. It rests, very simply, on the majority's lack of interest.

This indeed is one of the explicit themes of Jacobs's book: our urban institutions are, in their corruption, their racist assumptions, their disdain for the poor, an accurate mirror of the society that created and perpetuates them. Our institutional model is becoming paramilitary. The well-being of the organization takes precedence over the well-being of the people it was meant to serve. Order and efficiency become ends not means, and individual needs are irritably viewed as impediments to the smooth functioning of the system.

Jacobs believes that under the accumulated weight of

such treatment, the ghetto masses (he does not specifically differentiate between old and young) are now far angrier than they were when Gary Marx polled and analyzed them. From 1964 to 1966 the minority poor could have hoped, realistically, that the country had begun to mobilize its resources against poverty. Now, with the American majority ever more immunized against suffering (in Vietnam no less than in the ghettos), that comforting hope can no longer be sustained.

If, as a result, the ghetto masses—and especially the rightfully impatient young—are *not* notably more alienated in 1968 than in 1964, we can only wonder why not. Gary Marx's warning in the very last sentence of his book—"the continued failure to obtain meaningful integration or significant changes in the life situation of the average Negro may well relegate the findings reported here to a brief episode in a long historical struggle"—already begins to take on the stature of prophecy.

THE AUTOBIOGRAPHY OF
W. E. B. DU BOIS

In this review of Du Bois' autobiography, as in so many other pieces, I am anxious to preserve the individual qualities of a life, to avoid reducing them to a sociological category. Yet in regard to another theme in this volume, I am less consistent: though I speak elsewhere of my skepticism about the "utility" of historical study, I find that in this piece I take implicit comfort from a historical perspective—from the recognition that the shift in the Negro community from integrationist to separatist goals is not a new, but a recurring, phenomenon through time. Since I'm fond of my skepticism, let me immediately add that the recurrence of certain patterns in the past does not guarantee their recurrence in the future, that the current demand among black radicals for separation need not give way to yet another cycle of integration—that history, in short, can not be relied upon to repeat itself.

IN terms of the external patterns of his life, it is impossible to write of W.E.B. Du Bois as a representative figure in Afro-American history. In terms of his ideas, it is impossible not to.

His personal history is hardly that of a black Everyman. Born in 1868 in Great Barrington, Massachusetts, he was descended on his mother's side from Tom Burghardt, who was brought by Dutch slave traders to the Hudson valley around 1740 and whose service in the army during the Revolutionary War brought freedom for him and his family. On his father's side, Du Bois was descended from French Huguenots who migrated from Flanders to America more than 300 years ago. At the end of the eighteenth century, a Du Bois either married a free Negro woman or took a slave as concubine, and the descendants of that union were white enough to "pass." One of them, Alexander Du Bois, W.E.B.'s grandfather, was given a gentleman's education at Cheshire School in Connecticut and then— symbolism begins early in Du Bois' family history—was apprenticed to a shoemaker.

Alexander was a stern, hard man who secretly wrote poetry ("stilted, pleading things from a soul astray," comments his grandson), sired four children and, in his domineering way, proved a poor parent to all four. The fourth, Du Bois' father, bent, as Du Bois eloquently describes it, "but did not break—better if he had. He yielded and flared back, asked forgiveness and forgot why, became the harshly-bold favorite, who ran away and rioted and

This review of *The Autobiography of W.E.B. Du Bois* (International Publishers Co., Inc., New York) appeared in *The New Republic*, March 23, 1968.

roamed, and loved and married my brown mother." Soon after the baby William was born the couple split up; under the urging of her relatives, Du Bois' mother refused to join her husband in Connecticut where he had gone to establish a home, and so William never saw his father again. He grew up with his mother's family, the black Burghardts of Great Barrington.

His childhood was in no way typical of the experiences of most black youths of his day, for he had almost no personal encounter with segregation or even prejudice. There were only a few dozen blacks in a population of 5,000 and most had lived in the area for generations; the Burghardts were among the oldest inhabitants of the valley. Young Du Bois' schoolmates and friends were white, he joined freely in their games, was continually in and out of their homes and grew, like his companions, to associate poverty and ignorance not with the blacks, but with the recently arrived Irish.

In his condescension towards the Irish, as in so much else, Du Bois was the typical New England product of the late nineteenth century. He believed, above all, that success in life was in direct proportion to ability and hard work; property and ancestry might influence one's standing to some degree, but color would not. He absorbed, too, the New England definitions of good form and sound thinking. Volubility, emotionalism, dishonesty and ostentation were vices. Frugality, candor, control and earnestness were virtues. Christian dogma, the rightness of all things American and the inevitability of Progress, comprised the substance and the boundaries of acceptable opinion.

Du Bois grew into the familiar Yankee mold, into that unappetizing yet somehow admirable figure, the fastidious man of character. He never lied, drank alcohol or consorted with women. He believed that the sort of person a man became was far more important than what he knew or what he accomplished. He believed that Truth could be scientifically established, that rationality was man's most distinctive attribute and tireless work his surest path to redemption. He had never heard of colonialism or imperialism; he knew nothing of the history of Europe in Africa, of the slave trade which had helped to fuel the industrial revolution, of the rivalry among white nations for the control of raw material and labor. His hero was Bismarck.

As he grew older, Du Bois gradually discarded the intellectual assumptions of his New England upbringing, but the region's style remained forever engraved upon his personality. By his own description, he was a man always slow to make friends and always quick to speak his mind; his deep reserve put a distance between himself and others which a biting tongue made wider still. He was readily respected for his integrity, for the brilliance of his mind and the polish of his manners, but he was not readily loved. He was, in short, a New England Brahmin.

About a third of Du Bois' *Autobiography* is devoted to his New England youth and this constitutes, from a literary and psychological viewpoint, the most compelling part of the book. Lyric in tone, rich in detail, it is a wonderfully evocative account of life in a New England town of the late nineteenth century. Du Bois' achievement in recreating the period and its people is the more remarkable when we realize that the *Autobiography* was completed in his ninety-first year.

The larger part of the *Autobiography,* concerned with Du Bois' adult life, is less engrossing, though valuable for the new detail it provides on the various milestones of his public career. The book is especially rich in information on

The Autobiography of W.E.B. Du Bois

his confrontation with Booker T. Washington at the turn of the century, and on his role as a founder of the NAACP and as longtime editor of its journal, *The Crisis* (in this last regard, Du Bois' comments on Walter White's leadership of the NAACP are of particular interest: White was "one of the most selfish men I ever knew. . . . He seemed really to believe that his personal interests and the interest of his race and organization were identical"). On one episode, Du Bois' unfavorable reactions to Marcus Garvey's movement of black nationalism in the 1920's, the *Autobiography* is disappointingly sketchy; it does not make clear whether Du Bois, champion even then of "Pan-Africanism," was put off by particular ideological differences with Garvey or only by the latter's "lower class" life style and appeal.

Though Du Bois' personal narration of public events is well worth having, it does not provide the materials nor suggest the need for any large-scale reevaluation of Afro-American history; on the contrary, it corroborates rather than alters the general lines of our previous understanding. The same can be said of what the *Autobiography* reveals of Du Bois' own ideological progression. It fills in some details in the story of how a man who remained a New Englander in temperament was gradually, through his growing consciousness of color, weaned from the region's philosophical premises. But it does nothing to change our view of Du Bois as a man of paradox, nor to clear up any of the particular ambiguities in his thought. August Meier's fine study, *Negro Thought in America, 1880–1915*, laid bare the ambivalent attitudes central both to the man and to the protest movement he so often represented. The *Autobiography* confirms Meier's analysis without adding any new dimension to it. What it does do is give additional proof of the confusions produced in both the man and the movement by, as Du Bois himself phrased it, a sense of "two-ness," a dual identification with the Negro race and with the American nation.

For at least a hundred years, the Negro protest movement has shifted, as a result of that "two-ness," between conflicting goals. In periods of discouragement, when white resistance to equality has been pronounced, the black community has turned from the goal of integration to that of racial solidarity, self-help, the development of separate institutions and, in times of profound hopelessness, to actual emigration. During one such period a black man wrote he wished the United States "nothing but ill and endless misfortune" and only hoped he would live to see it "go down to ruin and its memory blotted from the pages of history. A man who loves a country that hates him is a human dog and not a man." Those lines were written not by H. Rap Brown in 1968, but by Henry M. Turner, bishop of the A.M.E. Church, in 1892.

It will not do to caricature Du Bois' idiosyncratic life by making of it a mere emblem of the Negro's struggle. There are too many ways in which Du Bois stood apart from the main stream of Negro thought—particularly in his elitist call for leadership by the "talented tenth," and in his Marxism (Du Bois died a confirmed Communist after having gone into self-imposed exile and having become a citizen of Ghana; by far the worst parts of the *Autobiography* are his mindless defenses of Soviet and Maoist societies, where "every opinion" is expressed and listened to, where "universal goodwill and love" are everywhere apparent). Yet in a lifetime lasting ninety-five years, Du Bois did embody most of the significant ideological twists and tactical turns of the Negro protest movement. This is especially true of the way in which his call for total integration alternated with his call for voluntary segregation.

The Autobiography of W.E.B. Du Bois

His attraction to separate Negro institutions, particularly in the economic sphere, reflected his fear that the mass of his people would never be allowed to participate fully in American life. He admits in the *Autobiography* that the Supreme Court decision in 1954 surprised him; he had not believed so substantial a victory against legal discrimination could be won so soon. Nonetheless he recognized—far in advance of most people—that for some time the victory would be in name only; it would take, he warned, twenty-five to fifty years before white Americans would abide by the Court's decision. In the interim, Du Bois argues, Negroes must undertake an "inner cooperative effort"; they must not make the mistake of the German Jews who "assumed that if the German nation received some of them as intellectual and social equals, the whole group would be safe. It took only a psychopathic criminal like Hitler to show them their tragic mistake. American Negroes may yet face a similar tragedy. They should prepare for such an eventuality." In sounding such a note, in calling on the Negro community to prepare its defenses through group cooperation, Du Bois prefigured by at least five years (the *Autobiography* was completed in 1960) the line of thought that has culminated in the philosophy of Black Power.

Nor is this the limit of Du Bois' prophetic powers. Other threads in his thought, those intimately related to his call for racial solidarity, are likewise finding new emphasis today: an identification with Africa, a stress on the distinctive qualities and achievements of Negro culture, a rhetoric that frequently hovers on the edge of reverse racism. Like his latter day counterparts in SNCC and CORE, Du Bois made mystic references throughout his life to the Negro's inherited qualities of sensuousness, rhythm, humor and pathos, and spoke of the Negro's duty to maintain his racial integrity so that he might fulfill his special mission to humanity. In his fury at white racism, in his determination to give his people the psychological weapons needed to defend themselves against white slander, Du Bois, like Rap Brown after him, sometimes resorted to the very terminology he ordinarily denounced, to that insistence on innate racial differences which in other moods he railed against so bitterly, and so justifiably.

Which perhaps only proves what the majority in this country has for so long denied: that Afro-Americans are, above all, Americans. Brought up in a racist culture, they, too, will sometimes exhibit symptoms of racism. When whites have for centuries hurled the thunderbolt of Race at blacks, it should come as no surprise that some blacks would finally learn to harness the lightning, to hurl back their own fiery slogans of négritude.

WILLIAM STYRON'S

NAT TURNER

AND

TEN BLACK WRITERS RESPOND

The two reviews that follow are both concerned with William Styron's The Confessions of Nat Turner. *The first is about Styron's novel itself; the second, a volume of essays written in response to the novel.*

The opening piece is subject to revision on two accounts. First, I now think I did an injustice to Kenneth Stampp's book on slavery by somewhat overstating the extent to which he portrays the slave as psychologically undamaged by the system's cruelties. Second, I was wrong in saying that Styron had kept scrupulously (too scrupulously, I argued, for the novel's own good) to all the details of Nat Turner's original "confessions." I had read those confessions so many times in the past that when I came to review Styron's novel I thought a quick rereading would suffice. I should have taken more pains. As so many blacks have angrily pointed out, Styron did change or omit a number of details in the confessions (though they have not pointed out that those confessions are themselves subject to challenge).

In any case, as I argue in the second piece, it does not follow from Styron's occasional distortion of detail that his intent was to "malign" Nat Turner, nor that his portrait runs counter to acceptable historical truth. To the contrary, I continue to be-

lieve that Styron's presentation of Turner is true in broad out-
line to the limited historical evidence we have. Indeed, where it
may be most suspect is in its insistence on humanizing Turner
by underplaying the religious fanaticism which seems to have
been the central component of his personality. I also continue to
believe that despite, or perhaps because of, certain invented
details in the novel, Styron's book is a superb work of history,
the most vivid evocation we have of the Old South and its
"peculiar institution."

There was considerable reaction to the second piece, rang-
ing from angry letters to the New York Times *to private ad-*
monitions from black friends (though perhaps what made me
most uncomfortable were the congratulations sent by a number
of white liberals whose opinions I thought I did not share). My
response to both the praise and blame is best summed up, I
think, in a section of the reply I wrote (and which was printed
only in part) in the Times:

My hope [that blacks could avoid the racism that has so long
characterized whites] may have been naïve (a naïvete, I might
add, widely shared and actively encouraged by many blacks
during the early years of the civil rights movement). I also
recognize, belatedly, that it is a subtle form of dehumanization
to regard anyone as a potential "hero" . . .

I would like to add here a point made by a friend in a private
letter to me. Although racism is as disturbing in blacks as in
whites, he wrote, it may not follow that all racisms should be
treated as equal in culpability. Whites, after all, started the
cycle, and the intractability of their racism may leave blacks
no way of surviving or of achieving "consciousness" other than
by adopting similar tactics. This friend further believes, following the arguments of Frantz Fanon, that while black racism
may be "a necessary stage in the psychological development of
many blacks, it is not really very satisfying for most of them,
and therefore is not likely to be permanent." I hope he is right,

William Styron's *Nat Turner*

but I am not convinced that racism is the only way blacks can achieve consciousness nor that there is any compelling reason for believing black racism need prove less durable than white . . .

The black essayists in *William Styron's Nat Turner* challenged Styron almost exclusively on historical grounds, and I therefore joined the debate on *their* chosen terms. When evaluating interpretations of the past, the criteria are inescapably those of accuracy and objectivity: "how well does the interpretation fit the known evidence?" Had I used criteria other than these in evaluating the interpretations offered by black writers, I could rightly have been accused of condescension. I suppose I might have taken the line that the black essayists were self-deceived— that they *thought* they were engaging in serious historical debate, but in fact were motivated by purely . . . [polemical] considerations. Surely this would have been a worse form of condescension. It would have put me in the position of presuming to know better than the black writers themselves what their real intentions were. Instead I accepted their purpose as they stated it: to argue the merits of Styron's novel as a work of history.

The reaction to the second article that most troubled me was raised privately by a black friend. He did not, he said, dispute the details of my review; indeed, he thought my points were well taken. But the piece, he added, should have been something more than a cold "taking to task," a scholar's hard insistence on the demands of "objectivity." What was also needed, he said, was some sympathy for the psychological needs forcing blacks into inventing usable myths, some sensitivity to their feeling that Styron, in denigrating Turner's virility, had assaulted their own, even some recognition of the natural resentment black writers would feel, after years of struggling to make a living, at the prospect of a white author's earning a million dollars from a book about a black hero.

I agree with my friend. It is not that I regret saying the things

I did in this review, for Styron had been ruthlessly and unfairly assaulted and, moreover, as a professional historian I did have the responsibility to take issue with the manipulation of historical data. But I regret that I did not say other things as well, did not make clear that although I was disquieted as an historian, I did sympathize as a man.

On a related topic treated by implication in these two pieces —the value of "Black Studies"—I might add that although I decidedly support such programs in our schools, I feel so much energy and hope is currently being invested in them that they could yet prove to be—to use the militants' vocabulary— counter-revolutionary. That is, the campus demand for Black Studies programs could come to overshadow other discontents (and tactics for change) in the black community, compressing a variety of grievances into a comparatively narrow channel. As Melvin Drimmer has recently reminded us, "Black History in itself will not put bread on the table, eliminate white racism, solve the problems of the cities, end the war in Viet Nam or wherever the next Viet Nam is going to take place, or reorient national priorities."

Faith in the importance of Black History, moreover, seems to me based on the double assumption—so uncommon in our culture—that the individual can best find fulfillment in the group, and that the group best gains an understanding of its future purpose by examining its own past history. To me, the opposite of these propositions seems truer: that the individual is most likely to find fulfillment by exploring his "specialness" —how he differs from all others—and that a group is most likely to formulate and pursue goals adequate to the needs of the present if it avoids intense involvement with or adulation of the past.

WILLIAM STYRON describes his latest novel as "a meditation on history." The phrase is provocative, suggesting a new form wherein history is converted into philosophy rather than, as in the case of most historical novels, romance. Yet the attempt to combine the novelist's imagination with the historian's devotion to "objective reality" (and to preserve both intact) may, on its face, be misguided. If one believes in the prime importance of subjectivity, of using materials from the past (or present) as grist for one's own mill, then some "re-arrangement" of those materials is inescapable. If one believes in the prime importance of objectivity, of staying within the strict limits of historical evidence, then invention must be curtailed. Styron's novel raises the question central to all efforts at historical fiction: can a writer simultaneously be true to the past and to himself?

Styron's concern for historical accuracy is manifest throughout the novel. In one sense, this scrupulosity was easily maintained, for there are few known facts about the 1831 slave revolt in Virginia which Nat Turner led. Yet Styron does more than simply narrate the events of that uprising. He attempts to re-create its social context, a context—the Old South—about which we have a great deal of information. Styron does remarkable justice to the subtleties and contradictions of that information.

Speaking as a professional historian, and one who has done most of his teaching and writing about the pre-Civil War years, I was astonished at Styron's mastery of both the details and interpretative themes of the period. There is

This review of William Styron's *The Confessions of Nat Turner* (Random House, Inc., New York) appeared in *The Village Voice,* December 14, 1967.

nowhere available a more richly patterned, evocative account of day-to-day life in the impoverished Virginia countryside around the year 1830. And Styron's portrait of the institution of slavery conveys its varieties of condition and experience with a subtlety unmatched by any academic historian.

There have been three major historians of American slavery: Ulrich Phillips, Kenneth Stampp, and Stanley Elkins. Phillips did most of his scholarly work in the early decades of the twentieth century, and until recently his views of slavery were the dominant ones. Phillips emphasized the mild, paternal aspects of the institution and underplayed its cruelties: severity, he claimed, was the exception, kindness the rule. Moreover, he believed slavery was a civilizing force: it removed Africans from their benighted homeland and introduced them to the blessings of Christianity and Progress. But the civilizing process could go only so far, for the Negro's childish temperament, however "amiable" and "ingratiating," made some form of subordinate status and guardianship inescapable. Phillips's characterization established the stereotype of Black Sambo, the shuffling, genial, happy darky. He saw Sambo's traits as genetic, not cultural—that is, given by nature, not acquired through learning.

Phillips's views had been challenged long before the appearance of Kenneth Stampp's *The Peculiar Institution* in 1956, but Stampp's well-researched and well-written volume swept away whatever lingering support for Phillips remained. (In the historical profession, as in politics, there is nothing so powerful as an idea whose time has come.) Investigating source materials that Phillips had not touched upon (though Phillips's scholarship had been no superficial thing), Stampp dispelled the idea that slavery was benevolent and easy-going. Yet curiously, he resisted the conclusion which seemed to follow from his own evidence: that a cruel and coercive system of labor must have had destructive psychological effects on its laborers.

Stampp's reluctance to pursue the pernicious consequences of slavery probably springs from his unwillingness to lend credence to the view that Negroes were—or are— "different." This humane concern has some unfortunate by-products. By insisting that "Negroes are, after all, only white men with black skins," Stampp is forced to minimize the special experience of slavery and to describe its effects in a way that threatens to replace Phillips's slanders and stereotypes with new unrealities. Stampp tends to see the slave, in full manliness and vigor, engaging in day-to-day resistance to oppression; his typical slave is closer to Toussaint L'Ouverture than to Black Sambo. Such a portrait, in a bizarre reversal of Stampp's actual intentions, ends by denying the Negro his common humanity, for he cannot be "like everyone else" if, unlike everyone else, he does not react to endless indignity and brutalization with some despair and self-hate.

In 1959 Stanley Elkins, in a book entitled *Slavery*, tried to cut through the standing debate about whether the Negro slave was child or hero, by introducing new questions and by employing new techniques of evaluation. Elkins compared slavery in the American South with slavery in Latin America and concluded that the former system was more rigid in structure and more harsh in practice (a conclusion since challenged by other historians). He then attempted to delineate the effects of the "closed" structure of Southern slavery on the personality of the slave. Using studies done on the personality disintegration of Jews in concentration camps, Elkins argued that a series of comparable "shocks" produced comparable "infantilization" among American slaves (a conclusion also challenged by other historians). In other words, Elkins, though rejecting Phillips's genetic explanation for Black Sambo, nonetheless accepts Sambo as the dominant personality type produced by Southern slavery. Nor, in Elkins's view, was Sambo merely role-playing. He did not consciously assume the role of Sambo in order to "get by"; he actually became Sambo.

Styron has profited from the special insights of these historians without climbing onto their special hobbyhorses. Nat Turner, the central figure in the *Confessions,* is Stampp's resistant, heroic Negro, but in his gallery of secondary characters, Styron makes room as well for the Sambo personality described by Phillips and Elkins. At the same time he makes sure that the Sambos who people his pages are too diverse a group to fit any of the explanatory or descriptive categories to which the social scientists, with their usual penchant for obliterating the individual in the abstraction, have tried to reduce them. One or two house servants in the novel do readily fit Elkins's psychograph of the brain-washed, infantilized slave (and no doubt there were such in the South), but most of the gullible, abject, semi-comic slaves in Styron's book deliberately adopt the Sambo role in order to deceive their masters and to preserve something of their inner life from scrutiny and control.

Yet Styron does not make it quite that simple either. He understands that when a man plays a role long enough, the role becomes internalized; that most behavior cannot be neatly divided into conscious and unconscious segments; that often we make inaccurate evaluations of our own actions, confuse our designs, sabotage our intentions. In the character of Hark, Nat Turner's closest associate, Styron fully dramatizes these ambiguities, fusing them into a moving portrait.

William Styron's *Nat Turner*

Hark is a wizard at "wise flattery"; he knows how to "gull a white man out of his very britches." Yet his obsequiousness is not wholly deliberate, for Hark confesses to feeling "blackassed" much of the time, and one can detect in his "womanish" eyes trust and dependence alternating with fear and furtiveness. Nat berates Hark for his servility, but though Hark does learn to direct some of his rage outward against the oppressor rather than inward against himself, the battle for self-respect is never fully won.

Styron's ability to recapture the nineteenth-century milieu is a function of his style as well as his intelligence. The leisurely rhythm of his prose, the lushness of imagery, the fondness for adjectives, the penchant for evoking time and place with set pieces of rhetorical description—all of these are nineteenth-century in form and feeling. Though style and subject matter generally complement each other, now and then the *Confessions* does seem merely old-fashioned. There are moments (rushing water falling "ineffable and pure through the tangle of grapevine and the honeysuckle and the tree-shadowed thickets of ivy and fern") when Styron echoes all too closely the more vapid and sentimental aspects of nineteenth-century prose. There are times (as when Nat, master of diplomacy, abruptly demands food from his new owners and gets a whip lash across the face instead) where, as in so many creaky nineteenth-century plots, plausibility of character is sacrificed to the need for narrative development.

But Styron does not often succumb to such excesses. Most of the time the *Confessions* manages to read like a contemporary nineteenth-century account without, miraculously, offending twentieth-century sensibilities. His success in combining the two is best seen in the way he develops the character of Margaret Whitehead, the young white girl whose love-hate relationship with Nat forms the book's central episode and metaphor. Styron takes great risks with Margaret, deliberately skirting cliché and parody. She is the young girl of pure heart and tender sympathies, well-intentioned, slightly simpering, thrilled by life's "spirituality." She is, in other words, the typical heroine of most bad, nineteenth-century romances. Yet Styron makes us accept her and care about her, in part because he himself believes absolutely in the authenticity of her type, in part because he individualizes her through subtle detailing. Styron's success in making Margaret at once an unattractive stereotype and an attractive person accounts for the effectiveness with which he is able to convey Nat's ambivalent feelings toward her. Nat's alternating tenderness and hatred for Margaret, the fact that he kills her during the rebellion—the only killing he is able to carry off—become not merely plausible, but psychologically compelling. Margaret's death and Nat's final vision of remorse and reconciliation—his near confusion of Margaret with God—are so moving that I found myself in tears at the end of the book. That, of course, is a very nineteenth-century reaction; not many twentieth-century books allow for it.

Just as Styron manages to avoid parody while creating believable, nineteenth-century personality types, so he manages to avoid over-simplification while drawing relevance out of the nineteenth-century experience. He has no easy message. He makes no vulgar equation between Nat's story and Rap Brown's, nor does he indulge in any gross generalizations about the utility, or inutility, of violence. Still, in its selection of detail and its choice of emphasis, Styron's particular reconstruction necessarily carries its particular message. He emphasizes that it is the Nat Turners, educated by their masters, given comparatively tender treatment, allowed to sleep an extra hour after their fellow slaves have been driven to the fields, who plot rebellion. ("Beat a nigger, starve him, leave him wallowing in his own shit, and he will be yours for life. Awe him by some unforeseen hint of philanthropy, tickle him with the idea of hope, and he will want to slice your throat.") But it is also the Nat Turners, unlike the brutalized field hands whom they lead, who, when the chips are down, draw back from personal participation in killing—to their own surprise and horror. Nat's script fails him; he acts in ways he neither planned nor wished. In his life, as in most, the unexpected and accidental control the movement of events.

What Styron seems to be saying is that the closer we look at human behavior, whether in the past or the present, the smaller the role played by reason; always it is impulse overcoming restraint, passion blinding intellect, caprice dominating logic. Where most historians try to wrap events into tidy bundles, crisply ticking off the "causes" of this, the "influences" on that, Styron gives us the whole aimless, unfathomable sprawl. He knows, as do few historians, that life is more like a happening than a planned performance, that even when an actor chooses his own part, he can discover on opening night that he is miscast in his role or has forgotten his cue. Styron is a superb historian because he understands people. Most historians understand ideas.

Styron also understands that the experience of an earlier generation can be made relevant without either distorting that experience or heavy-handedly pointing its moral. It is because he re-creates Nat Turner's revolt on its own terms and refuses to superimpose too precise a message, that the episode takes on pertinence and immediacy. Nothing is more fatal to the fragile prospect of learning from an event or a person widely separated in time or style from one's own than the insistence that they are not separated.

The young, who know better than their elders that the generations cannot be assimilated, quickly reject the matron in a mini-skirt, but they show some ability to appreciate those—an Erikson, say, or a Mills—who insist on speaking in their own, not the latest style. Authenticity (and the self-respect which underlies it) is the only possible mediation between strangers.

Yet Styron's success as an historian is intimately related, paradoxically, to the one major defect of the *Confessions,* a defect so serious as to compromise its success as a novel. I refer to the characterization of Nat Turner himself, the story's narrator and central figure. Though the book's secondary characters are vivid and believable, Nat is neither. Aside from his encounters with Margaret, in which we do get the sense of a particular man involved in a particular situation, Nat never comes alive as an individual. He speaks his lines well, but we sense a ventriloquist near at hand.

The root of the trouble, I believe, is Styron's very insistence on historical authenticity. With the secondary characters he felt free to invent, since only a miniscule amount of information has come down to us about any of them. Not a great deal more is available about Nat, but in his case we do have a twenty-odd-page document, the so-called "confessions," which he dictated, while awaiting execution, to a Virginia lawyer named Thomas Gray. There is little doubt that the document is not pure Nat Turner, that Gray filtered Nat's words through the prism of his own and his community's needs. Yet there is little doubt, too, from the document, that Nat Turner was a religious fanatic, a man who believed his actions inspired and sanctified by God.

In his determination to be true to the past Styron has preserved Nat as an Old Testament figure. Yet at the same time, he decided to make Nat the narrator of events. This means that Nat must simultaneously be a Hebraic prophet lost in visions of a coming blood-bath and a down-to-earth fellow observing and reporting all those minute details of everyday life on which Styron relies for his portrait of ante-bellum Virginia. The images of prophet and journalist comport badly; the deed Nat did and the book Nat has "written" do not synchronize.

Styron alludes to this dilemma—though apparently he did not see it as such—in an "author's note" at the front of the book. "I have allowed myself," he writes, "the utmost freedom of imagination in reconstructing events—yet I trust remaining within the bounds of what meager enlightenment history has left us. . . ." The two, unfortunately, are all but impossible to combine; fantasy and scholarship are antagonistic, not complementary, pursuits. In adhering to the historical Nat Turner, Styron has had to renounce those rich powers of invention which make his secondary characters so memorable.

And so William Styron has paid his scrupulous debt to the past, to a past that neither cares nor complains. One cannot serve all loyalties or preserve all integrities simultaneously. Choices are necessary, and Styron has made them. He has decided to put aside his subjective vision, his own truth, in order to serve those twenty-odd scraps of paper we call Nat Turner's "confessions," a document, ironically, which almost certainly distorts "what actually happened." My own feeling is that in delineating Nat's character Styron has succumbed to the wrong pieties and priorities and has thereby kept a fine novel about and in the vein of the nineteenth century, well this side of the masterpiece it has almost everywhere been acclaimed.

THIS is a depressing volume—for those who believe the past can and should be protected from the propagandists, for those with the lingering hope that the races in America can be reconciled, for those who have regarded the blacks as a saving remnant that might help our country become something better than what it has been.

The book is a commentary—perhaps "assault" would be the more appropriate word—by ten black writers on William Styron's novel, *The Confessions of Nat Turner*. There are legitimate complaints, historical and literary, to be made against Styron's book, and as presented by two of the ten essayists, Vincent Harding and Mike Thelwell, those complaints are cogently, even poignantly, set forth. Harding and Thelwell recognize that Styron, as a novelist, is entitled to certain prerogatives of invention and fantasy, but they point out that he has not been content to advertise his work as "fiction"; in the preface to the novel (and in a number of public comments and debates since its publication) Styron has insisted that he "rarely departed from the *known* facts about Nat Turner and the revolt of which he was the leader."

By inviting critics to treat his book as a work of history as well as one of fiction, Styron has increased his vulnerability to attack. Even had he not, the attack would have come, for as Thelwell points out, the acclaim given the novel by white critics and the terms in which that acclaim has been formulated (e.g., Styron reveals "the agonizing essence of Negro slavery") have turned the book into a cul-

This review of *William Styron's Nat Turner: Ten Black Writers Respond*, John Henrik Clarke, ed. (Beacon Press, Boston), appeared in *The New York Times Book Review*, August 11, 1968.

tural phenomenon about which extra-literary questions become more inescapable.

My own feelings about Styron's book are that, although seriously flawed as a novel, it is, at the same time, superlative history. By this, I do not mean that Styron cannot be faulted for the occasional omission or distortion of detail (an inescapable by-product of *any* work of history, no matter how rigorous and scrupulous the historian), but that the *Confessions* provides the most subtle, multifaceted view of antebellum Virginia, its institution of slavery and the effects of that institution on both slaves and masters, available in any single volume.

This opinion is furiously rebutted by the ten black writers in this collection. Three sets of "distortions" in the *"Confessions"* particularly outrage them. The first has to do with Turner's family background. By failing to credit the role played in Nat's upbringing by a black grandmother and father, and by de-emphasizing the influence of his mother, Styron has, it is charged, written a kind of early-day adjunct to the Moynihan Report, whereby the instability of black family life carries the inevitable corollary that the "significant others" in Nat's life had to be whites.

The second set of distortions concerns Nat Turner's sex life. Styron, it is said, has dropped Nat's black slave wife from history, has focused his desires instead on a young white girl and, by throwing a homosexual episode into the package, has ended by creating a Nat Turner who is all at once impotent, queer, sexually repressed, and full of secret lusts for white flesh.

The third indictment against Styron centers on his description of the revolt itself and the part Nat Turner played in it. Nat's vacillation at the moment of crisis, his refusal or inability to kill any white other than the young girl who had been the focus of his repressed desires, the inanity of his few black allies and the indifference or hostility of the other slaves, create the impression, Styron's critics argue, that Nat was a coward, a fool, an incompetent, or all three, and imply, moreover, that blacks are at all times incapable of engineering their own liberation.

These are the most detailed of the indictments made against Styron, but they by no means exhaust the grievances listed by the ten authors. Among the additional, more general charges made by individual essayists, is that Styron has exaggerated the benevolent aspects of slavery, that he has portrayed all or most Negroes in slavery as "Sambos," that he has minimized the powerful resistance blacks made to bondage, that he has misunderstood the black temper, the psychology of uprisings, the very nature of American society.

Some of the essayists insist that Styron's distortions are deliberate, the conscious design of (in Ernest Kaiser's phrase) a "vile racist imagination." Two or three of the writers are willing to entertain the notion that Styron may not have intentionally maligned the character and historical significance of Nat Turner (Alvin F. Poussaint, the Boston psychiatrist, even detects in many parts of the novel, the author's "strong empathy" for Nat), though they feel that his stereotypic liberal views have prevented him, despite good intentions, from understanding the black psyche and the black experience.

In drawing their charges, the essayists imply that in regard to all these matters—Nat Turner's personality, the institution of slavery, the psychology of insurrection, etc.—the historical evidence establishes clear patterns that run counter to those presented by Styron. They are certain, for example, that the "real" Nat Turner was, in the words of John Henrik Clarke, "a virile, commanding, courageous figure." It is as unthinkable to them that Turner could have been irresolute in battle or ambivalent about committing murder, as it is that he could have hankered after a white woman or not "dearly loved" his black wife.

According to their countermodel, Nat Turner was one of the world's great military geniuses and one of its most resolute white haters. (Poussaint chides Styron for suggesting that Turner could have believed in "the basic humanity of some slave-holders.") This would make Nat Turner, among other things, a dedicated killer and racist —qualities which I doubt most of the essayists would ordinarily single out for praise. In any case, they see Turner not as a human being, but as an epic force, a figure immune to the usual range of error, compassion and desire.

If this is what blacks mean by "rediscovering" black history and finding historical figures with whom black youths can identify, then the prospects are grim, for in the case of Turner at least, the figure they present for emulation is frighteningly one-dimensional, even pathological. It is a question, moreover, whether the new emphasis on black heroes really will demythologize our past (as is claimed and needed), or whether it will replace one set of myths with another. To give just one other example: We have heard much of late of Crispus Attucks, who, we are being told, was a runaway Negro slave killed in the "Boston Massacre"—the first blood to be shed in the American struggle for independence. The fact is we don't know whether Attucks was a Negro, a mulatto, an Indian, or even a runaway, and no one, of course, can assign the moment or the vein from which the "first blood" for independence spurted forth.

Blacks are entitled to their version of Turner, Attucks and others, but let them not pretend that those versions are incontestably validated by the historical evidence. As regards Turner, for example, the historical documentation is so skimpy and contradictory that only by embroidering or ignoring it (the very sins for which they denounce Styron) can the black writers in this collection establish their predetermined and dogmatic "lessons." The chief—indeed with the exception of a few scattered references in contemporary accounts—the only source on Nat Turner is the twenty-odd-page "confessions" taken down when he was in jail by a white racist lawyer named Thomas Gray.

The full text of these original confessions is printed as an appendix to this volume, as if to suggest that it carries some kind of unarguable certification for the views of the essayists. It does present some "facts," like Turner's family lineage, which contradict Styron's version—but even on this level, the black essayists should have been the first to remind us (as they do in so many other contexts) that Turner's confessions were filtered through the eyes and words of a white man and are therefore automatically suspect.

Since, to the contrary, most of the essayists seem to believe that the original confessions are Absolute Truth and that every account which deviates from them partakes of malignant intent, it is surprising they did not chastise Styron more severely for underplaying the one character trait of Turner's that emerges most clearly from those confessions—that he was a religious fanatic of terrifying, perhaps psychotic, proportions.

For matters incidental to Turner's own career—and especially for the view that rebellions like his were not rare (as Styron states) but rather frequent occurrences—the essayists rely heavily on Herbert Aptheker's *American Negro Slave Revolts*. But they do not mention that most historians consider Aptheker's evidence suspect, based as it often is on inference and rumor (nor that historians are equally leery of the "oral tradition" which some of the writers are reduced to citing).

The essayists wish to believe that the "craving for freedom" was to be found in every Negro breast, and that therefore there is no "big mystery," as John Oliver Killens puts it, about the causes of Nat Turner's rebellion. But since there were millions of slaves and very few revolutionaries, the phenomenon of Nat Turner does need further explanation—as does the failure of the vast majority of Negroes to rebel. Evidence of Negro apathy or acquiescence will not disappear by the mere reiteration that it never existed. Denmark Vesey's Charleston insurrection in 1822—to give but one example—is known to have been betrayed by black informers.

By insisting that all slaves "craved freedom," the essayists force themselves into a bizarre view of the institution of slavery. For slavery could not have been as barbaric as they otherwise insist if it inculcated self-love and masculine assertion in the slaves, rather than the self-hate and loss of identity more usually taken to be its products.

Only when slavery is viewed as an essentially benign institution (the position associated with the scholarship of Ulrich B. Phillips and bitterly denounced by the essayists), can it follow that it left no deep personality scars on its victims. But the weight of historical evidence and opinion suggests that American slavery was harsh enough to produce serious character disorders in many slaves. If this be "slander," then I suppose we shall now have to brand Bruno Bettelheim an anti-Semite for pointing out that prisoners in the concentration camps tended to identify with their S.S. guards and to become infantilized.

What makes Styron a better historian than any of his critics is that he will not bury unpleasant evidence or minimize the complexities of past experience in order to serve some presumed contemporary need. It seems to me grotesque to say as some of these writers do, that because Styron portrays an occasional master as kindly, he therefore believes slavery was benevolent; Styron recognizes that some slaves had kind masters *and* that slavery was abominable. It seems to me absurd to claim that Styron "dehumanizes every black person in the book" because he portrays some Negroes as Sambos and endows others with conflicts and uncertainties (traits which I hitherto took to be among the telltale signs of humanity); Styron recognizes that slavery produced Uncle Toms *and* rebels.

Finally, I think it is obscene to say that Styron is "an unreconstructed Southern rebel" and that his purposes in writing the *Confessions* were to confirm white racists in their view that Negroes are ingrates and incompetents and to defuse black militancy by suggesting that all rebellions are acts of futility. Styron's chief crime, it appears, is his refusal to reduce any man to caricature, whether as Hero or Oppressor. His chief disability—that is, to those who wish to exploit rather than to understand the past—is his insistence on holding contradictory views in tension, on embracing paradox.

After several hundred years of white myth-making and polemic, it looks as if we're now in for some innings by the blacks. One hoped it was going to be different this time around. But that, I suppose, was one of the more recent myths: that blacks in this country could somehow transcend the destructive racism that permeates our culture, that they, unlike the whites, might somehow avoid distorting the past as a way of inciting one half of mankind to hate the other.

THE AGONY OF THE
AMERICAN LEFT

In the first part of this review, I lament the tendency of radical critics of American life to multiply sects and to direct more of their fire at each other than at their common enemies. Yet I realize, with some discomfort, that later in the review I spend more time detailing my points of difference with Christopher Lasch than elucidating our common ground—which is considerable. I don't know how to account for this penchant on the Left for internecine bickering—or even whether the penchant is peculiar to the Left. Perhaps the trait is intrinsic to all social criticism, regardless of political persuasion, or even to all writing, concerned as it so centrally is with self-inflation.

Still more unfortunate, some of the differences between Lasch and myself that I pointed to in this review are apparently illusory. I now have it on Lasch's own authority that in advocating a "new party," he did not mean to associate himself with Marcus Raskin's group of that name. In Lasch's opinion, a new party will eventually be necessary, but it must be preceded by a good deal of theoretical and practical work—of a kind done in an earlier generation by the Fabian Society.

EPIGRAMS cannot do the work of analysis, but it is tempting to say of the left in the United States that as its numbers grow, its strength ebbs. More Americans are deeply dissatisfied with our society than at any time since the thirties, yet as the ranks of the discontented swell, they simultaneously break into fragments.

Black activists of CORE reject cooperation with white radicals of S.D.S.; Marxists in the Progressive Labor party scorn the ideological flabbiness of members of the Peace and Freedom party; the columns of *The New York Review of Books* are filled with radicals denouncing radicals (Harrington vs. Macdonald, Genovese vs. Lynd); *Hard Times* regards *The New Republic* as old hat; *Dissent* worries about the responsibility of *The Village Voice,* which in turn scolds hippies and "crazies," who couldn't care less so long as the Mexican pot fields don't go up in flames. The closest all come to a common voice is when faced with The Enemy —who is not, as the uninitiated may suppose, George Wallace or Max Rafferty or General Westmoreland—but rather that latest figure of left demonology, The Corporate Liberal.

In sorting out divisions on the left, one critical index is electoral politics. Though many of the young retain their faith in the ballot—like the students who worked in the Kennedy and McCarthy campaigns—the more radical among them increasingly doubt its usefulness for promoting change. Black militants became cynical about politics as far back as 1964, when the Mississippi Freedom Democratic party was denied its rightful place at the Democratic Convention. Many campus activists have never been at-

This review of Christopher Lasch's *The Agony of the American Left* (Alfred A. Knopf, Inc., New York) appeared in *The New York Times Book Review,* March 23, 1969.

tracted to politics as the top order of business, arguing that priority must go to building a radical constituency through community organizing.

Distrust of the electoral process is far less pronounced among older radicals. They, too, applaud community organizing and political education, but argue that the best way of curtailing corporate and military power is to use the ballot for gaining control of the only larger power complex in the country—the Federal Government.

Two organizations are currently bidding for the allegiance of those who believe in the strategy of electoral politics. The first, the New Democratic Coalition, came into existence during the closing hours of the Chicago Convention and now has chapters in about half the states. The N.D.C. believes in working within the Democratic party in the hope of ultimately capturing it (though its antagonists charge that a "capture" would only result in more of the same welfare statism), and has already drawn to its banner such men as Julian Bond, Allard Lowenstein, Paul Schrade, Michael Harrington, Arnold S. Kaufman and Adam Walinsky. The second organization calls for the formation of an entirely separate party (the New party); thus far it has less strength and fewer well-known names than the N.D.C., but does include among its advocates, Marcus Raskin, Dr. Benjamin Spock and Christopher Lasch.

For the last few years, Christopher Lasch's essays have been appearing in various periodicals (particularly *The New York Review*), and they have won wide respect for the way they combine a devotion to understanding the past with a passion for informing the present. Five of those essays—one each on Populism, Socialism, the Congress for Cultural Freedom, Black Power, and a concluding piece, "The Revival of Political Controversy in the Sixties," which has as its main theme the need for a new party—have been collected as *The Agony of the American Left*. All the essays contain brilliant provocations, and the one on Black Power seems to me extraordinary, especially for its discussion of the vitality of Negro culture in the rural South as compared with the ghetto North, and how this has affected the different reception given to Black Power in the two regions.

I do, however, quarrel with some of Lasch's historical judgments, particularly his indictment of the Wobblies, which I think underplays their anti-authoritarianism and overplays (as the researches of Joseph R. Conlin have made clear) their hostility to politics. And though I started with an open (which is to say, divided) mind in regard to a new party, I found Lasch's description of its potential shape so vague as to leave me unconvinced that it holds any decisive advantage over working for a new coalition within an old party.

Lasch argues that a new party, by "daring to call things by their proper name," would gather to itself the widespread discontent that currently exists. But the proper name that Lasch employs for the party—Socialist—is one that produces instant trauma in most Americans. Perhaps it is possible to define "Socialism" in such a way as to make it a feasible political label in this country, but Lasch does not provide that definition.

He rejects the "ugly overtones of bureaucracy, centralization and forcible repression," which the term has acquired from its association with existing Socialist regimes in underdeveloped countries, and he also disavows the diluted "social democratic" (or welfare state) connotations with which Socialism has been identified in advanced countries like Sweden or Great Britain. But he offers us nothing in place of those definitions other than the hint that the basis for a new Socialism might come from an "indigenous tradition of radical populism"—which he describes as "decentralization, local control and a generally antibureaucratic outlook."

But this is not very helpful, since that same tradition is claimed by the American Right. Moreover, a definition that relies on "decentralization," etc., seems to confine Socialism to a matter of means rather than ends. Yet if that is to be the case, why is there no discussion of the possible necessity and consequences of nationalization? Is its omission meant to imply that nationalization is too obvious—or too outmoded—to discuss? And in any case, what does Lasch then mean when he refers to "social planning"? Can that be achieved without state ownership, or at least state regulation, and if not, how would he then avoid the bureaucracy and centralization he so deplores?

It would be unfair to expect from Lasch a fully satisfying redefinition of Socialism, since no one else has been able to provide one. (When C. A. R. Crosland made his notable attempt a dozen years ago, he insisted that the constant in Socialism was its goals not its means, but he was reduced to so broad a definition of those goals—"a high priority for the relief of the unfortunate," etc.—that any welfare-stater could qualify as an adherent.) Still, if Lasch expects us to embrace the idea of a new party, its intentions will have to be made at least somewhat less obscure.

Besides, I am not convinced that electoral politics is going to prove the most significant catalyst or even the chief conduit for social reconstruction. I think what is most impressive about the radical young is not their politics or their social theories, but the cultural revolution they have inaugurated—the change in life style. If that revolution develops, it may well express itself politically (and to some extent already has), but that is not the same as arguing that the new culture must rely on political expression for its development.

The sources and manifestations of the revolution lie else-where—in a bewildering grab-bag that includes hallucinatory drugs, bi-sexuality, communal pads, dashikis and bluejeans, rock and soul, Eastern mystics, scientology, encounter groups, macrobiotic foods, astrology, street theaters and free stores. One may loathe some of the ingredients (as do many of the young themselves), or argue that they have not yet (and never will) crystallize into anything distinctive enough to be called a culture, but though the mix be unpleasant, shifting and inchoate, if it continues to locate its center in the senses and emotions, in participation and sharing, in the unexplored, the spontaneous, the casual, the experimental, we may well be witnessing a decisive break with our society's hitherto dominant values of rationalism, puritanism, materialism and individualism.

I think Lasch pays insufficient attention to this side of the youth revolt, though he has much to say about young radicals and much of value. Some of it is complimentary—he credits them with having communicated to many people a sense of crisis and an awareness that our system is unresponsive to the needs of millions of its citizens. Some of it is disparaging—he is angry at their tendency (present in only a few, it seems to me) to turn public questions into tests of personal "authenticity" and to talk glibly of guerrilla warfare or the advantages of right-wing repression.

Though Lasch is as eloquent in defense of their virtues as he is stern in censuring their failings, he nowhere credits the young with what may be their most revolutionary contribution—the forging of a new mode of living. This is the more ironic because Lasch himself, in the very last page of his book, calls for "an alternate culture and vision." It may be that his temperament, with its unqualified faith in rationality (historical analysis, he writes, is "the best way, maybe the only way, of gaining a clear understanding of social issues"), and its distrust of what he calls the "spiritual and philosophical chaos of American life," has blocked his access to the particular kind of alternate culture the radical young are in process of creating.

One quality Lasch assuredly shares with them—and it sets both apart from welfare-state liberals or the N.D.C.— is uncompromising anti-Americanism. That attitude in the main cannot be faulted—certainly not as regards the horrors of our war machine, our ghettos, our corporate greed, our violent, inequitable society. Yet even so, the case against us can be made too all-inclusive, and Lasch is sometimes guilty of this excess.

When he writes, for example, that "The American press is free, but it censors itself. The university is free, but it has purged itself of ideas. The literary intellectuals are free, but they use their freedom to propagandize for the state," one is willing to credit the statement only if Lasch has in mind some narrow definition which would exclude (to give only a few of many possible examples) *The New York Review of Books* from membership in the "press," would eliminate Harvard from the category of universities, and would deny the editors of *Partisan Review* (whom he elsewhere praises) the right to be called "literary intellectuals."

I doubt if Lasch himself believes that dissent is as "illusory" in this country as he sometimes seems to argue, for he implores radicals to guard against the suppression of free speech, and unless he is thinking only of its potential rather than its current value, he could not call for so determined an effort in defense of so "meaningless" a cause. It may be that in speaking of "illusory dissent" Lasch only means to deplore the fact that dissenters do not have the impact on official policy that they would like or that their numbers would sometimes justify; but as Johnson's decision not to seek re-election shows, that is not the same as saying dissent has no impact whatsoever.

Or it may be that Lasch only means that our society does

not value-free inquiry to the extent that it claims; but as the flood of anti-American books and periodicals demonstrates, that does not mean we *habitually* prevent free inquiry from proceeding. It is one thing to recognize that freedom of speech and of the press are diluted by self-censorship, by government indifference or harassment, and by vigilante attacks, but quite another to suggest that those freedoms do not exist at all. The distinction is not trivial. It would be tragic if radical critics, having taken the lead in challenging our country's mindless anti-Communism, encourage the substitution of mindless anti-Americanism.

At one point in his book, Lasch refers to Marx's insight that political issues must be seen in their social context. That same insight can be used to inquire into the determinants of our own rabid anti-Americanism, for it, too, is a social product—not only in the sense of being a response to our society's serious shortcomings, but also in being a reflection of our society's masochism, its furious self-hate. Our self-esteem as a nation has always rested on pride in material affluence. We have recently (all too recently) learned that millions of Americans do not share that affluence and, more heart-rending still to defenders of the faith, that additional millions of our middle-class youth who *have* shared in that affluence not only do not prize it, but consider it a positive handicap in the search for personal identity and national integrity.

Yet our worth as a people never did depend solely on our riches. It may be too late to recapture those other qualities, but one way of trying is to divert some of the energy that now goes into frenzied self-contempt into the very different and more promising channel of self-examination. Men like Christopher Lasch, Howard Zinn and Noam Chomsky are providing the materials for that self-examination. Now, if only people will read them.

BLACK POWER AND THE
AMERICAN RADICAL TRADITION

*Although this essay was originally written in the summer of
1966, I have placed it last in this section because in its present
form it did not appear until 1968, and because it sums up so
many of the themes of the preceding pages.*

*In its Spring 1968 issue, Partisan Review asked a dozen
people to comment on some of the issues the essay had raised.
It's worth pointing out—as a gauge of current sentiment—that
of the four Negro commentators (Ivanhoe Donaldson, Charles
V. Hamilton, William Melvin Kelley and Dr. Nathan Wright,
Jr.,), all but Dr. Wright expressed resentment at the idea
of a white's writing on the Black Power movement. Only
Charles V. Hamilton, however, offered a detailed critique of
my views. He began by objecting to self-styled "ghetto-
watchers" who spend their time "nit-picking with Black Power"
instead of devoting their energies to combatting racism within
the white community—a point well taken only if one believes that white radicals must allocate their energies in an
either/or way, which I do not. I am more ready to accept
Hamilton's other main objections to my essay: that I do not give
sufficient weight to Black Power's emphasis on "the culture and
heritage of black Americans"; and that I focus too much on the
positions taken by a few highly visible black leaders and seem
ignorant of less publicized and perhaps more constructive de-*

velopments which also characterize the Black Power movement —like the burgeoning organizations of black teachers devoted to developing "relevance" in the curricula of ghetto schools, and the recent meeting of black, middle-class professionals in Chicago to "map ways they can bring their skills to bear on the development of the black community."

Among the white commentators in Partisan Review's *symposium, Norman Mailer pressed for recognition of the fact that Negroes "have become on the average physically superior" to whites, a view which Irving Howe and Dr. H. Jack Geiger took issue with in* PR's *succeeding two numbers. They pointed out that if one uses the usual criteria of proneness to disease, infant mortality or life expectancy (which may not have been those Mailer had in mind), the statistics prove the opposite of Mailer's contention.*

Another commentator, Tom Kahn, raised an important issue about "coalition politics." Though thinking I was "rightly critical of the inadequacies of recent liberal legislation," Kahn feels my pessimism about "radicalism's immediate prospects" leaves us "stranded"; needlessly, he believes, for the organized labor movement, in his view, is more available for a new coalition on the left than I suggested—certainly as available as the New Class technocrats or unskilled, ununionized laborers whom I mentioned as possible allies. Kahn may be right that I overstate the availability of the latter two groups, but if so, that would leave me more, not less, pessimistic about the prospects for coalition politics. On the basis of the limited evidence I have seen, I don't think it means much (in terms of a radical coalition) to say, as Kahn does, that organized labor has "the most advanced economic policies of any major institution in American life." By "advanced," Kahn means a concern with "full employment, higher wages, expanded housing construction and increased federal spending for social purposes." These seem to me "advanced" goals only by New Deal definitions—though

Kahn is surely right that no major institution in America has moved beyond them. In any case, organized labor seems interested in advancing those goals chiefly for its own limited membership.

THE slogan of "Black Power" has caused widespread confusion and alarm. This is partly due to a problem inherent in language: words necessarily reduce complex attitudes or phenomena to symbols which, in their abbreviation, allow for a variety of interpretations. Stuart Chase has reported that in the thirties, when the word "fascism" was on every tongue, he asked 100 people from various walks of life what the word meant and got 100 widely differing definitions. And in 1953 when *The Capital Times* of Madison, Wisconsin, asked 200 people "What is a Communist?" not only was there no agreement, but five out of every eight admitted they couldn't define the term at all. So it is with "Black Power." Its definition depends on whom you ask, when you ask, where you ask, and not least, who does the asking.

Yet the phrase's ambiguity derives not only from the usual confusions of language, but from a failure of clarity (or is it frankness?) on the part of its advocates, and a failure of attention (or is it generosity?) from their critics. The leaders of SNCC and CORE who invented the slogan, including Stokely Carmichael and Floyd McKissick, have given Black Power different definitions on different occasions, in part because their own understanding of the term continues to develop, but in part, too, because their ex-

"Black Power and the American Radical Tradition" was first written as a series of newspaper articles in the summer of 1966. I revised it thoroughly when it was published in the Winter, 1968, issue of *Partisan Review* (under the title "Black Power in America") and then slightly altered it again for *Dissent: Explorations in the History of American Radicalism*, Alfred F. Young, ed., (Northern Illinois University Press, 1968). It is the last version of the essay which appears in this volume.

Black Power and the American Radical Tradition

planations have been tailored to their audiences.[1]

The confusion has been compounded by the press, which has frequently distorted the words of SNCC and CORE representatives, harping on every connotation of violence and racism, minimizing the central call for ethnic unity.

For all these reasons, it is still not clear whether "Black Power" is to be taken as a short-term tactical device or a long-range goal—that is, a postponement or a rejection of integration; whether it has been adapted as a lever for intimidating whites or organizing blacks, for instilling race hate or race pride; whether it necessitates, permits or encourages violence; whether it is a symptom of Negro despair or of Negro determination, a reaction to the lack of improvement in the daily lives of Negro-Americans or a sign that improved conditions are creating additional expectations and demands. Whether Black Power, furthermore, becomes a constructive psychological and political

---

[1] Jeremy Larner has recently pointed out ("Initiation for Whitey: Notes on Poverty and Riot," *Dissent*, November-December, 1967) that the young Negro in the ghetto mainly seeks the kind of knowledge which can serve as a "ready-made line, a set of hard-nosed aphorisms," and that both Malcolm X and Stokely Carmichael have understood this need. In this regard Larner quotes a speech by Carmichael to the students of Morgan State College, as transcribed in *The Movement*, June, 1967:

> Now then we come to the question of definitions . . . it is very, very important because I believe that people who can define are masters. I want to read a quote. It is one of my favorite quotes. It comes from *Alice In Wonderland*, Lewis Carroll. . . .
>> "When I use a word," Humpty Dumpty said in a rather scornful tone, "I mean just what I choose it to mean, neither more nor less."
>> "The question is," said Alice, "whether you can make words mean so many different things." "The question is," said Humpty Dumpty, "who is to be master."
> That is all. That is all. Understand that . . . the first need of a free people is to define their own terms.

As Larner comments, "Mr. Carmichael, unlike Mr. Carroll, identifies with Humpty Dumpty."

tactic or a destructive summons to separatism, violence and reverse racism will depend at least as much on developments outside the control of its advocates (like the war in Vietnam) as on their conscious determination. For all these reasons, it is too early for final evaluations; only time, and perhaps not even that, will provide them. At most, certain limited, and tentative, observations are possible.

If Black Power means only that Negroes should organize politically and economically in order to develop self-regard and to exert maximum pressure, then the new philosophy would be difficult to fault, for it would be based on the truism that minorities must argue from positions of strength rather than weakness, that the majority is far more likely to make concessions to power than to justice. To insist that Negro-Americans seek their goals as individuals and solely by appeals to conscience and "love," when white Americans have always relied on group association and organized power to achieve theirs, would be yet one more form of discrimination. Moreover, when whites decry SNCC's declaration that it is tired of turning the other cheek, that henceforth it will actively resist white brutality, they might do well to remember that they have always considered self-defense acceptable behavior for themselves; our textbooks, for example, view the refusal of the revolutionaries of 1776 to "sit supinely by" as the very essence of manhood.

Although Black Power makes good sense when defined to mean further organization and cooperation within the Negro community, the results which are likely to follow in terms of political leverage can easily be exaggerated. The impact is likely to be greatest at the county unit level in the deep South and in the urban ghettos of the North. In this regard, the "Black Panther" party of Lowndes County, Alabama, is the prototype.

Black Power and the American Radical Tradition

There are roughly 12,000 Negroes in Lowndes County and 3,000 whites, but until 1964 there was not a single Negro registered to vote, while white registration had reached 118 per cent of those eligible. Negro life in Lowndes, as Andrew Kopkind has graphically recounted,[2] was —and is—wretched. The median family income for whites is $4,400, for Negroes, $935; Negro farmhands earn $3.00 to $6.00 a day; half of the Negro women who work are maids in Montgomery (which requires a forty- to sixty-mile daily roundtrip) at $4.00 a day; few Negroes have farms, since 90 per cent of the land is owned by about 85 white families; the one large industrial plant in the area, the new Dan River Mills textile factory, will only employ Negroes in menial capacities; most Lowndes Negroes are functional illiterates, living in squalor and hopelessness.

The Black Panther party set out to change all this. The only path to change in Lowndes, and in much of the deep South, is to "take over the courthouse," the seat of local power. For generations the courthouse in Lowndes has been controlled by the Democratic party; indeed there is no Republican party in the county. Obviously it made little sense for SNCC organizers to hope to influence the local Democrats; no white moderates existed and no discussion of integration was tolerated. To have expected blacks to "bore from within," as Carmichael has said, would have been "like asking the Jews to reform the Nazi party."

Instead, Carmichael and his associates established the separate Black Panther party. After months of work SNCC organizers (with almost no assistance from federal agents) registered enough Negroes to hope for a numerical majority in the county. But in the election of November, 1966,

² "The Lair of the Black Panther," *The New Republic,* August 13, 1966.

the Black Panther party was defeated, for a variety of reasons which include Negro apathy or fear and white intimidation.[3] Despite this defeat, the possibility of a better life for Lowndes County Negroes does at last exist, and should the Black Panther party come into power at some future point, that possibility could become a reality.

Nonetheless, even on the local level and even in the deep South, Lowndes County is not representative. In Alabama, for example, only eleven of the state's sixty-seven counties have black majorities. Where these majorities do not exist, the only effect independent black political parties are likely to have is to consolidate the whites in opposition. Moreover, and more significantly, many of the basic ills from which Negro-Americans suffer—inadequate housing, inferior education, limited job opportunities—are national phenomena and require national resources to overcome. Whether these resources will be allocated in sufficient amounts will depend, in turn, on whether a national coalition can be formed to exert pressure on the federal government—a coalition of civil rights activists, church groups, campus radicals, New Class technocrats, unskilled, un-unionized laborers and certain elements in organized labor, such as the UAW or the United Federation of Teachers. Such a coalition, of course, would necessitate Negro-white unity, a unity Black Power at least temporarily rejects.[4]

[3] I have not seen a clear assessment of the causes for defeat. The "Newsletter" from the New York Office of SNCC of November, 1966, makes two points regarding the election: that according to a November report from the Southern Regional Council, 2,823 whites and 2,758 Negroes had registered in Lowndes County, though the white population eligible to vote was approximately 1,900; and that "the influential Baptist Alliance told Negroes throughout Alabama to vote the straight Democratic ticket."

[4] On this point, see what to me are the persuasive arguments made by Pat Watters, "The Negroes Enter Southern Politics," *Dissent,* July-August,

Black Power and the American Radical Tradition

The answer that Black Power advocates give to the "coalition argument" is of several pieces. The only kind of progressive coalition which can exist in this country, they say, is the mild, liberal variety which produced the civil rights legislation of recent years. And that kind of legislation has proven itself grossly inadequate. Its chief result has been to lull white liberals into believing that the major battles have been won, whereas in fact there has been almost no change, or change for the worse, in the daily lives of most blacks.[5]

The evidence for this last assertion is persuasive. Despite the Supreme Court decision of 1954, almost 85 per cent of school-age Negroes in the South still sit in segregated classrooms. Unemployment among Negroes has actually gone up in the past ten years. Title VI of the 1964 Civil Rights Act, with its promising provision for the withdrawal of federal funds in cases of discrimination, has been used in limited fashion in regard to the schools but not at all in regard to other forms of unequal treatment, such as segregated hospital facilities. Under the 1965 Voting Rights Act, only about 40 federal registrars have been sent into the South, though many areas have less than the 50 per cent registration figure which would legally warrant intervention. In short, the legislation produced by the liberal coalition of the early sixties has turned out to be little more than federally approved tokenism, a continuation of paper promises and ancient inequities.

If a *radical* coalition could be formed in this country, that is, one willing to scrutinize in depth the failings of

1966, and Bayard Rustin, "Black Power and Coalition Politics," *Commentary*, September, 1966.

[5] See, on this point, David Danzig, "In Defense of 'Black Power,'" *Commentary*, September, 1966.

our system, to suggest structural, not piecemeal, reforms, to see them executed with sustained rather than occasional vigor, then Black Power advocates might feel less need to separate themselves and to concentrate on local, marginal successes. But no responsible observer believes that in the foreseeable future a radical coalition on the Left can become the effective political majority in the United States; we will be fortunate if a radical coalition on the Right does not. And so to SNCC and CORE, talk of further cooperation with white liberals is only an invitation to further futility. It is better, they feel, to concentrate on encouraging Negroes everywhere to self-respect and self-help, and in certain local areas, where their numbers warrant it, to try to win actual political power.

As an adaptation to present realities, Black Power thus has a persuasive logic. But there is such a thing as being too present-minded; by concentrating on immediate prospects, the new doctrine may be jeopardizing larger possibilities for the future, those which could result from a national coalition with white allies. Though SNCC and CORE insist that they are not trying to cut whites out of the movement, that they merely want to redirect white energies into organizing whites so that at some future point a truly meaningful coalition of Negroes and whites can take place, there are grounds for doubting whether they really are interested in a future reconciliation, or if they are, whether some of the overtones of their present stance will allow for it. For example, SNCC's so-called position paper on Black Power attacks white radicals as well as white liberals, speaks vaguely of differing white and black "psyches," and seems to find all contact with all whites contaminating or intimidating ("whites are the ones who must try to raise themselves to our humanistic level").[6]

SNCC's bitterness at the hypocrisy and evasion of the white majority is understandable, yet the refusal to discriminate between degrees of inequity, the penchant instead for wholesale condemnation of all whites, is as unjust as it is self-defeating. The indictments and innuendos of SNCC's "position paper" give some credence to the view that the line between Black Power and black racism is a fine one easily erased, that, as always, means and ends tend to get confused, that a tactic of racial solidarity can turn into a goal of racial purity.

The philosophy of Black Power is thus a blend of varied, in part contending, elements, and it cannot be predicted with any certainty which will assume dominance. But a comparison between the Black Power movement and the personnel, programs and fates of earlier radical movements in this country can make some contribution toward understanding its dilemmas and its likely directions.

Any argument based on historical analogy can, of course,

[6] SNCC's "position paper" was printed in *The New York Times*, August 5, 1966. It is important to point out, however, that SNCC staffers have since denied the official nature of this paper; see for example Elizabeth Sutherland's letter to the editors of *Liberation* (November, 1966), in which she insists that it was "not a S.N.C.C. position paper but a document prepared by a group of workers on one S.N.C.C. project." (She goes on to note that the *Times* refused to print a SNCC letter to this effect). For other denials of the "racist" overtones in "Black Power," see Stokely Carmichael, "What We Want," *The New York Review of Books,* September 22, 1966, and C. E. Wilson, "Black Power and the Myth of Black Racism," *Liberation,* September, 1966. But Andrew Kopkind's report on SNCC staff conferences ("The Future of Black Power," *The New Republic,* January 7, 1967) makes me believe that the dangers of black racism are real and not merely the invention of frightened white liberals (see also James Peck, "Black Racism," *Liberation,* October, 1966).

241

become oversimplified and irresponsible. Historical events do not repeat themselves with anything like regularity, for every event is to a large degree embedded in its own special context. An additional danger in reasoning from historical analogy is that in the process we will limit rather than expand our options; by arguing that certain consequences seem always to follow from certain actions and that therefore only a set number of alternatives ever exist, we can prevent ourselves from seeing new possibilities or from utilizing old ones in creative ways. We must be careful, when attempting to predict the future from the past, that in the process we do not straitjacket the present. Bearing these cautions and limitations in mind, some insight can still be gained from a historical perspective. For if there are large variances through time between roughly analogous events, there are also some similarities, and it is these which make comparative study possible and profitable. In regard to Black Power, I think we gain particular insight by comparing it with the two earlier radical movements of Abolitionism and Anarchism.

The Abolitionists represented the left wing of the antislavery movement (a position comparable to the one SNCC and CORE occupy today in the civil rights movement) because they called for an *immediate* end to slavery everywhere in the United States. Most Northerners who disapproved of slavery were not willing to go as far or as fast as the Abolitionists, preferring instead a more ameliorative approach. The tactic which increasingly won the approval of the Northern majority was the doctrine of "nonextension": no further expansion of slavery would be allowed, but the institution would be left alone where it already

Black Power and the American Radical Tradition

existed. The principle of nonextension first came into prominence in the late eighteen-forties when fear developed in the North that territory acquired from our war with Mexico would be made into new slave states. Later the doctrine formed the basis of the Republican party which in 1860 elected Lincoln to the Presidency. The Abolitionists, in other words, with their demand for immediate (and uncompensated) emancipation, never became the major channel of Northern antislavery sentiment. They always remained a small sect, vilified by slavery's defenders and distrusted even by allies within the antislavery movement.

The parallels between the Abolitionists and the current defenders of Black Power seem to me numerous and striking. It is worth noting, first of all, that neither group started off with so-called "extremist" positions (the appropriateness of that word being, in any case, dubious).[7] The SNCC of 1967 is not the SNCC formed in 1960; both its personnel and its programs have shifted markedly. SNCC originally grew out of the sit-ins spontaneously begun in Greensboro, North Carolina, by four freshmen at the all-Negro North Carolina Agricultural and Technical College. The sit-in technique spread rapidly through the South, and within a few months the Student Non-Violent Coordinating Committee (SNCC) was formally inaugurated to channel and encourage further activities. At its inception SNCC's staff was interracial, religious in orientation, committed to the "American Dream," chiefly concerned with winning the right to share more equitably in that Dream and optimistic about the possibility of being allowed to do so. SNCC

[7] For a discussion of "extremism" and the confused uses to which the word can be and has been put, see Howard Zinn, "Abolitionists, Freedom Riders, and the Tactics of Agitation," *The Antislavery Vanguard*, Martin Duberman, ed. (Princeton, 1965), especially pp. 421–426.

placed its hopes on an appeal to the national conscience and this it expected to arouse by the examples of non-violence and redemptive love, and by the dramatic devices of sit-ins, freedom rides and protest marches.[8]

The Abolitionist movement, at the time of its inception, was similarly benign and sanguine. It, too, placed emphasis on "moral suasion," believing that the first order of business was to bring the iniquity of slavery to the country's attention, to arouse the average American's conscience. Once this was done, the Abolitionists felt, discussion then could, and would, begin on the particular ways and means best calculated to bring about rapid, orderly emancipation. Some of those Abolitionists who later became intransigent defenders of immediatism—including William Lloyd Garrison—were willing, early in their careers, to consider plans for preliminary apprenticeship. They were willing, in other words, to settle for gradual emancipation *immediately begun* instead of demanding that freedom itself be instantly achieved.

But this early flexibility received little encouragement. The appeal to conscience and the willingness to engage in debate over means alike brought meager results. In the North the Abolitionists encountered massive apathy, in the South massive resistance. Thus thwarted, and influenced as well by the discouraging British experiment with gradualism in the West Indies, the Abolitionists abandoned their earlier willingness to consider a variety of plans for prior education and training, and shifted to the position that emancipation had to take place at once and without compensation to the slaveholder. They also began

[8] For the shifting nature of SNCC see Howard Zinn, *SNCC: The New Abolitionists* (Boston, 1964), and Gene Roberts, "From 'Freedom High' to 'Black Power,'" *The New York Times*, September 25, 1966.

(especially in New England) to advocate such doctrines as "Dis-Union" and "No-Government," positions which directly parallel Black Power's recent advocacy of "separation" and "de-centralization," and which then as now produced discord and division within the movement, anger and denunciation without.

But the parallel of paramount importance I wish to draw between the two movements is their similar passage from "moderation" to "extremism." In both cases, there *was* a passage, a shift in attitude and program, and it is essential that this be recognized, for it demonstrates the developmental nature of these—of all—movements for social change. Or, to reduce the point to individuals (and to clichés): "revolutionaries are not born but made." Garrison did not start his career with the doctrine of "immediatism"; as a young man, he even had kind words for the American Colonization Society, a group devoted to deporting Negroes to Africa and Central America. And Stokely Carmichael did not begin his ideological voyage with the slogan of Black Power; as a teen-ager he was opposed to student sit-ins in the South. What makes a man shift from "reform" to "revolution" is, it seems to me, primarily to be explained by the intransigence or indifference of his society: either society refuses reforms or gives them in the form of tokens. Thus, *if* one views the Garrisons and Carmichaels as "extremists," one should at least place the blame for that extremism where it belongs—not on their individual temperaments, their genetic predispositions, but on a society which scorned or toyed with their initial pleas for justice.

In turning to the Anarchist movement, I think we can see between it and the new turn taken by SNCC and CORE (or, more comprehensively still, by much of the New Left) significant affinities of style and thought. These are largely unconscious and unexplored; I have seen almost no overt references to them either in the movement's official literature or in its unofficial pronouncements. Yet the affinities seem to me important.

But first I should make clear that in speaking of "Anarchism" as if it were a unified tradition, I am necessarily oversimplifying. The Anarchist movement contained a variety of contending factions, disparate personalities and differing national patterns. Some Anarchists believed in terrorism, others insisted upon nonviolence; some aimed for a communal life based on trade union "syndicates," others refused to bind the individual by organizational ties of any kind; some wished to retain private ownership of property, others demanded its collectivization.

Despite these differing perspectives, all Anarchists did share one major premise: a distrust of authority, the rejection of all forms of rule by man over man. They justified their opposition in the name of the individual; the Anarchists wished each man to develop his "specialness" without the inhibiting interference imposed by authority, be it political or economic, moral or intellectual. This does not mean that the Anarchists sanctioned the idea of "each against all." On the contrary, they believed that man was a social creature—that is, that he needed the affection and assistance of his fellows—and most Anarchist versions of the good life (Max Stirner would be the major exception) involved the idea of community. The Anarchists insisted, moreover, that it was not their vision of the future, but rather society as presently constructed, which represented chaos; with privilege the lot of the few and misery the lot of the many, society was currently the essence of *dis*order.

Black Power and the American Radical Tradition

The Anarchists envisioned a system which would substitute mutual aid for mutual exploitation, voluntarism for force, individual decision-making for centralized dictation.

All of these emphases find echo today in SNCC and CORE. The echoes are not perfect: "Black Power," after all, is above all a call to organization, and its acceptance of politics (and therefore of "governing") would offend a true Anarchist—as would such collectivist terms as "black psyche" or "black personality." Nonetheless, the affinities of SNCC and CORE with the Anarchist position are substantial.

There is, first of all, the same belief in the possibilities of "community" and the same insistence that community be the product of voluntary association. This in turn reflects a second and still more basic affinity: the distrust of centralized authority. SNCC and CORE's energies, and also those of other New Left groups like Students for a Democratic Society (SDS), are increasingly channeled into local, community organizing. On this level, it is felt, "participatory" democracy, as opposed to the authoritarianism of "representative" democracy, becomes possible. And in the Black Panther party, where the poor and disinherited do take a direct role in decision-making, theory has become reality (as it has, on the economic side, in the Mississippi-based "Poor People's Corporation," which to date has formed some fifteen cooperatives).[9]

Then, too, SNCC and CORE, like the Anarchists, talk increasingly of the supreme importance of the individual. They do so, paradoxically, in a rhetoric strongly reminiscent of that long associated with the Right. It could be Herbert

[9] See Art Goldberg, "Negro Self-Help," *The New Republic*, June 10, 1967, and Abbie Hoffman, "Liberty House/Poor People's Corporation," *Liberation*, April, 1967.

Hoover (or Booker T. Washington), but in fact it is Rap Brown who now reiterates the Negro's need to stand on his own two feet, to make his own decisions, to develop self-reliance and a sense of self-worth.[10] SNCC may be scornful of present-day liberals and "statism," but it seems hardly to realize that the laissez faire rhetoric it prefers, derives almost verbatim from the classic liberalism of John Stuart Mill.

A final, more intangible affinity between Anarchism and the entire New Left, including the advocates of Black Power, is in the area of personal style. Both hold up similar values for highest praise and emulation: simplicity, spontaneity, "naturalness" and "primitivism." Both reject modes of dress, music, personal relations, even of intoxication, which might be associated with the dominant middle-class culture. Both, finally, tend to link the basic virtues with "the people," and especially with the poor, the downtrodden, the alienated. It is this *lumpenproletariat*—long kept outside the "system" and thus uncorrupted by its values—who are looked to as a repository of virtue, an example of a better way. The New Left, even while demanding that the lot of the underclasses be improved, implicitly venerates that lot; the desire to cure poverty cohabits with the wish to emulate it.

[10] For more detailed discussions of the way in which the rhetoric of the New Left and the traditional Right have begun to merge, see Ronald Hamowy, "Left and Right Meet," *The New Republic*, March 12, 1966; Martin Duberman, "Anarchism Left and Right," *Partisan Review*, Fall, 1966; Paul Feldman, "The Pathos of 'Black Power,' " *Dissent*, Jan.-Feb., 1967; and Carl Oglesby and Richard Schaull, *Containment and Change* (Macmillan: 1967). Oglesby (on p. 167) seems actually to call for a merger between the two groups, arguing that both are "in the grain of American humanist individualism and voluntaristic associational action." He confuses, it seems to me, a similarity of rhetoric and means with a similarity of goals.

Black Power and the American Radical Tradition

The Anarchist movement in the United States never made much headway. A few individuals—Benjamin Tucker, Adin Ballou, Lysander Spooner, Stephen Pearl Andrews, Emma Goldman, Josiah Warren—are still faintly remembered, but more for the style of their lives than for any impact on their society.[11] It is not difficult to see what prevented them from attracting a large following. Their very distaste for organization and power precluded the traditional modes for exerting influence. More important, their philosophy ran directly counter to the national hierarchy of values, a system of beliefs, conscious and otherwise, which has always impeded the drive for rapid change in this country. And it is a system which constitutes a road block at least as formidable today as at any previous point in our history.

This value structure stresses, first of all, the prime virtue of "accumulation," chiefly of goods, but also of power and prestige. Any group—be it Anarchists or New Leftists—which challenges the soundness of that goal, which suggests that it interferes with the more important pursuits of self-realization and human fellowship, presents so basic a threat to our national and individual identities as to invite almost automatic rejection.

A second obstacle that our value structure places in the path of radical change is its insistence on the benevolence of history. To the average American, human history is the story of automatic progress. Every day in every way we have got better and better. *Ergo*, there is no need for a

[11] The only over-all study of American Anarchism is Eunice M. Schuster, *Native American Anarchism* (Northampton: 1932), but some useful biographies exist of individual figures in the movement; see especially Richard Drinnon, *Rebel in Paradise: A Biography of Emma Goldman* (Chicago: 1961).

frontal assault on our ills; time alone will be sufficient to cure them. Thus it is that many whites today consider the "Negro Problem" solved by the recent passage of civil rights legislation. They choose to ignore the fact that the daily lives of most Negroes have changed but slightly—or, as in the case of unemployment, for the worse. They ignore, too, the group of hard-core problems which have only recently emerged: maldistribution of income, urban slums, disparities in education and training, the breakdown of family structure in the ghetto, technological unemployment—problems which show no signs of yielding to time, but which will require concentrated energy and resources for solution.

Without a massive assault on these basic ills, ours will continue to be a society where the gap between rich and poor widens, where the major rewards go to the few (who are not to be confused with the best). Yet it seems highly unlikely, as of 1968, that the public pressure needed for such an assault will be forthcoming. Most Americans still prefer to believe that ours is either already the best of all possible worlds or will shortly, and without any special effort, become such. It is this deep-seated smugness, this intractable optimism, which must be reckoned with—which, indeed, will almost certainly destroy any call for substantive change.

A further obstacle facing the New Left today, Black Power advocates and otherwise, is that its Anarchist style and mood run directly counter to prevailing tendencies in our national life, especially of conformity and centralization. The conformity has been commented on too often to bear repetition, except to point out that the young radicals' unorthodox mores (sexual, social, cultural) are in themselves enough to produce uneasiness and anger in the average American. In insisting on the right of the individual to please himself and to rely on his own judgment (whether in dress, speech, music, sex or stimulants), SNCC and SDS may be solidly within the American tradition—indeed may be its main stream—but this tradition is now more central to our rhetoric than to our behavior.

The Anarchist focus in SNCC and SDS on decentralization, on participatory democracy and on community organizing, likewise runs counter to dominant national trends. Consolidation, not dispersion, is currently king. There are some signs that a counter-development has begun—such as the pending decentralization of the New York City school system—but as yet the overwhelming pattern continues to be consolidation. Both big government and big business are getting bigger and, more ominous still, are coming into ever closer partnership. As Richard J. Barber has recently documented, the federal government is not only failing to block the growth of huge "conglomerate" firms by antitrust action, but it is contributing to that growth through procurement contracts and the exchange of personnel.[12] The traditional hostility between business and government has rapidly drawn to a close. Washington is no longer interested in restraining the giant corporations, and the corporations have lost much of their fear of federal intentions. The two, in happy tandem, are moving the country still further along the road to oligopoly, militarism, economic imperialism and greater privileges for the already privileged. The trend is so pronounced, and there is so little effective opposition to it, that it begins to take on an irrevocable, even irreversible, quality.

[12] Richard J. Barber, "The New Partnership: Big Government and Big Business," *The New Republic*, Aug. 13, 1966. But see, too, Alexander Bickel's article in the same journal for May 20, 1967.

In the face of these monoliths of national power, Black Power in Lowndes County is pathetic by comparison. Yet while the formation of the Black Panther party in Lowndes brought out paroxysms of fear in the nation at large, the announcement that General Motors' 1965 sales totaled $21 billion—exceeding the gross national product of all but nine countries in the world—produced barely a tremor of apprehension. The unspoken assumption can only be something like this: It is less dangerous for a few whites to control the whole nation than for a local majority of Negroes to control their own community. The Kafkaesque dimension of life in America continues to grow.

Black Power is both a product of our society and a repudiation of it. Confronted with the continuing indifference of the majority of whites to the Negro's plight, SNCC and CORE have lost faith in conscience and time, and have shifted to a position which the white majority finds infuriating. The nation as a whole—as in the case of the Abolitionists over a hundred years ago—has created the climate in which earlier tactics no longer seem relevant, in which new directions become mandatory if frustration is to be met and hope maintained. And if the new turn proves a wrong one, if Black Power forecloses rather than animates further debate on the Negro's condition, if it destroys previous alliances without opening up promising new options, it is the nation as a whole that must bear the responsibility. There seems little likelihood that the American majority will admit to that responsibility. Let us at least hope it will not fail to recognize the rage which Black Power represents, to hear the message at the movement's core:

Black Power and the American Radical Tradition

Sweethearts, the script has changed . . .
And with it the stage directions which advise
Lowered voices, genteel asides,
And the white hand slowly turning the dark page.[13]

---

[13] Kay Boyle, "On Black Power," *Liberation,* January, 1967.

PART III

The Crisis of the Universities

THE CRISIS OF THE
UNIVERSITIES

*THE four articles which follow only begin to touch on the var-
ied issues of today's crisis in the universities. Even as regards
classroom procedures—the starting point and still the central
focus of my own concern—I feel I have only begun to discover
what is wrong and what may be done to right it. All the problems
confronting the university involve difficult and interconnected
questions. For example, the relationship of the university to the
surrounding community hinges on a definition of what kind of
institution a university is—is it best seen as a corporation? a
family? a public agency? a combination of these? an entity sui
generis? Linked to this question are others: What are the sanctions and restraints of power within the university structure?
Who legitimately holds and/or actually exercises that power?
What, ideally, should be the roles played by state and federal
governments, trustees, administrators, faculty and students?
Are the latter, children to be watched over and disciplined, or
consumers whose needs must be met, or constituents whose
voices must be heard? These are but a few of the intertwined,
complex issues which must—and hopefully will—be debated in
the years ahead.*

*For all the earlier pieces in this collection I have appended
prefatory remarks that suggest my second, or even counter,
thoughts about what I had originally written. But in this section, possibly because the pieces are quite recent, I haven't had
any substantial changes of mind. However, about the last of
them, "On Misunderstanding Student Rebels," I do want to
make one thing clearer than it might already be.*

Much as I admire the campus activists, I think some tend-

encies in some few of them are to be guarded against: using civil disobedience as a first rather than as a last resort (a precipitousness shared by most administrators when calling the police), interfering with the free speech of others, employing the rhetoric and sometimes the fact of violence, talking glibly of the advantages to be gained from right-wing repression, arguing that the university is the incarnation of evil—the chief enemy—rather than an antique institution whose renovation might well provide the major power base in the struggle for a new society. Though real, these tendencies are characteristic of only a small number of student activists and should not be used, as so many have used them, to slander the entire movement.

AN EXPERIMENT IN EDUCATION

In the fall of 1966, at the beginning of a new term, I received permission from the Course of Study Committee at Princeton University to drop all grades from my undergraduate seminar on "American Radicalism." It was agreed that the record of each student taking the course would show only an asterisk in the space where a grade would ordinarily appear, and that the attached explanation would read: "Experimental course; no grades given." It was further agreed that the experiment would be for a single term only, and that at its end I would present a formal report to the Committee describing the results. This is my report.

※　　　※　　　※

I have been an educator for ten years, but I have really been interested in education only for the past year or so.

"An Experiment in Education" appeared in *Daedalus*, Winter, 1968.

Before that I was chiefly interested in my career. I still am, but having got tenure three years ago, it became possible for me (this was not conscious: I see it only in retrospect) to concern myself solely with how I evaluated the success of my teaching and not how the senior members of my department did. My experience with teaching bears out the central point that I will be trying to make about learning: that only when the necessity to please others is removed, can the main job of *self*-evaluation begin. Most young teachers, like most students, are afraid much of the time they are in class, and fear guarantees that energy will go into defensive strategies rather than creative explorations.

Various threads besides the "release" which tenure gave me helped to produce my new concern with teaching and learning. Perhaps the original germ had been planted in 1962 when some students suggested that I read A. S. Neill's *Summerhill*. I did, and was moved by Neill's candor and exhilarated by his demonstration that children flourish when they are allowed freedom. After discovering Neill, I read Paul Goodman, Edgar Z. Friedenberg, and, most significantly and most recently, John Holt—in other words, the "romantics" of educational theory, as they have been dubbed by their critics. I had also, within the past two years, read a great deal about Anarchism, in line with a play I was then writing on Emma Goldman. I strongly identified with Anarchism's anti-authoritarian basis; it was the closest I had come to feeling at home in a philosophical tradition. (I'm aware that this effort—that all such efforts —at charting "influences" is a little foolish. For all I know, the true cause of my developing interest in unstructured education may have been familial—an unresolved authority problem?—or even metabolic.)

But to continue the exercise: My experience in group

therapy must also be taken into account. I cannot fully demonstrate why, but I feel that membership in a therapy group for the past three years may have been the most profound of the influences prompting me to re-evaluate my role as an educator. In the therapy group, I became aware of how many levels of the person can be "educated" simultaneously when a group is functioning well—that is, when an atmosphere of mutual trust and forbearance prevails. The willingness to suspend judgment of one another in the name of understanding, the tolerance of mistakes, the opportunity to reveal and examine one's inner self without fear of penalty—all encourage growth.

My experience in therapy made me impatient with other group enterprises that were narrowly functional—like a university seminar that *merely* engaged in the transmission of factual information. I knew that much more than information could be exchanged when a permissive, nonjudgmental atmosphere prevailed. Indeed, little important information can be transmitted if an emotional transaction is not simultaneously in process, for an individual will not expose his deepest assumptions nor be able to perceive those of another if their relationship is purely intellectual. (I continue to use outmoded, dualistic terminology like *intellectual* and *emotional* because more accurate vocabulary is not yet available.)

Much of what I have outlined thus far became clear to me belatedly. At the time I petitioned the Course of Study Committee for permission to drop grades, I knew only that my dissatisfaction with traditional methods of teaching had accumulated to the point of irritability. I wanted something more and different from my classroom experience. I felt that most students did also. For years I had heard graduating seniors speak unhappily of their education ("I still don't know who the hell I am"; "I still don't know what I want to do with my life"; "I don't even know if such questions matter to me any more") and express bewilderment at how eager, curious freshmen had been turned, four years later, into prototypes of articulate emptiness.

The job of self-discovery is never, of course, complete; it is hardly surprising that twenty-one-year-olds do not fully know "who the hell they are." But the point is that they have not begun to know. In many cases, four years of college do not initiate or further, but dampen or destroy efforts at self-exploration. This may not be the intent, but it is nonetheless the result of the tactics employed by those who administer and teach in a university. They make certain that the student's energies are directed at fulfilling tasks set by them rather than by himself; they encourage him to define his worth in terms of his success in winning their approval: high grades, good letters of recommendation, departmental honors, prizes. He is taught to regard these tangible signs of election as the only important evidence or kind of achievement, and as the indispensable precondition, almost the guarantee, of a satisfying life. What he is not taught is that orientation toward gaining the approval of others carries high costs: the acceptance of disguise as a necessity of life; the unconscious determination to manipulate others in the way one has been manipulated; the conviction that productivity is more important than character and "success" superior to satisfaction; the loss of curiosity, of a willingness to ask questions, of the capacity to take risks.

The removal of grades is a necessary, but hardly sufficient means for reversing this disastrous orientation. Grading is but one way in which we turn potentially creative individuals into data-processing machines, adapting them to their society but alienating them from themselves. More than grades must go. The entire superstructure of authoritarian control in our schools must give way if we are to enable people to assume responsibility for and to take pleasure in their own lives. We cannot expect aliveness and involvement when we are busy inculcating docility and compliance.

In this regard, the false distinctions that separate student from teacher must be broken down. What do we think titles like "professor," "sir," or "mister" achieve? Perhaps the illusion of respect, but certainly not its reality. Those qualities which are worth admiring in a given person—perception, experience, honesty, empathy, openness—will be admired regardless of title, and no title can create admiration when such qualities are absent. But a title can—and often does—establish a pattern of formality that prevents free exchange and the common pursuit by student and teacher of understanding. Titles also provide the professor with a subtle means of discipline and a false sense of self-importance, neither of which is conducive to humanness or communication.

Then there is the matter of "requirements." John Holt has written a brilliant critique of the notion that certain bits and pieces of knowledge are "essential," that adults know which these are and at what point and in what way they can best be fed to the young. It seems to Holt, and to me, that this is dangerous nonsense. There is no agreement as to what knowledge is essential. (Should everyone read *Crime and Punishment*? understand ego psychology? study Greek civilization? learn about quasar theory? All of these? None of these?)

The individual young have their own interests and timetables, and if these are stifled by the teacher's imposed demands, the result may be a certain number of facts temporarily absorbed, but at the cost of knowledge becoming irrelevant and curiosity being destroyed. Schools, as Holt puts it, should be places where students "learn what they most want to know, instead of what we think they ought to know." In any given seminar, it is far less important to convey the particular body of information that the professor happens to care about than to seek the information that the student cares about. It is far more valuable for the student to let a course on, say, the American Revolution wander off during a given session into a discussion of the "utility of violence" than to insist on the day's set topic of the British Navigation Acts; the latter will stick for about as long as it takes the student to walk out the door, while the former could provide grist for a personal re-evaluation of lasting significance. Moreover, if knowledge is made relevant to the student's current needs, it is henceforth viewed as a desirable commodity. A student who is allowed to ask questions that matter to him soon learns the habit of self-generating inquiry.

Finally, there is the matter of leadership. A crucial distinction must be made between authority and authoritarianism. The former represents accumulated experience, knowledge, and insight. The latter represents their counterfeits: age masquerading as maturity, information as understanding, technique as originality. Authoritarianism is forced to demand the respect that authority draws naturally to itself. The former, like all demands, is likely to meet with hostility; the latter, like all authenticity, with emulation. Our universities—our schools at every level—are rife with authoritarianism, all but devoid of authority.

In any given seminar the teacher, expounding on the subject of his choice, almost always knows more facts than anyone else. He is also older and has had more professional training. These are the raw materials—information, experience, discipline—out of which authority can come, but they do not guarantee authority. If information has not been digested and personalized, if years have added grayness rather than growth, if training has submerged the person in the specialist, then the potential authority turns into a mere authoritarian. And it is the rare authoritarian when given power—when put, say, in charge of adolescents —who can resist the satisfaction of reducing them to his level. So it is that one generation, desperate lest its own achievement be exceeded, corrupts the next—all the while protesting benevolence. Fathers are not known to encourage patricide—and few youths grow to manhood.

But let us look at the authority, rather than the authoritarian. Even the genuine authority—no one realizes this better than he—is limited in perspective. The ideal Professor Jones, a master of both Shakespeare and himself, knows that he can be surprised. He knows that Joe Smith, freshman from Dubuque, has some special experience that can illuminate a word or passage from *Hamlet*: Joe may be oblivious to generations of scholarship, but he knows something about sons. And he will tell it—if the climate is right, if Professor Jones has made it clear that no one has a corner on truth, that competence is never across the board, and that therefore leadership (in a classroom discussion, in life) should shift as areas of competence shift. If he can convey that much to Joe Smith, Professor Jones will have given him the one encouragement essential to true education: Ultimately each man can, must, become his own authority. This is the one path to adulthood—and democracy.

I suppose some will feel that I have put the cart before the horse. Theory is supposed to follow fact, not vice versa. The arrangement of this report is, however, true to my experience. Previous to the experiment in "History 308: American Radicalism," I did have decided views on education—otherwise I would never have conceived the experiment. This is not to say that the seminar merely confirmed my earlier views. On the contrary, it did not neatly bear out my theories, nor was it a wholly satisfying experience, either for myself or for the students. Nevertheless, it *was* a qualified confirmation, and given the context in which the experiment took place, with all that meant by way of obstacles and inexperience, even a qualified success seems to me significant. My evaluation can best be tested, however, by a detailed look at what actually took place in the seminar.

I limited the enrollment in History 308 to twenty-four students so that I could break the group into two sections of twelve, thereby making a seminar format feasible. At the first meeting, however, we met as one group, so that I could explain the content of the course and its "experimental" features. (Most of the students already knew my intentions from having talked with me earlier.)

The course was to be structured, I said, by the over-all topic "American Radicalism," but the specific topic for any given week could and should vary in response to what they, as a group, felt would be most logical and useful. The two groups, I added, could go in entirely different directions. One, for example, might feel the need to discuss the Radical Right in detail, the other might choose to omit the Radical Right altogether. What was important, I felt, was that each group develop, as a group, its own personality and direction. There would, of course, be individual variations in interest and need, and the group should not be so determined in its collective purpose as to prevent these individual requirements from being met.

I hoped to accomplish both purposes—group identity and individual variety—through "open-ended" reading lists. I had prepared in advance, I told them in that first session, about a dozen topics which I felt could concern us during the term: the Abolitionists, the Wobblies, the Socialists, the Populists, and so forth. None of these topics was mandatory; after each session we would discuss, as a group, what we wanted to do the following week. I expected each group to reject some of my suggested topics, to deal with others only in passing, and to suggest alternative topics of its own. In order to preserve individual preference, I would make no assignment on any given subject, but would prepare lengthy reading lists, describe each book in detail, and encourage the student to choose that aspect or approach to a given topic which most appealed to him and to read those books which related to it.

On some topics one book might be so outstanding—like David Shannon's volume on American Socialism—that I would strongly recommend that everyone read it, but not because I felt a common reading list was necessary to produce discussion, nor because I was trying to sneak in a requirement under the guise of a recommendation. Nothing, I made clear in that first session, was required: neither reading, nor attendance, nor "performance." If, throughout the term, some students chose to do only a minimum of work or none at all, there would be no reprisals, since the course would not have grades, exams, or papers. (In this regard, I added that if anyone wished to write down anything at any point, I and no doubt others would be glad to read it—and this happened several times during the term.)

During the first meeting we also decided on the membership of the two groups. I had hoped for a fairly even division, and a tally of preferences showed an exact split of twelve and twelve. Although this was accidental, the membership of each seminar was less random than might appear. Friends tended to sign up for the same seminar, with the result that the two groups differed significantly from each other.

Everyone in the evening seminar, it turned out, was a senior, whereas the afternoon group included four juniors and one sophomore. This was significant because, as all the undergraduates agreed when we discussed these matters at the end of the term, seniors are more "deadened," more cynical and disinterested, than those who have not yet "been through the system." The undergraduates also pointed out that fewer members of the afternoon group had previously known one another or been friendly. This they considered a decided *advantage*. It was easier, they felt, to discuss the "big questions," to generalize and speculate, in front of comparative strangers.

The students also pointed to the different pattern between the two groups in terms of "eating club" affiliations.[1] The afternoon seminar included more Woodrow Wilson members and more "independents"; moreover, only two of

---

[1] Princeton's private, alumni-subsidized eating clubs resemble fraternities except that they have no national affiliations and offer no dormitory facilities. Nearly all upperclassmen (90 per cent in 1967) join one of the fifteen clubs, each of which numbers about one hundred members. The admissions process (called "bicker") is highly selective, and most students would admit to a strict social hierarchy among the clubs (the prestigious "big five" clubs being the "inner circle"). Because few alternative social facilities exist, few students "go independent" (only 6 per cent) or join the university-subsidized Woodrow Wilson Society, whose fellowship and facilities are open to all. Annual club membership costs about $1,100; Wilson Society membership about $700.

[AUTHOR'S NOTE: In 1969 alternative facilities are increasingly available and fewer upperclassmen at Princeton are now "bickering."]

its members belonged to "big five" clubs, whereas almost all of the evening group did. Members of the "big five," the students agreed, emphasized "keeping cool," remaining detached, "above it all," presenting only the superficial aspects of self. In a seminar, such values would manifest themselves as an unwillingness to allow emotion to enter into discussion, to expose one's deeply held values, to engage another person in any full confrontation of opinion and belief. The "big five" personality was further described as involving a distrust of anything "different," "strange," "off-beat," a tendency to value and to adhere to that which is traditional and respectable. I should stress that those members of the seminar who were themselves in the "big five" clubs fully agreed with this diagnosis.

Finally, the undergraduates came to believe, and I concur, that the afternoon group was simply lucky in its "chemistry"—a factor beyond prediction and not susceptible to close analysis. By "chemistry" they meant that the members of the group took to one another early and well. Mutual respect and trust were established among people of widely different viewpoints; this made it possible to expose feelings and to engage in debate without excessive fear of "being made a fool of."

Following the organizational meeting, the first full session of both groups was devoted to the "New Left." I had suggested, and the suggestion had been adopted, that we begin our study of "American Radicalism" with the contemporary scene and then go back in time to study other radical movements, such as the Abolitionists, the Socialists, or the Wobblies—though the actual choice of topic would depend on group decision each week.

The afternoon group took off in a blaze, without even a brief period of awkwardness or hesitation. Indeed, the rapid-fire exchanges, the passionate interruptions and debates worried me a little. The pace and tone seemed to smack of hysteria. People were not listening carefully to one another; they were briefly silent in order to prepare their next broadside, rather than to digest what someone else was saying.

Though the general feeling was that things were going swimmingly, I was not alone in having doubts. After the second session, a student named Paul[2] handed me a typewritten statement he had prepared. (I had encouraged the students from the beginning to let me know—in whatever form they wished—their opinions on how things were going, and especially if they felt any discontent.) Paul, who up to that point had not said a word in seminar, was decidedly discontented. He found the seminar "anarchic more than democratic," merely "a series of chain reactions." This especially bothered him "on a personal basis" because he felt unable to participate in discussions if he could do so only by fighting for the opportunity:

I refuse to out-shout or vie with someone who begins to speak at the same time I do. To participate in the seminar requires of me a combativeness, a competitiveness, and a disregard for others which I do not want to cultivate in myself.

I agreed with Paul, but thought he was exaggerating, and doing so in order to avoid his own share of responsibility. I knew Paul well; his statement represented his ideal of himself more than his actual self. He had, in fact, a pronounced combative streak of his own, but preferred to deny it. He was frightened by his aggression, and it was

[2] All the names in this account are fictitious.

270

An Experiment in Education

this, more than the group climate, which prevented him from participating.

Still, he had made a legitimate point, and the point needed airing. An opportunity presented itself at the next session. We had spent the meeting, our third, on the Abolitionists. I had played a more active role which, by the end of the session, left me uneasy, so I asked whether the group thought the meeting had been too structured in comparison with the earlier sessions, and my role too prominent. The reactions were varied. The more we talked, the more I began to see that the source of uneasiness, mine and theirs, was that leadership had shifted into new hands. I had earlier outlined this as one of our chief aims, yet when it did happen, a number of us were made uncomfortable.

Toward the end of this session, one member suggested that some mechanism be established for allowing people to make points without having to interrupt or to concentrate their attention on finding an opening into which they could jump. In the discussion which followed, we agreed that we did not always listen carefully to one another and that it was not always possible to speak without interrupting. We also agreed, however, that there seemed no way to correct these occasional defects without re-introducing, through some such device as hand-raising, a formality which we felt was less desirable still. The student who had brought the matter up, when pressed, had no suggestion as to how we might improve communication. The general feeling was that on the whole the group functioned unusually well, that perfect communication was impossible and the expectation of it unrealistic, and that additional devices for trying to achieve it would defeat the spontaneity and ease of the sessions. Better, we concluded, to leave it to each individual to assume increased responsibility for talking only when and as long as he had something to say and for listening closely when someone else was talking.

In my view, this discussion had good effect. By the next (fourth) session, the hysteria had notably abated, members were listening to one another more attentively, and the group had begun to function as a group—that is, to work together toward understanding, each for himself, the material. The "shakedown" period for the afternoon seminar was over and its prospects seemed promising.

The evening group had a quite different history. Its first session, on the New Left, was not so lively as the afternoon one had been, but I thought that was all to the good. Some restraint was natural during the phase of getting to know one another and was to be preferred to the hyperactivity of the afternoon group. In the following three weeks, unfortunately, the restraint grew and the liveliness diminished. Later, when the term was over, some of the students wrote (on a voluntary basis) retrospective evaluations in which they offered explanations for the failure of the evening group to catch fire. (Significantly, only four members from the evening section turned in evaluations whereas eight from the afternoon group did.)

The explanations offered by these four students stressed the hampering effect of a chronological approach, the minimal interest of some members of the seminar in its subject matter and experimental format, and the initial uneasiness at the lack of factual emphasis—an uneasiness, they agreed, which later gave way to appreciation as they came to question their previous definition of what was "useful" knowledge. These explanations are, to my mind, peripheral at best. Much more important in understanding the failure of the evening session, I believe, is the collective personality of the group. In this regard, I have already discussed the "cool" presentation of self stressed by the "big five" mentality. Another attribute, which I have not yet touched upon, may, in fact, be the most crucial of all—passivity.

I became aware of this problem only gradually, as various comments and bits of behavior began to add up to a coherent pattern. One student, for example, early tipped me off with his complaint about "the dominating nature" of certain members of the evening group. There were many times, he said, "when one person or another would try to add something to a discussion and either be unable or cut short." He then added, and I think significantly: "These people, including myself, were not forceful enough to interject their ideas until they were no longer pertinent."

Another bit of evidence came from Norm, a student I knew from previous courses to be uncommonly docile and dependent; he had insisted on "guidance" at every step, but when I had tried to guide rather than to direct him, to help him find his own way rather than to insist that he follow mine, he had always become uneasy. On the way home from the third session, Norm told me he was "confused." He did not know "what was going on," "what was expected of him." I tried to suggest that nothing was expected of him, that the point of dropping grades and exams was to encourage him to meet his own expectations rather than someone else's. The conversation then went something like this:

Couldn't you at least assign readings?

Why would that be valuable?

Because then I'd know what to read.

But you do know. I suggest a number of books each week, and I tell you what each book is like. You then read those that tie in with your interests.

But I don't have any special interests.

We talked in this vein for some time. I tried to encourage Norm to rely more on himself. I told him I knew this was difficult when for eighteen years or so he had been trained to rely on everyone but himself, but that he had to start at some point. Either that, or he would spend his life in dependency, doing what others told him was important, but never finding out what was important *for him*. He seemed to agree, or said he did, but in fact he never came alive in the seminar. He remained for the rest of the term on the periphery, a nonparticipant, the least affected student (at least consciously) in the group. Yet, as his talk with me indicated, initially he *was* shaken up by the experience of self-regulation. Apparently the challenge proved too frightening. His passivity represents, in extreme form, what I take to have been the central problem of the evening seminar, a problem which finally came to focus during the fourth session.

We had, by then, shifted our meeting place. At first we had met in my office, but that had proved to be too cramped. We then moved to a larger room down the hall, but this proved to be too "diffuse." Still hoping that a shift in scene might produce a shift in attitude, we started to meet in one of the student's living rooms, which was spacious and comfortable. In an additional, rather desperate effort to get things going, I agreed to the suggestion that if anyone wanted beer, he could bring it. I probably should not have agreed. Instead of contributing to informality and helping to loosen us up, the beer seemed to underscore the prevailing attitude of unseriousness. Instead of encouraging responsible commitment to the discussions, it seemed to confirm their view that learning was an irrelevant game.

The subject under discussion at the fourth session was Pragmatism. A student had suggested the topic at the end of the previous meeting, as a natural follow-up to our discussion of the Abolitionists' "absolutist" approach to social change. Few of the others seemed enthused at the suggestion, but there was still less enthusiasm for discussing Populism, partly because that was the topic on which the afternoon group had settled. By this time, as I gathered from occasional comments made during the seminars, a certain amount of ill-feeling had developed between the two sections: The evening section referred to the members of the afternoon one as "wild-eyed fanatics," the latter referred to the former as "proto-fascists."

Earlier in the term I had suggested it might be a good idea to invite outside guests who had special interest or expertise in the day's topic, and at almost every session, some guest did attend—dates, other undergraduates, and once a group of four or five dropouts from Harlem who were spending the day in Princeton under the sponsorship of the Urban League. I invited Mrs. Green, an expert on Dewey and James, to the fourth session because I myself felt inadequate to discuss Pragmatism, and I deduced that no one else in the seminar had much knowledge of the topic or much incentive to gain it. In retrospect I think the invitation reflected my own inability to "let things happen." I had not the time nor interest myself to bone up on Pragmatism, and I feared a leaderless and lethargic session. I could have tolerated this had the seminar been going well, but I hadn't the guts to sit through another lifeless meeting. Perhaps if I had, we all would have learned more from it, if only the knowledge of our inadequacies.

It became clear early in the evening that no one had done much reading on Pragmatism. For forty-five minutes, the group struggled with the topic, but our ineptness, our inability to utilize the talents of Mrs. Green, became increasingly embarrassing. When someone, in passing, mentioned the New Left, the group shifted to that topic with a rush of relief. There then followed an unusually animated discussion of Princeton's SDS chapter and why it had not drawn support on campus. During the discussion, the passive orientation of most members of the group was clearly exposed.

A view much expressed was that those who joined SDS did so for the simple reason that they were not members of the "in" group on campus. Not only were their motives highly suspect, it was said, but their personal style was distasteful: They dressed like "weirdos," they "smelled bad," they were "dirty." How about their position on current issues? I asked. Was SDS right in its diagnoses? Did it point to real ills in our society? There was general agreement that it did. Then why, I asked, did they not join SDS? Was it really because the personal style of its members put them off, or were they using that as a convenient excuse for not becoming active in behalf of their own beliefs?

Mrs. Green joined the discussion at this point. She said that the refusal to take responsibility for one's own life—or, as a subdivision of that, to assume direction for one's own education—was probably the single most characteristic trait of Princeton (perhaps of all American) undergraduates. Her remarks cut deep. A few admitted the indictment, painfully. More protested it, though not with much conviction. Later, with leisure to digest Mrs. Green's remarks and to confront them in privacy, others came to admit their validity.

An Experiment in Education

Three weeks later, the issue of passivity was again brought up, this time by one of the members of the seminar. Hank had been one of two students in the evening group who had persistently tried to establish active discussion. Discouraged at the meager results and hearing of the success of the afternoon section, he decided to sit in on one of its meetings to see if a different climate did in fact prevail, and if so, why. He brought up his findings that same evening.

In a quiet way, without trying to provoke guilt, he reported that he had attended the afternoon session, had been amazed at the intensity and intelligence of the discussion, and had wondered "why we don't swing the way they do." His tone and attitude were free enough of hostility and of accusations against individuals that no one felt especially threatened, and a discussion followed which, I felt, was frank and searching.

As Hank saw it, he said, the basic failure had to do with their refusal to accept responsibility for themselves as individuals and also for the group of which they were a part. They preferred to continue in the traditional mold, to hope that someone else would, as always, "do it for them," and to encourage me, especially, to be that doer. In short, they preferred dependency to active exertion in their own behalf.

At this point, I spoke up. I agreed, I said, with Hank's diagnosis, and moreover it had set me to thinking about the utility of the kind of experiment we had been attempting. Perhaps, I said, it was too late by age eighteen to begin encouraging people to exercise control over their own lives, to discover and respond to the pressures within rather than to directions from without. Their pre-Princeton experience in authoritarian homes and schools may have established the habit of docility so firmly that subsequent encouragement to self-regulation could do little—other than confuse. Perhaps the real surprise, I said, was not that the evening section had had trouble functioning in a permissive climate, but that the afternoon group had not had trouble; perhaps the chief puzzle to be solved was not why most Princetonians do not know what to do with freedom, but why a few do.

I said, too, that despite all this I thought we had to be careful in our definitions and estimates of what made a "successful" seminar. I, for one, did not feel that mere noise or vociferousness was proof that something was happening. Activity, when manic, was itself a form of passivity, though disguised to look like its opposite. "Busyness," like "boredom," could serve as a device for avoiding self-confrontation. Passivity was best measured not by how often a student spoke, but by what he said. The passive person surrendered direction of his life, and this could be accomplished in varied, even directly opposite ways—by being inarticulate or by being overarticulate. The active person was present in his own life and concentrated his energies on engaging, not avoiding, himself.

In drawing this definition, I had, curiously, Hank himself in mind (though I never said so). Hank's eagerness to talk, his discomfort at silence, and his determination to make the seminar "work" had chiefly represented, I felt, the desire to please me. Though his tactics and personal style were different from those of the majority, Hank was only slightly less passive than those he labeled as such. As if to confirm my estimate, Hank broke into the discussion to say that he had been eager to do a "conscientious job" mostly because I had "stuck my neck out" for them in arranging the seminar on an ungraded basis, and he felt that in return he had an obligation to me to make the seminar a success.

An Experiment in Education

I replied, in what I hope was a fairly gentle tone, that he didn't owe me a thing. I had set up the seminar on an experimental basis, I said, chiefly for my own sake. My discontent with authoritarian education and its negative results had accumulated to the point where in order to maintain my interest—to justify my existence—I had to try a new approach.

As the discussion proceeded, only two students tried to shift responsibility for their apathy from themselves to the group as a whole. One insisted that his unresponsiveness had been due solely to intellectual discontent. He had become distrustful of the "tenuous analogies" constantly being drawn in seminar between what he took to be wholly dissimilar protest movements; he felt we were straining to make the past relevant to the present. (Even if he had invented his argument to avoid personal responsibility, and I think he had, that did not mean the argument was necessarily false; indeed it led us into a side discussion of "the utility of history," which ended in a whole session being devoted to that topic.)

The second student protested that a few verbal types had monopolized discussions, leaving no opportunity for others to participate. In reply, one of the "verbalizers" said that he had talked only to fill gaping silences and would have welcomed interruption at any time; the fact that it rarely came was, he said, not his fault but theirs. I think he was right—not in having talked to fill a void, but in pointing out that anyone really wanting an opportunity to speak could have made one.

These two exceptions aside, the seminar members agreed that "passivity" did correctly describe the dominant mood, and that responsibility for ending that mood rested with each individual. One student closed the discussion by pointing out—I thought eloquently—that if we could truly accept, each for himself, the diagnosis of passivity, the seminar could then be accounted a large success, though little had been read or remembered, though the discussions had been banal and the interchanges superficial. The seminar would have been successful because it would have provided new self-awareness for each member. If we had the courage to realize, he said, that when offered the opportunity of self-regulation, we had been unequal to it, that when given freedom we had either not wished or not been able to utilize it, then we would recognize to what an alarming degree we had already become automatons. To achieve that kind of insight was to fulfill the chief aim of education.

As a result of this self-examination, the remaining meetings of the evening section seemed to me more fruitful; there was wider participation and the discussions were better informed, more centered on matters of substance, and more lucid in content. After the final meeting, one student commented, "too bad this wasn't the first instead of the last." Another claimed (though I do not agree) that "in a less dynamic way" the members of the evening group ultimately "got as much" out of their seminar experience as the afternoon group had.

The afternoon section, while maintaining consistently high levels of participation and enthusiasm, developed frictions of its own. They centered around Sherm, who at one point in almost every meeting tried to reintroduce, under various guises, some form of authoritarian structure. Each of his suggestions was greeted with loud opposition, some derision, and considerable impatience.

Someone pointed out to him that his chief, almost sole, criterion for a useful discussion was efficiency, and that he

measured efficiency, in turn, by how much factual information was amassed and how closely the group stuck to the
stated topic of discussion. These criteria, it was said, were
shallow. As it was impossible to "cover" most of the topics
we discussed, the group should focus on those aspects
which most interested it, since only these would be re-
tained anyway. Moreover, when the group did wander off
into a discussion of some peripheral matter which had
come up—taking drugs, say—the lack of immediate relevance to the over-all topic at hand was more than compensated for by its broader relevance to the lives of those
involved. The seminar should hold one and only one pursuit sacrosanct: self-knowledge through group interaction.
"Rituals of legitimacy," as one student put it, should not
take precedence over the unorthodox and the unexpected,
especially since the latter could often produce authentic
experience.

Sherm took these reprimands in good spirit; indeed he
largely ignored them, tenaciously returning every week or
two to his pet schemes. Nor was he intimidated by the outcry against him; not only did he continue to participate
actively in the seminar, but in fact helped to initiate what
we came to call our "lab work."

In about the fourth week, Sherm and a few others suggested that since the seminar was studying radicalism and
was itself a radical experiment in education, it followed
that its members should take the lead in "radicalizing" its
own community—namely, Princeton University. Aside
from the inherent value of the undertaking, it would, secondarily, enable seminar members to discover empirically
the problems characteristic of all radical movements.

I made it clear from the outset that if a movement for
change at Princeton were to develop, it would have to be
their movement. I would be glad to participate in strategy

sessions, but, as in the seminar itself, I did not intend to play, either openly or covertly, the role of Gray Eminence. It was agreed that those interested in the "Princeton movement" would get together at 10:15 P.M. once a week, after the close of the evening seminar.

These sessions went on, irregularly, throughout the term, with attendance varying a good bit. In the beginning fifteen of the twenty-four seminar members attended, ten of whom were from the afternoon group. Only one member of the evening group, Hank, showed up with any regularity. I myself attended almost all of the meetings, occasionally contributing a comment or question, but more often simply sitting in and listening. As the term proceeded and as pressure from other course work mounted, attrition set in. At some meetings only six or seven students showed up, and now and then a meeting would be called off entirely "because of midterm exams" or the like.

In the first few meetings, an effort was made to thrash out what a university ideally should be and to what degree Princeton met those specifications. A voluntary committee of four formed to draw up a "Statement of Principles," and after innumerable delays and false starts, it presented a draft statement to the full group, where suggestions were made and new drafts subsequently drawn. Two such statements were eventually mimeographed, but by then exams and papers had descended, and still further inroads were made in attendance. I know that one "Statement of Principles" was circulated privately to various student leaders, faculty members, and administrative personnel, but beyond this the movement brought no concrete results.

That nothing more materialized can be laid, I believe, not only to the competing demands of course work and campus activities, but also to the division of views on tactics and theory which existed among the seminar members and to their feeling, assumed from the first, that any sizable campus-wide interest in behalf of change was unlikely. Yet the sessions themselves, which probed, often with sophistication, into basic aspects of university structure and educational theory proved of considerable value to those who attended—certainly to me. Members of the movement did gain insight into the kinds of social obstacles that have often defeated radicals in the past, into the nature of the Princeton community, and, perhaps most important, into their own inability to resist the pressures of conformity and routine, to place their concern (often deep) about public malfunctions above their fear of personal reprisals.

At the final meeting of the term, the two sections again met as one to evaluate the seminar experience. The views expressed in that meeting, in combination with material presented by those who turned in written evaluations, make up the topical summary which follows.

Grades and Exams

There was no dissent from the view that the elimination of grades and tests had been liberating. One student expressed appreciation for being "treated as if we wanted to learn," for the recognition that it was possible to discover and nurture internal incentives in place of external ones —a substitution especially welcome because the latter encouraged not curiosity and satisfaction, but merely competition and showmanship. Another student expressed relief, apparently shared by all, that the "stultifying effect" of exams had been removed. For once, he said, "students were not required to tailor thoughts to those useless three-hour blitzes and were allowed to let their thinking run free."

The only regret expressed was that grades and tests could not be eliminated from all courses. So long as those devices remained operative in the rest of the university, so long as "professorial retribution" continued to hang over them in other courses, they could never take full advantage of the liberating potential of a single unstructured seminar. One student put the matter this way:

When one is taking three other subjects, two of them departmentals, which are all-important to grad-school admission, which in turn will supposedly determine much of one's future life, the tendency is to put off the ungraded work, as we all did.

It is often said that grades are necessary "training for life," for the competition that defines and measures all aspects of adulthood. While one may agree that competition is omnipresent, one can question its desirability and necessity. To the extent that we know anything about human nature, and we don't know much, there is little reason to believe that the competitive drive is an instinctual and therefore inevitable component of behavior (witness the human product of the *kibbutzim* in Israel). Competition continues to be the hallmark of our society because we continue to train our youth to act competitively, to measure their worth in terms of how successfully they dominate others rather than themselves.

The grading system also trains young Americans to be more adept at judging others than at understanding them, and at judging, moreover, on the basis of limited and largely unattractive qualities: how well an individual "performs" in public; how readily he assimilates established values; how responsive he is to pressure situations; how

An Experiment in Education

adept he is at memorizing and verbalizing; how mechanically he can provide "right" answers; how obediently he can avoid "wrong" questions.

I do not doubt that tests and grades prepare the student for the American life style. The question is whether we approve of that style and wish to perpetuate it.

Readings

When the coercive power of the grading system is eliminated, can we rely on any alternative stimulus to motivate students to learn?

Quite a few seminar members felt that "natural curiosity" was a sufficient motivating force for learning, but a number of rebuttals were and can be made to this assumption. First of all, even if "natural curiosity" is innate, it can be argued that the deadening procedures of pre-Princeton schooling will have bred this quality out of many undergraduates. Those whose curiosity has at least partially survived are then subjected to, and often defeated by, the rituals of the Princeton system.

Moreover, there is reason to doubt, as Bernard Z. Friedlander has recently argued, whether "natural curiosity," "hunger for learning," or "joy in knowledge" can be relied upon as a sufficient incentive for academic learning. Friedlander points out that young children are chiefly curious about matters that relate to sexuality and that such curiosity is not automatically transferable, as the child grows older, to scholastic topics. Indeed, if curiosity about sex is not satisfied—and in our society it is more usually disapproved and suppressed—the child's interest in asking questions may be permanently destroyed. Having been given no answers or false answers to questions of pressing urgency, he is not likely to consider raising questions about matters of less potent interest.

All of which raises the pessimistic possibility that curriculum reform on the college level may be an enterprise of marginal value only. By age eighteen, it could be said, it is too late to salvage curiosity. One could answer that those who arrive as freshmen at college, especially at a "prestige" college, can be assumed to be those whose early craving for information was satisfied and encouraged. This answer is not, however, very persuasive. The arrival of freshman Joe Brown at Princeton's portals means only that he has distinguished himself in a secondary school, that he has performed better in meeting its requirements than most of his classmates. Since those requirements are usually geared to satisfying the needs of teachers rather than students, Joe Brown's high grades may directly reflect, in inverse ratio, the slow strangulation of his own curiosity.

At discouraging moments during the seminar, one thought kept occurring to me: Anyone interested in education should teach on the primary-school level, where there is still some chance of it mattering. At other moments, however, I preferred this more sanguine syllogism: The curiosity of many students arriving at Princeton has already been destroyed; it is too late in any significant degree either to harm them or to help them; nevertheless, some freshmen are still eager and alive, and it matters very much whether they are subjected to destructive discipline or encouraged to seek, without fear of retribution, honest answers to honest questions. The experience of History 308 provides evidence to confirm both the discouraging thought and the sanguine syllogism.

With a single exception, the students admitted that they

did less reading and studying in the seminar than they did in courses with assignments and grades. The confessional chorus was loud and long—lamentations of *mea culpa* generously interspersed with recriminations against a "system" that "feeds our worst impulses." A few students, in their extremity, were reduced to suggesting as a remedy the very coercions against which they otherwise protested. "I think," wrote one, "that it may have been worthwhile if I had been expected to present a paper or perhaps an oral presentation. . . . This would have forced me to do reading in areas where I was lax . . . to gather my thoughts about radicalism in general." Yet in another part of his written evaluation this same student expressed the opinion that my method of indicating the subject matter and value of each book on a list of suggested titles was preferable to the usual system of assigning a common set of readings. The conflict in this student's feelings—the way in which he simultaneously called for more coercion in written and oral work even while expressing appreciation for being allowed to set his own reading pattern—accurately represents, I believe, the blurred reactions of the majority. They were excited by freedom and yet, because they failed by their own (perhaps excessively demanding) standards fully to grasp its opportunities, repelled by it.

Discussions

The strengths and weaknesses of our seminar discussions were best perceived, it seems to me, by members of the afternoon group, perhaps because they were convinced of the over-all value of the discussions and so felt less inhibited about articulating its incidental deficiencies. The

chief complaint centered on what was called "formless-
ness," or "lack of direction." Only a minority viewed this
as a deficiency, and no two people who did shared the
same reasons for thinking it so. The most extreme statement came from a student who claimed to be "basically
happy" with his seminar experience, but felt that he could
have got still more out of it had the sessions been tightly
organized. He suggested—and this, I feel, is yet another
example of an endemic unwillingness or inability to exercise individual responsibility—that since "it would have
been very difficult for any of us to impose this kind of
discipline successfully," the solution was for me to impose
it on them. He did not suggest how I could do this without
inhibiting spontaneity and destroying "the relationship of
complete equality between professor and student" that he
himself felt had "contributed so much to making our discussions worthwhile."

This position, shared by others, was sharply rebutted by
the majority. They agreed that discussion frequently became generalized, unknowledgeable, and discursive, that
the "bull-shit quotient" was often high and that "a snarling
five-man cacophony" often replaced thoughtful dialogue.
But such "dysfunctions" are to be expected, they said, are
perhaps even necessary by-products, of an alive atmosphere. Talk, by its very nature, is spasmodic, discursive,
repetitive, even at times incoherent. To try to trim it into
neat, orderly packages is to drain it of life.

The important point they were making, it seems to me,
is that human exchange is fullest when it operates on a
variety of levels, including the emotional, the irrational,
the fantastic. Unfortunately, most educational situations
concentrate on only one level of human interaction—the
rational. In doing so, they try to make people into what

An Experiment in Education

they are not—thinking machines—and end by turning the average seminar into an exercise rather than an experience.

The chief function of a university should not be, as is currently assumed, the accumulation and dissemination of knowledge, but rather the encouragement of individual growth. Factual information can aid in that growth, but to do so it must be made relevant to the individual's needs; it must pose some problem, extend some challenge, answer some longing, if it is to be incorporated rather than merely appended.

There is no one way to make knowledge relevant. Any seminar is composed of a variety of individuals with disparate life styles and contrasting perspectives. Moreover, the needs of a seminar group as a whole, like those of the individuals who make it up, do not remain constant. A seminar's structure must, therefore, remain flexible enough to register shifts in mood, and its climate permissive enough to allow individual variety in the approach and solution of problems. Some discipline is necessary to a coherent discussion, but it should be imposed not from above, but by the individual on himself when he senses that the group's collective need demands a shift in attitude and approach.

The central point, it seems to me, is that a seminar must involve more than intellectual exchange. Opinions and values are most likely to be revealed when the atmosphere encourages rather than suppresses emotional interaction. Opinions, never shaped solely by reasoning, are always influenced by personal relationships and encounters, themselves freighted with emotion, and thus are most likely to be exposed and examined in an environment that contains an emotional dimension. We want students to "re-examine their beliefs"; that, we like to say, is the whole point of education. Since those beliefs were first formed in a multi-dimensional setting, they cannot be successfully challenged in a setting that is one-dimensional.

This was, I think, the main reason why so many of the students in History 308 came away from the seminar feeling, as one put it, that "no course I have ever had in this university has challenged and changed my attitudes and views as much as this 'bull session.' " The term *bull session* is instructive; it was used by a number of the students to connote the sense of a discussion among friends, one more free of formality and constraint than most, one in which more of the person gets exposed and involved than it does in a seminar discussion narrowly confined to a selected topic or issue. To my mind, the frequent use of the term *bull session* to describe our meetings is a testimony to their success.

Perhaps someone might object that I had confused the purpose of a university seminar with that of a group-therapy session, that my function as a professor was not to treat personalities, but to develop minds. I would answer such an accusation in part by denying it and in part by embracing it. I would deny that the seminar was chiefly designed to encourage members to reveal pathology, that our purpose in coming together was "medicinal." Yet neuroses were revealed, and something which could be called "therapy" did take place. In the process of actively engaging one another, the students exposed personality traits of all kinds. To the extent that a given individual became aware of what he had revealed about himself and chose to ponder it (I do not mean openly, in seminar, but privately, with himself), some personality changes could have ensued. Henry Anderson has said: "Any experience that is humanizing might be called psychotherapeutic." If History 308 did partake of psychotherapy, I would, therefore, not only welcome the news, but consider it the best possible vindication of the seminar—for I do not know what "education" is if not self-examination and change.

This does not necessarily mean that I believe education and therapy should henceforth become interchangeable processes. (I am not sure that I believe the opposite, either.) I do feel, however, that the simple dualism which pretends that education is concerned solely with "informing the mind," and therapy with "understanding the emotions" falsifies our everyday experience. No one actually functions on the basis of such neat categories; our emotions always color our intellectual views, and our minds are continually "ordering" our emotional responses.

It would be grotesque and dangerous for a professor of history to claim the insight and skill needed to conduct group-therapy sessions, just as it would be foolish for a psychiatrist to conduct a seminar on Plato for his patients. But this is not to say that a university seminar does not influence the emotions of its members. We need to recognize that when a seminar is functioning well, the emotions of its members *are* engaged and, once engaged, will be transmuted.

Intellectual development does not, cannot, take place *in vacuo*. Indeed, it can be argued that intellectual development is predicated on the simultaneous development of the emotions. By intellectual development, I do not mean the amassing of facts (we all know walking encyclopedias who are emotional infants), but rather what William Kessen, professor of psychology at Yale, has called the individual's "delight in the solution of problems, pursuit of the orderly, joy in his own active inquiry, the relief and excitement of setting his own goals." For that kind of intellectual development, one needs emotional growth as well. The two are inextricably linked, and it is because we have tried to separate them—have tried to exclude emotion from the class-room—that we have turned out many more pedants and parrots than human beings.

Postscript

I tried the experimental course described in the preceding article for two years. At the final session of the second year, the students and I spent more than three hours evaluating the course; it was a discussion that helped greatly to clarify in my own mind what still needed doing in the way of classroom reforms. It led me to formulate plans for a new experiment which is best described in a memo I circulated to members of my department at Princeton. It read in part:

Most undergraduates, I believe, are starving on the standard diet of course work which is tailored more to the professors' interests than to their own and which concentrates on the absorption of information.

The chief defect of our current seminar set-up, it seems to me, is that we acknowledge only one form of interaction: rational discourse concerned with the mastery of factual detail and the interpretation of it. I have no wish to minimize the importance of this function. My point is that other levels of interaction are also present in every seminar, though we do not choose to acknowledge them, and that these—if acknowledged—could be of immense value in advancing what I take to be the basic purpose of education: self-discovery. These other levels of interaction are often non-rational, non-verbal, even unconscious. They involve all those processes which currently go under the rubric of "group dynamics," that is, "what happens" when a group of five or more people come together—how each individual presents himself and his ideas, what roles he chooses to play, what roles he projects onto others, how he reacts to challenge and debate, what forms of discussion he finds most congenial (or most threatening), etc., etc. We are all, as teachers, necessarily involved in group dynamics, whether or not we like the idea. Since we cannot escape that involvement, it seems to me we should try to deal with it more responsibly than we do. That would mean facing the fact that a variety of interactions do take place in our seminar meetings, that these interactions influence the form, the content and the retention of "rational discourse," and that they are therefore important to excavate and understand.

My tentative view is that in the long run this can probably best be done by giving all graduate students, regardless of their field of specialization, training in group dynamics. This would give them some of the insights and skills needed, when they become seminar leaders, to deal with certain classroom processes which are now handled by evasion, both conscious and otherwise.

I myself have not had the benefit of such training. As a result I do not feel able, other than on an intuitive basis, to explore the processes of group dynamics with competence. But I am eager to learn more about these processes—both so that I might make more considered suggestions in the future as to what form graduate training in group dynamics might take, and also to enrich the current experiences of myself and my students in the classroom. I should stress that I do not wish to abandon or minimize the intellectual content of university work, but, on the contrary, to find out more about those hidden transactions which inevitably influence intellectual exchange. I feel I know a good deal at this point in my life about what it means to be a professional historian, about research and writing in the field of my special interest. I feel I know very little about what it means to be a teacher of history (or of anything), about what kinds of strategies succeed with what kinds of students, about what can be exchanged between teacher and student.

Since I myself lack the necessary training to explore these matters as far as I would like, I decided the most sensible (and responsible) approach would be to have someone who is trained in group dynamics sit in on my seminar. The professionals with *most experience in this area are the group therapists. I have managed to locate a man—Dr. Cornelius Beukenkamp—who is not only a widely admired practitioner, but is as well one of the few psychotherapists with a deep interest in bridging the worlds of education and psychology; he has written and talked on the subject, and has also had a great deal of experience in university teaching. . . .*

The chief purpose of this experiment, as I saw it, was to seek new ways of establishing the kind of emotional climate of trust and honesty (so absent in most seminars) which would in turn make possible an authentic exchange of ideas. Though my department approved the proposal, it was subsequently vetoed by the Princeton Administration on "financial and pedagogical" grounds. Dr. Beukenkamp and I then decided to take the course to another university. Hunter College in New York City received us enthusiastically, and we began the course there in the spring term of 1969.

THE DISSENTING ACADEMY

THE colleges of our country, in contrast to those of most of the world, have a long tradition of quiescence. They have been islands of passivity and irrelevance rather than centers of ferment and innovation. The faculties have tended their scholarly gardens of rare herbs and leafless plants. The students, like dutiful inmates, have put in their time.

In the past few years this has begun to change, most, though not all of the change, for the better. A growing minority of students is no longer willing to settle for mechanical exercises in which it has little interest and less control. Younger faculty have begun questioning both the traditional forms of education—lectures, grades, requirements, exams—and the traditional emphasis on morally

This review of *The Dissenting Academy*, Theodore Roszak, ed. (Pantheon Books, New York) appeared in *The New York Times Book Review*, March 17, 1968.

neutral research and on the withdrawal of the scholar from active participation in public issues. Meanwhile, senior faculty have begun to find their expertise in wide demand by government and industry, and have gained proportionately in status and income.

It is this last development which gives grounds more for worry than for congratulation: with the jet schedules of some faculty members, especially in the physical and natural sciences, beginning to rival those of Princess Pignatelli's set, there is growing concern that teaching is being shortchanged and that the academic's "search for truth" has become compromised by his association with the centers of economic and political power.

Pantheon Books, under the imaginative leadership of André Schiffrin, has decided to give voice to the developing dissidence on campus by issuing a series of "anti-textbooks." *The Dissenting Academy* is the first in the series; it attempts to examine the university as a whole, thus preparing the ground for subsequent volumes that will deal with specific disciplines. *The Dissenting Academy* is not meant, however, to be an exhaustive survey of all recent trends on the campus. It concentrates on presenting the objections of scholars to the way their subjects are currently being researched and taught, and to the role academics are playing in society as a whole. Theodore Roszak, the editor, sums up the volume's double indictment of university practices as "mindless collaboration on the one hand and irrelevant research on the other."

Both parts of this indictment are cogently, at times even brilliantly made. Both parts seem to me irrefutable, though each raises questions that the volume does not fully explore.

The first charge, that of indiscriminate collaboration by the academy with the American military-industrial establishment, is well documented. At the University of Pennsylvania, biologists have worked—under secret contract—on chemical-biological weaponry. The Army's counter-insurgency Project Agile in Thailand enlisted a large group of anthropologists,° and the notorious Project Camelot, designed by our government to subvert the revolutionary aspirations of Latin America's underclasses, attracted a flock of social scientists. The professed ideal of the academic community is the relentless pursuit of truth, a pursuit that cares nothing for established piety or organized privilege. But our academics, more often than not, have been co-opted as defenders of the status quo, delighted to be on the Great Stage even if it means carrying a spear in some modern dress *Götterdämmerung*.

Sordid as this state of affairs is, no simple cure is available. Are all ties between government and the academy offensive, and should all be ended? If so, where will needed research funds come from? From the business community? From the foundations? From trustees? Are these sources likely to be any less pernicious in their influence? Besides, if we close the lines of communication between the academic community and the government, will we have any right to complain if our government then suffers from lack of information and expertise? If we do want the campuses to contribute personnel and ideas to Washington, what boundaries should we set, and who shall set them? These are all hard questions. Among the essayists, only Marshall Windmiller raises them, and he only in part.

The second half of the indictment is no less valid than the first—and no less troublesome. The eleven essayists agree that all their disciplines are rife with what Roszak

---

° Clark E. Cunningham pointed out to me after the publication of this review that the number of anthropologists connected with Project Agile has been greatly exaggerated.

calls "mindless specialization and irrelevant pedantry." The anthropological journals, for example, are full of articles on kinship terms or the Tzental words for "firewood," but, as Kathleen Gough points out, they almost never contain speculation on such crucial matters as the dynamics of neo-imperialism or the genesis of guerrilla movements.

Sumner Rosen argues that the economists are doing little better; most of them assume rather than test the validity of doctrines central to the economic tradition of the West —free markets, efficiency, growth—and concentrate their energies instead on improving quantitative methods of measurement and on tinkering with peripheral matters like the manipulation of interest rates. Staughton Lynd does a similar job on the historians, Louis Kampf on the literary critics, John Wilkinson on the philosophers, Robert Engler and Christian Bay on the sociologists and political scientists. All the disciplines, to quote Engler (the most gifted phrase-maker in a uniformly well-written volume), are characterized by a deplorable combination of "small-scale research backed by large-scale grants."

The essayists further argue that since a value-free social science is impossible anyway, its practitioners should be ashamed rather than proud of their moral detachment, for the pride is based on a misunderstanding of both the limitations and responsibilities of their profession. Pseudo-scientific, pseudo-objective pretensions must be replaced by an ideal dating back at least as far as the Enlightenment: How can we as intellectuals "help men to live more fully and creatively and to expand their dignity, self-direction, and freedom"?

The problem comes—for some of the essayists as well as for myself—when we get down to specifics, for although the indictment is well-substantiated and well-deserved in general outline, it has at its core, some uncertain definitions. Roszak, for example, calls for an end to "fastidious but morally undirected research" and charges the scholar "to intervene in society for the defense of civilized values," to "clarify reality" so that his fellow citizens "can reason toward the solution of their problems." But what does it mean to "clarify reality," and exactly what kind of research should we discard as "fastidious but morally undirected"? Roszak himself explicitly rejects the notion that we should abandon all scholarly research that does not relate immediately to social criticism; such a call, he says, would be "little more than philistine."

Yet another contributor to the volume, Louis Kampf, comes very close to sounding that call when he disparages the announcement of a new Henry James Journal as an example of the "more exquisite levels of absurdity" scholars continue to attain. But I see nothing inherently absurd in such a journal, though its topic is of interest to only a few and though its relevance to social problems is probably minute. The fact is it will give pleasure to those few, and to banish it haughtily from our Brave New World is to inaugurate a brand of Puritanism different perhaps from that of Anthony Comstock, but no less pernicious.

Besides, if we posit a Henry James scholar who is eager to be socially responsible, he will not find Kampf's guidelines of much help. Kampf calls on teachers of poetry to dedicate themselves "to the human ends of poetry—to men's desire for the true, the good, and the beautiful"—but he never pauses to define those fine sentiments. It might even be that a Henry James Journal, concerned with style and performance rather than with "content," devoted, that is, to explicating the possibilities of language, the multiple meanings which adhere to words, the subtleties of communication, would make its own contribution to "the true, the good, and the beautiful." Kampf's essay embodies the

chief short-coming of *The Dissenting Academy* as a whole
—its inability to elucidate an alternate model, to make
clear what kinds of knowledge a scholar would be pursuing
and in what ways he would pursue it, if he were indeed
functioning for both his own and his society's best interests.

What the volume does establish beyond dispute is that
most academics are careerists: they will accept any offer
or, alternatively, slight any responsibility (to their students,
their profession, their society) in the name of augmenting
their own prestige. In the meantime urgent social problems go unresolved, basic questions of international responsibility go unasked, and the older view of an intellectual community devoted to keeping alive the tension
between what man is and what he might and ought to be,
goes untended.

We would probably all agree (all but the Ayn Rands,
that is) that nothing in man's genetic make-up forces him
to behave in so self-enclosed a manner. The academy's
failures are due to culture, not nature. One can hardly grow
up in the American ethos of each-against-all individualism,
in an atmosphere which emphasizes the virtue of accumulation (goods, power, prestige), and at the same time develop
concern for one's neighbors, profession or community. The
corruptions of the academy are, writ small, the corruptions
of our society. A change in society's values must therefore
precede (or at least parallel) any change in those of academia.

That a parallel re-evaluation *has* begun can be seen in
the growing discontent of both students and younger faculty with traditional practices. They are finding a common
voice, a voice that calls for value-oriented research, for
teaching that concentrates on fundamental issues rather
than marketable skills, for an interaction with the larger
community based on a critical rather than worshipful

stance. *The Dissenting Academy* salutes this new, more humane spirit, and makes its own substantial contribution to its further growth. That spirit needs what nourishment it can get. For in our colleges, as in so many areas of our national life, an internal conflict is being waged: an increase in knowledge, compassion and social consciousness has been matched, and is currently dwarfed, by the growth of pedantry, neutralism and careerism.

Academia, in other words, like so much else in our country, is in both better and worse shape than it was a generation ago. The worst tendencies at present have the upper hand. But it is good to know that the others exist and have not given up the field.

THE ACADEMIC REVOLUTION

CHRISTOPHER JENCKS and David Riesman were not meant to rule, but to arbitrate, to serve as mediators—within the universities, between the generations—and they have written a book which exactly fulfills that thankless role.

Mediation has its pitfalls. In trying to understand all positions, there can lurk the refusal to establish one's own; in attempting to allow all voices their say, one can lose the power of distinctive speech. Jencks and Riesman do not entirely avoid these pitfalls, but one of the many achievements of *The Academic Revolution* is that its authors insist on evaluating as well as describing the myriad patterns, attitudes, interest groups and controversies which comprise the current academic scene. They even venture general theories about the development of American uni-

This review of Christopher Jencks and David Riesman's *The Academic Revolution* (Doubleday & Company, Inc., New York) appeared in *The New Republic*, June 22, 1968.

versities and, more ambitious still, the social context in which that development took place.

Given their range of inquiry—from cultural stratification in America to the future of private Negro colleges—some weak spots in research and some contradictory conclusions are inescapable. But throughout the book, the authors admit their limitations and uncertainties; when they give an impressionistic judgment, they so label it, when they lack data for a firm conclusion, they openly confess it. Their candor is the more engaging for coming from men whose credentials and thoroughness (the book has been in preparation for ten years) would have warranted the kind of positivistic, pseudo-scientific claims so often indulged in by their less subtle, less talented colleagues.

I can only begin to acknowledge the many points at which the book has corrected or sharpened my own opinions. It contains, for example, the best brief discussion of class in the United States that I have ever read—just one instance of the authors' success in writing a book about education which, because of their insistence on a large framework of reference, becomes a book about America's social arrangements and value structure. In the same way, they also make a startling and convincing case for viewing the development of colleges in nineteenth-century America not as another symptom of the country's fluidity—the usual interpretation—but rather as a reaction *against* the rapid change everywhere apparent.

In regard to the contemporary academic scene, Jencks and Riesman challenge conventional wisdom at many points. Though colleges believe that the more money they spend, the better job they do (and thus justify their endless appeals to alumni and legislatures), that claim, the authors assert, may be illusory. Does a university that hires an academic superstar at, say, $40,000 a year, get a hundred percent greater return on its money (especially in effective teaching) than if it had hired a less well-known specialist at half the price? Or, even more suspect, does the construction of one more $10 million classroom complex serve any true educational purpose—which is not to be confused with serving the ego needs of alumni? But then, as Jencks and Riesman remark, we should no longer pretend that the prime function of our universities *is* to educate. They are, and it is time we faced it, institutes for certification. They sort and label the young for the convenience and, usually, the deception (for, as the authors also demonstrate, there is no correlation between performance in college and on the job) of future employers.

If our universities were interested in education, which is to say in helping the young to grow in self-awareness, it would follow that they would be deeply interested in teaching. They are not. Nothing demonstrates this more clearly than the kind of training Ph.D. candidates get. Almost every doctoral candidate will some day be teaching as well as researching and writing in the field of his special choice. But graduate training concentrates almost exclusively on preparing a man for scholarship. (And that, at least in the humanities and social sciences, is done by settling for still more course work on the undergraduate pattern—for no one really knows, and few will even acknowledge the problem of what it means to "train" a man to be, say, a historian. Among other difficulties, historians are themselves deeply divided about what a good historian does: describe actions or probe motives? concentrate on similarities in the behavior of groups of men or on the idiosyncratic performance of individuals? treat the data as a novelist might, with subjective dash, or as a machine might, with neutral dispassion?) We know almost nothing about what does or does not work in a classroom—especially with this generation—and, to put it bluntly, most faculty don't give a damn anyway. Teaching is how a scholar makes a living. It is not an integral part of how he justifies his life or gets his kicks.

I would like to have seen Jencks and Riesman devote more space to teaching and learning, since their incidental comments show that they themselves feel strongly about this scandal of avoidance. There are a number of good reasons why they have not. They have much to cover in their broadly conceived volume, and besides, we lack data on what does or could go on in the college classroom. But I think, too, that the authors tend to slight the classroom because, unlike a growing portion of the student body, they do basically believe in the university as an institution and in rationality as a way of life. Their stance in *The Academic Revolution* is, to be sure, critical of many aspects of academia, but in the way Woodrow Wilson was critical of capitalism: let's do away with the excesses so that an enterprise, good in itself, might once more flourish.

Today's student radicals are far more disenchanted than Jencks and Riesman. Their disgust with traditional procedures is grounded in a growing distrust of rationality itself, of the importance of gathering and transmitting factual information and technical expertise. They are angry because they know that their growth depends on more than the accumulation of information. The kind of growth they value—increased openness to a range of experience, emotional honesty, personal interaction—seems actually threatened and compromised by additional proficiency in the manipulation of ideas and things. In a brilliant article in *The Nation,* Michael Crozier, professor of sociology at the University of Paris, has recently put his finger on the source of current student unrest in this country: it is a rebellion against the new hyper-rationalist world, where the capacity for abstract reasoning is considered the gauge of human worth and the precondition for human happiness. Or, as Berger, one of the hippie heroes of *Hair* succinctly puts it to his teachers: "Screw your logic and reason." The rationalist tradition, as the student rebels see it, has produced a race of deformed human beings, or rather, a race of thinking machines: heads (the old-fashioned kind) without bodies or feelings. The new generation does not wish men to become mindless; they wish them to become something more than minds. Unlike Robespierre, who enthroned reason, these revolutionaries search for a way to topple it.

Jencks and Riesman are far more open to and appreciative of the needs and values of this generation than most adults. They explicitly state that it is a mistake to try to teach only "traditional academic subjects by traditional academic methods," and they call for a wide variety of curriculum experiments, a search for new ways of teaching and learning through the incorporation of materials from the teen-age culture of folk-rock and films. They would further supplement (not, sensibly, replace) academic disciplines by deliberately adding to the faculty men who have done field work or who have had clinical experience in a wide variety of fields that currently interest the young. They are firm opponents of the rigidities that now characterize departments and disciplines within the university, and especially of the traditional emphasis in the graduate schools "on training men to write papers rather than to communicate with students on a face-to-face basis." They are angry with current practices which encourage the student to "repress himself and become a passive instrument 'used' by his methods and his disciplinary colleagues." They wish to make a place for, and to give weight to, knowledge that is derived from "individual subjective experience," so that the student might be put in closer touch with himself and so that the various aspects of his person might find integrated focus. They are less concerned with what a student can verbalize or repeat on an exam than with what, as a person, he becomes.

Yet at other points in their discussion Jencks and Riesman sound strangely smug about the human product the colleges are currently turning out, and to that extent, ambivalent or hostile to the demands being made by student malcontents. Thus they are "reasonably clear that today's B.A.'s know more in absolute terms than their predecessors in any earlier era." But isn't the point, as they themselves ask elsewhere: more knowledge about what and for what? They are also prone to congratulating faculties for not only being "better" but "often more interested" than previously. Here, too, they seem to be contradicting their own earlier strictures on faculty absorption in research and on faculty indifference to all but strictly academic communication with students. Finally, they insist, "there are very few colleges where an enterprising student cannot get an education if he tries, and none of us can think of where this is more difficult today than in the past." But an education in what besides technique, and for what purpose other than certification?—both of which Jencks and Riesman deplore.

When they turn "from the narrow question of academic competence to the broader question of human growth," the authors conclude, again in contradiction to much of their earlier argument, that "the academic revolution . . . strikes us as a progressive development." Indeed, they "see relatively little ground for nostalgia, and considerable reason for satisfaction with the consequences to date of academic power." Well, they promised in their introduction that their "prejudices are many [and] . . . often contradictory . . .," and that they would be ambivalent on certain issues. In regard to the basic question of whether the colleges as currently structured can really be considered educative institutions, that promise of ambivalence is fulfilled.

But I don't wish to end on an ironic or negative note. Because my own interests are increasingly focused on the teaching/learning process, I may have harped unfairly on the one issue which *The Academic Revolution* handles least well. On dozens of other topics, Jencks and Riesman are more exhaustive in their treatment, more certain of their own position, more satisfying in their conclusions. This is, in sum, a rich, brilliant volume, essential background for understanding the current worldwide crisis of the university.

ON MISUNDERSTANDING
STUDENT REBELS

THE young, it is becoming clear, are regarded with considerable hatred in our country. Resentment against them cannot be explained simply as a reaction to the style of a particular generation, for in recent years the young have been attacked on such divergent grounds that the grounds themselves take on the appearance of pretext. In the 1950s we denounced students for their inertia, their indifference to public questions, their absorption in the rituals of fraternities and football, their dutiful pursuit of "achievement." In the 1960s we condemn them for the opposite qualities: for their passion, their absorption in public questions, their disgust with the trivia of college parties and athletics, their refusal to settle for mechanical processes of education.

Since the past two college generations have been denounced with equal vehemence for opposite inclinations,

"On Misunderstanding Student Rebels" appeared in *The Atlantic Monthly*, November, 1968.

it seems plausible to conclude that it is not those inclinations but the very fact of their youth that makes them the target for so much murderous abuse. This conclusion may seem to contradict the fact that American society, above all others, is known for its adoration of youth. But that itself, paradoxically, is one cause of adult hostility: our youth-obsessed elders resent the eighteen-year-old's easy possession of the good looks and high spirits they so desperately simulate.

Adult anger at the physical superiority of the young has usually been contained by the comforting assumption that eighteen-year-olds are at least the moral, intellectual, and emotional inferiors of their elders. College students have traditionally been viewed as apprentices, almost as supplicants. And until recently they accepted their role as dutiful petitioners for entry into the world of adult insight and skill.

As no one needs reminding, they no longer accept that role, though most of their elders continue the struggle to confine them to it. Today's eighteen-to-twenty-year-old considers himself an adult, by which he does not mean (as so many forty-year-olds unconsciously do) that he has ceased growing, but that he has grown up enough to make his own decisions. In every sense, even statistically, his case is a strong one.

The weight of recent physiological and psychological evidence establishes the student claim that today's eighteen-year-olds mature more rapidly than those of earlier generations. Physically, they are taller and heavier than their counterparts at the turn of the century. Boys reach puberty around age fourteen, and girls begin to menstruate at the average age of twelve years, nine months (in both cases almost two years earlier than in 1900).

On Misunderstanding Student Rebels

Moreover, there is much evidence that this earlier physical maturity is matched by emotional and intellectual precocity. According to Dr. C. Keith Conners, director of the Child Development Laboratory at Massachusetts General Hospital, both emotional and intellectual growth are today largely completed by age eighteen. By this Dr. Conners means that the difficult trials of adolescence are over, the basic patterns of personality have become stabilized, and the ability to reason abstractly—to form hypotheses and make deductions—has been established. This does not mean, of course, that no further maturity is possible after age eighteen. Additional information and experience do (or at least should) provide material for continuing reassessments. But that, of course, is (or should be) true of all of us.

In terms of knowledge already possessed, moreover, the graduating high school senior of today, thanks both to the media and to the stepped-up pace of academic work, is well informed on any number of topics—the new math, say, or the physical properties of the atom—of which his elders are ignorant. And as for experience, I am not at all sure that the eighteen-year-old who has had his senses activated by early sexual relations, strobe lights, pot, soul, and rock, and his political instincts honed by Vietnam, the draft, and the civil rights movement, should not be considered more vitally alive, more instinctually sound, than the typical forty-year-old who has spent his additional twenty years glued to the tube, the routinized job, the baseball and stock statistics.

It is bad enough that we have refused to extend to students the rights and responsibilities which their maturity warrants. What is perhaps worse is that many of those who hold positions of power or prestige in our universities have learned so little from the upheavals which that refusal has

311

produced. A recent spate of books and articles by such men demonstrates anew their uneducability; they make it clear, by their continuing patronization and belittlement, that students still have an uphill fight in their struggle to be taken seriously.

One case in point, though not the most egregious, is that of George F. Kennan. When Kennan's article "Rebels Without a Program" (aptly characterized by Richard Poirier as "a new containment policy for youth") appeared in the *New York Times* Sunday Magazine for January 21, 1968, it drew such an unprecedented reply from students and teachers (including a letter from me) that the Atlantic Monthly Press decided to issue the article, the replies, and a lengthy rebuttal by Kennan as a separate volume, *Democracy and the Student Left.* In that rebuttal, Kennan does acknowledge that the public questions agitating the country are indeed "so harrowing" and "harbor such apocalyptic implications that it is silly to suggest," as he originally had, that college students should go about their studies as usual.

But having acknowledged that "harrowing" problems face the country, Kennan proceeds, by a curious indirection, to minimize them. He lectures student activists on their "inability to see and enjoy the element of absurdity in human behavior" (adding, gratuitously, that he suspects their love lives, no less than their politics, are "tense, anxious, defiant and joyless"), on their "social science" rhetoric, and on their indifference to "nature as a possible compensation or sustaining factor in the face of social or political frustration." Kennan fails, however, to make clear how the merit of the issues the students raise in any way depends on the "inadequate" manner in which they raise them. I, for one, cannot see how the Vietnam War or the plight of our ghetto-dwellers might become more attractive or tolerable if viewed with an awareness of "the element of absurdity in human behavior" or described in a rhetoric free of social science jargon or escaped from by periodic trips to the wilderness.

Kennan insists that the students' obliviousness to nature, etc., is symptomatic of their "lack of interest in the creation of any real style and distinction of personal life generally." By which he means, as he goes on to specify, their lack of "manners," their untidiness, their disinterest in "personal hygiene," their refusal to cultivate the "amenities." It is debatable that this description is either accurate or significant as applied to the nonpolitical, drug-oriented "hippies," but it is certainly not a valid description of campus activists, the ostensible subjects of Kennan's critique.

The main point, of course, is not that the new generation lacks "any real style," but that Kennan is unable to perceive much of its distinctiveness. Kennan is a good eighteenth-century *philosophe*, distrustful of "enthusiasm," and preoccupied with the rationalist credo of restraint and temperance in all things. Since "passion" is suspect, it follows (albeit unconsciously) that no injustice warrants fervent disapproval. What the new generation believes and Kennan apparently does not, is that "moderation" can itself become a form of paralysis, even of immorality—like the moderate protest of Pope Pius XII against the extermination of Jews.

If Kennan's condescension toward the different life-style of the young were peculiar to him, it could be more readily ignored. But in fact his attitude is the characteristic response of the older generation to the young. Any number of other examples are possible, but I will mention only two of the more prominent: Sidney Hook and Jacques Barzun.

Hook has published two statements (that I know of) on the recent ferment at Columbia, a long article, "The Prospects of Academe," in *Encounter* for August, 1968, and a brief note in the *Psychiatry and Social Science Review* for July, 1968. It is difficult to choose between them in deciding the high point to date for gray-bearded arrogance. In the shorter piece Hook flatly states that the Columbia rebels "had no grievances," and that they were interested solely in "violence, obscenity and hysterical insult." In the longer article Hook characterizes the protesters as "callow and immature adolescents" whose dominant mood, like that of all adolescents, is "irrationalism." While denouncing students for their passion, this self-appointed defender of "reason" and of the university as the "citadel of reason," himself indulges in a rhetoric so inflamed ("Fanatics don't lack sincerity. . . . They drip with sincerity—and when they have power, with blood—other people's blood") that by comparison the most apocalyptic students seem models of sobriety. Hook even declares that "there are some things one should not be moderate about"—which is exactly what the student activists (and Barry Goldwater) have said. The students, of course, mean it is acceptable to be passionately against war and racism. Hook (and Goldwater) mean it is acceptable to be passionately against those who passionately protest war and racism.

Hook's themes—that college students are adolescents, that the best proof of their childishness is that they are "emotional" and that emotion (in others) is bad—are to be found in their most explicit form in Jacques Barzun's new book, *The American University*. In a note in the book's preface Barzun, who was dean of faculties and provost at Columbia from 1958 to 1967, explains that the manuscript was in the hands of the publisher six weeks before the student outbreak on April 23, 1968. But lest we be tempted on that account to excuse some of the positions he adopts in his book, Barzun further adds that despite the outbreak he has "found no reason to change or add to the substance

On Misunderstanding Student Rebels

of what I had written months earlier." Among the views he has found no need to modify is his statement that Grayson Kirk has always shown himself "ready and eager for progressive changes." Barzun does not pause to define "progressive," but one can't help thinking he uses the word in its original sense to describe the reforms that preceded World War I. Certainly nothing in his attitude toward students would place him beyond the year 1915.

Barzun begins his discussion of the college population by adopting the Olympian view: they are, after all, young men, and that means "turbulence is to be expected, heightened nowadays by the presence of girls. . . ." In other words, a certain amount of inherent anger adheres to the condition of being young (it *is* a "condition," in Barzun's view), and anger must find its outlet. The nature of the outlet is almost a matter of indifference: if "the people of the town" do not provide a convenient target, well then, it might just as well be politics.

Still in the Olympian vein, Barzun further suggests— it is as close as he ever comes to implicating society—that "perhaps our lack of proper ceremonies for initiation into the tribe leaves the young to devise their own proof of manhood." Barzun loves dismissing the young with this kind of casual irony. Its elegant offhandedness is a useful device for keeping a proper distance between the generations. It is also useful—though of this Barzun seems unaware—for expressing the savagery which he likes to think is confined to the student population. Barzun claims the undergraduates would themselves welcome rites of initiation, for what they really want, he insists, is more, not less, discipline. When they speak of the impersonality of the university, they mean, it seems, "the looseness of its grip upon them." Kennan makes the same point in almost the same words: students are currently objecting to parietal rules, he asserts, because "the rules have relaxed too much rather than that they have been relaxed too little." According to both men, students are starved for structure, are desperate to be introduced to the rigors of logic. In Barzun's phrasing, they are looking for "order," for "intellectual habits"; they sense that this is the balance they need, for like all youngsters they are in a "fever and frenzy," "their mind is monopolized by their inner life."

To meet this "rage for order," Barzun and Kennan posit a properly antiseptic university, a place of "respite and meditation" whose "proper work," in Barzun's phrase, is "in the catacombs under the strife-torn crossroads." He fills this subterranean cemetery with properly lifeless figures; they are "somewhat hushed," they give pause, as at Chartres, to the "spiritual grandeur of their surroundings." Yet just as one begins to feel, in the rush of Christian imagery, that Barzun has spent so many years surrounded by campus Gothic as to have lost all sense of distinction between the university and the church, he stoutly declares that *his* catacombs will not be peopled by early Christians. He dislikes that breed; it was marked by the same distasteful qualities he associates with today's young radicals: "indifference to clothes and cleanliness, a distrust and neglect of reasoning . . . a freedom in sexuality, which is really a lowering of its intensity and value . . . and—most symptomatic—a free field given to the growth of hair."

Barzun also shares with Kennan and Hook the proposition that "emotion" has no place on campus, and that since student rebels tend to be emotional, it can be safely assumed they are also unreliable. All three men equate (and thereby confuse) "emotion" with "irrationality," and all employ a vocabulary of neat opposites—"reason" versus "emotion"—that separates what our experience combines.

On Misunderstanding Student Rebels

They see education as "the cultivation and tempering of the mind" but fail to see that "enthusiasm" is one path by which tempering proceeds. (For an understanding of the role emotion might and should play in learning, they would do well to read a remarkable new book by George B. Leonard, *Education and Ecstasy*. Though Leonard's discussion is chiefly centered on the lower grades, almost everything he says has applicability to higher education as well, especially his remark that schools as presently structured tame the "unnamed powers" of their students—their chief effect is to "limit possibilities, narrow perceptions and bring the individual's career as a learner (changer) to an end." Leonard foresees schools where the children will not emerge as mere knowledge machines but as beings who have also learned about their bodies, emotions, and senses. His is as authentically the voice of the future as Barzun's is that of the past.)

Barzun is also huffy at other "nonsense" currently being peddled about teaching, especially the idea that teacher and student should explore together, each learning from the other. This view, he asserts, has done "immense harm to both parties. The teacher has relaxed his efforts while the student has unleashed his conceit." And of what does that "conceit" consist? Barzun is quick to tell us: the conviction that they (the students) have something to contribute. "Only rarely," he declares, with a hauteur appropriate to the century from which most of his ideas spring, does a teacher "hear from a student a fact he does not know or a thought that is original and true . . . to make believe that their knowledge and his are equal is an abdication and a lie."

And so we are back, as always in Barzun's schema, to the confinement of his starting assumption: students are

children and, usually, fools. His contempt for undergraduates is pervasive. They are, very simply, not to be trusted;
"student reliability is at a low ebb," he warns, and especially among radical students, who have but one purpose: to destroy. The evidence Barzun marshals to justify
his contempt is so exasperatingly trivial (as well as suspect in its accuracy) that it demeans its compiler far more
than the students. The undergraduates, he asserts, cheat
a lot on exams and papers; they obtain pocket money by
stealing books from the college bookstore; they keep library
books out as long as they like and let fines go unpaid; they
deny their roommates "the slightest considerateness"; students of both sexes live "pig-style" in their dormitories;
their conversations "usually cannot follow a logical pattern," and so on.

The first thing to be said about these accusations is that
Barzun has seized upon the occasional practices of a few
undergraduates in order to damn a whole generation. The
second is that even if these qualities did characterize a
whole generation, they hardly seem heinous when compared with the sins of the fathers—when compared, that is,
with racism at home and imperialism abroad.

The distressing consequence of this obsession with the
peccadillos of the young is an avoidance of those genuinely
important problems to which the young are calling attention. Mandarins like Barzun, Kennan, and Hook are so
preoccupied with manners that they forget matter. They
are so certain of the rightness of their own patterns of
thought and action and so eager to denounce all deviations
by the young from those patterns that they blind themselves (and others) to the serious questions this new generation has raised—questions about the nature of education, the proper functions of a university, the very quality
of American life.

On Misunderstanding Student Rebels

. . .

A dozen or so studies have been made of student activists at a variety of universities, and the findings have been conveniently summarized in a recent essay by Stanford's Nevitt Sanford.[1] The group portrait that emerges (confirmed by Kenneth Keniston's new book, *Young Radicals*) is strikingly different from the slanderous one being peddled by Messrs. Barzun and Hook.

The activists, first of all, constitute only a small minority, though a growing one, of all college students; at Berkeley, for example, their number is put at about 15 percent. Second, there are important differences, in almost all measurable categories, between activists on the campus and other students. The activists score consistently higher on a wide variety of personality tests, including theoretical skills, aesthetic sensitivity, degree of psychological autonomy, and social maturity. They are also the better students, with significantly higher grade-point averages than the nonactivists. In trying to account for the recent emergence of student activism, Sanford points to various changes since the 1930s in family life and child training. But he feels that student activism is primarily a response to social conditions both within the university and in the world at large. Since the latter are the more widely known determinants of student rebelliousness, I will confine my remarks to conditions in the university.

One set of grievances on the campus centers on what does—or does not—go on in the classroom. As David Riesman has written, "Colleges on the whole have been very backward as compared with industry or the Army in their curiosity about their own inner processes." Until recently they have accepted lectures, grading, and examinations as

[1] Nevitt Sanford, "The College Student of 1980," *Campus 1980*, Alvin C. Eurich, ed. (Delacorte, New York).

part of the Natural Order of Things and have seen no reason to question the long-standing assumptions that Teacher is the possessor and arbiter of Truth, that his function is to transmit knowledge (narrowly defined as accumulated information) to students, and that their function is to memorize it.

Any challenge to this conventional wisdom is still viewed with scorn by the vast majority of faculty and administrators—and of the student population as well. Barzun, for example, gives short shrift to any protest against grades and tests; "no person by way of being educated," he announces, "resents examinations; they are so instructive." Should a student activist or one of his allies among the younger faculty reply that exams and grades chiefly instruct students in how to please their professors, in how to compete with one another, in how to settle for orthodox questions and answers, and in how to suppress their own originality, Barzun's answer would be—hogwash. He sees the activists' demand for autonomy and for the freedom to pursue their own lines of inquiry as cant, as another example of their "mental confusion." By way of proof, Barzun triumphantly recounts a recent episode in a large Midwestern university: when students in a philosophy of education class of 300 complained that they had little say in their own education, the professor asked how many did in fact want to take responsibility for their work, and only ten hands went up. The moral, as Barzun draws it, is that students calling for self-regulation merely "ape the advertiser's soapy mind." But that is not the moral at all. Our educational system has been so successful in turning out automatons that the vast majority of its products are terrified at the thought of taking over responsibility for their own lives. The fact that only ten hands went up is itself a

On Misunderstanding Student Rebels

severe indictment of our educational practices. Instead of proving that "all is well," it proves that we are in desperate trouble—that maybe only 3.3 percent of our *citizens* are willing to make their own decisions.

Barzun similarly misses the point the undergraduate dissenters are making about the lecture system. That point has been well put in the April, 1968, issue of the *Yale Alumni Magazine* by Alan Weiner, a graduating senior. The present system, he wrote, encourages "debilitating dependence"; each student, taking dutiful notes at lecture, produces by the end of the semester (and for exams) a "paraphrased copy" of the lecturer's text, "one copy differing from the other less in content than in penmanship." Weiner recognizes that lectures, at their best, can be useful—a good lecture can provide a lucid introduction to some particularly difficult area of study so that the student "is spared the initial paralysis of venturing alone into *terra incognita*"; it can offer a fundamental reinterpretation not yet published or widely accepted; and it can "show a brilliant man in the process of putting ideas together." But such moments in the lecture room are rare, so rare that they do not justify the maintenance of a system which far more typically inculcates sloppiness, omniscience, plagiarism, and theatricality in the lecturer, and passivity, boredom, resentment, and cynicism in the student.

And what is the answer of men like Barzun to the growing resentment of the lecture system? That the protesters do not understand the true nature of their dissatisfaction. The real trouble, Barzun declares, is that the university has "let lapse the *formality* of lecturing—its form—which was its principal merit." What is wanted by way of change, in other words, is not to dismantle the lecture system but to return it to its pristine shape, to reintroduce "formal presentation" and even "staginess and rhetorical effects," since these impart something Barzun labels "didactic energy." Given this gross misreading of student discontent, it might be well to remember in speaking hereafter of the "generation gap" that incomprehension is not confined to one side.

Discontent with teaching practices in our universities embraces more than the lecture system. Even where small seminars or discussion groups prevail (an expensive device few universities can afford), the needs of the students are not given anything like equal consideration with the needs of teachers. As two students in the *Yale Daily News* recently put it, the present system fails to help undergraduates appropriate facts and skills "in the interest of making lives, not just livings." In assuming that the university's main, almost exclusive, function is to produce and transmit information, we have given top priority to promoting those faculty members most likely to assist in the manufacture of knowledge. This means, of course, that the university has come to be staffed chiefly by those concerned with research and writing rather than those concerned with educating the young—that is, with helping them to discover what their interests and talents are, in helping them to change. As Alfred North Whitehead said long ago, "So far as the mere imparting of information is concerned, no university has had any justification for existence since the popularisation of printing in the fifteenth century." Yet most professors do look on the imparting of information as the sum and substance of their responsibility. They make little or no effort to show, either in their subject or in their person, how knowledge can influence conduct and inform action (which, as William Arrowsmith has pointed out, is not really surprising, since they are themselves products of the same noneducation).

On Misunderstanding Student Rebels

Most professors are interested only in students who are themselves potential scholars; they are concerned with training future colleagues, not with helping the individual young person grow in his own directions. The lack of interest taken by most professors in most students, their refusal to reveal or engage more than a small share of their own selves, have made many of the best students cynical about knowledge and about those who purvey it. They hoped to find in their professors models on whom they might pattern their lives; instead they find narrow specialists busy with careers, with government contracts, with the augmentation of status and income. They hoped to find a curriculum which would help them to uncover and pursue their interests; instead they find one primarily tailored to the needs of the faculty specialists. They hoped to discover a mode of living which would help them to integrate their intellectual curiosity with the demands of their senses and emotions; instead they find, in Erich Fromm's words, an education "more and more cerebral . . . [where] people are taught concepts, but are not taught or confronted with the experience which corresponds to these concepts." They hoped to find some acknowledgment of their worth and some encouragement toward its further development; instead they find disinterest, patronization, overt dislike. They find, in short, what Nietzsche called "the advancement of learning at the expense of man."

With considerable justice, therefore, the students, particularly the more talented and sensitive ones, reject the university and its faculty as self-serving, self-justifying, self-enclosed. They learn to seek their education—the expanding of insight and option—outside the formal academic curriculum, to seek it in talk and games with friends, in films, clothes and cars, in Sergeant Pepper's Lonely

323

Hearts Club Band, in the lyrics of Bob Dylan, in the Doors, in pot and acid. And if some of these sources prove as phony or as dangerous as the mechanical exercises of the campus, surely much of the responsibility lies with an academic community that has encouraged, almost forced, its students to look for life-enhancement where they can.

Most of the powers within the academic community will not even acknowledge the right of students to complain, let alone the cogency of those complaints. To the request that they be allowed a voice in planning the curriculum, a Jacques Barzun replies that they have done nothing to "earn" a voice. To the lament that their studies seem outmoded or irrelevant, Barzun retorts that "relevance is a relationship in the mind and not a property of things"— which apparently means that although students might want to study urban affairs, if they will instead study cockle shells *in the right way,* they will discover all there is to know about life in the ghettos. And to the students' suggestion that they have some formal power in such matters as choosing faculty, passing on applications for admission, or helping to decide on the expansion of the physical plant, Barzun responds with hoots of derision and George Kennan with cold anger.

Both gentlemen remind the undergraduates that the university is not, and was never meant to be, a democracy. Barzun does believe that students should have the right of self-government in their own dormitories, for he acknowledges that they are "socially mature enough not to need domestic proctoring" (a curious and seemingly arbitrary departure from his usual premise that undergraduates are children). But Kennan will not go even this far in extending power to undergraduates. The university, by virtue of

On Misunderstanding Student Rebels

its position as owner of the dormitories, has no choice in Kennan's view but "to lay down certain minimal norms for the manner in which that use can proceed. This would be true," he insists, "even if the inhabitants were older people." But it is not true, for Kennan's (and my own) university, Princeton, owns a great deal of faculty housing, and in none of it are the tenants subjected to the demeaning regulations in regard to visitors, and so on, which are imposed upon the students.

With the exception of this disagreement over parietal rules, Barzun and Kennan are firmly united in their contention that the university cannot and should not be a democracy. Kennan, in this instance, is the more peremptory of the two. "Even if university trustees and administrators had a right to shift a portion of their responsibilities for university affairs to the student, which they do not," he writes, the student would in any case "be unqualified to receive it." The very suggestion, he warns, is part of the current tendency of American society "to press upon the child a premature external adulthood."

Barzun rests most of his case on the grounds of impracticality. The university cannot function as a democracy, he argues, because it is "extremely difficult to get from student bodies either a significant vote, or a council or committee that is representative. . . . Add that student newspapers have long ceased to purvey anything approaching a public opinion, and it is clear that democracy is the last name a political scientist would apply to the government by outcry which has lately gained favor as an extracurricular activity." The absurdity of this argument (and its loaded terminology) is best seen when placed in another context. Is it *easy* to get a "significant" or "representative" vote from the United States Congress? Do our commercial newspapers "purvey anything approaching a public opinion"? Shall we, on those accounts, abandon both the Congress and the public press as unworkable institutions? In trying to make a case against democracy in the university, in other words, Barzun has forced himself—I assume, inadvertently—into making a case against democracy in general. The "insurmountable obstacles" which he finds to democratic institutions on the campus are likewise in the path of democracy within the larger society. Indeed, they loom less large on campus; given the limited size of a university, the opinions of its constituency could be canvassed and tabulated far more easily than in the society as a whole —that is, if the will to do so existed.

The other argument most often heard for denying students any say in university affairs is that they are "mere transients." True, but so are many professors, and so (to change the context) are members of the House of Representatives, who are elected for only two years. Besides, the *interests* of the student population do not shift as often as the population itself; Clark Kerr, in fact, detects signs that students are beginning to look upon themselves as a "class." But even if the interests of the undergraduates did continually change (and they probably should), life does, after all, belong to the living, or, in the case of the universities, a campus to its *present* constituents.

In addition to student grievances over what happens in the classroom and on the campus, there is another major source of disaffection: the university's relationship to the world around it—its role as landlord of neighboring property, and, on the broader canvas, its role as the recipient of government largesse and provider of government expertise.

The upheavals of last spring at Columbia brought to focus the problem of the university's relationship to the society at large. One of two key issues during that upheaval was Columbia's pending construction of a gym in a public park used by Harlem residents. This issue by itself might be thought of minor importance (if, that is, one is not a resident of Harlem), but in fact it was the latest of a long series of encroachments by Columbia into the surrounding ghetto, an encroachment which usually involved evicting tenants with little concern for their wishes and welfare. (Even now Columbia continues its encroachment; as James Ridgeway reports in his new book, *The Closed Corporation: American Universities in Crisis*, Columbia is still secretly extending its real estate holdings in Harlem, and its "relocation office" is still forcing families out of buildings it wants to tear down.)

Various groups, including students, faculty, Harlem residents, and the city, had appealed to the Columbia administration to review its policies on the gym construction —all to no avail. It is simply false to say, as Sidney Hook has, that "instead of seeking peacefully to resolve them [grievances] through existing channels of consultation and deliberation, the SDS seeks to inflame them." Not only did student groups, including SDS, attempt to get a peaceful hearing, but they had to make those attempts against formidable obstacles, for as Amitai Etzioni, professor of sociology at Columbia, has written, "due process, even in the loose sense of established channels for expression and participation, is not institutionalized at Columbia or at most other universities."[1]

Even after the upheavals of last spring, the suggestion that precise channels be established for student participation continues to infuriate men like Barzun. One would

[1] *Psychiatry and Social Science Review,* July, 1968, p. 10.

think that anyone who so deplores student "immaturity" would at least recognize the standard argument of psychologists that immaturity is prolonged, even heightened, by an exclusion from responsibility. But apparently, despite his rhetoric in defense of "orderly process," Barzun prefers occasional barricades to regularized communication.

He even goes so far as to deny the reality of issues like the gym construction. Universities must expand, he argues, and expansion inevitably brings conflict with the university's immediate neighbors. But shall the needs of several hundred citizens, he rhetorically asks, "prevail over the needs of . . . a national university?" Besides, the area around a university is usually a "deteriorating" one (as regards Columbia, Barzun has elsewhere referred to its surrounding neighborhood as "uninviting, abnormal, sinister, dangerous"), so it is a matter of simple "self-protection" for the university to take "steps." The "steps," as Barzun defines them, include "bringing in the police against crime and vice, hiring special patrols, and buying real estate as fast as funds and the market permit." This might look, Barzun concedes, like "waging war on the inhabitants," but what they forget is that with the university's expansion goes "increased employment and trade." The residents of Harlem apparently do not see it that way, and they and their student allies have decided that all else failing, it becomes necessary to invoke the doctrine of "self-protection" for themselves as well. (In his long book, Barzun has almost no discussion of Columbia's relations with Harlem; when I came to a chapter entitled "Poverty in the Midst of Plenty," I thought I had finally come to a detailed review of those relations, but the chapter turned out instead to be about the financial problems of the university.)

The second major issue in the Columbia dispute last

spring concerned the university's affiliation with the Institute for Defense Analyses (IDA), an affiliation which in turn symbolized the university's dependence on government grants and involvement with government research. Barzun and others like to defend the university as a "center of research," and they contrast that "proper" function with the "misguided" one of the university becoming a center of "experience." But it is one thing to defend the university theoretically as a research center, and quite another to ask specifically "research in what and for what?"

The multiple and tangled relationships that have developed between our leading universities and the large corporations and the federal government raise doubts about the proper boundaries of "research." This is especially true of what James Ridgeway calls the university's "war machinery"—its complicity in everything from antisubmarine-warfare research at Columbia to counterinsurgency planning at the University of Michigan. Today more than two thirds of university research funds come from agencies of the federal government closely connected with defense matters, and about one quarter of the 200 largest industrial corporations in the country have university officials on their boards of directors. It is certainly an open question these days whether the university is engaged in research in order to pursue "truth" or to acquire status, power, and profit. Columbia's own farcical involvement with the Strickman cigarette filter is but one of many examples of the university's placing greed ahead of integrity.

There are, I should stress, no simple formulas for establishing the "right" relationship universities should form with public corporations and governments. It is *because* there are no easy answers that the matter should be subjected to open debate, with all interested parties bringing to bear their insights and perspectives. And by "all," I include students. They are rightly disturbed over the university's entanglement with war and private profit, and they ask that their concern be registered and their views considered. They are entitled to nothing less, for until students began to protest such matters as IDA affiliation, the universities were doing business as usual, blind to the implications of their own actions. The same is true of the university's record regarding innovation in education and the procedures of campus government—I mean real innovation, not the substitution of blue tape for red. Before student activists began forcing a variety of campus and classroom issues into the open, the university's concern was minimal.

What we are witnessing, then, is not a sporadic and superficial, but a sustained and far-reaching, attack on the university's smug and antique bearing. The student activists are not rebelling against their parents' values, but applying those values to the institutions with which they find themselves involved. They are not confused children, uncertain of their motives or aims, but determined adults who have found their education and their society seriously wanting.

I doubt if we have ever had a generation—or at least a minority of one—that has engaged itself so earnestly on the side of principled action, that valued people so dearly and possessions so little, that cared enough about our country to jeopardize their own careers within it, that wanted so desperately to lead open, honest lives and to have institutions and a society which would make such lives possible. It is a generation for which we should be immensely grateful and of which we should be immensely proud. Instead, we tell them that they are frenzied children; that we will try to be patient with them but that they should not push us too far; that they too in time will grow to understand the *real* ways of the world. To say that this condescension or blindness on the part of the older generation is a "pity" does not fit the dimensions of the case. It is a crime.

PART IV

ON BECOMING AN HISTORIAN

I have placed this essay last in the collection not merely because it is the most recent in point of time, but more, because it both sums up many preceding themes (especially what I take to be the limitations of a "life in history") and, by embracing rather than shunning the personal, looks ahead to what I hope will be a new emphasis in my writing.

Some friends who have seen the piece in advance of publication think that it might be read as a valedictory to the research, writing and teaching of history. That was not as I intended. What the essay does represent is my intention in the future to make more of an effort at combining historical data with personal reflection—though I am unsure what forms that effort might take. Perhaps all I am saying is that these days I think of myself more as a writer than an historian.

MANY historians are today discontented with their profession. The younger malcontents chiefly bemoan its "irrelevance"; historians, they argue, are not sufficiently engaged, either in their own lives or in their scholarship, with the pressing social problems of the day. The counter-model these malcontents suggest is an academic whose professional energies would be devoted to some such topic as the history of racist thought in America, and whose person, time and money would be actively committed to movements championing egalitarianism. The historical investigations of such a man would provide contemporaries with perspective on current problems, and his personal engagement would contribute directly to the eradication of those problems.

A second, far smaller and older group of historians is dissatisfied with the profession for what I would call philosophical reasons—not primarily because of its unwillingness to help solve contemporary problems, but because of its inability to do so even where the will is present. These historians are unhappy because of what they take to be limitations inherent in the nature of their work. And especially two limitations: insufficient data, which makes it difficult, and in many cases impossible, to reconstruct the past with any fullness of detail or certainty of interpretation; and, secondly, the fallible abilities of any single historian commenting on the data. Because of the first limitation—the skimpiness of evidence—studies of the past are better at cataloguing particulars than extracting universals,

"On Becoming an Historian" appeared in *Evergreen Review*, April, 1969.

and more adept at recounting actions than explaining the motives behind them. And because of the second limitation, human fallibility, any given historian is likely to project his subjective perspective onto the limited data before him, thereby further falsifying it.

In other words, discontent within the historical profession today can be roughly divided into two groupings. First, a large number of young historians who seem to have little doubt that the past can yield rich relevance for the present if only we decide that it should, and second, a small number of older historians who find the limitations that adhere to historical investigation so decisive that they do not believe the past can yield guidelines for the present even though the historian may be determined that it will (unless, that is, the historian turns propagandist, manipulating limited evidence in order to make resounding pronouncements about What the Past Tells the Present).

In trying to sort out my own discontents with history (I mean, of course, with history as a profession, not with history as the actual sum of man's past—we are all discontented with that, no matter how we read its partial remains), I find that they are drawn from both the activist and philosophical positions. This was probably predictable, given where I "fit" among the current generations of practicing historians. I am thirty-eight years old, a product of the campus ethos of the early 1950s, a member of the "silent generation." Preceding us was a generation fascinated by ideas, particularly those of Karl Marx; following us, there is a generation, typified by SDS, more interested in action. The generation preceding my own, true to its youthful devotion to ideas, makes up the small ranks of philosophical objectors to history as a discipline. The generation following mine, true to its disinterest in ideas, makes up the large ranks of young instructors who place chief emphasis on history as a tool for the active conversion of society.

My generation was the in-between one, never as attracted to a system of ideas as our predecessors had been, never as committed to active resistance to American society as our SDS successors currently are. Those of us in our mid- to late-thirties are the "floaters" of today's academic community. As undergraduates we equated a commitment to ideology with a religious turn of mind, one which required certainty and completeness at the expense of complexity (to us a synonym for "truth"). At the same time we regarded anyone with a commitment to "action politics" as probably more deranged still, for we felt, in the complacent fifties, that such injustices as existed in our country would be set right simply by continuing the ameliorative policies of the New Deal.

We matured, in other words, in an atmosphere distrustful of (or disinterested in) both ideas and action. Our obsessions instead were wholly traditional—grades, athletics, fraternities, sex—and perhaps the best that can be said of us, in retrospect, is that somewhere we seemed to have recognized our pettiness for what it was, for we adopted a cool, I-don't-give-a-damn-about-anything manner, as if to say that we knew our concerns didn't warrant the zeal we were investing in them.

In the last few years we have been educated somewhat by events. We now know the need for active opposition to some of the crippling policies and institutional arrangements in our country. We now know—if for no other reason than from watching the young activists, whom many of us admire, flounder in their search for philosophical underpinnings—that ideas, perhaps even those old-fashioned Marxist ones, are necessary for focusing action and sustaining commitment. Learning these lessons, we have, to some degree, changed. We are less scornful of systematic thought and less reluctant to commit ourselves to an active role in politics. Yet the scorn and the reluctance alike remain, residual testimony to the way my generation was programmed. It is still difficult for us to work up enthusiasm over ideas (for example, Herbert Marcuse's) or to feel in our gut that the United States is so rotten as to warrant an outright assault against the entire "system." (I am, of course, over-generalizing; there are historians of roughly my own age—like Staughton Lynd or Eugene Genovese —who have less difficulty than most of us in committing themselves either to a philosophy or to organized action.)

Being a member of this particular generation, with its pervasive suspicion of advocacy, helped to condition the "mid-way" position that I discover I hold between the two centers of discontent—activist or philosophical— within the historical profession. But my conditioning as a member of the silent generation is only part of the explanation for my mid-way position—what might be called the sociological part. No one can understand himself simply by listing the cultural influences that worked upon him. Something more is needed: those unique relationships and events which make up his—and only his—experience. The way I have come to regard history as a profession is due at least as much (indeed, I think, more) to my personal history as to my shared membership in a particular generation. I would like to try to recall the relevant parts of that personal history. I apologize for the egotism involved, but discussing my own history is the best way I know of illustrating certain general propositions I would like to make about the historical profession itself.

. . .

339

When I set out to answer the question "How did I become an historian?" I soon discovered that my experience as a biographer failed to prepare me for the difficulties involved in autobiography. The biographer has before him only such tangible remains of his subject's life as have survived—letters, journals, published writings and the like. But the autobiographer has another kind of evidence to confront as well: all those hazy impressions of early events which are too vague even to be dignified by the word "memory." These recollections, the origins and outlines of which are so uncertain, keep the autobiographer perplexed about whether he is writing a true history of his own life or some fictionalized account in which events become merely the starting point, the pretext, for some invention whose necessity is itself not understood. The biographer can afford to pronounce on the "meaning" of this, the "motivation" for that, because his conclusions need only meet the evidence accumulated on his work desk. The autobiographer, haunted as well by all the unwritten, unendurable fragments, knows that what is piled on the work desk is not the whole story but some accidental, refracted trace of it. Biographers write about skeletons, autobiographers about remembered flesh.

As the biographer of Charles Francis Adams, for example, I had little difficulty describing why he decided to become a lawyer: the legal profession in his day carried promise of prestige and income; he came from a long line of lawyers; he wanted to demonstrate pecuniary and emotional stability to his future father-in-law; he doubted if he had the talent or interest to pursue any other work. These, at least, are the reasons I gave in my biography of Adams. Now, eight years after writing that book, I doubt the sufficiency, perhaps even the centrality of those reasons. It may well be that Adams' choice of career hinged on re-

lationships or episodes about which we now have little or
no evidence. Perhaps the real force behind his entering
law school was the hope of duplicating the achievements
of his father, John Quincy Adams, just as his ambivalence
about the decision may have reflected his fear that he
would not measure up to his father. Or it may be that
some particular event, now entirely lost to us, proved to be
the true catalyst—like a temporary fascination with a legal
treatise or opinion; the subtle pressures of his fiancée to
enter a prestigious calling; an unsuccessful attempt to
write fiction.

As an autobiographer trying to discover why I became
an historian, I find I can make up a neat little list for myself
in much the way I once did as a biographer when trying
to explain why Adams became a lawyer. The list would
include a number of items special to my own circumstances, especially my friendship as an undergraduate with
a young history instructor (my admiration for him led me
to adopt his profession in the confused belief that thereby
I would reproduce for myself his life style and personality
as well). The list would also include a number of items
standard for any academic: the influence of a few outstanding teachers, courses or books in high school and college,
and a kind of generic fascination with what we like to call
finding out "what makes this country tick," "what made it
what it is."

It's this last factor that I have most trouble accounting
for. *Why* was I fascinated with this country's past? Indeed,
was I, or did the fascination represent some elaborate game
of concealment I was playing with myself? In trying to
answer these questions, I've hit on many possibilities, all
of which seem to me true, though whether true to my
current needs or to my actual feelings of fifteen years ago,
I'm not sure. Nor do I know how to weigh their significance

in relation to each other—which, in other words, were of minor and which of decisive importance.

I thought, for example, of the influence of my father's history on my own. He was already twenty years old when he emigrated to this country from Russia, a man without formal education and without any knowledge of English. He never talked to me about Russia; I knew of no antecedents, heard no tales of the Old Days. That is, with one exception: the story that my father, a peasant on a large estate, had stolen away to America in the dead of night —taking his own aged father with him—in order to avoid being drafted into the Russian army.

Thinking to check this story, I mentioned it recently at a family gathering. To my astonishment my mother's version turned out to be markedly different from the one I had long believed to be true. As she told it, my father had been an overseer on a beet plantation (the only Jew, she added, who worked there). He did suddenly leave Russia to avoid the army but didn't bring his own father over to this country until several years later. At this point in her narrative my mother was interrupted by a cousin also present at the family gathering. "You've got it all wrong," he said; "just before Joe [my father] died, he gave me a complete account of what happened. He didn't run away to avoid the draft, he ran away *from* the army after he had already been inducted." After much discussion (and considerable shell-shock) all around, my mother finally decided that my cousin's version was the correct one; she was persuaded by recalling that a "laundry chute" had been involved in my father's escape and the chute only seemed to make sense in connection with an army barracks.

One thing was clear: *my* recollection had been almost wholly inaccurate; my father did not escape in the dead of night and did not bring his own father with him. How I came by that tale remains a mystery. Perhaps I invented it to supply some version of a father-son cooperative venture which in fantasy held enormous appeal for me because of the lack of communion with my own father. Or perhaps my father himself told me the story, producing it out of some obscure wish to save us both from what he took to be a less digestible truth. In any case I believe I have made the point that I know almost nothing of my father's past (and perhaps secondarily have also provided an apologue of how both "first-hand" accounts and the historian himself can create obstacles to "reconstructing the past").

It was not only my father, but my mother, too, who seemed devoid of antecedents. Her family had come to the United States two generations earlier from Austria, but I was given no sense of what that background had meant. My mother always seemed to me (as did her parents) one of those present-minded Americans whose very insistence on living exclusively from day to day suggests, as a correlative, a suffusing dislike of what has gone before. It may well be that I became an historian in order to compensate for this lack of family roots. It may be that I became an historian of the United States out of some unconscious drive to end our displaced status within it. To have this country depend upon me for its official interpretation was in some way to possess it, to achieve over it the kind of mastery for which my father seemed unequipped, and my mother uninterested.

But that is not the whole story either. A "life in history" held out attractions for me for reasons still more personal. I had, in fact, grown up the family "presentist" *par excellence*. My life lacked continuum, connections with what preceded. Every day seemed new, unrelated to others; events, feelings, relationships, did not so much build on each other as cancel each other out. I seemed as little able to retain the satisfactions of yesterday as its pain. It was as if an enormous blackboard eraser were suspended down my back to the floor and as I walked it instantly erased all trace of my footsteps.

Why this was so, I hardly begin to understand. In part I had simply internalized an attitude common to my family: the past was something to forget as rapidly as possible; it was an encumbrance, the source of useless anguish rather than useful experience. For a long time I liked to think of this attitude as an emblem of emancipation. The moment was what counted, I said, and the moment could be most fully experienced when the fewest preconceptions were brought to it.

But as I belatedly came to understand, when I talked of "living in the moment" I was theorizing about my life rather than describing it. In fact I was as little committed to the present as to the past. I disliked depth experience of any kind, today's as well as yesterday's, and if, by some chance, I found myself undergoing such an experience, my impulse was to terminate it as rapidly as I could and obliterate its traces as fully as I was able. I preferred, in other words, to pass quickly from one mild encounter to another, avoiding as much as possible binding associations, for those I tended to link with the threat of pain.

It seems bizarre that someone so eager to dissociate himself from his own past should decide to devote his life to collecting and explaining other people's pasts. But that paradox itself contains the heart of the explanation. It is one that eluded me until a few years ago when I found myself trying to express the contrast between my professional devotion to history and my personal distrust of it, in a short poem I called "Historian":

> I am a guardian of memories,
> collective ones, the race—

> to give it all the best light.
> My own I do not care for,
> fear the shadow line they throw,
> suppress their bite.
> Neat balance for a life,
> If one believes a blank brings peace—
> and fright.

Apparently my personal amnesia—the "blank"—frightened me more than I could consciously admit. Skating on a thin layer of ice (and on a new pond) every day carried special thrills; but at the same time, I recognized the dangers involved and longed for some thickness beneath the surface —especially if it could be artificially manufactured from someone else's refrigerator.

In short, though I had little sense of it at the time, I now think I became an historian largely out of the need to find some balance for a life tipped heavily toward the immediate, the momentary, the present occasion. There was little in my motivation which had to do with what might be called a "passion to know" about the American past—certainly not one which I can separate from my subjective need for "ballast." My guess is that such subjective needs are the chief ingredients of any historian's pursuit of the past. Doubtless those needs vary widely with individuals; some historians may be drawn to the seeming stability of a world of "hard" facts, some to the isolation (and safety) of dealing with the dead, some to the authoritarian pleasures of being able to pass judgment on others without fear of retaliation.

But if my main motive for joining the historical profession was one of personal compensation, my actual experience within the profession has modified that motive. From the first I found myself asking questions of the past which carried me a good distance from my starting point.

This broadening of my concerns was a matter of fits and starts, a development that took place almost behind my own back. Only when its accumulated force became pronounced did I become conscious of what had been going on in my professional life for some time.

My first book—that biography of Charles Francis Adams —was inspired by accident and finished by will power. When I entered graduate school at Harvard in 1952, I was put in a dormitory room with a student whose mother had at one time been social secretary to Brooks Adams and who was currently curator of The Adams Mansion in Quincy, Massachusetts. She invited me out to Sunday dinner, gave me a tour of Adams memorabilia and further caught my interest with her private storehouse of anecdotes and recollections. At about the same time, The Adams Trust announced that the family's enormous collection of private papers, so long withheld from scholars, would henceforth be open for research.

This conjunction of personal exposure to the Adams milieu and the public availability of the family's papers seemed to me, when the time came to choose a topic for my doctoral dissertation, something like a mandate. Like most graduate students, I had no one burning interest I was eager to pursue, but rather a desultory half dozen or so. Such burning as I felt was knowing that a thesis topic had to be chosen and had to be chosen expeditiously lest I lose my hard-won status as a graduate student Seriously Devoted to the Study of Our Past. And so I chose—not, as it turned out, wisely or well.

In truth, most of the five years I ended up devoting to the Adams biography was drudgery. This is not hindsight but in fact the way I felt at the time. For a brief period in graduate school I kept a diary (I think because I needed an outlet for my feelings which my academic work was not providing), and in rereading that diary recently, I find my discontent with working on Adams' biography pervasive. In one entry I wrote that my research into state politics of the 1850s was proving so "exasperatingly dull and inconsequential" that all the familiar doubts about being a professional historian had begun to return. "*Why* the academic life," I wrote. "*What* the significance of scholarship either as a vehicle for my self-expression or as a tool for others?" On another day I wrote:

I don't really give a healthy damn for "the past," nor for scholarship and its laborious recollections . . . I *use* the past, I do not purposely elucidate it. I write about Charles Francis Adams because I wish to write *a good book* . . . I don't give a damn for his personality, nor do I wish to immortalize his achievements. He is a vehicle, nothing more. Does anyone feel differently? I doubt it . . . How *can* one feel interest in the past "for its own sake"? One can only feel *from* oneself. True, if personality has become meaningless, if one wishes to submerge oneself in someone else's life, or times, then selflessness can be approached. But then it is the devotion of a nonentity . . .

Yet I persisted with the Adams biography. At first because I wanted to get my doctorate; then, the doctorate completed, because I wanted to publish a book, and with two years of my life already invested in studying Adams' career, it seemed uneconomical to start all over on a new topic. I also persisted for what some might call "better" reasons (though these were never uppermost), primarily the interest I had begun to develop in Adams' leadership of the moderate "free-soil" wing of the antislavery movement. I found the issue of slavery in politics increasingly absorbing and the position Adams took on it increasingly persuasive. "Spent most of the day," I wrote at one point in my diary, reading the *Boston Whig* in New England Deposit [library]—not bad work—the slavery issue is absorbing—I lean more and more to outright sympathy with the overtly aggressive position of the antislavery leaders—though some abolitionist tactics were deplorable. Many parallels with today & the desegregation issue: what to do?—to insist forcefully on equal rights or to leave improvement to "time" & Southern evolution? Reaction knows no progress; stability or worse is its operational level. Yet force must be tempered with a reasonable understanding of the complexity of the problem—a thin line to define & tread—but Charles Francis (and *not* the abolitionists) once managed to do so. He presents an admirable ideal (if disagreeable personality)—the "right," moderately insisted upon.

I should add, immediately, that in the dozen years since writing those lines I have felt ever diminishing sympathy for the Adams' moderates and ever increasing admiration for those who, like William Lloyd Garrison, called for outright abolition of slavery. This radicalization of my views might have come about simply as a response to public events of the last dozen years, events which have demonstrated clearly that the white majority in this country does not wish to give the American Negro equal access to the benefits of our society, and that a large and determined minority still believes in the Negro's biological inferiority. These events, as I say, might alone have moved me "leftwards," have made me realize the necessity for firm resistance to racism. But aside from the education of public events, I was also moved to a more radical stance as a result of my historical studies themselves (though because my scholarship itself probably took the particular turns it did under the influence of public events, I would say my historical researches reinforced rather than initiated my changing opinions).

What happened was that when I finished the Adams

On Becoming an Historian

biography in 1961, I decided to pursue further the one strand in it that had consistently sustained my interest —the antislavery movement. For a while I thought of writing a full-scale history of the movement, or perhaps of its radical wing, abolitionism. But my temperament worked against that idea. I've always been more inclined toward the particular than the general and more interested in the workings of human personality than in the panorama of public affairs. How individuals differ from each other concerns me more than how they are alike; biography and intellectual history—the study of what made a few men, and their works, special—holds far more fascination for me than sociology, the study of group behavior, of what a disparate collection of individuals have in common. To study the abolitionists as a *group* would have meant concentrating on impersonal factors and shared traits, whereas I preferred to investigate idiosyncratic ones.

I finally satisfied such interest as I had in the abolitionist movement as a movement by writing two speculative articles and by putting together a volume of new essays by young historians entitled *The Antislavery Vanguard,* a volume aimed at providing enough new evidence and perspective to touch off the full-scale reevaluation I thought needed. I turned the bulk of my energies toward writing a new biography, this time of James Russell Lowell.

I had been attracted to Lowell on several levels. Though his aristocratic New England background was similar to that of Adams, Lowell had taken up a more radical position in the antislavery struggle by becoming an active abolitionist. I wanted to know why he had (and why Adams had not), chiefly, I think, in order to find out more about where I stood (and why I stood there) in the current spectrum of opinion on the Civil Rights struggle.

I was also interested in Lowell as a literary man. By 1962,

when I began work on his biography, I was feeling the constrictions of my role as an "objective" historian. I wanted to get more of myself into my writing, and it was this need (among others) which led me in 1963 to write the documentary play *In White America,* and which has led me since then to spend increasing amounts of my time writing plays. In other words, more and more attracted to "literature" as an outlet and career for myself, I was drawn to the prospect of finding out more about what made a literary man "tick." Writing a biography of Lowell seemed the ideal way to focus and go further with two matters of concern to me—the Civil Rights movement and literature.

I again spent close to five years on the Lowell book. The years were much more pleasant than those given over to Adams, largely because Lowell was a far more genial companion. I came to like him enormously as a man, and to feel—as I had not with Adams—involvement in his life. There was also drudgery and discouragement, as with any book, but on the whole I felt the time with Lowell well spent.

The trouble is, I'm not sure why. When I finished the biography, I wrote another poem, entitled "A Biographer to His Subject":

> *Upon your grave*
> *a wreath of words,*
> *circling about your life.*
>
> *Joint commemoration:*
> *Your image molded now in time;*
> *My own, unsettled by the mime.*

What I was trying to express in that poem was my general sense of uneasiness at what had happened—to Lowell and to me. I felt glad to have gotten to know Lowell and somewhat changed by the contact. But I wasn't sure how much I had been in touch with the actual Lowell, as opposed to my reconstruction of him, and therefore, whether I had been changed by contact with another person or with my own fantasies; nor in any case, could I have said *how* I had been changed. Finally, though I knew in some vague way that I had profited from writing the book, I wasn't at all convinced anyone else would profit from reading it.

For the fact was I had found out very little about those matters that had originally led me to undertake Lowell's biography. The kind of introspective evidence I needed to help me understand why Lowell became a radical in the antislavery movement, and what inspired or drove him to seek a life in literature, was available only in fragments. Nor do I think its paucity is peculiar to a study of Lowell. In fact a comparatively large number of his private papers have survived and his formal writings were voluminous. It is true he did not keep a continuous diary and that he was not a particularly introspective man. But although Charles Francis Adams did keep a journal almost every day of his life and did tend to brood (although in a rather stereotypic way) about the motives behind his actions, I am equally unable to tell you why Adams became a "free-soiler" rather than an abolitionist or why he did not devote his life to literature.

I can, of course, tell you something of what went into the decisions of both men; I don't mean to overstate the case. I can (and did), for example, describe the atmosphere in Lowell's home when he was growing up—his father's strong antislavery views and his mother's deep interest in literature; I discussed the Christian radicalism of his first wife, Maria White; I tried to delineate the literary ferment operative in ante-bellum Cambridge—and so forth. But these hardly satisfy me as *sufficient* explanations for Lowell's major decisions in life. Many boys grew up in

New England under influences seemingly comparable in every way to those surrounding Lowell, but they did not become abolitionists or writers. Moreover, when I look at the actual turning points in Lowell's life—the points at which he decided to abandon the law for poetry and decided to take out membership in the Massachusetts Anti-Slavery Society—I am as unclear about what immediate events precipitated those decisions as I am about the preconditioning that disposed Lowell to regard those events as critical.

What I am saying, in other words, is that I cannot tell you what made Lowell tick, and to that very large extent, therefore, I cannot tell you much about what ever makes for literature or for political radicalism. I can describe the dominant outlines of Lowell's personality—its buoyancy, its grace, its wit—and I can describe most of his activities in behalf of literature and abolition—his writings, his attendance at meetings, his positions on public questions, etc.—but I cannot *explain* why his personality or his activities took on the particular shape they did. I find the source of his motivation pretty much cut off from my view —as indeed, it may have been from his own, for few of us can master (even when we have the will) that maze of impulse, determination and sheer circumstance that leads us to do or say certain things and not others.

Did I—to focus on one of the two questions which were of central concern to me—learn *anything* from studying Lowell's life about the impulses that lie behind political radicalism? Not much. I think I learned that radicals are made, not born, that childhood experiences produce certain predispositions which public events then activate. In Lowell's case, for example, I found that his upbringing predisposed him to be compassionate toward the suffering of others and particularly toward the black slave; and that this predisposition was activated by his marriage to Maria White, who was already deeply committed to the abolitionist cause, and also by certain public developments, especially the growing threat in the early 1840s that slavery's boundaries would be extended through the annexation of land belonging to Mexico.

But that is all I can tell you, and it doesn't seem to me much. I can't tell you *precisely* what influences in Lowell's home or what attitudes in the surrounding community may have predisposed him to public protest, and therefore I can't come close to generalizing about what kinds of upbringing produce which predispositions in the young. Many New Englanders grew up in homes much like Lowell's; the subtle areas in which they differed are crucial for understanding what does or does not produce "radicals," but it is exactly these fine points of difference which are least available for historical scrutiny. We can say only that although many New Englanders were aware of the growing threat of slavery's expansion, few joined Lowell in advocating abolition—just as today many are aware of the inequities in our society but few become active members of SDS or the Peace and Freedom Party.

It seems to me that *if* we are interested in finding out what produces radicals, we would learn far more by studying radicals today than by investigating the life histories of radicals in our past. The studies done on contemporary radicals by social scientists like Kenneth Keniston, Nevitt Sanford and Richard Flacks provide that very abundance of detail and analysis so absent in historical efforts. Because men like Keniston deal with live subjects who can be interviewed directly and repeatedly, and who can be subjected to a sophisticated variety of testing devices and laboratory controls, they have been able to tell us much about the kinds of environmental stimuli that produce disaffection and protest in the young. Their techniques, of course, are subject to challenge, but not, it seems to me, much challenge, given the fact that the dozen or so studies thus far completed were made independently of each other and yet closely agree in their major findings (for example, that young radicals tend to come from liberal, middle-class homes, to have been brought up permissively, and to be more mature and more intelligent than their non-activist counterparts).

In other words, if an historian is interested in the past primarily because of the light he hopes it will throw on present-day problems (his own or his society's), he would do better, it seems to me, to study the present itself. If, for example, he is interested in the phenomenon of youthful radicalism today, he will learn a great deal more about it from reading the psychological and sociological work done by Keniston and others than he will from studying previous groups of radicals in our history—for the latter operated in a widely different context and, in any case, have left only fragmentary evidence on the roots and shape of their activism.

One can, of course, be interested in history for any number of reasons other than "problem-solving" and could thereby justify its study by any number of other rationales. One could claim, for example, that the chief reason for studying past experience is not to help us *solve* the problems that confront us, but only to make us aware of how those problems developed through time, how, in other words, we got into the predicament in which we currently find ourselves. Thus it could be said that we must know the history of slavery in this country before we can understand the current crisis in race relations. (A plausible rationale, though also a debatable one, for the fact is that historians differ so widely among themselves about the nature and effect of the slave experience that it is difficult to say *precisely* what contribution it made to our current dilemma.)

Or one could eschew the "problem" approach entirely as extrinsic to the study of history—and yet still defend that study for its relevance (of a more generalized kind) to our life today. One could, for example, insist that investigating past experience makes us aware that people have at times behaved according to different norms from those we know and sanction—and that discovering this puts us in touch with our own potential range. Or one could claim that by learning how difficult it is to "account" for past events, we become more aware of the complexity of contemporary ones, become more able to recognize and sustain uncertainty, more humble in the face of it.

My point in this essay is not to argue these or other possible justifications for the study of history. It is only to say that *my* dissatisfactions with history (as a source of insight, as a way of life) reflect my initial expectation (shared, I feel sure, by many other historians) that it *could* help us "problem-solve," could help us to understand not only how we got where we are, but also where we want to go and how to get there. Like many of the younger historians, I am increasingly disturbed that we spend so much of our time investigating materials (in my case, ten years in writing the lives of two men) of so little immediate import either to ourselves or to the society at large. Like them, I wish we could find a way of making the past yield information of vital concern to contemporary needs. But unlike them, I have little hope that we can. Here I join the older group of philosophical skeptics who feel that the limited evidence available from the past, the very different context in which past experience took place, and the clouded perspective of any historian trying to evaluate that limited evidence and that changed context, all combine to keep historical study of marginal utility for those concerned with acting in the present.

There cannot be a New History, in the sense our younger malcontents are calling for it—that is, a History researched, written and taught in such a way as to aid directly in the eradication of social ills—because we can neither manufacture the needed data for "problem-solving" nor decontaminate the scholars who will deal with it. For those among the young, historians and otherwise, who are chiefly interested in changing the present, I can only say, speaking from my own experience, that they doom themselves to bitter disappointment if they seek their guides to action in a study of the past. Though I have tried to make it otherwise, I have found that a "life in history" has given me very limited information or perspective with which to understand the central concerns of my own life and my own times.

Index

Index

Index

Index

Index

Index

Index

Index